A graduate of Monash University with a degree in sociology, Cecilia Dart-Thornton is the author of the internationally acclaimed Bitterbynde Trilogy and the Crowthistle Chronicles. Her interests include animal rights, wilderness conservation and digital media. She lives with her family in Australia.

Visit Cecilia's website: www.dartthornton.com

FALLOWBLADE

Cecilia
Dart-Thornton

FALLOWBLADE
Second Edition, updated

Cataloguing-in-publication data is available from the National Library of Australia

ISBN 978-0-9875001-4-4

Map by Elizabeth Alger
Cover by Ran Valerhon

ABN 67 099 575 078
PO Box 9113, Brighton, 3186, Victoria, Australia

Dedicated to Geoff.

Author's Note

To the innumerable fans of the Bitterbynde Trilogy who wrote to
me asking for another character like Morragan:
You might find him within these pages.

CONTENTS

GLOSSARY

Ádh: luck, fortune (AWE); one of the four Fates of the Sanctorum

Álainna Machnamh (AWE-lana Mac-NAV)

Aonarán: loner, recluse (AY-an-ar-AWN)

a mhuirnín: darling (a wirr-NEEN)

a stór: darling (a STOR)

athair: father (AH-hir)

brí: the power possessed by weathermasters, enabling them
    to predict and control the dynamics of pressure systems and
    temperature, winds and other meteorological phenomena

Cailleach Bheur: The Winter Hag (cal-yach vare or cail-yach vyure)

carlin: wise woman

Cinniúint: destiny, fate, chance (kin-YOO-int); one of the four
    Fates of the Sanctorum

Cuiva (KWEE-va) In the Irish language this name is spelled
    'Caoimhe'

Earnán (AIR-nawn)

Eldritch: supernatural

Eoin (OWE-in)

Fedlamid macDall (FEH-limy mac-dawl)

Fionnbar (FIN-bar or FYUN-bar)

Fionnuala (Fin-NOO-la)

gariníon: grand-daughter (gar-in-EE-an)

garmhac: grandson (gar-VOC)

Gearóid (gar-ODE)

Genan of Áth Midbine (AWE mid-BINNA)

gramarye: magic

gramercie: expression of thanks

Lannóir: Goldenblade or Fallowblade, the golden sword, the only
   one of its kind, slayer of goblins and heirloom of the House of
   Stormbringer (lann-OR)

Liadán (LEE-dawn)

Luchóg (la-HOGE)

Maolmórdha (mwale-MORGA)

máthair: mother (MAW-hir)

Mí-ádh: bad luck, misfortune (mee-AWE); one of the four Fates of
   the Sanctorum

Míchinniúint: doom, ill-fate (mee-kin-YOO-int); one of the four
   Fates of the Sanctorum

Ó Maoldúin (oh mwale-DOON)

Páid (PAWD)

Risteárd Mac Brádaigh (reesh-TARD Mac BRAW-dig)

Saibh (SAY-EVE)

To *sain* is to bless, or call for protection from unseelie forces

seanáthair: grandfather (shan-AH-hir)

seanmháthair: grandmother (shan-WAW-hir. 'Waw' rhymes with
   'au' in 'Maud')

seelie: benevolent to humankind

Uabhar (OO-a-var)

Uile: the All, or universe (ILLE, 'e' as in 'best')

unseelie: malevolent to humankind

SIGNIFICANT CHARACTERS & PLACES

The Kingdom of Ashqalêth (Capital city: Jhallavad)

Chohrab Shechem II: King of Ashqalêth.

Duke Rahim: King Chohrab's brother-in-law, brother of Parvaneh.

Parvaneh Shechem: Queen of Ashqalêth.

Shahzadeh: King Chohrab's eldest daughter, the Princes Royal of
Ashqalêth.

The Kingdom of Grimnørsland (Capital city: Trøndelheim)

Gunnlaug Torkilsalven: youngest son of Thorgild.

Halfrida Torkilsalven: Queen of Grimnørsland.

Halvdan Torkilsalven: second son of Thorgild.

Hrosskel Torkilsalven: eldest son of Thorgild, and Crown Prince of
Grïmnørsland.

Solveig Torkilsalven: third child and only daughter of Thorgild.

Thorgild Torkilsalven: King of Grïmnørsland.

The District of High Darioneth (Principal seat: Rowan Green)

Aglaval Maelstronnar (Stormbringer): Storm Lord in days of yore.

Albiona: Dristan Maelstronnar's wife.

Alfardēne Maelstronnar (Stormbringer): eldest son of Avalloc.

Asrăthiel Heronswood Maelstronnar: only daughter of
Jewel and Arran.

Avalloc Maelstronnar (Stormbringer): the current Storm Lord and
member of the Council of Ellenhall.

Avolundar Maelstronnar (Stormbringer): the warrior mage who
wielded Fallowblade during the Goblin wars.

Cavalon: son of Dristan and Albiona Maelstronnar.

Corisande: daughter of Dristan and Albiona Maelstronnar.

Desmond Brooks: swordmaster at High Darioneth.

Dristan Maelstronnar (Stormbringer): youngest son of Avalloc.

Jewel Heronswood Jaravhor: wife of Arran and mother of Asrăthiel.

Lidoine Galenrithar (Gale Rider): carlin at Rowan Green.

The Kingdom of Narngalis (Capital city: King's Winterbourne)

Giles: Asrăthiel's butler at The Laurels in Lime Grove.

Lecelina: eldest daughter of King Warwick, the Princess Royal of
Narngalis.

Linnet: Asrăthiel maid at The Laurels.

Lord Hallingbury: the Lord Chamberlain.

Mistress Draycott Parslow: Asrăthiel landlady, the owner of The
Laurels in Lime Grove.

Saranna: youngest daughter of King Warwick.

Sir Gelead Torrington: King Warwick's lieutenant-general.

Sir Huelin Lathallan: Knight-Commander of the Companions of
the Cup.

Sir Torold Tetbury: the Lord Privy Seal.

Walter Wyverstone: second son of King Warwick.

Warwick Wyverstone: King of Narngalis.

/

William Wyverstone: eldest son of King Warwick, and Crown Prince of Narngalis

Winona: second daughter of King Warwick.

The Kingdom of Slievmordhu (Capital city: Cathair Rua)

Adiuvo Constanto Clementer: a druid who renounced the Sanctorum.

Almus Agnellus, 'Declan of the Wildwoods': a druid who renounced the Sanctorum.

Conall 'Two-Swords' Gearnach: Commander-in-Chief of the Knights of the Brand.

Cormac Ó Maoldúin: third son of Uabhar.

Fedlamid macDall: Queen Saibh's most trusted servant.

Fergus Ó Maoldúin: fourth son of Uabhar.

Fionnbar Aonarán: an enemy of Arran Maelstronnar.

Fionnuala Aonarán: Fionnbar's sister.

Grak: a Marauder.

Kieran Ó Maoldúin: eldest son of Uabhar, and Crown Prince of Slievmordhu.

Krorb: a Marauder captain.

Lord Genan of Áth Midbine: a courtier.

Luchóg: a minstrel at Uabhar's court.

Primoris Asper Virosus: the Druid Imperius.

Risteárd Mac Brádaigh: High Commander of the Slievmordhuan armed forces.

Ronin Ó Maoldúin: second son of Uabhar.

Ruurt: a Marauder captain.

Saibh: Queen of Slievmordhu, wife to Uabhar.

Scroop: a Marauder.

The spawn Mother: a progenitrix of the Marauders.

Uabhar Ó Maoldúin: King of Slievmordhu.

THE STORY SO FAR

Fallowblade is the fourth book in the CROWTHISTLE CHRONICLES.

Book 1: *The Iron Tree*, told of Jarred, a young man who lived in a village in the desert kingdom of Ashqalêth, and possessed an amulet that apparently made him invulnerable. He and his comrades decided to travel to seek their fortunes in distant realms. On the way, they visited a town built amongst the intricate waterways of the Great Marsh of Slievmordhu, where Jarred fell in love with a Marsh daughter named Lilith.

Slievmordhu is a kingdom situated in the south-west of Tir, a continent throughout which grows a disliked but beautiful common weed called 'crowthistle'. Eldritch wights dwell in the Marsh but seldom harm the Marsh folk, who understand them and their ways. An urisk, a seelie wight like a dwarfish man with the legs of a goat, often loitered near Lilith's cottage, where she lived with her mother Liadán, her stepfather Earnán, Earnán's son Eoin and Earnán's mother Eolacha, who was a wise carlin. Nearby lived Old Man Connick, a demented and elderly man who was the father of Liadán. Lilith's mother Liadán kept thinking she could hear footsteps invisibly following her, and privately sensed that she was falling prey to a mysterious madness.

When Jarred and Lilith fell in love, Lilith's stepbrother, Eoin, became jealous. Jarred and his comrades departed from the Marsh and continued on their travels, but Jarred could not stop thinking about Lilith. Back at the Marsh, Lilith's mother tried to flee from her growing madness, but instead was accidentally drowned. Jarred made excuses to his friends and returned to the Marsh to settle. His arrival helped Lilith endure her grief over the inexplicable death of her mother.

Jarred learned the ways of the Marsh dwellers and began to court Lilith. Around his neck he still wore the protective amulet. Rivalry grew between him and Eoin, who was resentful of Lilith's affection for Jarred, and who guessed the power of the amulet.

During celebrations of the traditional Festival of Rushbearing, Lilith became lost and injured. The urisk, usually surly but in this case benevolent, helped Jarred find her. Upon her rescue the two young people plighted their troth. Jarred gave his bride-to-be a ring, and his amulet.

Their happiness, however, was short-lived. After Old Man Connick died, completely insane, the carlin Eolacha and young Lilith realised that there was some kind of curse on Lilith's bloodline. Lilith declared she must never marry and beget another doomed generation. Jarred swore he would find the cause of the curse, and break it.

Lilith and other members of her household travelled to the Autumn Fair at the capital city of Slievmordhu, Cathair Rua. There they saw druids of the Sanctorum, who are the official 'intermediaries' between the people of Tir and the 'Four Fates'. In the city, Jarred sought to learn the history of Old Man Connick. He visited apothecaries and made enquiries, but to no avail. Eventually a dirty street urchin called Fionnbar Aonarán led Jarred to the hovel of half-senile Ruairc McGabhann. The old man told the decades-old story of the brave man Tierney A'Connacht, who rescued beautiful

Álainna Machnamh from Janus Jaravhor, the long-dead sorcerer of
the sealed and abandoned Dome of Strang.

Jaravhor, powerful and malign, cursed the heirs of Tierney
A'Connacht and Álainna Machnamh with madness and death.
Old Man Connick, his daughter Liadán and her daughter Lilith
were all descended from the cursed couple. This tale of the past
explained the nature of the malediction, but not how to break it.
Jarred returned to his friends and sweetheart and told them what
he had learned. The news cast a pall of gloom upon them all.

On a subsequent visit to the city Fionnbar appeared for a second
time, and guided Jarred back to Ruairc's hovel. On the way he led
Jarred near a strange tree that grew in the city. Enclosed inaccessibly
within the Iron Thorn's fretwork of cruel boughs hung an extraordinary, sparkling jewel. Jarred was tricked into retrieving the jewel,
a feat no man had been able to achieve before, thus inadvertently
proving he was the grandson of the sorcerer. It was further revealed
that Jarred's amulet had no power, but Jarred himself was immune
to harm because the sorcerer had left an enchantment of invulnerability on all those of his own bloodline. Despising his malicious
forefather, Jarred flung the jewel back into the tree and vowed to
have nothing more to do with the sorcerer of Strang.

Joyfully, Jarred and Lilith returned to the Marsh. They believed
that they could now safely marry: the benison on Jarred's blood
would surely cancel the curse on Lilith's. Eoin was not so happy,
despite the fact that recently he had happened to do a good turn for
some eldritch wights, who granted him good fortune. His jealousy
festered. He became prosperous, and built himself a floating house,
while Jarred remained in poverty.

A year after her marriage to Jarred, Lilith gave birth to a
daughter. They named her 'Jewel'. Despite his earlier misgivings,
Eoin discovered he adored the child.

Lilith and Jarred enjoyed twelve years of happiness together. They were convinced the curse had been broken. However, Eolacha the old carlin eventually died and, as if her grief were a trigger, Lilith began to fall prey to the ancestral madness. She heard the first, distant footsteps of paranoia.

Desperate to save his wife, Jarred travelled to Cathair Rua in search of a druid called Adiuvo Constanto Clementer, who was reputed to be a healer of madness. In order to pay the healer, Jarred once again retrieved the jewel from the Iron Tree, but a passer-by spied the deed. Soon, word of this stranger came to the ears of King Maolmórdha and his dysfunctional family, including the conniving eldest son, Crown Prince Uabhar. They suspected Jarred was of the sorcerer's blood. Only a descendent of the sorcerer had the power to open the sealed Dome and reveal the reputed treasures hidden within. Uabhar convinced his weak father that it was in the Crown's interests to capture this 'jewel thief' and make him unlock the Dome of Strang.

Ruairc McGabhann's niece, the drudge Fionnuala Aonarán (half-sister to Fionnbar), came in haste to Jarred, whom she loved. She informed him that the king's men were hunting him, and any offspring he may have. Jarred wished to have nothing to do with the mysterious Dome. Besides, he knew the king was untrustworthy and would probably harm him. Fervently he hoped Uabhar was not aware he had a daughter. Fionnuala and Fionnbar helped Jarred to escape, on the proviso that Jarred would later leave his family and go with them to unlock the secrets of the Dome.

Eoin, also in the city, witnessed a strange funeral, conducted by eldritch wights. When he looked into the coffin he saw his own face and understood, to his horror, that he had witnessed an omen of his own death.

With the king's men hot on his heels, Jarred hurried back to the Marsh. On the road he met Eoin, who eventually admitted that his jealousy had led him to betray Jarred to the king, not realising that in betraying his rival he would also be bringing danger to Lilith's daughter Jewel.

At the Marsh Jarred angrily bade Eoin help him, and told Lilith and eleven-year-old Jewel to make ready to set out in secret for the safe haven of Narngalis. But before they had a chance to leave the Marsh the madness came upon Lilith again, triggered by the fear of pursuit. Running in terror, Lilith fell over a cliff and was mortally injured. Jarred, trying to retrieve her broken body, slipped and fell a short distance. His heart was pierced by a branch of mistletoe sprouting from a tree leaning out from the cliff part-way down. Mistletoe was the only thing in the world (besides old age) from which the Sorcerer's enchantment could not protect him.

Jarred and Lilith had perished, but their child lived on. In later days it was said that the wraiths of the doomed lovers could be seen walking happily, hand in hand, through the Marsh twilight.

Jewel's parents were now both dead, and Eoin, racked by the agony of remorse, was determined to save the child on his own. They set out together in their boat - just in time; the king's cavalry arrived at the Marsh soon after they had left.

Book 2: *The Well of Tears*, told how Jewel and Eoin fled across the countryside from their native Slievmordhu into the northern kingdom of Narngalis. Along the way they experienced many bizarre adventures. Ultimately, Eoin was slain by unseelie wights and Jewel was left alone in the wilderness. She discovered that her father's legacy - the sorcerer Jaravhor's enchanted blood - protected her from harm, including starvation.

Lost in a mountainous region, Jewel chanced upon a party of people who dwelled at High Darioneth, the home of the Weathermasters of Rowan Green and the plateau dwellers. These kindly folk took pity on the homeless waif, brought her with them, and gave her shelter. With nowhere else to go, and no one else to aid her, she went to live with a family called the Millers, at the nut mill on the plateau. There the orphan grew up.

The famous building in which the weathermasters held their councils was called Ellenhall under Wychwood Storth. The weathermaster's leader was the Storm Lord, Avalloc Maelstronnar-Stormbringer, whose eldest son was Arran, and whose nephew was Ryence Darglistel-Blackfrost. Over the mantelpiece at Avalloc's house hung the famous sword Fallowblade, long ago forged to defeat unseelie goblin hordes and once employed to cut off the hand of the sorcerer Jaravhor. High Darioneth was teeming with brownies and other eldritch wights; the source of many remarkable events, causing both joy and dismay. Jewel met an urisk and realised that it was the same one that used to belong to her mother's household at the Marsh. The urisk had followed her; yet it was most uncouth and unresponsive when she tried to draw it into conversation, and never appeared for long.

Curious about her heritage, Jewel decided to journey to Orielthir and see if she could unlock the secrets of the sorcerer's mysterious building. She and Arran, the son of the Storm Lord, discovered the sorcerer's book recording the existence of certain Wells, each of which held a few drops of the Water of Eternal Life. On their quest to find these wells they were tracked and thwarted by Fionnbar Aonarán, a boy grown to be a heartless rogue of a man. Through cunning and cruelty Aonarán obtained the first of the three draughts of immortality, which he swallowed. Arran was forced to drink the second, and the third was lost.

Now there was no chance that Jewel could match Arran's immortality. Visualising a future in which he lived on eternally, without Jewel at his side, Arran was gripped by rage. He swore vengeance on Fionnbar and Fionnbar's half-sister Fionnuala. After embarking on a hunt, he trapped Fionnbar in a cave in the far north-eastern mountains of Slievmordhu, telling his prisoner that he must dwell there forever, immortal, suffering loneliness and exile. This was the punishment for forcing him, Arran, to drink the Draught of Immortality while stealing eternal life from his bride, Jewel.

Fionnuala Aonarán hated Arran, blaming him for the death of her lover, Cathal Weaponmonger. She knew she could no longer harm the weathermaster, so decided, in her bitterness, to do harm to the one he loved best. She infiltrated the Marsh and learned the manner of Jarred's death. Now she understood the nature of Jewel's bane, and having stalked Jewel, mortally wounded her with an arrow of mistletoe.

At this, Arran was inconsolable. As for Fionnuala, in sudden repentance and shame she hanged herself from the boughs of the Iron Thorn, but at the last minute she was unexpectedly saved. She changed her ways and devoted the rest of her life to making a beautiful garden.

It seemed certain that the story would end unhappily, but the ex-druid Almus Agnellus chanced upon a revelation:

'Agnellus spoke. 'After I left here I had cause to consult my notes and books of lore, and as I was searching among my papers I came across a scroll which I could swear I had never seen before. On it were words written in an archaic tongue, but fortunately I am learned in that speech and was able to decipher it. I learned this: that a woman who mothers an immortal child must inevitably be tinged by that immortality. If she is fatally wounded she shall not die, but shall instead fall into a deep and lasting sleep that resembles death.' He drew breath and appended, 'Jewel lives.'

And it was true.'

They raised Jewel from her grave. She lived, but appeared to be in a deep slumber, and could not be wakened. The beauteous sleeper was placed on a silken couch on the glass cupola atop the

Maelstronnar house. Wild roses entwined their stems about the cupola, framing the eight panes with leaves and their five-petalled rosettes.

Declaring he would seek forever, until he could find a way to bring back his lost bride, Arran abandoned his child, his home and his inheritance, including the golden sword Fallowblade, leaving them all with his father, Avalloc. The grieving weathermage, with the faithful impet Fridayweed in his pocket, disappeared out of men's knowledge. It was said he wandered far in the Unknown lands north of the northernmost mountains.

By then, Jewel's young daughter Astăriel had encountered the very same urisk that used to be attached to her grandmother's cottage in the Marsh. Towards the end of The Well of Tears, the girl had grown used to the wight's companionship, little guessing that the creature was hiding an extraordinary secret.

Book 3: *Weatherwitch*, told of a mysterious burrower digging its way beneath the mountains of the north. The story described, also, the bond of comradeship between Conall Gearnach - Commander-in-Chief of Slievmordhu's Knights of the Brand - and Prince Halvdan of Grïmnørsland. Halvdan's sister Solveig was betrothed to Prince Kieran of Slievmordhu, Halvdan's lifelong friend.

King Uabhar of Slievmordhu had made a secret pact with the Marauders – mutant brigands, huge of stature, who dwelled in outlying caves and prey on the citizens of the four kingdoms of Tir. Uabhar allowed these 'swarmsmen' to raid some of his villages so that he could justify the levelling of higher taxes, with which to prepare – clandestinely – for his forthcoming invasion of Narngalis, the first stage of his attempt to seize sovereignty of the whole of Tir. Uabhar was in cahoots with King Chohrab of Ashqalêth, whom he controlled with eloquence, rhetoric and drugged wine.

Asrăthiel (erstwhile Astăriel), daughter of Jewel and Arran, grandchild of Storm Lord Avalloc Maelstronnar, lived at the stronghold of the weathermasters, her kindred.

She had an unlikely confidant – the cynical faerie creature called an urisk, who appeared only to her, but who caused trouble in the Maelstronnar household.

An ardent advocate of rights for animals, an expert weather-wielder and a skilled swordswoman, Asrăthiel left the stronghold of the weathermasters at Rowan Green and took up a position in the city of King's Winterbourne, as weathermage to King Warwick of Narngalis. Warwick's eldest son, William, was in love with Asrăthiel, but, although she was fond of him, she found herself unable to love him in return. She was pleased, however, when the urisk, who later revealed he was called 'Crowthistle', appeared at her new lodgings, and their casual meetings continued as before.

Meanwhile, unknown to above-ground dwellers, the mysterious burrower broke through a stony wall into a cavern, only to discover something truly awe-inspiring and terrible.

King Uabhar wanted the weathermasters out of the way so that they could not prevent his bid for power. He paid gossips to put about rumours to malign them, then lured most of them to his royal city, Cathair Rua where, by means of trickery, he destroyed them in secret. Unbeknownst to him his appalling deed was witnessed by Cat Soup, the itinerant beggar, who hastened away in terror after what he had seen.

Meanwhile, in King's Winterbourne, Asrăthiel heard reports that in the northern hamlet of Silverton some unknown agency was expertly and ruthlessly slaying the villagers. She and King Warwick's cavalry were dispatched to investigate.

Having destroyed most of the weathermasters by means of trickery, King Uabhar mobilised his troops – as well as those of his ally, King Chohrab – readying them to march north to invade Narngalis. The Four Kingdoms of Tir were on the brink of war.

FALLOWBLADE

The Four Kingdoms of Tir

1

WAR

A wondrous sword was Fallowblade, the finest weapon ever seen;
Forged in the far-flung Inglefire, wrought by the hand of Alfardēne,
Famed mastersmith and weathermage. Of gold and platinum 'twas made:
Iridium for reinforcement, gold to coat the shining blade,
Delved from the streams of Windlestone; bright gold for slaying wicked
wights,
Fell goblins, bane of mortalkind, that roamed and ruled the mountain
heights
Upon a dark time long ago.

A VERSE FROM THE SONG OF THE GOLDEN SWORD.

Oceans of billowing clouds surged through the frozen peaks of the far North. White vapours seethed, misting the glittering sharpness of ice and precipice. Timeless and serene beyond man's measure, the mountains themselves stood firm against this tide, their razor crags forever slashing the sky. Below their foundations a terror had lately been unleashed in a burst of silver light; something ancient and lethal, entombed long ago. Now free, it was on the move.

On the other side of the Four Kingdoms of Tir, hundreds of leagues away, a more mundane force was also moving.

Watching from a high turret window, unseen, Queen Saibh observed her four strapping sons, the noble concourse on the palace battlements, the swarming crowds of men and horses below. As she gazed upon the departing battalions she was grieving most bitterly. These days she wept often. Her ladies-in-waiting murmured amongst themselves that her sad and wistful loveliness reminded them of a faded flower drooping beneath a fine rain.

Uabhar had been pleased to view his wife's red-rimmed, swollen eyes, gleeful at her lamentation, contemptuous at her inability to master her emotions. He thought it was for him.

'Weep for your husband,' he had bidden her, greatly encouraging. 'Weep for me, as I charge joyously into battle. You see, madam, if a king laughs at his foes and seems unafraid to confront them, his own subjects will believe the Fates are on his side. That will give the troops greater courage to risk their lives for his cause. I must laugh but you must cry, for soon I will depart to face great danger - perhaps I will not return. Then you will be widowed, and all that I have given you will be taken away; your status as queen, your jewels, your fine palace apartments. You will become nothing. Weep for me, madam, as a wife ought.' As a parting shot he added, 'My sons will ride beside me, to glory or death.'

And the fading-flower queen had wept more bitterly than ever, but shed no tear for him; it was for her four brave sons, and also for her servant Fedlamid macDall, who had never returned.

Below Saibh's window the King of Slievmordhu, Uabhar Ó Maoldúin, looked out from his battlements across the Fair Field of Cathair Rua, whose well-trodden acres teemed with armed men, horses, chariots and ordnance. Chohrab Shechem, King of Ashqalêth watched from this vantage point too, lying on a cloth-of-gold-draped litter. Uabhar's favoured ministers were stationed a few paces back, shoulder to shoulder with numerous household officials and courtiers, though no snowy-robed druids gleamed like pale candles amongst this jewelled and embroidered assembly. The courtiers' raiment blazed with rich dyes; the blood-flame-wine-soaked reds of Slievmordhu mingling with the sun-sand-fired-clay shades of Ashqalêth. All eyes were fixed on the field, where the last of a vast and clamorous display of battle-ready troops was forming into marching order and moving off. Noises resounded; the ground trembled with the stamp of hoofs, the trample of boots, the mutter of heavy iron wheels crushing gravel. The dusty air racketed with the yelling of orders, shrill whistle blasts, whip cracks, drum rattles, trumpet blasts, and shouts of approval from the civilian onlookers amassed around the periphery of the field.

Tidings of imminent invasion from the south had not yet escaped from Slievmordhu's royal city, Cathair Rua, to reach the northern kingdom of Narngalis. Uabhar had placed a ban on the news. Nor had he openly declared war according to ancient, honourable custom. Instead he left it to his foes to discover belatedly, so that he could take them by surprise. As the ultimate controller of his kingdom's communications network he had made every effort to suppress the information for as long as possible. He silenced the semaphores of Slievmordhu. He prohibited the flying of carrier pigeons. For the first time in history, pigeon pie was encouraged as a patriotic dish; if any such birds were observed in the skies, wild or tame, they were targeted with sling stones or arrows. Throughout the realm of Slievmordhu, northbound travellers were intercepted on the road, and interrogated, and their bags searched for letters, and if they were suspected as spies, or at the whim of their captors, they were taken prisoner. Despite Uabhar's exertions rumours of unrest had begun to trickle from his net; nonetheless, no clear-cut evidence of his plans had yet reached the lands he intended to seize.

This censorship lasted long enough for the military commanders of the two southern kingdoms to mobilize their armies in secret.

The infantry battalions of the Slievmordhuan and Ashqalêthan vanguards, comprising longbowmen, shortbowmen and cross-bowmen, had long since departed from Cathair Rua, led by High Commander Risteárd Mac Brádaigh riding beside his Ashqalêthan counterpart. Sixty companies of archers had gone striding forth, bearded and burly, carrying their round shields on their backs, their yew bows thrusting up from behind their shoulders. At each man's belt hung sword or axe, according to his disposition, and over the right hip there jutted out the leathern quiver, with its tufts of goose, pigeon, and peacock feathers. Behind each company of bowmen marched two drummers beating their nakirs, and two trumpeters in particoloured clothes. The beat was brisk; no laggards would be suffered.

After their departure a tremendous press had thronged into formation on the field. The main-battle of each army consisted of two battalions of foot soldiers - spearmen and archers - and four of heavy armoured cavalry equipped with swords and lances, geared up to charge enemy formations. Of the cavalry, the principals were Ashqalêth's foremost knights, the Desert Paladins, under their own leader, and several companies of Slievmordhu's elite chevaliers, the Knights of the Brand.

One of the latter companies, led by Conall 'Two-Swords' Gearnach, was notably missing. King Uabhar had sent the Commander-in-Chief of the Red Lodge on an expedition to the South-Eastern moors, and he had not yet returned. Though he was a popular officer his absence at this time was not entirely unwelcome to those who were close to him. Since the feast that had been hosted for King Thorgild at Orielthir, Gearnach's own knights often hesitated to traffic with their hitherto approachable leader. In private they asserted that he had turned into a live volcano, ready to erupt into fiery wrath at the slightest provocation, and without notice. His unstable temper was attributable; Uabhar Ó Maoldúin had used their leader badly. The king had compromised the knight's honour, trapping him between two vows, so that he could not help but be forsworn either way. Subsequently, while the Knights of the Brand were absent from the Red City at the feast in Orielthir, Uabhar had burned down the Red Lodge in order to betray and capture the weathermasters on the fabricated pretext of treason. Those of Gearnach's men who rode out from Cathair Rua alongside the Desert Paladins wondered how their leader would respond when he received the tidings of Uabhar's decision to attack Narngalis, aided by his ally, King Chohrab of Ashqalêth. It could only make matters worse for the Red Lodge's Commander. If the west-kingdom, Grïmnørsland, should come to the aid of Narngalis – which was a certainty – Gearnach would be forced to do battle against the military forces of King Thorgild Torkilsalven, father of Prince Halvdan. The prince and the knight had always held each other in high esteem, and, after Gearnach saved Halvdan's life during a hunting trip, an unbreakable bond of friendship had formed between the two.

Gearnach's warriors did not doubt, nonetheless, that in spite of his liege's transgressions their Commander-in-Chief remained steadfast in his loyalty to the crown of Slievmordhu. He viewed the trials that Uabhar brought on him as a true test of his merit as a knight, a patriot and a man who kept his word; and he desired above all things to redeem his self-worth by proving the constancy of his fidelity. For this his knights esteemed him, and despite his volcanic temperament, or because of it, there were many at Cathair Rua who wished he rode with them on that day.

Hour by hour the main-battles of Slievmordhu and Ashqalêth had surged in ostentatious procession through the streets of Cathair Rua so that Uabhar's subjects could admire and applaud the formidable military forces promoting the country's cause. Out through the city gates the columns proceeded, bristling with standards, oriflammes, banners and flags, to the accompaniment of stirring tunes on pipe and drum. Six battalions of light horse from both realms comprised the rearguard. After them trudged columns of sumpter horses carrying cloth, spare arms, spurs, wedges, cooking kettles, horseshoes, bags of nails and rivets, and a myriad other items. Supply wagons rolled in their wake, piled with food, fodder, ammunition, tools and parts for repairs, galenicals and other apothecaries' supplies, tent poles and canvas, assorted construction materials and sundries such as spiked stakes and siege ladders. Last of all trailed the heavy artillery - various types of catapults and trebuchets, hauled by teams of oxen. This part of the convoy would move slowest on the road, so it travelled behind the columns to avoid impeding their progress. Milling crowds of citizens cheered wildly as the troops quit the city and marched off to war.

Eight regiments of Slievmordhu's regular army, the Household Division, were to remain in Cathair Rua. The king himself was their colonel-in-chief, and they were charged with the special duty of guarding the city when their sovereign fared forth to lead his army. On the Fair Field the Royal Horse Guards and the Royal Dragoons now lined up for review, resplendent in dress uniform for the occasion; scarlet tunics, white helmet plumes and white leather breeches, a steel cuirass of breast and back plates. Their cloaks, vermilion with sapphire-blue linings, flowed from their shoulders to cover the haunches of their horses. An amalgamation of the aforementioned battalions, the Blues and Royals, strutted in azure tunics and crimson helmet plumes. The Foot Guards: the Bellaghmoon Guards, the Royal Regiment of Guards, Eastmarch Guards, Valley Guards and Orielthir Guards flaunted their equal magnificence, no less well drilled.

It was an exhilarating day for King Uabhar Ó Maoldúin.

Uabhar's royal neighbour and ally, however, seemed less than enthusiastic. King Chohrab's appearance indicated he was suffering from ill health. Jaundiced and sagging was his countenance, his eyes drowning in drains of shadow. The desert ruler sprawled upon a canopied litter, waited upon by eight brawny attendants, as if it were too exhausting to balance on his slippered feet. He had, nonetheless, rallied after his former palpitations and attempted to rise to the challenge of war. His apothecaries busied themselves mixing invigorating potions for him, while his wife's brother, Duke Rahim, at his side, lent him confidence.

The show was less inspiring, too, for Uabhar's eldest son Kieran, who had been sojourning in Orielthir with his brother Ronin. Fergus and Cormac had joined them on the way home, and all four princes arrived in the middle of the pageantry. They were hardly able to believe what they saw, for they had left Cathair Rua with no idea that war was imminent. Without pausing to refresh themselves or remove their riding gear, the young men went straight to their father on the battlements for explanation.

On bended knee the princes kissed their father's hand. Uabhar, as persuasive as ever, was ready with his carefully constructed web of lies, so often repeated that he was beginning to believe them himself. A domineering father, his lifelong manipulation of his children's beliefs and feelings had had such a profound and disturbing effect on them that it their mother, powerless in the face of Uabhar's subtle eloquence, doubted in her anguished heart whether the princes would ever be able to penetrate the devious jungles of his influence sufficiently even to recognise the abuse, let alone rebel against it. He soon convinced his sons that King Warwick of Narngalis intended to overrun Ashqalêth, claiming that Warwick's enmity had been exposed when he sent the majority of the weathermasters to Cathair Rua where they wounded Chohrab's servant, and then, heaping injury upon injury, burned down the Red Lodge with their lightnings. Uabhar concealed the fact that he had ordered the slaying of the weathermasters. His glib tongue could not yet find an excuse for such an atrocity - even for his sons, blind in the filial devotion he had cultivated with every stern look, critical remark, lecture, inconsistent reward and hard knock, beginning in their infancy. The king fabricated a story that he had promptly ordered the weathermasters to be seized and locked into one of the palace towers, where, according to him, they dwelled in comfort as befitted their station. 'They are dangerous still,' he added. 'All visitors are forbidden, even you, my sons.'

Prince Fergus swore obscenely. 'They deserve to be flogged for their foul work!' he cried. 'They should be punished, for the wrongs they have done to us!'

'They hold the power of storms in their hands,' said Uabhar with a philosophical shrug. 'Keeping them bound and gagged is punishment enough, is it not? Without speech or movement there are unable to work their magicks. But we have wasted enough breath on the puddler-makers. Our main objective now is to attack Narngalis and teach Wyverstone a lesson, before he and Torkilsalven execute their scheme to invade Ashqalêth.'

'Torkilsalven?' Prince Kieran said quickly. 'Is Thorgild part of this scheme?'

'If not already, then likely soon,' his father replied impatiently. 'He and Wyverstone have ever been in cahoots.'

The Crown Prince felt sickened that his country was likely to come into conflict with Narngalis' ally Grïmnørsland, the homeland of his bride-to-be, Solveig, and his best friend Prince Halvdan. He kept his feelings of disgust to himself, however, because he was a dutiful son above all, and would not gainsay his father, even in such extreme circumstances.

Prince Ronin said quietly, 'Alas that Tir's peace should be broken.'

'We must fight for justice!' shouted Prince Cormac. 'Justice and freedom!'

'Come,' barked their father, 'to the armoury! This is no time for chatter. Let us prepare ourselves to do our duty.'

Away they hastened.

The southern armies were marching to cause havoc in Narngalis, but already the northern realm was suffering mayhem of another kind.

Since early in the year, villages in the region of Silverton, in the shadow of the mountains, had been subject to a spate of grisly episodes. People who ventured out of doors after dark suffered a ghastly fate; in the morning their corpses were found, butchered with surgical exactness. There were no survivors, no thefts. Neither was any quarter given - young or old, male or female, crippled or hale, the victims were slain without discrimination. No one had yet caught a glimpse of the perpetrators, but through that region strange mists had begun arising from the ground between sunset and sunrise and, taking into account all evidence, general opinion held that unseelie wights of some uncommon and truly horrifying kind were at work.

At evening on a Salt's day early in Mai, Asrăthiel returned home to the Narngalish royal city of King's Winterbourne from Silverton, where she and William of Narngalis had been helping the king's reeves and bailiffs and constables in their endeavours to uncover clues about the mysterious night attacks. Her sky-balloon *Lightfast* coasted along beneath clouds underlit by the pink glow of sunset. She leaned out over the edge of the wicker basket. Far below, gold and ruby tones highlighted the deepening hues of the landscape. Weather conditions were excellent, the surface winds light, visibility good and the air stable. For a while the excitement of flight, the exhilaration of being at one with the extreme power of the elements, overcame the worries of her daily life. It was a thrill that never dulled.

The aircraft gently dropped several feet, and a lower altitude current began to push it around to the east, off course. Weathermasters strove to employ natural energies whenever possible, instead of summoning elements that would disrupt the atmosphere's complicated balance. Asrăthiel allowed heat to escape from the great sun crystal trussed in its cradle, thereby warming the air inside the envelope and lowering its density. Slowly the aerostat responded to fundamental forces, rising as air pressure and gravity combined to create buoyancy. The pilot let her aircraft ascend to the altitude of a southerly current she had sensed above, and ride with the world's wind. It was blowing faster, too.

The balloon, a quicksilver teardrop, glided in the river of the sky.

Tilting back her head so that her rain hood fell back across her shoulders, the weathermage looked up past the suspended cradle and the skirt of the envelope into the domed interior. It resembled a huge, symmetrical flower, glimmery white. The long gores, extending from the base of the envelope to the crown, served as the petals, striped by the seams of the panels and the shadow of a trailing line; the parachute valve cord. Beyond the flower she could espy floating mid-level layers of rosy altocumulus clouds; flattened globular masses in wavy rows, their base hovering at about twelve thousand feet. This was what people called a 'buttermilk sky', though currently it was tinged the delicate colour of orchids. Withdrawing her weathersenses for a single instant, Asrăthiel abandoned herself to exhilaration. Time seemed suspended as the world drifted past tranquilly below. The joy of lighter-than-air flight never tarnished. 'When once you have tasted flight,' she quoted aloud, 'you will for ever walk with your eyes turned skyward, for there you have been, and there you will always long to return.'

But how much sweeter it would be, she thought fleetingly, to actually swoop and soar with true freedom, on the wings of birds…

The wide green lawns of her home, The Laurels, hove into view beneath the gondola of woven willow. Down there, the miniature figures of the ground crew could be spied waiting; they had been keeping watch for the aerostat ever since the semaphores notified them of their mistress's imminent arrival. A small knot of other observers waited also; Asrăthiel's landlady Mrs. Draycott Parslow and her household never seemed to tire of the spectacle of balloon launches and landings.

Asrăthiel worked the cord to let air escape from the parachute valve atop the envelope, thereby decreasing the inner air temperature. As the balloon commenced to sink she manoeuvred deftly, using the brí to call tiny puffs of wind that aligned the aircraft with the landing site. The landing was a little rougher than usual – as she neared the ground her mind kept straying to other matters - but as an experienced pilot she allowed the wicker gondola to bump along the grass a short distance, minimizing the impact, and gradually coming to a halt. The ground crew held down the basket as soon as it had stopped, and ensured it was properly anchored. With the swiftness born of much practice they spread out a tarpaulin to protect the aircraft from dirt and damage. Asrăthiel opened the parachute valve to its fullest extent, then gracefully vaulted out of the basket. Warm gases fled out from the apex of the envelope into the atmosphere, whereupon the crew seized hold of a cord fastened to the top of the balloon and hauled the envelope over onto the tarpaulin. Expertly they began to squeeze out the remaining air. They would flatten out the flower of silk-light linen before cramming it into the storage bag.

After leaving the aircraft the damsel greeted her landlady and household staff with fondness. They followed as she made her way indoors, tugging off her rain hood as she walked, and shaking out her long black tresses. Her companions were accustomed to her striking looks, but a stranger would have marvelled. So blue were her eyes, and so translucent her skin, that her lids seemed brushed with powdered sky, like the two wings of a bluebird.

Bemusement clouded those remarkable eyes. No explanation for the spate of outlandish butchery at Silverton had been found. The outbreak had spread to the surrounding countryside as far south as the Harrowgate Fells and the outskirts of Paper Mill, then inexplicably ceased. From time to time a few nebulae of preternatural mists had continued to emerge, here and there, still as unaccountable as ever. King Warwick's wardens remained vigilant, but for now it seemed there was nothing more that Asrăthiel, official weathermage to King's Winterbourne, could do; she reverted, instead, to her customary duties.

After dinner the weathermage retired somewhat discontentedly to her favourite haven, the upstairs parlour, where low-burning embers in the grate warmed the room against the cool airs of late Spring. She did not suffer from the cold – indeed she was wearing a light gown of ruched linen – however the housemaid who tended the fireplaces was ignorant of her invulnerability, or incapable of comprehending it, or a slave to habit. Instead of opening a book Asrăthiel reclined upon a buttoned divan, resting the back of her head on an embroidered cushion and staring pensively at the ceiling, where reflected firelight played amidst the mouldings of beaten copper.

For a long while all was quiet save for the low murmur of flames. Then, an interruption.

'That prince, so lordly,' sneered the voice of Asrăthiel's occasional visitor, the urisk. 'You would make a good queen for him. No doubt you dream of him this instant, believing you are in love with him.'

It was remarkable how silently the wight could move, despite his horny hooves. Asrăthiel was by now accustomed to his unheralded appearances and inflammatory statements. Rather than growing indignant at his baiting she replied with studied offhandedness, 'No doubt.'

The little ragged wight, resembling a man from the waist upwards, but with goatlike legs, was seated cross-legged, precariously, atop a cabinet of mahogany that stood against a wall. Regarding her with a cynical air he said, 'I daresay you are consumed by what you believe to be true love. Humankind like best to deceive themselves, and the substances that flow through their brains collude with them in this pastime.'

'Of course our brains conspire,' Asrăthiel retorted, fully rousing herself from her reverie to engage in the usual verbal sparring. She levered herself to sit upright. 'Their primary purpose is to ensure we continue to survive and procreate. All the rest of the brain's contrivances, such as the capacity to enjoy art and music, to fall in love, to philosophize, are born from that single supreme purpose. The bonding of a man and a woman is a tactic that helps guarantee the continuation of our kind. Romantic love arises from the success of that strategy. Do not think I am ignorant.'

'I am overjoyed to learn you harbour no delusions,' said the wight.

The damsel allowed the corners of her mouth to twitch in the beginnings of a smile, pleased to have disarmed her opponent, though she guessed it would be only a temporary victory. 'The truth is obvious, nevertheless love is no less enjoyable for knowing its basis.'

'Would it be less enjoyable were you to be aware of the exact operations of the gelatinous walnut housed within human skulls?'

She rejoined, 'Were I to reply 'yes' or 'no', would that dissuade you from explanation?'

The creature ignored the question. 'There is much that eldritch beings understand about your kind, of which you yourselves are oblivious. The sense of elation accompanying so-called love in its infancy is caused by a mixture of dopamine and phenylethylamine swilling about in the cranium.'

'Your terms are unfamiliar to me,' Asrăthiel retorted. 'I have no idea what you are talking about.'

Her visitor barely paused. 'In new lovers the state of irresistible passion lasts for about two years; the lifespan of neurotrophins in the human system. As lust wanes, the formation of close relationships evolves because of the effect on the brain of oxytocin, which yields a temperate, drifting, affectionate state. Oxytocin is related to opiate-like substances in the brain, which is why the mechanisms of 'love' resemble addiction. Humankind never has a good grasp of the truth at the best of times, but people in the thrall of this maelstrom of chemicals are uncommonly dissociated from reality.'

'It would appear,' said Asrăthiel, 'you are proposing that romantic love is a type of insanity stimulated by alchemies within the brain.'

'For humankind, that's all it is. Such an absurd foundation for the organisation of societies.'

'It has served us well enough.'

'Has it indeed? Think again.'

'You are forever cynical.'

'Merely realistic.'

'Pray, leave us some few of the illusions we hold dear!' the damsel said wryly, smiling.

'Recall, next time you behold your prince,' said the urisk, 'that what you call 'passions' are not lofty sentiments at all, but chemical survival systems embedded in the very flesh, which have arisen in order to make your kind avoid peril and desire that which may be of advantage.'

It appeared to Asrăthiel that the wight believed she had formed a close attachment to William. Furthermore, he seemed scornful of such a relationship, possibly even resentful. Well, let the creature stew. It was his own fault if the idea bothered him – a comeuppance for being so presumptuous as to pry into her personal affairs. Where she chose to bestow her affections was none of his business.

It was true that as time passed she had come to regard William with increasing partiality. She could not help but be aware of the depth and constancy of the prince's fondness for her. It would melt even the hardest heart to be steadfastly loved and held in high regard by anyone, let alone a young man so estimable. Always, she had loved the prince as she would love a brother, but of late she found herself beginning to consider him more as an especially cherished friend. It saddened her that she could not summon stronger sentiments for him, for she felt that he deserved to be loved as ardently as he loved. If it were possible for her to give her heart to any man, she told herself, it would be William.

All at once the wight's harping about the good-natured prince seemed petulant and unbearably tiresome. 'You can be cruel,' Asrăthiel chided, dropping her façade of light-hearted indifference.

Uncharacteristically, the wight seemed to repent. He looked away. 'Yes,' he said. 'That is true.'

After an uncomfortable silence the weathermage said, 'If you would care to know what I was truly thinking of before you showed yourself, I was musing about something that occurred several days ago.'

'What might that be?'

'There was a most curious stirring in the atmosphere, the like of which is rarely manifested. So strong it was, so antagonistic to natural law. . . 'twas evident that there had been some powerful wielding of the brí, somewhere in the southern regions. Weathermasters were at work in no small way. Yet no messenger brought tidings of anything untoward. It will be long ere the patterns return to normal, yet I have no notion of what caused the disturbance. My grandfather would have sent word, were it of consequence, yet I have heard no ill news from him. It is strange. I feel uneasy.'

'You, with your faculties that grasp the nature of the elements!' said the urisk. 'There is much you comprehend that is beyond the reach of commonkind.' Glancing at the pyre of rubies in the hearth as if he saw through them to some remote, incomprehensible place or state of being, he added softly, 'Much, too, that you have no inkling of.'

'Of course there is,' Asrăthiel said, experiencing a sudden rush of fondness for her intermittent and tetchy but intriguingly unpredictable companion. 'However, you have taught me things I could never have learned from books or human scholars.'

During their conversations of the past season, the urisk had told her truths about the world that she had never known, had answered questions she had never dreamed of asking, despite the fact that at Rowan Green she had been well tutored in the lore accumulated by humankind over the centuries.

'Such as?'

'Such as stories about the outer rim of the heavens.' The wight had often spoken of the stars; it seemed he was as attuned to astronomy as bri-wielders were cognizant of weather; linked to the stars by something more than mere observation and study, as if he were, in some way, related by blood to celestial phenomena. 'You sense the slowing of the world's spin,' said Asrăthiel, 'caused by the drag of the tides. You tell of the five hundred and thirty-two year lunar-solar cycle, the exact orbit of the moon, the existence of black holes in the sky beyond the sky, the births and deaths of stars, the equations governing time; incredibly, you even measure the speed of light.'

'Ah,' said the eldritch savant, 'and well might I speak of the stars. For we are all fashioned from star-dust.'

All fashioned from star-dust. It was an extraordinary assertion, one that he had made before, but which Asrăthiel held like treasure in the storehouse of her mind. She considered the concept strangely comforting; it was as if she too were related by blood to the entire universe. It occurred to her, then, that she had not yet tapped the wight's store of knowledge for answers to a more recent mystery. 'Wight, do you know aught of the unseelie killings in the north?' Before she had finished speaking, a lurid glare abruptly licked up the opposite wall. The leaded panes of the windows flared to a bloody radiance. 'What's astir?' Asrăthiel sprang up, ran to the casements and peered out. Through the windows she perceived a small sun rising on the distant heights. 'The Watchmen have kindled the beacon fires! What can it mean?'

No sooner had she asked the question than someone rapped urgently at the parlour door.

'Enter!' she cried.

Her butler, Giles, appeared and bowed. 'My lady, pray forgive me for this interruption. A post rider has just now arrived from the palace.'

'Usher him to me forthwith!' Asrăthiel's heart thudded. Beacons or no beacons, she hoped, desperately, that the messenger would be bringing a long-overdue communication from her weathermaster kindred who had journeyed to Cathair Rua on what she considered to be a perilous mission.

Foreseeably, the urisk Crowthistle was nowhere to be found during the time that Giles or King Warwick's post rider occupied the parlour. The incoming envoy swept his hat from his head and saluted the weathermage on bended knee, as she stood, tall and elegant, beside the divan, anxiously awaiting his news.

'Most esteemed Storm Lady,' said the messenger, 'King Warwick has charged me to proffer you his most cordial greetings. He begs to inform you, my lady, that grave tidings have lately reached King's Winterbourne.'

'Tell on.'

'My lady, the countries of Slievmordhu and Ashqalêth have mobilised in war against Narngalis.'

Asrăthiel said nothing, but her left hand gripped the back of the divan as if she required support to remain on her feet.

'The armies of King Uabhar and King Chohrab are on the march,' the post rider continued. 'At their current rate of progress they will reach the borders of our country in ten days, maybe as few as eight. The defenders of Narngalis are being called to arms. Battle will be joined anon.'

'Has Grïmnørsland been informed?'

'Indeed, my lady. Semaphores confirm that King Thorgild has been notified and is preparing to come to our assistance.'

The damsel quizzed the envoy further as to what else he knew. When she was satisfied that he could tell her no more she dismissed him, bidding Giles attend to his needs. For a while she remained in taut silence. The only sounds in the parlour were the crackle of flames, the soft swoosh as a burned-through log shifted, the mutter and moan of a rising breeze against the leaded window panes.

The Councillors of Ellenhall and their companions had long been absent from Rowan Green, ostensibly enjoying King Uabhar's hospitality in Cathair Rua. Only a single message had they sent home. In it, they stated that all was well. In sudden hindsight, Asrăthiel wondered whether the communication had been concocted by Uabhar, to mislead Avalloc and herself. The weathermasters had failed to return, and now Slievmordhu marched to war. All was now terribly clear. With his military offensive in mind, the king had undoubtedly taken the weathermasters hostage to prevent their opposition. Ruthless intriguer that he was, he had betrayed his own guests. In all likelihood they were at this very moment chained in his dungeons. It must have been their attempts to save themselves that had caused the atmospheric disturbances that had so unsettled her.

Asrăthiel could barely contain her anger when the treachery of Uabhar was borne out by the tidings of war. Her initial impulse was to fly *Lightfast* to Cathair Rua so that she might rescue her kinfolk. Even as she commenced to plan the excursion, however, she recalled to her chagrin that it was possible for sky balloons to be shot down. The envelope's fabric could not resist metal barbs; besides, Uabhar's archers could launch flaming arrows at it and at the wicker basket, so that *Lightfast* would catch fire and fall from the sky like a meteor. Even though Asrăthiel could not be harmed, if she were captured and thrown into prison she, like the others, would be unable to aid Narngalis against the invaders. With her impetuous scheme of action in tatters, she could only bluster and fume.

As she pictured her beloved kindred and friends chained to the walls of some dank cellar, the damsel's rage redoubled. Yet she mastered her temper swiftly; this was no time for tantrums;

there was work to be done. To ensure their freedom, Uabhar must be quelled.

She had no doubt the urisk still lurked nearby. 'Urisk,' she said then into the shadows – for unaccountably she could never bring herself to address him by the odd name he had once revealed to her - 'you have heard the news; 'tis grim indeed! I can scarcely believe it! I must hasten, forthwith, to King Warwick's aid. It may be that I shall not return to The Laurels for some long time.' She hesitated, made as if to impart more, then subsided, her mind racing.

'Well then,' said the voice of the wight, 'so be it.' The urisk moved from the gloom into the firelight and stood on the hearth rug, the coarse, curly hair of his head haloed in gold. 'You must leave this place, and so must I.'

'You?' The declaration startled Asrăthiel, jerking her out of her state of feverish abstraction. 'What can you mean?'

'What do you mean, 'what can I mean'? Did you suppose I had made your brick pile my home, as if I were some stray hound you'd adopted?'

'Nay, of course not,' the damsel bluffed, although she had assumed exactly that. 'Where will you go?'

'Where I will.'

Feeling fractious because this blow fell on the back of the first, the damsel sought to dissuade him. 'These are dangerous times.'

Firelight laved the ragged and diminutive form of the wight. He uttered no word, but his nonchalant pose and the contemptuous tilt of his goateed chin communicated, Do you truly believe I am unaware of that? Do you suppose I care?

Asrăthiel was smitten by an unexpected sense of loss. She had presumed that the urisk would remain at The Laurels, even while she travelled about on the king's business, and that he would be there to converse with her, delight her and vex her whenever she came home. Understanding afresh that nothing eldritch could ever be truly tamed she felt bereft, as if something valuable had been stolen away.

All at once there seemed to be countless matters stored in her mind that she had intended to discuss with the creature, yet had never mentioned. She tried to recall them all, but in the urgency of the moment most of them eluded her. Seating herself on the edge of the divan and twisting her hands together in her lap she said, endeavouring to keep plaintiveness out of her tone, 'Why do you want to go? Have I offended you?'

'My reasons are my own. No, you have not.' The wight crossed to the window and leaped agilely up onto the ledge. Resting his forearm against the panes and his brow on the back of his wrist, he stared moodily out towards the far-off beacon fire. In the fireplace the black husk of a log imploded, setting off a brief fireworks display and conjuring a swathe of smoke ghosts.

At length the damsel said resignedly, 'I see you keep your own counsel, as ever. I will not pry. Allow me to say, though, that I will be sorry at your departure. Long have I believed you to be - ' she broke off, paused, then stammered with gaucherie that surprised herself, 'extraordinary. That is to say,' she went on hurriedly, 'I believe you are different in most respects from other wights of your kind. I have learned that you possess deep knowledge of the great sciences, encompassing vast lore that reaches from the paths of the stars, to the minds of humankind, down to the roots of the mountains. You will tell me that I am not as well acquainted with other wights as I am with you, and therefore have no basis for comparison. Yet many tales are told about eldritch creatures, and not in any of them is there reference to one such as you.'

'Every living being is unique.'

'Are you the king of the urisks?'

The urisk laughed, but with no good humour. 'Quit conjecture,' he said. 'Keep to your weatherworking, which you are better at. Urisks are solitaries, and have no king, as anybody knows.'

'Are you determined to leave this house?'

'I am.'

'Will you sometimes return? Will you visit?' she persisted.

'Weatherwitch,' the wight said, 'I seldom make promises.'

Asrăthiel nodded, struggling to keep her face from crumpling into an expression of disappointment.

'But this I avow,' he went on. 'In your most bitter hour, look for me. I will come to you.'

Touched by this unusual gesture of kindness from a creature prone to be as prickly as his namesake, the weed crowthistle, Asrăthiel was on the verge of thanking him for his offer of protection, before recalling the eldritch prohibition on that form of expressing gratitude.

'Your courtesy is appreciated,' was all she could manage, shyly, suddenly awkward for no reason that she could fathom. Ridiculously, she almost laughed at the concept of such a small, innocuous object, no matter how unlike other urisks he was, proposing to aid a weathermage. Promises made by immortal entities, however, always held fast, and eldritch protection could be formidable even when offered by a dwarfish domestic creature who walked on the hooves of a goat.

Giles rapped at the door a second time, and during the ensuing bustle the urisk disappeared. Later, when her thoughts turned to her odd companion once more, it came to Asrăthiel that it should be no surprise the wight would wish to emigrate now that battle loomed nigh. The quarrels of men would hardly be to the taste of one such as he, who considered himself infinitely superior to the human race, and it was unlikely he would risk accidentally becoming embroiled in them.

Over the years his companionship had pleased her more than she had ever admitted to herself. They had shared numerous jests. Her confidence in him was such that she had entrusted him with many of her innermost thoughts and feelings. Besides, she would grievously miss his treasuries of knowledge. The erudition of this immortal being seemed boundless; she supposed he had lived long enough to know practically everything. He could describe events of the dim past as if they were still fresh in his memory. He proved himself master of the lore of hidden things. Once, he had described to her the strata buried miles below the surface of the ground, the layer upon layer of clays and shales and sandstones; the fossils held frozen in time within those layers...

Had the weathermage but known it, one of those fossil-bearing layers ran deep beneath The Laurels, its carbonate-rich beds preserving a wide variety of petrified invertebrates. Sporadically other such shale strata stretched underground for many leagues; beneath mountain ranges, rivers and lakes, beyond the Riddlecombe Steeps, all the way to the caverns perforating the great Eastern Ranges in Slievmordhu.

From those exact stenchful caverns the last of the Marauders were marching out to make war. They issued forth in no orderly way, not in ranks or files, not marching in step nor organised into battalions and regiments but in ragged groups or pairs or alone, each making his way as he thought fit. These haphazard crowds had been instructed by their leaders that their only purpose was to attack soldiers who wore the battledress of Narngalis or Grïmnørsland, and to leave the other uniforms alone – for now. Later, when otherkind – the rest of the human race, including their allies - had been weakened and their numbers thinned by their struggle against each other, and their farms and villages left unprotected; when they were at their most vulnerable, then would the Marauders turn upon them all, and rend them. But for now the comswarms must appear compliant.

The tardiest stragglers amongst them, Scroop and Grak, were reluctant conscripts. They had spent the evening endeavouring to keep a low profile - no simple task, with profiles that resembled barnacle-covered flotsam - and in their efforts to spy on everyone else, they had inadvertently become witness to a large company drove of trows gliding northwards, flitting almost soundlessly through the twilight like bundles of tattered webs on spindly sticks. The uncanny sight had unnerved them further.

'Shake an 'ind leg, ya misfits,' their captain bellowed, pinning the stragglers with a baleful eye. 'Do not think I cannot see youse loitering be'ind, up to ya sly tricks. Youse are comin' to 'elp us foight, by 'ook or by crook, ya cowards!'

Unwillingly the pair loped along in the wake of their cohorts.

'Gunna get skewered if we obey orders,' Grak said to Scroop, out of the side of his mouth.

Scroop blinked two of his eyes and nodded. 'Yeah,' he replied in his peculiar, high-pitched voice. 'Kings' war boys got wicked weapons. Skewered, all right.'

'Don't wanna get skewered.'

'Nope.'

'Captin's takin' us north, inta Narngalis, inta the 'ome territory of the Narngalishes.'

'Them with reel sharp swords.'

'We ortta disguise ourselves. Ittud be safer.'

'Yeah.'

They scratched their flea-bitten ears.

The same stars glittering peacefully above the caverns of the Marauders also glimmered above the city of King's Winterbourne. Their light silver-plated the basalt battlements of Wyverstone Castle. Within that fortress much urgent discussion was taking place. Royal personages were consulting with advisors, secretaries of state, bailiffs and other well-informed members of the household. Around this inner conclave soared oak-panelled walls, detailed in gilt and hung with crimson damask. Through traceried windows the stars were shining, but it was lamplight that sparkled upon the gold-threaded fabrics and jewellery of the room's occupants.

Asrăthiel was present, clad in a travelling cloak almost as blue as her eyes, and a square-necked gown of brocade. Upon her head she wore a stiffened coif whose front edge was decorated by a band of fine silverwork set with moonstones. The white jewel that had belonged to her mother glistened on a fine chain hanging about her neck. In honour of her parents she had taken to wearing it; a token of her father who wandered afar in mapless marches, and her mother, safe at home but doomed to sleep endlessly, high against the wind-scoured alpine sky in a glass cupola fretted with roses.

The damsel had just received a semaphore message from her

grandfather at High Darioneth, the contents of which she made known to the conclave. Uabhar's display of military aggression had confirmed Avalloc's suspicions. Like Asrăthiel, he and the few remaining weathermasters were now convinced that the King of Slievmordhu had captured their kinsfolk; that he was holding them prisoner, bound and gagged, so that they would be unable to use their powers to interfere in the conflict. The first investigators Avalloc had dispatched from Rowan Green had mysteriously failed to return. Since then the Storm Lord had sent a second company of daring and capable men on a mission to infiltrate the palace at Cathair Rua, by use of deception, or disguise, or whatever means were required. They intended, if necessary, to break into Uabhar's very dungeons. To locate the captives and set them free was their purpose.

'Even if this rescue expedition meets with no success, my kinsmen will surely find a way to escape,' Asrăthiel said to King Warwick and his two sons. 'Surely Uabhar cannot keep their hands and tongues immobile forever. A few words, a slight movement of the fingers will be all that is needed to command the brí, then wind and fire and water will burst lock and key asunder! When we have defeated Ó Maoldúin I will destroy his dungeons. How dare he treat my kinsmen so foully! Let us to the battle front forthwith!'

'We ride south this night for the Eldroth Fields,' said the king, 'but you, Asrăthiel, will not accompany us. I would fain keep you safe from the fighting. You must remain here at the castle. If my troops cannot achieve victory on the field without your aid, we do not deserve to win.'

'What? By your leave, Majesty, I yearn to avenge the wrong done to Rowan Green!'

'Rest assured, I will send for you if needs be.'

'Harm cannot be done to me.' It cost the damsel dearly to reconfirm the qualities that set her apart from the rest of the human race, especially in front of Prince William, whose sudden recollection of her immortality was manifested only in a flicker of his facial muscles. 'I beg of you, my liege…'

Warwick cut short Asrăthiel's speech. 'Of course I fully understand that you are invulnerable, Lady Maelstronnar, however I direct you to remain here, for now. I am not willing to put you at risk of being captured.'

Despite her yearnings, the damsel knew she must comply with the commands of her sovereign. To indicate acquiescence she bowed to him, somewhat stiffly. Inwardly, she seethed. Masking her frustration with the accomplishment of a true diplomat she asked, 'How long will it be before Thorgild's reinforcements reach us?'

The king nodded to his eldest son, and William answered, 'We estimate that if he can marshal his troops within a week, then make a forced march across country, he will arrive in the middle of Juyn.'

'So late!' Asrăthiel cried in dismay.

'By then we will have the victory,' William's brother Walter said a little too loudly, as if by sheer force of conviction he could overcome the formidable odds.

'If not, we can, at least, hold out until then,' William said resolutely. 'We are on home ground. Our troops are familiar with the terrain, unlike the southern invaders. It is not merely by chance or necessity that we have chosen the Eldroth Fields to make our stand. We possess maps of the maze of ancient Fridean delvings beneath the landscape. The largest of these tunnels and channels can be used for communications, and as fortified trenches for defence. Our nimblest raiders may suddenly appear in the midst of the foe, cause mayhem, then disappear, bringing down rockfalls behind them to seal the passageways. Ó Maoldúin knows nothing of this. The Fields of Eldroth will prove to be our allies.'

'We need all the allies we can muster,' Asrăthiel said bitterly, picturing the noble councillors of Ellenhall under lock and key. She addressed the king. 'My liege, I beg you to allow me to go and meet Thorgild on the road so that I may protect him and his troops, in case Ó Maoldúin sends a swift vanguard to ambush him, or in case unseelie wights waylay them. I will not be at the battle front, yet I will be aiding your efforts.'

The king pondered. 'A splendid scheme,' he answered presently. 'Do so Asrăthiel, and choose any of my people to accompany you.'

When Asrăthiel looked up, her gaze locked with William's. His expression said, 'Would that I could be numbered amongst your escort,' but they both knew he could not leave his father's side.

'Gramercie, my liege,' Asrăthiel said, 'but I need very little assistance and my aerostat is not capacious. I will take only my maid, if she is willing, for I have trained her to help with the take-off and landing of aircraft.'

'What of the situation in the far north, at Silverton and the Harrowgate Fells?' Prince Walter asked his father. 'Is Narngalis to be pinched in the claws of baneful tongs, between weapons of steel and weapons of gramarye?'

'According to the last report all remains tranquil throughout that region,' replied the king. 'The local shrievalties remain on alert, and sentinels have been posted in strategic locations to keep vigil, in case the unseelie slayings should recommence. For now, that danger sleeps. But enough of this talk! It is time to gird our-selves and hasten to defend the kingdom. Farewell, Asrăthiel!'

On Mai the twenty-second, a date Asrăthiel used to celebrate as Highland Mai Day when she dwelled in the Mountain Ring, Uabhar and Chohrab crossed the border and entered Narngalis. Their armies in colours of blood-flame and sun-fire advanced into the north-kingdom, marching rapidly. Through blossoming fields they trampled - crushing the buttercups underfoot - and along muddy highways. The metal wheels of their supply wagons and ordnance carriages smashed the hedges bordering the roadsides; the hobnailed boots of the infantry clattered across bridges of wood and stone. Slender spears and pikes and standards surged like some storm-driven forest, and the cavalrymen made an awesome spectacle as they sashayed forth, resplendent, beneath regimental banners.

King Uabhar himself rode with his troops amidst his retinue of bodyguards, their fleet-footed horses having caught up with the slow-moving columns. King Chohrab, too, travelled at the head of his own army, although initially he had lagged somewhat behind the King of Slievmordhu. In fact, he had not intended to venture from the safety of the city walls at all, until Uabhar suddenly took his leave, declaring that he was heading for the battlefront.

'But why?' Chohrab had cried, rousing from his waking nightmares. 'Surely your commanders are competent enough to make decisions on the spot. Why risk your own person?'

'My wife nagged me until I could endure it no longer,' Uabhar replied ruefully. 'Pity me, for she can be a tyrant behind closed doors. Go and prove your courage, she harped. People will laugh at me if I have a craven husband! Chide me not, Chohrab, fool that I am, for being ruled by womanhood.'

Chohrab did not question that this was so, for he had never taken much note of the reticent Queen Saibh and knew next to nothing of her true character. Try as he might, he could not visualise Uabhar enthusiastically charging head first into battle at risk of life and limb, so he supposed that his ally's motive for his proposed heroics was valid.

'I must go to the front also,' declared Chohrab, 'otherwise I will be named a coward.'

'Not at all!' Uabhar protested. 'Everyone knows you suffer from ill health and are too delicate to fare abroad. No one will blame you, brother. Ádh be with you!' And he departed precipitately.

Chohrab, however, seethed with discontent and a smattering of suspicion. 'Uabhar will recite words of inspiration to his men,' he said to his brother-in-law, Rahim. 'He will appear to be a better leader than I. To him will go the glory and the power when we triumph. I wonder whether he truly has my interests at heart, for he takes precious little note of my opinions. In future I shall stand up to him! ' He had his apothecaries mix a strong stimulant, which he quaffed without delay, then girded himself for war and followed after.

Day by day, rumour proliferated that Uabhar was openly in league with Marauders; that he had sealed a peace agreement with several large comswarms, promising to cease harassing them in return for their cooperation against his enemies. Uabhar's paid gossip-mongers made certain to conceal the truth about the exact date this treaty had been ratified, asserting that, if such a compact existed, it would have been a recent development forced upon the king by the exigencies of war.

Despite the false rumours being put about, some of the Knights of the Brand and a small proportion of the civilian populace guessed the truth; that the alliance had been struck in secret, long ago. Uabhar had been allowing the Marauders to persecute his own subjects in order to terrorise them into paying higher taxes, purportedly for protection. Though their outrage knew no limits, no one had the courage to speak out. Those who had deduced the facts began - in private - to question their sovereign's methods.

Many Slievmordhuan subjects believed that if the tales of alliance were true their king ought to be feted for such a cunning move, as it would guarantee their security. Others, mistrusting the comswarms, dreaded the ultimate outcome of a league so incongruous. Those citizens of Slievmordhu who did not applaud their sovereign, and in fact cursed him and all his schemes, chiefly resided in the villages that lined the war machine's northward route, for Uabhar and Chohrab supplemented the provisions of their forces by allowing the soldiers to strip the countryside bare of victuals and fodder as they travelled. Nor were the troops gentle with those from whom they pillaged, despite that they were fellow countrymen.

By the time the foremost newly mobilised battalions of King Warwick had swept southwards over the Black Crags and down past the Eldroth Fields to meet the invasion, the Slievmordhuan and Ashqalêthan vanguard had reached the crossroads known as Blacksmith's Corner, where the byway to the Mountain Ring branched off to the west. Had they turned onto that path, they would at length have arrived at the very gates of High Darioneth. They made no effort, however, to steer for the stronghold of the weatherlords. Their goal lay in another direction.

At the forefront of the invading columns small groups of Sliev-mordhuan and Ashqalêthan foot soldiers continually conducted patrols, scouring terrain which might hide infantry waiting in ambush, and keeping a lookout for enemy scouts. Near the cross-roads they finally confronted the first of the defenders; an advance patrol of Narngalish bowmen, who immediately loosed a hail of arrows on the southerners.

Messengers raced back to inform Commander Mac Brádaigh that hostile archers were concealed in the hedges and deep lanes, and that, further along the road ranks of infantry were lined up and waiting, armed with bow, pike, war-hammer and axe. Without delay Mac Brádaigh ordered his leading troops to halt and deploy in combat formation, while the first companies of the main-battle caught up.

Before the southerners had time to arrange themselves in fight-ing order King Warwick's vanguard surged forward in the attack. The Narngalish archers continued to shoot over the shields of their infantry into the invading troops, who were still frantically preparing to return the volleys and suffered numerous casualties. Mac Brádaigh, however, soon had them manoeuvred into a posi-tion to withstand the onslaught, whereupon his infantry retaliated with their own barrage.

Thus began the first encounter of the war – the battle of Black-smith's Corner.

2
A WICKEDNESS

Why goest thou hence, my lovely lord,
Upon thy snow-white stallion?
Why leave thy home to fare abroad,
Without me riding pillion?

Say, is it to the tourney field
For prizes and medallions?
Tiest thou my favour on thy shield
Amongst the gay pavilions?

I dreamed the brazen trumpets sang,
Bells chimed in loud carillon,
And tents like stripèd flowers sprang,
Green, saffron and vermilion.

Alas! Not for the tourney bound
Art thou, with brave battalions.
Thine object is some battleground
Drenched with the blood of millions.

Farewell. Now I am left to sigh
Amidst bereft civilians.
I wonder - wilt thou live or die
Before the bright pavilions?

Hill and valley rang with the sound of eldritch weepers lamenting. Anyone who managed to catch a glimpse of one of these wights would have beheld a ragged little washerwoman on her knees at the banks of a stream, sobbing as she scrubbed at a bloodstained shirt. It was rarely, however, that humankind laid eyes on these elusive incarnations, though their voices were loud enough to be heard at great distances. The weepers' cries prophesied the deaths of men, and at Blacksmith's Corner there was much to foretell. Their keening continued incessantly, behind the music of war: the screams and yells, the clash of weapons, the trumpets and drums.

For three days the conflict raged back and forth, waxing and waning. Slievmordhu's Knights of the Brand fought well, but they were short of their best company; furthermore, without their leader, Conall Gearnach, they lacked their usual zeal. Nonetheless their ranks were as well disciplined as Narngalis' elite knights, the Companions of the Cup – in contrast to their compeers, the heavy cavalry of Ashqalêth. The Desert Paladins believed they deserved the honourable stations in the front lines. They jockeyed for position, not only vying against the Knights of the Brand but also against each other, often ignoring orders in their quest for individual glory. This lack of compliance caused disorder amongst the allied ranks of Slievmordhu and Ashqalêth.

Perceiving the increasing disarray that was thwarting his strategies, Mac Brádaigh decided to employ fresh tactics. He had been eagerly looking forward to the moment when Marauders would begin pouring into the battlefield like flies to a carcass, in response to the messages carried to them by his own officers. The enemy, he knew, would be dismayed when confronted unexpectedly by the vicious swarmsmen. When he began receiving reports that confirmed the first of the cave dwellers were, at last, converging on the scene of action, he judged that the time was right for an added surprise.

King Uabhar had entrusted Mac Brádaigh with the strange artefact discovered amongst the ruins of the Dome of Strang, the Sylvan Comb, along with the secret that governed it. Spurring his steed through the front lines into the very heart of the fighting, the High Commander hurled the goblin artefact to the ground, articulating the Word.

The Comb's nineteen teeth bit into the dust.

His own men and their allies were prepared for what happened next. The raising of certain flags and the sounding of drums and trumpets had signalled the alert: Ware the enchantment! The southerners fell back, having been instructed as to what would occur, but even they were astonished. As for the opposing troops, they were taken by surprise and thrown into confusion.

A sudden wood of silvery trees, most wonderful and uncanny, sprang up around and amongst the fighting men. Their bark seemed etched with spirals and flowing designs, their leaves shimmered and sighed in a nonexistent breeze. Dark vapours coiled between the trees, as if sentient. Eerie shiftings and blinkings in the forest's shadowy depths gave suggestion that unguessable creatures lurked there. The skulls of the soldiers who found themselves in this wood of weirdness became flooded with a subdued oceanic roar, and a dry rattling like dead leaves shaking in an Autumn wind. They felt dizzy and dislocated, as if transported to some eldritch realm in which nothing they had ever known made sense. A feeling of impending doom and tragedy tainted their awe.

If the Comb's illusions cast the defenders into turmoil, the incoming Marauders augmented their disorder. At their first appearance, both invaders and defenders were astounded. Mac Brádaigh had issued no forewarning of this to his own troops or Ashqalêth's. Uabhar's bizarre alliance had never been openly acknowledged; it had been a secret guarded as closely as possible - given men's fondness for gossip – until the last moment, for if the southern troops had known, the knowledge would soon have been gleaned by the northerners, one way or another. Soldiers in all camps reacted sharply to the intrusion of their traditional antagonists, until commands rippled through the ranks of the southern allies – 'Stand unafraid, for the swarmsmen are on our side'.

Huge and powerful as oxen, the swarmsmen ploughed havoc amongst the Narngalish. Amongst the fighting men astonishment dawned, as they comprehended that the hearsay had been true, and Uabhar had indeed struck some bargain with the monsters. Outrage and disgust flamed, even as they continued to do battle against each other, but when men in the uniforms of Slievmordhu and Ashqalêth remained unscathed by the monsters, and the southerners witnessed the carnage the swarmsmen wrought on their behalf, they took heart, and many began to approve of the unusual manoeuvre.

Outnumbered, demoralised and unable to shield themselves from the debilitating effects of the Comb's supernatural visions, the northern forces were eventually driven back. King Warwick's officers endeavoured to beat an orderly retreat so that they might rally the troops, carry the injured with them, and review their tactics. The invaders pursued, skirmishing and picking off the few stragglers, until Mac Brádaigh summoned them to fall back and regroup. Both sides had sustained substantial casualties, but the southerners successfully took control of Blacksmith's Corner. For King Uabhar the invasion had begun well.

That night his triumphant troops, their spirits high, sang songs of ancient battles as they drank their ration of ale around their campfires:

'Time bygone, wicked goblinkind came down from north-
    ern heights,
Laid siege to lands of mortal men and ruled the death-dark
    nights.
Through many battles terrible, both wights and men
    engaged,
But Silver Hill was named amongst the greatest ever waged.

'From mountain-halls the goblin hordes poured forth with
    eerie sound,
But, combat-ripe, the Slievmordhuan soldiers stood their
    ground.
Ever toward the south men turned, expecting soon to see
Three companies of reinforcements, armoured cap-a-pie.

'"We'll hold this camp," their captains cried, "Until relief
   arrives!"
We'll not surrender Silver Hill. Defend it with your lives!
Noble Sir Seán of Bellaghmoon commands us in the fray –
No bolder or more valiant man ever saw light of day."

Yet goblins thronged, wave upon wave, in numbers
   unforetold.
Alas! The ranks of mortalkind boasted few swords of gold.
They found themselves outnumbered - yet, unyielding,
   pressed the fight.
"The north-bound troops will join us soon! We're sure to
   win the night!"

But ere the goblins issued from their vast and sunless caves
In secrecy they had dispatched their crafty kobold slaves,
Who, under cover of the dark, by pathless ways had crept.
They struck the northbound companies and slew them as
   they slept.

All through the night at Silver Hill Sir Seán of Bellaghmoon
Fought on beside his men. At last the sun rose, none
   too soon.
For, as night's shade gave way to day the goblins had
   withdrawn.
A bitter scene of carnage spread beneath the rays of dawn.

'"Alas!" cried Bellaghmoon. Sore anguish creased his noble
   brow.
"Ill fate has met our soldiers, else they'd be beside us now!"
"We must retreat," his captains urged, "Before the setting sun,
For goblins move in darkness. They outmatch us two
   to one."
'But bold Sir Seán of Bellaghmoon cried, "Never shall
   we flee,
I've sworn to fight for Silver Hill, though death should
   be my fee."

His troops thus stayed upon the mount, aware there was
no chance,
And when the sun began to fall they sharpened sword
and lance.

As darkness came a-creeping, goblins overthrew them all,
Hewed off the head of Bellaghmoon and of his captains tall,
Hoisting the severed polls on pikes. Unto their eldritch halls
They bore their dreadful prizes, for to nail them on the walls.

Above the gates of goblin-realm they hung their grisly
plunder.
The mourning winds keened through the vales, the
mountains rang with thunder.
But proud Sir Seán who fought so well, he did not die
in vain.
Ye bards and minstrels, sing his praise and eulogise his name.
For, hard against all odds he would not let his sovereign down
And through harshest adversity stayed loyal to the crown."

All the while, high above and far away from the clamour of
war, Asrăthiel journeyed westwards in her sky-balloon accompanied by her maid, Linnet. The servant leaned on the basket's rim,
gazing dreamily at the landscape over which they were gliding.
She enjoyed flight, and her mistress had tutored her well in the
rudiments of crewmanship.

Preoccupied with the straitened circumstances of her kindred
and worried about her friends who must defend Narngalis, the
weathermage was piloting the aerostat somewhat absentmindedly.
It was sufficient. After numerous flying hours she had no need to
consider what to do next. Her intuitive perception of altitude, and
of wind speed and direction, combined with her own observa-
tions, enabled her to find the right level to catch the currents she
required. Without having to think about it she let heat escape from
the sun-crystal a short while before she wanted to ascend, and shut

it off a few moments before she wanted to stop rising. Inexperienced pilots often overshot, rising too high before leveling off, but Asrăthiel, to whom the elements were as extensions of her own faculties, never erred.

A thin layer of wispy clouds drifted at an altitude of about five hundred feet, spread on a horizontal plane. Above it stood a deep chasm of cloudless sky, roofed by thick, fast-moving cumulus, like clumps of lamb's wool borne on a clear tide. The river meandered below, grey as polished pewter, its shores braided by dark green knots of trees. Dense flosses of foliage mottled the landscape as far as the eye could see. Through the dense cover the road could seldom be glimpsed. Occasionally Asrăthiel and her passenger would see a curve of it engraved into the foliage, with pocket-handkerchief fields and meadows fanning out from the verges, studded with square-cut buttons that were the roofs of buildings.

It was easy to spy the marching columns of King Thorgild's cavalcades and infantry columns; an articulated serpent in gleaming mail winding its way along the River Road towards Narngalis, pennants flying. The troops who walked or rode below the aerostat looked up to behold two beautifully dressed young women gliding upon the air, borne up by a silver-white sphere, and they were struck with awe by the sight. They welcomed the presence of a weathermage to aid them in their journey. Asrăthiel guided her aircraft with a precision that pilots lacking the brí could only dream of, until the basket hovered just above the treetops at the head of the column, matching the pace of the marchers. Flocks of crows scattered from the trees as the balloon passed by.

King Thorgild rode in the lead with his three sons Hrosskel, Halvdan and Gunnlaug. Unhelmed were they, their hair shining copper-gold whenever the sun broke through the clouds. The emblem of the square-sailed longboat was embroidered against the turquoise background of their velvet tabards, and peacock plumes adorned the harness of their steeds. Beneath the tabards they were armed, but not yet heavily armoured for war. Over the rattle and shriek of the startled crows, Asrăthiel exchanged greetings with the royal family and gave them such advice as she could: The way seemed clear before them, she had sighted no danger on the road, and King Warwick's troops were south-bound to meet the first spear thrust of the invasion. She emphasized the fact that haste was imperative, for against the combined forces of Slievmordhu and Ashqalêth, Narngalis would be outnumbered and hard-pressed.

Well after the sun had set the columns continued to march, but eventually, when they had penetrated a lush and fertile river valley, Thorgild issued the command to halt and make camp for the night. Speed was essential, it was true, but the troops must arrive at their destination in good order, not exhausted and underfed. Within the hour, a city of portable shelters sprang up all along the valley floor.

Having known a long period of peace, Grïmnørsland was not equipped with the latest in tentage for military campaigns. Many of the structures were aged. Most had originally been fashioned for use at tournaments, state ceremonies, picnics or hunting expeditions. Made from heavy sailcloth first dyed with weld then overdyed with woad to produce a deep blue-green shade, the tents were triangular or wedge shaped, with finials cast in the design of fishes. The royal compound dominated the encampment, its vertical sides adorned with heraldic devices, banners flying from the tips of its pointy roofs. Here it was that Thorgild sheltered his horses and the upper echelons of his household. The main structure in the compound consisted of twelve single- and double-peaked pavilions with tasselled valances, all connected by passages. Four of the edifices were for the use of Thorgild - a pavilion for the council of state, a bath pavilion, an arming pavilion and so on - the rest were for his sons. As royal pavilions went, it was austere.

It was not until Asrăthiel and Linnet had landed the balloon and joined the royal family in their lodgings that the weathermage spoke of the rumours of Uabhar's alliance with the Marauders, the unsolved mysteries of Silverton and, above all, the undoubted betrayal and imprisonment of the weathermasters. She had had no wish to dampen the spirits of the troops by shouting such disturbing tidings over their heads from the balloon's gondola.

Propped against piles of brocade cushions strewn about the carpeted floor, her audience remained in silence while she made her report. Lamps, hanging on long chains from the ridgepole, glowed like faceted gems, their light casting a muted sheen on the wall hangings and the satin festoons billowing from the ceiling. The youngest prince, Gunnlaug, sat cross-legged with a dish of garlic sausage on his knee, chewing while he listened.

'I am grieved that Sir Isleif and the Shield Champions were unable to protect the weathermasters from Uabhar's treachery,' Thorgild said heavily, when Asrăthiel had finished speaking. 'My knights never returned from that mission. Uabhar sent word that they had been slain by Marauders on the road as they journeyed, not two leagues from Cathair Rua, but I did not believe a word of it. No barbarian cave dwellers could overcome such fine warriors. I am now convinced they met with foul play from Ó Maoldúin, but there is no way to prove it.'

'I grieve also, at this loss,' said Asrăthiel. 'The fame of the Shield Champions was widespread. Sir Isleif was greatly esteemed.'

'He was a man most honourable,' agreed Prince Halvdan, 'a defender of his people, oath-bound to uphold truth and justice.'

'And in all things wise, level-headed and determined,' his elder brother Hrosskel appended.

'But it seems,' Gunnlaug put in through a mouthful of food, 'he was bested in the end. Ó Maoldúin is indeed a formidable foe.'

Hearing these words King Thorgild wrinkled his brow in exasperation, and Hrosskel turned a disapproving look upon his youngest brother.

'Formidable and ruthless,' Asrăthiel agreed, to break the uncomfortable silence.

'Methinks you have been consorting again with the druids, Gunnlaug,' the monarch said sharply. 'Stay away from them! They meddle overmuch in affairs of state, and poison men's minds with insidious advocacy of causes that enhance their own veiled interests – which, I'll warrant, do not lie with us. Slievmordhu is not as redoubtable as they would have you believe.'

Putting aside his dish, Gunnlaug counted on his fingers: 'Ó Maoldúin owns an eldritch weapon, and a covenant with our pretty friends of the caves. He has stifled his most powerful adversaries, convinced the desert king to aid him, and jumped first, while the rest of us were asleep.'

'He also has his weaknesses,' said Halvdan.

'They are hard to see, from where I am sitting,' said Gunnlaug, 'but I long to find them out with my axe.'

'It will take more than your axe to finish Ó Maoldúin,' observed Hrosskel. Clearly he intended it as a jest, but Gunnlaug gave him a filthy look.

'Think you?' the youngest prince thrust out his chin. 'Perchance you think you could do it all by yourself, eh? Or you and Hrosskel shoulder to shoulder, champions of Grïmnørsland!'

'Save your hero's boasts,' Thorgild said, directing his gaze at all three of his sons, but his words to only one. Gunnlaug subsided, and Asrăthiel seized the opportunity to lead the discussion to a topic close to her heart. For a while the youngest prince listened without making a contribution, obviously bored. Presently he got up and wandered away.

During the previous exchange Asrăthiel had been bracing herself to broach a certain subject with the king. Of all political causes, that of the rights of nonhumans was dearest to her, but it was also the only subject that won her disfavour amongst many of her friends. They were all good people, she knew, but cultural mores had made them blind to the suffering they caused by their actions or inaction. Risking dislike by speaking out was hard, but remaining silent would have been harder.

'I would that this war had never begun,' the damsel said to Thorgild, 'not least because of the terrible toll humankind's battles take on horses. It is injustice beyond belief that innocent beasts, grass-eaters, should be used as war machines and, usually, end up thrashing and dying in agony at the end of a spear. Our quarrels are not theirs. To use them thus is inhumane in the extreme. The employment of cavalry is unjust and cruel.'

This was tactless of her, she was aware – particularly at such a time, but contrary to her own best interests she was driven, as ever, by compassionate ideals, even to the extent of sacrificing the kind opinion of those who would review her.

Thorgild's increased displeasure was evident. 'Have you spoken of your concerns with Warwick?' he asked.

'Indeed, sir, I speak often to him on this subject. He is sympathetic to the cause, however he says he can find no alternative.'

'And there is no alternative, if we are to defend our realms against an enemy who has no such qualms about using horses in warfare,' Thorgild said firmly.

'Yet that does not diminish the wrongness of it,' the weathermage persisted.

'With respect, Lady Maelstronnar,' the king said formally, 'I am grateful to you for your help and I value your friendship. Nonetheless, I will no longer listen to your lectures. I fear you are in danger of becoming a pedant.'

The weathermage's efforts had come to naught, as she had rather suspected they would. She could only hope that by sheer repetition, illumination and persistence she might cause humankind to question the existing state of affairs. She disliked admonishing people in this way and always had to steel herself to the task. The entire business of abuse and exploitation was hateful enough, without that it made her feel obliged to say and do things that grated on the sensibilities of others; it felt like swimming upstream against a fast current, when by nature she would rather have simply crossed to the other side and gone about her business.

Bowing coldly, the damsel said, 'Compassionate folk have to show opposition to cruelty, sir, and at times we have to run the risk of having unflattering labels placed on us, because there are some things for which we should display no tolerance.'

She and the king spoke no more to each other that evening and Thorgild initiated a discussion of strategies with his generals. Prince Halvdan and Asrăthiel were the last to seek their couches that night; they conversed until late. 'Like you I am sorely grieved

that this war has come to pass,' the prince told her. 'I do not want
to fight against Slievmordhu. Because of this war I have lost my
friends at Ó Maoldúin's court.'

'You will not lose the goodwill of the Crown Prince,' said
Asrăthiel, 'nor of Two-Swords Gearnach.'

'You think not?'

'Kieran and Conall, above all men, understand the concept of
duty. They will absolve you from all blame.'

'I can only hope that the conflict will soon be over,' said
Halvdan, 'and that peace and amicability will be restored between
our realms.'

A pavilion was set up for Asrăthiel, and an overnight watch posted on *Lightfast*. Next morning the entire tent city was dismantled
and the army was on the move before sunrise. The weathermage
and her maid accompanied them in the aerostat, hovering near the
head of the procession at a height of two hundred feet so that she
might keep watch for signs of danger. Some of the gawping soldiers
took to calling the weathermage 'The Lady in the Moon'.

She had temporarily set aside her efforts on behalf of horses
used in battle, for no one would listen. Her vexation became part
of the general turmoil within her breast. Wrath at Uabhar's sub-
jugation of her kinsmen ate at her like a canker, and her thumbs
twitched with desire to summon thunderbolts. The anger was a lid
that battened over dread. Since King Thorgild's revelation that he
believed Uabhar had lied about the way his knights met their end,
she had begun to fear, within some secret recess of her heart, that a
fate worse than captivity had been inflicted upon her kinfolk. She
would not, however, permit herself to dwell on the possibility, and
deliberately concealed the tumult within her mind.

As for King Thorgild, he brooded, speaking only when it was
absolutely necessary, even during the nightly meals he took with
his sons and Asrăthiel. He was filled with self-reproach for having
invested his faith in Uabhar Ó Maoldúin, and unable to forgive
himself for his role, no matter how unwitting, in the betrayal of the
weathermasters. Nobody, not even his sons who rode beside him,

could rouse him from his gloomy abstraction.

Having prevailed at the Battle of Blacksmith's Corner, the southern troops speedily regrouped. Shortly thereafter they began to press on towards that region in Narngalis known as the Eldroth Fields, in the wake of the retreating defenders. Marauders skulked along the fringes of the marching battalions, like predatory beasts seeking the weakest of the herd. Scouts and reconnaissance parties kept a wary eye on the swarmsmen, who in spite of alliances and promises, appeared ready to pounce on any man they might encounter.

A company of Ashqalêthan cavalry was crossing a hillside meadow when the outriders spied a scuffle breaking out amongst the willows lining the stream at the bottom of the slope. From a distance it looked as if the circling Marauders had stumbled upon two Narngalish stragglers, whom they set upon with a vengeance. To the astonishment of the observers the Narngalishmen broke free of their attackers and ran away, doffing their garments one by one, with each stride, throwing them wildly to the winds. Hats and jackets were tossed into the air, and shirts, and belts, and even – after some stumbling, rolling and hopping - breeches. The Marauders gave chase. Soon the hunt disappeared into a grove of alders.

'Ha! The freaks prove their worth,' one of the horsemen said, snickering contemptuously.

Another shrugged. 'And the Narngalish, faced with defeat, are losing their wits.'

Had the audience stayed to keep watch on the alder grove they might have seen, some while later, two threadbare figures cautiously emerging.

'Rotten as a tooth!' said a high-pitched voice 'Uniforms! He sez the uniforms of the sharp-swords will keep us safe! Rotten idea.' Scroop rubbed his bruised shoulders and squinting at the world from his least swollen eye.

Grak's uneven gait was more pronounced than usual. 'Get a better one,' he challenged.

At the northern marches of the Eldroth Fields King Warwick's troops reassembled, dug themselves in, and set up their indigo and ivory pavilions, ready to take a second stand against the invaders, with the Companions of the Cup in the front lines.

There was little assistance to be had from the most powerful allies of the north-kingdom, the weathermasters. No full-fledged mages remained in the Mountain Ring, save for the Storm Lord, but the few prentices who could be spared had flown out to join Warwick at his field encampment. What limited support the king's troops received from Rowan Green was heartily welcomed. The odds were quite clearly stacked against the Narngalish. In alliance, the military forces of the southern kingdoms outnumbered the defenders. Already the soldiers could hear the wails of eldritch weepers mourning for men whose lives would soon be cut short, and they jested to each other, 'Hark, the wights weep for our foes and wash Slievmordhuan blood from their rags and tatters!' But the unease behind their eyes belied their jocularity. Fervently the northerners prayed that King Thorgild's reinforcements would arrive speedily. They were acutely aware, nonetheless, that many perilous leagues lay between Narngalis and the western kingdom.

As the invaders pressed further into Narngalis the rumour of their advance precipitated panic. Retreating Narngalish troops had warned the civilians that pillaging aggressors were on the way, so the villagers had packed their belongings and fled with them, or hidden them in secret cellars, or buried them. They drove their herds before them, or, if their haste was too great, turned them free so that the beasts stood a chance against the arrows of the foraging infantry. Every village through which the southerners marched was deserted. They found slender pickings – a few hens, an overlooked sack of rye – and it was too early in the season for ripe fruit, or they would have stripped bare the orchards. Nonetheless, the columns carried with them sufficient provisions, and were never in danger of starving. Angry that the peasants had thwarted them, some called for firing the thatch of the empty cottages, but their superior officers warned them there was to be no wanton destruction. 'These hamlets now belong to the crown. Anyone caught wilfully damaging the king's property will be flogged.' Which crown, that of Slievmordhu or Ashqalêth, was deliberately left unclear.

The allies surged forward in an eager wave across the countryside until they reached the outskirts of the Eldroth Fields, where the foe waited on the other side. There Uabhar called a halt. A belt of green turf, half a mile wide, separated the armies of north and south. Sitting astride his destrier Mac Brádaigh shaded his eyes against the sun's glare, staring across the open acres at the glittering fence of troops ranged across the furthest border of the fields. The wily strategist chafed at the slightest delay, knowing they should waste no time in the assault. The decision, however, was out of his hands. For the moment, his liege lord refused to let him act.

There was much perplexity in the Narngalish camp as to why the southerners did not attack straight away, driving home their advantage. Each hour that passed without engaging in warfare enabled the northerners to strengthen their position; throwing up embankments and redoubts, distributing provisions, honing arms and preparing armour. Had they known it, squabbles had broken out between Uabhar and Chohrab as to the most effective strategy, and the bickering led to an impasse. No fighting was in progress but the tension throughout the bivouacs was almost palpable. Each side was watching for the other to make the first move, alert for the slightest signal that the foe was on the point of launching assault.

Late that afternoon one of Uabhar's sentries noted a couple of peasants skulking at the edges of the Slievmordhuan encampment. His captain was about to issue orders to challenge the lurkers when he perceived that a patrolling band of Marauders, having also spotted the prowlers, was rushing to the attack.

'So much for our new-pledged brother swarmsmen obeying orders to refrain from setting upon civilians,' grunted one of the captains. 'Not only do they have the look of wild beasts, they act like them.'

'Ought we to go the rescue of the farmhands sir?' his lieutenant asked.

''Twould be a waste of manpower. Either those churls are wondrous fools to wander so close to armed and twitchy troops, or they are spies. In both cases they deserve the doom they have brought upon themselves.'

The peasants disappeared from view, the Marauders hot on their heels, and the officers pondered no more on the matter.

As darkness drew in and day gave way to evening, five eyes appeared above the surface of a muddy pool behind a stone fence at the eastern borders of the Eldroth Fields.

"Disguise ourselves as peasants,' he sez! 'Be safe from both sides', he sez! Pity ya didn't tell that to Krorb and Ruurt,' a shrill voice bubbled from beneath the cluster of three eyes.

'Ya've got to admit, this is a good hoiding spot.' The other two eyes belonged to Grak, who flicked a tadpole out of his ear and scanned his surroundings for something to distract Scroop from his recriminations. 'Look!' he said raising a dripping claw out of the slime and pointing to a pair of small humps that appeared to the rounded backs of semiaquatic rodents floating in the water pool. 'Water rats! A tasty supper.'

Scroop's three eyes blinked, then narrowed to a trio of squints as he took a sighting in readiness to pounce on the prey. Beneath the water the two made ready to spring, but even as they lunged forwards Grak screamed. In mid air they both managed to twist sideways and fling themselves towards the banks of the pool. They vaulted out of the water, jumped over the fence and took to their heels. Two bleak sockets, punched into the velvety skull that had risen from the pool, regarded their escape unblinkingly. In their depths a remote flame coldly flickered. Waterweed trailed from the wicked muzzle. Presently the flesh-eating fuath submerged itself once more, slowly and silently, engendering scarcely a ripple. The last portions of the head to disappear were two bony swellings on the crown. The two bedraggled Marauders had made another narrow escape.

By day the mellow sunshine of early Summer warmed the landscape, gleaming off spear and helm, while birds sang. By night thousands of campfires sprang up on either side of the Eldroth Fields, red chrysanthemums floating in a dark abyss. The stalemate between Uabhar and Chohrab came to an end on the evening of the second of Juyn, when the desert king unexpectedly developed a fever and took to the featherbed installed in his gigantic, ornate pavilion. Claiming that he had been poisoned, he complained of palpitations of the heart, falling sickness, shortness of breath and toothache. Chohrab left his troops under the command of his generals, who soon found themselves answering to Uabhar. Just before dawn on the third of Juyn, under cover of darkness, Ashqalêth's foot soldiers attempted to encircle the northern troops with the intent of taking them by surprise. Warwick's patrols discovered the plan, and fighting broke out on all flanks. Uabhar employed these distractions to his advantage. While attention was directed at the skirmishing, Slievmordhu launched an assault.

Narngalis, however, was ready.

The front ranks of foot soldiers rushed together in two colliding waves, each breaking upon the other. As the infantry engaged, the light cavalry of both armies waited in serried ranks behind them. Clad in knee-length hauberks and helms plumed with long tassels of horsehair, the mounted soldiers were armed with longbows. At a signal from their captains the riders charged, shooting to right and left as they drove through the seething masses of the enemy. The heavy cavalry followed; knights on armoured steeds, hurling lances, smiting and hacking with swords. Churned by the hooves of horses and the boots of men, blood and mire mingled with crushed wildflowers on the Eldroth Fields.

The battle rampaged, hour after hour. Princes William and Walter of Narngalis donned battle harness and took their places in the fray, but were summoned back behind the lines to their father's side towards noon, during something of a lull in the fighting.

Located at a prudent distance from the battlefield, high on a ridge where the watchmen could scan the surroundings without difficulty, the Narngalish encampment embellished the verdant slopes like a garden of ivory and indigo blossoms. The tents of linen canvas were round or oval in shape, with vertical walls and domed tops, or tall, conical roofs, gently flared. Some were supported by a single shaft; others were double-peaked. Deeply scalloped valances depended from the lower edge of each roof, like the eaves of a house. Banners fluttered above the spike-and-ball shaped finials that topped the central poles. In the centre of this flowerbed stood the royal pavilion, simple and elegant in design, with many apartments, and tracery decoration in gold.

King Warwick was holding a war council with his sons and several officers in one of the chambers of the royal pavilion, when they were interrupted by a commotion at the entrance. Vexed at the interruption, Crown Prince William strode to the portal and pushed aside the curtain of purple silk, saying sternly, 'Who disturbs the King's Council?'

On the grass outside the pavilion half a dozen pikemen saluted and stood to attention when they beheld the king's son. In front of them a dirty, dishevelled horseman in the livery of Narngalis doffed his helm and threw himself to his knees at the prince's feet. 'Your Royal Highness,' he said, 'pray forgive me. I bear tidings of the gravest importance.'

The brow of the prince darkened. 'Enter and speak.'

The rider took a few paces forward, onto the patterned carpet. At his back the silk curtain swished shut. After saluting his sovereign and the council members the newcomer declared, 'Two messengers from the far north have come riding in haste. They arrived in King's Winterbourne this very morning, bringing urgent news.'

King Warwick was seated at a trestle table covered with maps, inkpots and quills. Above his head a bronze hoop-chandelier hung from the ridgepole, unlit. 'From the far north, you say?' he demanded, his eyebrows bristling and all his attention fixed on the man.

'From the watch stationed at Silverton, my liege, and the other hamlets around the Harrowgate Fells. The sentries, the villagers - all are fleeing from the district, calling for the weathermasters. They are being pursued, pursued by...' The messenger stammered, hesitated, took a deep breath and blurted, 'Great numbers of eldritch beings are issuing from the Northern Ramparts, and it is reported they are mounted on nightmarish steeds. No one knows what species of wight they are, though it is certain they are of the same unseelie kind that has been haunting that region these past weeks. By night they travel, under starlight and moonlight, but it is said that on cloudy days when the sun's light is weak they conjure eerie fogs to obscure it even further. In darkness, or surrounded by these mists they move swiftly. They are deadly. They mow down all who encounter them.'

Warwick's officers had been standing silently around the table. They stirred, muttering exclamations of astonishment. 'What are these creatures that kill with such gruesome expertise?' one of them wondered again. 'It was bad enough when there were but a few of them striking down folk who travelled by night. Now they seem to have multiplied and found mounts for themselves! This threat could not have arisen at a more inopportune hour.'

'Describe them!' the king demanded of the messenger. 'And tell us how many!'

'None can tell what they look like, sire, nor estimate their numbers. It is impossible to discern them in the shadows and fog, and those who get close enough to do so never live long enough to pass on the knowledge. If people try to escape, they are ridden down. It is conjectured that these riders are mountain wights, the dreadful gwyllion, pouring out of the ranges in unprecedented numbers, as if they have been mustering in secret amidst the heights.'

The officers interrogated the courier further. When they were content that he had told them all he could, he was dismissed, and the pavilion's occupants subsided into silence, awaiting the king's pronouncement.

Sombre of countenance, Warwick said, 'This news is surprising and most disturbing.' He pushed back his chair and rose to his feet. 'If what this messenger says is true, and not an exaggeration born of panic, it would appear that we are now interposed between two active assailants. A calamitous coincidence indeed.'

'The gwyllion are murderous,' said Lord Hallingbury, 'but they can be defeated.'

Prince William said, 'If they advance only by night or by dim day, that is a weakness we might exploit.'

His father nodded approval at this suggestion before continuing, 'There is more at risk here than heretofore guessed. Creatures of unseelie loathe humankind. Our destruction is their delight. If there is indeed a formidable eldritch menace surging southward, then it threatens the entire human population of Tir, not merely a single kingdom.' Murmurs of concord greeted his words. 'These reports must first be verified so that we can act wisely. Let fresh scouts be despatched!'

The Battle of Eldroth Fields stormed on into the next day, and the day after. Overnight the conflict tended to ebb. This was not for reasons of courtesy, but because during the sunless hours, no matter how many bonfires were set aflame on the Fields, it was difficult to tell friend from foe. Warwick's use of the Fridean tunnels compensated, to a certain degree, for the fact that the Narngalish were vastly outnumbered. For a while it seemed that neither side was gaining the upper hand, and the northerners began to fan the flames of hope that they might hold out until Thorgild's arrival. Their optimism took a beating, however, when on the morning of Juyn the sixth word came to the royal pavilion, relayed by carrier pigeon, semaphore and rider, confirming the dire accounts of the messengers from the north. It was, without doubt, a fact that unseelie hordes were pouring out of the Northern Ramparts and flooding down past Silverton into the Harrowgate Fells. Anyone who stood against them was destroyed. They were slaying all human beings in their path, and giving no quarter.

Warwick convened an urgent conference. He and his sons gathered beneath the silken folds of the canopy in the council-of-state pavilion, with their senior advisors and those officers who could be spared from their stations in the battlefield. Most of the men were garbed in plate armour or chain mail, beneath murrey tabards embroidered with the emblem of an unsheathed broadsword. Weapons of Narngalish steel depended from their baldrics and belts. They were prepared to re-enter the fray at any moment, should they be called.

'We find ourselves trapped between two adversaries,' Warwick announced to the gathering, 'one of whom evidently prosecutes wholesale genocide. Entire households are fleeing from their homes in the north of the realm, just as others are evacuating the villages further south. The dispossessed converge in the middle, assailed on every front.'

Prince Walter muttered in his elder brother's ear, 'At this rate the entire population of Narngalis will end up in King's Winterbourne.' William nodded acknowledgement.

Pausing briefly, his father surveyed the careworn visages of his audience. 'Thus far,' he went on, 'the life of every man who has challenged these fell mountain-wights has been forfeit. Their uncanny mists accompany them, and out of that haze no living human being ever emerges. Dim fogs crawl across Silverton and the Harrowgate Fells, the lands taken by the gwyllion - if that is what species of wight they be.

'Should these unseelie hordes be as numerous and as powerful as our patrols report, then it may be that even Thorgild's reinforcements cannot save the day. I say again – it is not impossible that this new danger threatens all of humankind across the Four Kingdoms of Tir. We can only cling to the hope that we will find a way to stop them; that by engaging them in battle, somehow our troops can learn enough about these foes to discover their weaknesses. Combat, too, will delay the unseelie onslaught, giving us a little extra time to develop a strategy. The very least I can do is immediately despatch two regiments to the Harrowgate Fells. This will weaken our position here, but I cannot leave my northern lands undefended.'

Nobody said aloud what all were thinking, Those regiments will march to certain death. Yet they could offer no alternative plan.

One of the officers said, 'My liege, as soon as Slievmordhu learns that our forces are diminished he will drive home the advantage.'

'The information must be kept secret from him for as long as possible, of course,' said Warwick.

Prince William said, 'If their numbers are even half as great as reported and their ferocity only half as bad, then as you say, Father, these wights threaten to exterminate our entire race. Surely Ó Maoldúin can be made to understand that we must abandon this senseless conflict between kingdoms and amalgamate our forces. If we are to survive, humankind must stand united against this horde! More particularly, it is the weathermasters we need now. They would be our strongest shields against eldritch foes.'

'Ó Maoldúin is like a side-blinkered horse,' said Walter. 'He can see only the prize he believes lies ahead of him and looks neither to right nor to left in his pursuit of it. 'Twill be nigh impossible to convince him there exists a peril great enough to necessitate abandoning his conqueror's ambitions.'

'Aye,' agreed Warwick's Secretary of State. 'The man is blind to all but his own dreams.'

'Still,' the king said, 'we must try to wake him up.' To a servant he added, 'Fetch writing materials.'

'What of Ashqalêth?' asked another officer, addressing the assembly at large.

'Shechem is naught but a pawn in the other's game,' the Lord Chancellor responded. 'He no longer judges for himself, if he ever did.'

'Nevertheless,' Prince William persisted, 'we must demand that Ó Maoldúin release the weathermasters forthwith. Although,' he added, 'even with the support of the mages a worldwide alliance might be our only chance of survival. We must try to persuade our foes to unite with us.'

'Even so. We will offer parley,' his father responded. 'But any emissaries of mine who approach Ó Maoldúin must be volunteers. Their lives will be in jeopardy. I have little faith that Ó Maoldúin, unprincipled traitor that he is, will honour the white flag.'

Later that day as the sun was melting above the distant peaks of the mountain ring in the west, and the south wind was blowing harder, the two armies broke apart as if by mutual consent and another pause ensued in the conflict.   King Warwick seized his opportunity. It was then that two riders picked their way slowly, alone, across the wide band of mud and corpses that lay between the rivals.   The young men wore neither plate nor mail, but shirts of bleached linen and breeches of woollen weave, and their heads were bare, their hair streaming behind them on the breeze. No arms did they bear, but in their hands they carried tall staffs, from which white standards were fluttering against the crimson banners of the sky. The flags were unadorned, for they signified a request for talks of mediation. By the rules of combat, flags of parley protected the bearers. No man sought to block their way, no spear was flung; neither blade nor axe nor bow was raised against them.

'We seek the kings of Slievmordhu and Ashqalêth,' said they when they came amongst the front lines of their enemies. The captains of the south came to ride alongside them, as guides.

'These are brave knights,' the officers said to each other.

To the pavilion of Uabhar went Warwick's two emissaries, seeking conference, as beyond the mountains the last flares of the sun dissolved into evening mist. Darkness closed in.

Concealed behind earthworks close to the northern battle front, Warwick waited in suspense with his sons and commanders. Ever their eyes turned in the direction of enemy lines, and their mood was grave, their spirits straitened.

'I would fain be there with them,' William murmured vehemently.

The battle lull lengthened. Night drew out the hours like thread from a distaff.

Towards midnight a shout was heard from the Narngalish sentries. Two horses were returning across no man's land, but they were riderless. Troopers led the steeds swiftly to the king. From each saddle hung a lidded basket which, when opened, revealed Uabhar's reply to the request for parley.

When Warwick witnessed the baskets' contents his countenance became that of a dead man. Walter gave a cry of horror, and William hoarsely uttered a curse.

Slievmordhu had sent back the severed heads of the two young knights.

Tidings of Uabhar's crime passed rapidly though the northern ranks and a shout of anger went up from the men of Narngalis. As for the two princes, they drew their swords, and, upon the naked blades, vowed to avenge the deaths of the brave envoys.

Lord Hallingbury grimly declared, 'The situation is clear. Except for the men of the west-kingdom, who are too far away, we are without friends. Only the weathermasters can save Tir now. Let us hope the Storm Lord's bold rescue expedition will swiftly release them from Uabhar's dungeons!'

King Warwick made no reply, but a shadow and a bleak coldness lay upon him, as of premature Winter.

William said into the silence, 'Let a billet be despatched to King's Winterbourne!'

Day and night, post riders went galloping back and forth along the Mountain Road between the battlefield and King's Winterbourne, where Warwick's daughters abided at Wyverstone Castle. The couriers' task was chiefly to back up and augment the semaphore network. Across the Four Kingdoms of Tir the wooden arms of the semaphore towers clacked and rotated almost incessantly. While men fought and died on the Eldroth Fields, messages were being relayed between the chains of semaphore stations that criss-crossed the countryside, as in peacetime. The difference now was that the signals had been re-encrypted to prevent the enemy from intercepting important information. Asrăthiel herself had delivered the new codes along the King's Winterbourne – Trøndelheim chain, as she flew her sky-balloon to join the marching columns of Grïmnørsland. When Thorgild's travelling columns passed within view of any station the signalmen would send word of their progress to King's Winterbourne, from whence the news was relayed by courier to King Warwick's encampment. As she journeyed with the army Asrăthiel took it upon herself to ferry tidings and reports between Thorgild and the nearby stations, for her aerostat was swifter and surer than any post rider.

On the evening the two Narngalish knights crossed the El-droth Fields under the white flag to seek parley, the Storm Lord's granddaughter, attended by her maid, was floating in the wicker gondola of *Lightfast* above Thorgild's troops as they marched through the wild country north of High Darioneth. Asrăthiel gazed out across hills and valleys striped with long shadows. The bloom of Summer was on the land and the blowing forests were festive with flowers. Streams leaped noisily down from the hills, and herds of deer grazed on the slopes. Southward reared the jagged rim of the mountain ring. Draped in their cloaks of tattered cloth-of-silver, the peaks towered in splendour. The sky-balloon's shadow danced across grassy meadows sparkling with dew. At last the aeronaut spied the hilltop semaphore station she had been looking for, a collection of low stone buildings surrounding a taller edifice crowned by its two-armed tower. She descended, letting the airy pearl glide smoothly down the currents.

'What news from the battlefront for King Thorgild?' she asked the signal operators.

'The fighting rages on at the Eldroth Fields,' they answered in apprehensive tones. 'But worse tidings are at hand. The station at King's Winterbourne sends reports of unseelie tribes on horseback swarming down into Narngalis from the ranges.'

'Great heavens!' Asrăthiel was taken aback. She rifled through the written notes the signalmen had provided, her brow furrowed with concentration, concern and frustration. At length she said, half to herself, 'If there are clues to these mysteries, I can make nothing of them.'

'Tir is in great danger, my lady,' said the Chief Signalman. 'We are fortunate we have the weathermasters to shield us from any unseelie scourge.' And he bowed deeply.

'As we are fortunate we have scrupulous signallers to man their posts, come what may,' Asrăthiel said, returning the compliment.

'Now I must hasten back to the King's encampment with this news. Farewell!'

Asrăthiel guided her aerostat to the meadow where Grïmnørsland's troops had halted to rest themselves and their horses. King Thorgild and his sons were taking a hasty supper, seated upon wood-and-canvas folding chairs beneath the spreading eaves of a leafy beech wood that bordered the grassland. Gunnlaug sat a little apart from the rest, in the shadow of a gnarled bole, gnawing on a bone and drinking beer.

Thorgild's commanders gathered around to hear what the weathermage had to say. When the monarch heard her report he let the bread and meat fall from his hand. Foreboding inscribed his ruddy countenance. He shook his head as if gravely discouraged, and his eyes hardened like stones. 'An unhappy accident,' he said, in echo of Warwick's sentiments, 'that eldritch wights should choose to assail Narngalis at time of war. Yet,' he added presently, 'I am puzzled. I have never heard of the gwyllion riding upon horses.'

'Neither have I,' said Prince Halvdan, close at his father's side. 'I cannot help but wonder what manner of unseelie manifestation we are confronted with.'

'I wonder also,' said Asrăthiel. 'The signalmen's notes state that the few living folk who have, from afar, descried these raiders-in-the-mists assert that their mounts are not true horses. They avow they are eldritch steeds.'

She handed the billets to Halvdan, who perused them, saying, 'I daresay they are waterhorses, then; tame brags or vicious kelpies maybe.'

'Yet,' said Asrăthiel, 'if that is so, then they are unlike any waterhorse I have ever heard of. One witness claimed he glimpsed, from afar, manes and tails that glow like green fire ...'

Thorgild muttered a curse. 'Eldritch steeds with fiery manes? This is most strange. It reminds me of a tale I learned at my old nurse's knee, a tale of daemon horses, the trollhästen. Lanky, light-some and fell were they, and faster than falling stars, and passing comely. The story was my delight, and I used to dream of having a

horse like that, though in vain, for they would never allow themselves to be ridden by mortalkind. As far as I know such steeds have
not trod the grasses of Tir for many lives of men. If I recall rightly,
only one species of wight ever leagued with the trollhästen, but for
the life of me I cannot, at this moment, remember which one.'

His commanders shook their heads and exchanged comments,
declaring that they had no recollection of any such tales.

Addressing his eldest sons, Thorgild said, 'Both of you have
studied the records of ancient battles and the archives of eldritch
lore stored in the libraries of Trøndelheim. Have you ever read
aught about the trollhästen?'

The princes contributed their theories, after which general
discussion ensued. Gunnlaug watched his father and brothers
over the top of the knuckle of ham on which he was chewing. At
the first pause in the conversation he said, 'What about me, sir?
You have not asked me for my rede.'

Thorgild drew a deep and silent breath. 'What is your rede,
Gunnlaug?'

'I am planning a strategy to win this war. When it is ready I
will tell it to you, but in the mean time I take it ill that my brothers
should be consulted and not me. All three of us have played war
games and trained with the defence forces since boyhood.'

'You are indeed a man of action, Gunnlaug, but Hrosskel and
Halvdan have spent long hours studying the tactics used to win
battles of yore.' The king refrained from adding that although
Gunnlaug was indeed a warrior of considerable might and prowess, his team had always lost the mock battles. Their leader was
prone to ignore pre-planned manoeuvres and charge headlong
with a single goal: to inflict harm upon his opponents. 'I did not
consider that you were much interested in sitting around tables
debating logistics. You have always been the hunter, the wrestler,
the pugilist.'

'You have read me wrongly,' said Gunnlaug, 'for warfare in
every aspect is my obsession, and you should make me a general.
I am a better warrior than anyone under this wood –' he stared

meaningfully at Hrosskel and Halvdan – 'and were I to lead the troops we would smash our enemies and kick their bloody heads around the field for sport.'

'I will not use my sons in military positions.'

'Then you are unwise.'

'That is enough!' Thorgild roared, standing up and advancing on his son.

Gunnlaug was on his feet also, holding his ground, daring to bait his father. 'We need a wise leader if we are to win against this unseelie onslaught. Uabhar is wise, even the druids say so. His might is growing. The druids say he might someday be High King of Tir.'

The onlookers gasped.

Father and son confronted one another, separated by a hand's breadth. Softly, so that none could overhear, Thorgild said, 'If you ever utter such treasonous nonsense again, I will exile you.' They held each other's challenging stare for a moment, before Gunnlaug dropped his eyes. Throwing down the remnants of his meal he slunk away.

He took a shortcut to his tent by way of a thicket that jutted from the beech wood, keeping to the shadows, but careful to stay within view of the glimmering campfires between the trees. No one overheard him savagely muttering to himself, 'Fools! The might of Slievmordhu is greater than you bargain for, and shortly you will be forced to learn that at your peril. You ought to be grateful that you have a warrior such as I to defend us against Ó Maoldúin – instead you treat me like a cur. Soon you will come to know my quality!'

Oblivious of his son's vituperations Thorgild said to the gathering, 'Now, let us to our beds with no further ado, for early in the morning we must take to the road. If Warwick is forced to weaken his defences by sending troops to defend the north, we have all the more reason to make haste!'

On the lavender-scented linen of the couch in her pavilion Asrăthiel lay wide awake while her maid Linnet slumbered peacefully nearby. The weathermage's mind was a whirlpool of conjectures, questions, and overlapping trains of thought. The questions, in particular, harassed her. Would her grandfather's rescue expedition be able to free her weathermaster kindred from Uabhar's dungeons? Were her loved ones hale, or had Uabhar mistreated them? If the ruthless king had slain their guardians, King Thorgild's Shield Champions, might he not do the same to them? What would the four princes of Slievmordhu think of their father's unpardonable crime against Rowan Green? Who were the eldritch riders, and what measure of menace did they present? Were they gwyllion, or something else? What if her father happened to return home at this dangerous time, and encountered the unseelie hordes on the road? What if he never returned home? What was happening at the Eldroth Fields? Would the Narngalish troops be able to hold out until the Grïmnørslanders came to their aid?

For an instant she wished the urisk could be in the tent with her. His extensive knowledge would be useful; he would be sure to know all about those wicked wights. Moreover, she realised in hindsight that she had found comfort in his presence, as if they shared something, perhaps a bond of fellowship derived from both being unlike their own kind. She missed the creature to an extent that surprised her; it was like having a bruise in her side, or maybe even some deeper wound. To soothe the ache she reminded herself what pain he had given her in person - his unwarranted derision of Prince William, for example.

'Ah, William!' she sighed, turning over on her pillowed couch, and her thoughts flew to King Warwick's encampment...

In the middle of the night a ragged vagrant limped amongst the Narngalish tents, tripped over a series of guy ropes and was seized by a pair of halberdiers.

'Who are you? What are you doing here? Are you a spy?' the guards demanded sternly.

'By the bones of Ádh, I am no spy!' said the beggar, quailing and rolling his eyes in fear. 'I only came to bring valuable tidings and this is how I am treated!' His accent was unidentifiable; besides which he was practically toothless, and mumbled.

'From whence do you hail?'

'I have travelled here from Cathair Rua, and a harrowing journey it was, too.'

'If you are of Slievmordhu, then you are our enemy!'

'I am not of Slievmordhu. I am a proud Narngalishman.'

'And a good liar, no doubt! You are a cunning fellow if you managed to slip through the lines of the southerners.'

'Nobody notices me if I set my mind to it,' said the beggar, a hint of conceit bizarrely mingling with his abject fear. 'I bring valuable tidings, I tell you!'

Upon hearing the commotion one of Warwick's captains strode up to the beggar and halberdiers. 'We shall not treat you unkindly,' he said, 'if you do indeed bear important news and are no troublemaker. What is your name?'

'They call me Cat Soup. I am so hungry I can barely speak,' whined the beggar. He rubbed his bony hands together. The finger joints were pink and swollen.

'Tell us first and we shall feed you afterwards.'

The old man cowered, looked up at the soldiers who loomed over him, and sniffed the cooking smells from a stew pot bubbling over a campfire.

'Do you give your word?'

'You are in no position to demand promises!' snapped the captain. 'Speak now!'

'All right,' Cat Soup said placatingly, blinking strands of greasy hair out of his red-rimmed eyes. 'I will tell you what felonies I saw lately at Cathair Rua.'

And he began to relate his gruesome tale.

Uabhar hardly slept, so feverishly preoccupied was he with his machinations. In the first hour after sunrise he paced to and fro within his compound, at a safe distance from the action.

His royal lodgings consisted of a series of four huge rectangular pavilions linked together by galleries. Decorations of gold knotwork ran along the tops of the ridge-beams. Round pavilions with conical roofs jutted from this formation, five on each side. Every component was made from matching material; a heavy, close-woven woollen fabric dyed madder red, figured with gorgeous motifs of contrasting colours. Scores of guy ropes held the entire arrangement in place, and the finials were shaped like beasts from myth.

Not to be outdone by the royal tent makers, Uabhar's personal valets made certain the king was magnificently dressed at all times, even in the throes of war. The crimson lining and gold stitch work of Uabhar's doublet contrasted sharply with his breeches of black velvet, and he wore spurs upon his boot heels, heedless of the damage they caused to the splendid rugs strewn about the floor.

'By rights we ought to have defeated them by now,' he raged at the cringing valets, momentarily losing any vestige of restraint. 'Narngalis should be ours! I am surrounded by imbeciles!'

His bodyguard heralded the arrival of High Commander Risteárd Mac Brádaigh. The soldier entered the luxuriously furnished chamber carrying his helm beneath one arm, bowed - to the accompanying sound of rustling chain mail - kissed the back of the king's proffered hand and waited with barely concealed impatience.

Uabhar dismissed his attendants. 'Speak!' he said to Mac Brádaigh.

'My liege,' said the soldier, 'All is in turmoil this morning. Rumours are spreading amongst the troops. It is said that swarms of deadly wights are issuing out of the highlands in the north and flooding across Tir, slaying all who stand in their way.'

'I have heard these rumours,' Uabhar said, his eyes darting rapidly from side to side. 'They are false. Narngalis is attempting to terrify and undermine us with wild stories. He will fail.'

'Men say the inhabitants of Narngalis' northern villages are deserting their abodes. They are crowding the roads, not heading due south but making south-east and south-west, so as to avoid encountering Your Majesty's troops.'

'But this is a pack of lies!' Uabhar roared. 'Are you really fool enough to believe it, Mac Brádaigh? Who is broadcasting this nonsense? Where did it come from?'

The soldier's visage turned brick-red with ire, but his voice was carefully controlled. 'The stories started with the two Narngalish knights who rode under the flag of parley. They spoke of the matter to the captains who escorted them to the royal pavilion. Their words were overheard by many others. Such news spreads swiftly through an encampment.'

'Scare-mongers will be discovered and chastised.'

'Sire,' the High Commander continued levelly, 'that is not the only source of the tales. The troops on the Narngalish front line have been shouting across the Fields. When the wind is in the north their words can sometimes be deciphered.'

'Purely a strategy to weaken our resolve. A worn-out trick. Only dupes would heed the agitations of the enemy.'

Mac Brádaigh was about to say something more, but Uabhar's sentries announced the advent of a despatch rider. The courier burst through the notched doorway like a gust of wind. He was breathing hard.

'Your Majesty,' said the courier, flinging himself at the king's feet, 'I come on the business of Lord Genan of Áth Midbine. Overnight my lord captured a Narngalish scout. Before he perished, the Narngalishman told my lord all he knew. He spoke of deadly riders, and daemon horses of green fire. Unseelie hordes are coming to destroy the world.'

'Áth Midbine's interrogator brings out the truth in men,' Mac Brádaigh interjected, seizing the opportunity.

'The truth as they believe it,' snapped Uabhar. 'Narngalis propagates falsehoods amongst his own troops to achieve his ends, knowing they will infect us with his lies.'

Mac Brádaigh said, 'My liege, the men are restless. They are ready to battle against a foe they can see with their own eyes, an enemy who submits to the laws of life and death, but it is a different matter if they find themselves pitted against an adversary they cannot understand. There are concerns amongst the captains that fear might drive them to mutiny ...'

'Rebels will be hanged!' shouted Uabhar. 'There are no unseelie hordes! They do not exist!' He cocked his head to one side, then added, 'And if they do, then let those hordes hasten south, for they will find Wyverstone barring their way before they encounter Slievmordhu. Let them destroy my enemies for me!' To the messenger kneeling on the floor he said curtly, 'Go back and tell that to Áth Midbine!'

'That is not all. There is other news, sire,' said the messenger.

'Say!'

'This very hour we shot down a carrier bird flying from the Narngalish encampment. It bore a message meant for Storm Lord Avalloc. Warwick has come to believe that the weathermasters have been slain by trickery.'

'And at whose door does that deluded inventor of fancies lay this charge?'

'At the door of Slievmordhu, sire.'

'Rumour and hearsay! Fancies and delusions! Is that all the information my noble officers have to send me? Tell them this,' said Uabhar; 'any man who spreads sedition will be boiled alive. I will not tolerate the broadcasting of alarm and despondency amongst my troops. Now begone, bearer of bad news, begone! You too, Mac Brádaigh!' Brusquely he extended his hand.

The High Commander gave a peremptory bow, brushed his lips against the back of Uabhar's hand and made a swift exit, followed by the courier. After they had gone Uabhar's second son appeared from behind an embroidered hanging where he had been seated upon a chair of carved walnut, reading dispatches. 'Sir,' he said, 'is it true?' The face of young Prince Ronin was as pale as if cast in plaster. His shoulders were draped with a cloak of rich brocade, lined with scarlet satin, and loose tendrils of dark brown hair straggled across his cheeks.

'Is what true?'

'Have you indeed slain the weathermasters?'

'You foolish whelp, I have merely caused the meddlers to be removed from our path. They are Narngalish subjects, and ever in alliance with Wyverstone. Do you suppose our campaign would have advanced even this far, had they been free to do as they wished? Well, do you?'

'I suppose not,' replied Ronin, but his voice was scarcely audible, and his lips were compressed to two smudged lines against the whiteness of his flesh. 'But I thought you had merely imprisoned them. Pray tell me whether - '

He broke off, as Crown Prince Kieran entered the royal pavilion, throwing off his mud-spattered cloak. Having heard that the High Commander and a messenger had paid a visit, Kieran was about to enquire after the latest news, but checked himself when he perceived the situation between his father and brother. The anxiety he always experienced when attending Uabhar sharpened to dread.

Uabhar ignored the presence of his eldest son, focussing his scrutiny on Ronin. 'Do you have quarrel with my procedures?' he barked.

The younger prince waited a moment before replying, 'You are my sovereign and sire.'

'Precisely. And all that I do, I do that the dynasty of Ó Maoldúin may prosper. You are second in line to the throne, an heir of this dynasty.'

'As one of your heirs,' Ronin said, leaving his seat and kneeling in homage to his father, 'I ask you, as before, for your leave to join the ranks and fight for Slievmordhu.'

'And as before I refuse the request. It is because you are one of my successors that I will not allow you to ride out to war, you understand? My sons will not risk their lives. It is for the ordinary soldiery to become spear fodder.'

Up jumped Ronin, overturning the chair. 'You tie our hands no matter which way we turn!' he cried despairingly. 'You refuse to let us fight, you refuse to allow us any part in the decision-making, you refuse to hearken to our counsel!'

This was too much for Kieran. From infancy he had been

schooled to loathe his father's wrath, and to go to any lengths to appease it. His reaction was reflexive, rather than calculated. 'How can you, in good conscience, address our father with such discourtesy?' he loudly reprimanded his brother. 'Obedience and loyalty above all! Recollect yourself!'

'Be silent, sirrah!' The king rounded on his eldest son. 'Do not presume to speak on my behalf!' Embarrassed and shocked that he was perceived to have erred, the Crown Prince bowed low and apologised. Returning his attention to Ronin, Uabhar said smoothly and with ominous civility, 'Prithee, give me your counsel now, my son. I would fain be privy to what discomposes you.'

'Already you know what troubles me, father!' the young man said in agitation. 'A Wickedness is on the way and the weathermasters, our best defenders, are betrayed. It is we who betrayed them, while they were unarmed, and guests beneath our roof! If the weathermasters still live you must set them free.'

'They live not.'

Ronin doubled over, as if his father had punched him just beneath the ribs. A sickly pallor washed over him as if he had taken ill, and he mumbled strings of phrases under his breath, one after the other. His elder brother sat down quickly upon the lid of an ark as if his knees had given way beneath him. Kieran passed one hand across his brow, wiping off sudden beads of cold sweat.

'Truth will out,' said Uabhar. 'Eventually it will become common knowledge, in any case, that the weathermasters are slain. Why should I not be the one to reveal it to you? I have nothing to hide! I remain as guileless as always. Leave off your prayers to the Fates, Ronin; they are not listening. And do not berate yourself, for you had no part in it. Most of that sad affair was the fault of the druids.'

Lifting his head Ronin said, 'Be that as it may, it is with Slievmordhu that the responsibility lies. Without the weathermasters, humankind is all but powerless before the wickedness of unseelie hordes.'

'There are no hordes. It is a false report that has been blown wildly out of proportion. I myself germinated the original hearsay in a clever tactical manoeuvre, when I concocted tales of unseelie wights gathering on the South-Eastern Moors.'

'They say these monsters are issuing from the north. Many folk claim to have seen them.'

'It is a trick.'

'What if it is no trick?'

'Then the first obstacles on their southbound route will be the armies of Narngalis. I consider that no inconvenience.'

'And after they have slaughtered the Narngalish, what then? A man's loyalty is of no concern to wicked wights. Being human, alone, is enough cause for them to put us to death. They hate humankind, and would destroy us all.'

'What would you have me do?' Uabhar asked with exaggerated politeness.

'Put aside all quarrels and join with Warwick in alliance against the unseelie threat.'

'That is treasonous talk! How dare you suggest it?' the king roared. 'Unworthy son! Have I taught you nothing? Would you bring dishonour upon your own father?'

Quietly Kieran subjoined, 'You show yourself a traitor, Ronin,' but his tone was a warning to his brother to shield himself, rather than an accusation with which to persecute him. Ronin was dear to him, and in the most secret recesses of his heart he agreed with much that he was saying, though this caused him untold anguish and confusion, for it threatened to undermine the very foundations on which his life had been built. They were not weak-minded, these young men – not in the slightest. It was an insidious, invisible influence they had to contend with; one that has ensnared and ultimately ruined many a mighty man.

The king addressed Ronin. 'Observe your brother, who stands closer to the throne than you do, praise the Fates. Of all my sons Kieran is the best, the most dutiful and steadfast. Of all my sons you are the worst. Take heed of your elder brother.

Model yourself on him. He obeys his father without question, and by this he proves himself worthy as my heir.'

'If I am a traitor and disloyal son, if I am the worst of all offenders, then let it be proclaimed,' declared Ronin. 'Let me be reviled for all time, but I cannot in good conscience commit treason against the whole of humanity.'

Uabhar thrust his face close to that of his second son. 'Were you not my flesh and blood I would see you hanged,' he hissed corrosively. The young prince flinched, but stood his ground, avoiding his father's eye.

'I apologise for speaking out against you, father,' he said tightly. 'If you knew what it has cost me…'

'You should have held your tongue, sirrah! I deny all you have said, and 'twould be better for you if you had never said it. Now I will reconsider my ban after all, and you will find out how generously I can reach a compromise. Put on your armour. Go forth to fight for king and country. See if you can find it in your faithless heart to wage war against the very realms with whom you so ardently desire to form alliance, and if you cannot do it in good conscience then do it while stung by guilt. Should you perish on the battlefield, at least you will have given your last strength while proving yourself no disloyal son. In that, maybe you will salvage some honour for the name of Ó Maoldúin.'

The king stretched out his hand.

Ronin stood as wan and still as an image painted on the silk draperies. He was lost, utterly lost. A moment later the training of a lifetime reasserted itself and he saw, again, the only path he knew, the familiar, deep-rutted track along which he had been driven so often that it had become the only way he could find. He stooped, pressing his lips to his father's hand in the gesture of fealty and acknowledgement.

Dismissively his father turned away and began speaking to Kieran, diverting his attention to matters of war.

'The wicked hordes are coming,' Ronin said under his breath, intentionally unheard and unheeded. To his hands that he had lifted, upturned and empty as shells, he whispered, 'and the weathermasters are betrayed.'

Then he went to put on his battle gear.

3

IRONSTONE KEEP

True friendship is worth more than can be measured,
A quality forever to be treasured.
True friends will staunchly stand beside each other,
As loyally as brother shieldeth brother,
Remaining firm in spite of war and strife,
In poverty or sickness, throughout life.
True friendship doth endure while comrades age
From boy to youth, from warrior to sage.

'TRUE FRIENDS'
(A SONG FAVOURED BY MAUDLIN DRUNKARDS THROUGHOUT TIR.)

A pair of eagles had flown over the crimson pavilions of Uabhar just as the despatch rider was making his exit. Swift though the rider was as he headed for the lodgings of Lord Genan, he could not outrace birds on the wing. The eagles soared and glided on their way north-west against the morning breeze, across hill and dale, over reedy brook and rushing river, until they reached a region where no war was being waged amongst humankind.

A shimmering orb hovered in the sky.

Matching the wind's speed, Asrăthiel's sky-balloon floated

amid airborne motes of thistledown and flocks of ravens whose cries tore open the throat of the wind. The basket was filled to capacity, though the weathermage had dispensed with the services of her maid, Linnet, bidding her return to King's Winterbourne out of harm's way. Beside her stood two tall men garbed in gleaming chain mail and tabards of darkest aquamarine. King Thorgild Torkilsalven scanned the horizon through eyes creased by the salt winds of the western sea, while Prince Halvdan leaned over the side of the gondola. The prince surveyed the marvellous spectacle below; burnished battalions were filing as sinuously as dragons through the countryside. The heavy drumming of marching feet was punctuated by the ravens' calls, the creaking of the basketwork, and the haphazard flapping of the envelope when buffeted by a sudden gust. Now and then Asrăthiel murmured a brí-command to the local currents, or to the sun-crystal in its cradle; ẞyřñ, ¥ē £ÿř-§țåṇâ,' and executed a quick, practised gesture, elusive to her companions. Sensing air pressure without effort, she was aware of her exact height above the ground.

Presently the weathermage worked a vent-line to release puffs of air from the balloon's crown, decreasing buoyancy. The aerostat descended at a steep angle. She guided it with precision until its woven floor scraped the ground beside the next hilltop semaphore station. The assistant signalman was waiting with the station's man-servant to help anchor the balloon to hooks hammered into the rocky ground. She waved them away and saw to it herself, with the help of her royal companions, instructing Halvdan how to throw out the ropes, before vaulting over the side as gracefully as a leaping deer, despite her encumbering skirts. The wind was strong; not only did it batter at her garments, it also buffeted the envelope as if it were a punching bag. To decrease the strain on seams and fabric Asrăthiel allowed some air to escape before tying everything down securely.

Having watched the approach of the Lady in the Moon, the station chief had hastened to finish deciphering the latest messages, writing in careful script on thick sheets of paper. When the crew alighted he was astounded to behold not only a weathermage but also a prince and the King of Grïmnørsland, his locks shining like iron-streaked copper as they swept his shoulders.

It took him some while to recover his usual placidity and he spoke to them breathlessly. 'Your Majesty, Your Royal Highness and my lady, two communications have come in this very hour,' he said, saluting and offering them the pages as soon as they entered the signal tower. The first message was from Avalloc, at High Darioneth; Asrăthiel had been keeping him informed of her whereabouts. The damsel scanned the message quickly, eager for her grandfather's counsel, and proceeded to read it aloud. '"Avalloc Storm Lord and Declan of the Wildwoods do greet Lady Asrăthiel."'

'Who is Declan of the Wildwoods?' Thorgild interrupted.

'He is a friend of my grandfather's, a scholar,' Asrăthiel replied without taking her eyes from the pages. 'Sometimes he sojourns at High Darioneth.'

The king nodded. 'Go on.'

First, the Storm Lord informed his granddaughter that the rescue mission despatched to Cathair Rua had not yet sent back any word of the weathermasters' whereabouts or welfare. Next, the Storm Lord revealed that he had discovered an astonishing fact about the unseelie strangers from the northern mountains.

Asrăthiel read out, 'Maelstronnar house brownie claims unseelie attackers are - what?' she broke off, staring in perplexity at the billet in her hand. 'But that is impossible!'

'What does he say of the attackers? And how can a brownie have anything to do with the matter?' the king demanded.

Slowly, shaking her head bemusedly, Asrăthiel continued. '"Maelstronnar house brownie claims unseelie attackers are goblin-kind, escaped from caves." She looked up and stared at her audience. 'Goblins? I thought they were all wiped out years ago. Surely the brownie is deluded. How could that sequestered wight be privy to such information, in any case, when better informed folk are in ignorance?'

'Read on!' Thorgild urged.

Eyes wide with astonishment, Asrăthiel continued, '"Brownie terrified. Lethal force. Beware."' Avalloc's message, all the more alarming in its conciseness, came to an end.

Dumbfounded the three companions gazed at one another. The hilltop wind whistled through a crack beneath the closed door, whirled up the spiral staircase and rattled the windows in the tiny observation chamber overhead.

'Goblins!' Thorgild cried suddenly. 'That was it, goblins! They were the only wights that ever associated with the fiery-maned trollhästen.' He laughed disbelievingly. 'Odds fish! As you say, Asrăthiel, by all accounts those ridiculous imps were wiped out decades ago.'

'It appears not,' said the weathermage. 'At least, my grandfather believes so, and I have never known him to blunder.'

'They had their own eldritch slaves, as I recall,' said Thorgild, pacing back and forth agitatedly as he sifted through his memories. 'It is all coming back to me now.'

'It makes no sense, if these riders are goblins,' said Halvdan. 'Such feeble and foolish manikins ought to be defeated with ease, yet they have proved beyond doubt to be dangerous.'

'The Storm Lord takes the brownie at its word. He asserts they are both goblinkind and a lethal force, and I doubt him not,' said Thorgild. 'I am confounded, to think that all these years they must have been lying in wait in some hidden place, some cave, by Avalloc's report. Yet this does arouse an indistinct memory…'

Said Halvdan, 'Why should the tales assert that they were all destroyed?'

'Not all the tales gave the same account,' said his father. 'As I dwell more and more on this conundrum, it seems to me that I recall fragments; stories of another kind of doom.'

'What doom?' Asrăthiel asked.

'Imprisonment. That fits with the Storm Lord's account. Yet, it is all so hard to credit…'

'A lethal force, he declares!' repeated the prince. 'If these Tom

Thumbs have escaped from solitary confinement, then it is possible they have grown stronger during their decades of isolation. Should that be the case, the weathermasters may be Tir's only hope.'

'Indeed,' the damsel replied quickly. 'Yet there is no news from those who are trying to rescue them. My kindred remain in the clutches of our enemy. May they return safely and swiftly!' Her blue eyes appeared darker than usual.

'How came the goblins to be locked into caves?' Halvdan asked his father. 'Can you recall?'

'If reminiscence serves me well, it was the greatest weathermaster of yore who drove the wights under the mountains.'

'Ah! So they can be defeated by lightning and hurricanes!'

'It was not with storms he foiled them. It was with Fallowblade,' said the king.

Asrăthiel glanced up sharply.

'It is now clear why the trow population of Tir has been moving north,' Thorgild went on. 'They wish to serve the goblins, whom they traditionally view as their masters. Since Avalloc has discovered the truth with relative ease others will soon find it out also, by questioning brownies, or urisks, or other seelie wights. Scholars will deduce as we have done, from the clues of the fire-maned steeds. Word will spread. Panic may spread also.'

Halvdan said, 'Conversely, if word gets about that this influx of wights is of goblinkind, the fears of many folk may be lulled. After all, popular stories and puppet plays ridicule goblins for being puny and stupid and easily defeated.'

'Let us hope those stories are true,' his father said grimly. 'Let us hope the Storm Lord's brownie is mistaken.' It was plain that the king nurtured few shreds of such hope. 'Goblins are unseelie,' he said, 'They have always hated humankind – all the more so, no doubt, after the weathermasters jailed them. It is now evident that contrary to their reputation they are a formidable host. Somehow these goblins and their daemon horses - and probably their dreadful slaves to boot - have broken free from their centuries-old incarceration, and they have caught us unprepared. Who knows, but their plan might be to sweep across the kingdoms of Tir and slaughter every member of the human race! Your brownie, at any rate, Asrăthiel, implies they are bent on further atrocities. As soon as we return to camp I will order a forced march. Let us make short work of this other report and hasten away without delay.'

The weathermage shuffled the pages of Avalloc's message while Halvdan perused the second bulletin, a brief note that had been sent from the battlefield by Prince William. As the prince commenced to read the contents aloud, one of the signalmen, ever vigilant at the view-windows in the room at the top of the stairs, applied a spyglass to his eye. He directed the instrument towards a neighbouring station, situated high on a remote peak across the valley. The distant semaphore's arms were rotating. While the watcher described the code sequence his assistant transcribed it to paper, ready for deciphering.

Paying no attention to the activities of the signalmen above, Halvdan read: "Unseelie hordes unstoppable. Nor can we hold off southerners much longer. Look forward to your swift arrival." The prince folded the paper and slipped it into his satchel.

To the station chief, who was hovering near at hand in a state of agitation, Asrăthiel said, 'Send Prince William a message informing him that the weathermasters cannot be found and that the Storm Lord names the hordes as goblinkind, broken loose from age-old confinement.'

The man bowed smartly.

'Let's go,' said Thorgild. 'There is no time to lose. Signalmen, remain at your post. We need no help relaunching the balloon.'

Asrăthiel had hardly finished giving instructions to the chief signalman and thanking him before her two companions were out the door and striding across the grass towards the mooring spot where *Lightfast* bobbed and tugged at her lines. Their hair and cloaks flapped wildly in the wind as they knelt on the short turf to untie the tethering guys from the iron ground hooks. Asrăthiel leaped into the gondola and summoned a blast of heat from the great sun-crystal in its cradle. As they all watched the balloon's sagging, wind-tortured envelope gradually expand she said, 'Another semaphore message is coming through. We ought to wait for it.'

'There's no time,' said Thorgild, raising his voice above the wailing gusts and the boom of billowing fabric. 'Every moment we delay is a moment lost to Narngalis and might mean the difference between life and death for Tir. Are we ready for lift-off?'

'Not yet.'

Halvdan braced himself as he pulled hard on a rope to steady the bucking aircraft. 'Asrăthiel, how could your grandfather's house brownie possibly be able to name the unseelie hordes?' he shouted over the wind. 'Domestic wights seldom leave their abodes. How could a humble brownie of Rowan Green learn about events hundreds of leagues away?' He sprang into the basket beside Asrăthiel, still grasping the rope.

'I cannot say, sir,' she answered distractedly, as her hands shaped the gestures of weatherworking. 'The ways of wights are not easily penetrated. Perhaps trows carry these tidings back and forth, in their ceaseless peregrinations.'

It came to the weathermage that Crowthistle might somehow have played some part in the brownie's acquisition of strange tidings, but she decided to make no mention of her suspicions. The urisk had attached himself to the Maelstronnar house for some while, during which he had harassed the brownie to the point at which it had almost departed from the premises forever. Being a wight itself, the brownie undoubtedly knew more about Crowthistle's comings and goings than any mortal being, and it was not impossible that the domestic wight had caught the news from him.

Beside the basket the king was coiling a hawser with the dexterity of a seasoned fisherman. Rope in hand, he climbed in beside his son. 'Are we set?' he asked the weathermage.

'Almost!' she cried, keeping an eye on the blazing sun-crystal. 'Three crewmembers is a full load and I must wait for sufficient buoyancy. To take off too soon would be risky.'

The wind veered. A shower of leaves blasted in their faces. The basket was jumping, held in place only by two ropes in the grip of the king and his son, which passed through a pair of ground hooks.

Asrăthiel stared up with irritated impatience at the inflating envelope. Her mind was worrying at Avalloc's news as a dog
gnaws a bone. 'My grandfather declares that the brownie itself was
frightened,' she called out, 'which disturbs me greatly. But the creature's words must be true, because it is unable to tell falsehoods,
and as for whether it is suffering from delusions, why the Storm
Lord has been acquainted with the wight all his life, and would
doubtless perceive any alteration in its outlook.'

The balloon had swelled taut and become buoyant enough to
lift the load. Asrăthiel was about to tell her companions to cast off
when the chief signalman, who had just completed his latest task,
burst out of the tower door and came running towards them. He
was waving a piece of paper and begging the visitors to tarry.

'This report has just now arrived,' the man said hoarsely, thrust-
ing the leaf into Asrăthiel's hand. It was a communication from King
Warwick himself, from his encampment, via King's Winterbourne.
The message was short, as if hastily composed.

After silently scanning the note the weathermage inhaled sharply. She uttered no word, but crumpled the paper in her fist and let
it drop from her fingers. It was snatched away by the gusts.

Halvdan brushed tousled amber filaments out of his eyes.
'What's amiss, Asrăthiel?' he asked in concern.

The weathermage simply stood, gazing into emptiness, making no move, unbreathing. As if in extension of her body the wind
faded to a mere sigh.

'What is it?' Thorgild turned his attention to the bearer of the
note. 'What was the message?'

A row of jackdaws that had been perched on the semaphore
tower took off in a storm of flapping pinions and a clamour of
shrieks, like fragments of burnt fabric. They scattered, startled by
the sudden sound. Perhaps even they, with their alien, avian minds
unattuned to human passions, were pierced by the sharp note of
utter grief and desolation in Asrăthiel's scream.

The signalman whispered, as if the words were too appalling
to be spoken aloud, 'It said, 'Regret to inform you Uabhar Ó
Maoldúin has slain your kindred.'"

The alarmed jackdaws reassembled themselves in flight formation and flapped across the pouring skies into the distance.

A long bank of lilac-bellied cloud was rolling in from the west,
promising rain. Intermittent shafts of sunlight slanted from the
darkening firmament like lances of fallow gold. Soon the indigo
clouds let loose their burden. Across Narngalis showers came
pouring down, all that day and through the night.

The long veils of rain that swept in from the coast and settled
in for several days failed to stop the fighting on the Eldroth Fields
– the weather merely contributed to the difficulties faced by the
troops on both sides. Fires went out and could not be relit, and the
ground became slippery with mire. Heavy mud encased the boots
of those who fought and the armour of those who fell. The showers
were finally easing when the Lord Privy Seal: Sir Torold Tetbury –
a small, dapper gentleman with a neat black moustache - arrived
from northern Narngalis at the indigo and ivory panelled pavilions
of King Warwick.

'How go the preparations at Ironstone Keep?' was the king's
first question. He had directed his stewards to open the abandoned
fortress at the mountain pass and provision it, in case the Narngalish
troops were beaten back as far as the Black Crags before Thorgild's
reinforcements arrived.

'All is in readiness. If our fears are realised, we will at least be
able to retreat to a well-supplied stronghold,' Tetbury replied.

'And further north, what of the goblins from underground, as
the Storm Lord reports that his drudge-wight names them?'

'Night itself has become the enemy, my liege. These creatures
are advancing slowly. Their secretive habits continue, for they
prefer the rays of stars and moon to those of the sun, and they
evoke opaque vapours to block out the daylight. Within these vapours they move cunningly. Their progress is like a thick wall of
fog creeping across the land. Through the haze, daring folk may
glimpse movement, a flicker of green fire, a glitter, the outline of an
ugly head. Ominous mutterings issue from that cloud, and, sometimes, harsh laughter. In the heart of the darkness daemon hoofs

thunder, and eldritch blades slay. Then the clouds engulf all, and when they pass none of our people are left alive. Through Mountain Cross and Trowbridge the mists come rolling, and nothing can stop them.'

'These things are far from being as innocuous as fashion would have had people believe,' said the king, shaking his head in dismay. 'They are mistaken, who deem goblins to be feeble wights.'

'How could it have happened, sir, that such convincing tales of their impotence and easy defeat have arisen since their incarceration at the hands of our ancestors?'

'On this I have pondered,' the king said. 'It is an age-old human trait; if men can scoff at the dark they do not fear it. If a menace is reduced to a joke, it is threatening no longer. When the goblins had been overcome and sealed away – as we thought, forever - mankind wished to make mockery of their longstanding foes so that they might banish their terror and become more confident in themselves. All the more reason for us now to verify the facts. We must know what foe we face.'

Tetbury shrugged. 'Odd. I would have thought it more likely for folk to embellish tales of past enemies, making them seem more dangerous rather than weaker, so that our heroes' feats in conquering them would seem more glorious!' As one of the royal advisors he was forthright in giving his opinion.

'Then you must brush up on your history, Torold,' said the king. 'Ridiculing genocidal monsters as figures of fun is humanity's custom. It diminishes them; their stature, their power, their menace. All tales evolve over the years, and no doubt the portrayal of goblins, which was originally fuelled by fear and hatred, became fuelled - after the unseelie threat was removed and people felt safe - by scorn and mockery. People took to depicting them as weak and foolish - a caricature that would certainly have benefited puppeteers, for example, who are always seeking a target to lampoon.'

Tetbury bowed in acknowledgement of his lord's argument. 'My clerks have been plundering the libraries of King's Winterbourne,' he said, 'digging out every scrap of information about these little terrors. Silver was ever their metal of choice, which is perhaps one of the reasons the trows loved them so. Indeed, they were called the Silver Goblins. In olden days, as a warning to humankind, the silver-mining towns were named for the goblins that plagued them, and named also for the trows that fawned on the goblins. Now the imps return by their old haunts; by Silver Hill, Silver Moss, and Silvercrags, through Yardley Goblin and Elphinstone. They cut down all human beings in their path, although, curiously, they do not pursue those who flee. Villagers are escaping southwards in ever increasing numbers.'

'Most of what you say is not news to me, Torold,' said the king, 'but I thank you for it.'

Later, when Warwick held counsel with his sons and advisors, Tetbury repeated his account, after which the king made known the latest news from Rowan Green. 'When he learned of the fate of his kindred the Storm Lord was struck down by a fit. He has taken to his bed. His son's wife nurses him, and he is too weak to travel. His mind, nonetheless, remains sharp. As you are aware, he communicates daily with me.' The king's grey eyes rested calmly upon his audience. 'Avalloc, of all men living, is most learned in goblin lore. He confirms what Torold has told us - that they love silver, and are therefore named the Silver Goblins. As to defending ourselves against these wights and driving them back, he advises that the best weapon is gold. As silver is their joy, so gold is anathema to them. Therefore we shall gather together all the gold in the kingdom and melt it, to plate our steel blades.'

Prince Walter said, 'What of the famous weapon of the weathermasters, Fallowblade? Once the golden sword was employed to defeat the goblins. Why not again?'

'Indeed,' said his father, 'that question has occupied my thoughts. I shall ask Asrăthiel, on her return, if she will fetch the sword from its keeping place.'

William gave a start as Asrăthiel's name was spoken. 'But Fallowblade is useless!' he cried. 'No ordinary man can wield it.'

'An ordinary man called Tierney A'Connacht handled Fallowblade in days of yore,' stated King Warwick, 'and to good effect, too, or so say the lore-books of Rowan Green.'

William countered, 'Maybe Aglaval Stormbringer put some forgotten charm on the weapon, or some old magick of Alfardēne was still clinging to it. Only a weathermage with years of training may use that weapon without danger to himself.'

'Aye. Asrăthiel alone has learned the secrets of the sword.'

'You cannot ask her to do this. Would you send a girl to fight the goblin hordes?'

'Will,' said his father, 'I cannot speak for Asrăthiel. It is for her to choose.'

'Even so,' replied the prince, scowling, 'but she must choose in full knowledge of the peril she would face if she confronted them, and the hopelessness of making such a stand. In his letters the Storm Lord continually emphasizes the fact that goblinkind is no force to be trifled with, for they possess supernatural arts, and they have no compunction. The slayings around Silverton bear that out. In days of yore they slaughtered hundreds of thousands – a fact conveniently overlooked by storytellers who would make them out to be easily duped bunglers - and in their wickedness they would have wiped humanity from the face of the known world.'

'If not for Fallowblade,' subjoined Warwick.

William made no reply, but his look was thunderous.

Next morning, as the rising sun made a burning battlefield of the cloud-barred heavens, the armies of Slievmordhu and Ashqalêth gathered their resources and launched a determined, well-or-chestrated onslaught. On the eleventh of Juyn by virtue of their superior numbers they succeeded in driving the defenders from their fortified trenches and embankments. The army of Narngalis was forced, once again, to retreat. Warwick quickly withdrew his troops from the Eldroth Fields, leaving their tents standing, and hastening northward while the rear-guard shielded their backs. They went precipitately, but also in orderly fashion, pushing ahead with great swiftness, and they did not pause until they arrived at

Ironstone Pass, high amongst the Black Crags, where the highway passed over a saddle between two peaks.

The Black Crags, a long range of hills running right across Narngalis from the North Eastern Moors to the Mountain Ring, were so named because their peaks were formed of a type of black basalt upon which vegetation – aside from mosses and lichens - refused to take root. Trees clothed their flanks, but their heads were bare, and sliced by deep ravines. Only mountaineers could cross those heights, except where a gap between two steep hills allowed the passage of a road. In order to reach King's Winterbourne the southerners would be obliged to cross the Black Crags, and Ironstone Pass was the most accessible way through the mountains for miles around.

The Narngalish troops were too numerous to file through the narrow gorge before the pursuers caught up and cut a swathe through their rearguard. Warwick ordered several battalions to rally and make a final stand at Ironstone Keep, defending the pass while the rest crossed it and rode on to King's Winterbourne. There they would swell the ranks of the household guard as they prepared the city to face possible siege. If the southerners won victory, then for those who remained at the Keep there would be no way out.

Frowning from its cliff top vantage, the massive fortress of Ironstone Keep overlooked the pass. It was once the main stronghold of the kings of Narngalis. Built long ago, it had been left in the care of a succession of stewards for almost two centuries, before ultimately being abandoned eighty-seven years earlier - but not neglected entirely, because successive monarchs had kept it in good repair. The old fortress, hewn partly out of natural rock, was well defended by the rugged terrain; moreover, arrow loops slitted its towering walls, and machicolations crowned it. All the windows and smaller portals had been sealed with stone and mortar when the last steward departed, and fifty years ago a mighty avalanche had blocked the main entrance, so that these days the only access was through a siege tunnel, large enough for two men riding abreast to pass through.

Small bands of Warwick's crack marksmen distributed themselves in redoubts, caverns and makeshift places of refuge throughout the highlands surrounding the stronghold, ready to harass the enemy with lightning raids and sniper-action. Warwick and his sons entered the rocky vaults of the Keep, along with the chosen troops. Although outnumbered, they were determined to hold out against the invaders for as long as possible, at least until Thorgild's reinforcements arrived, or until the eldritch mists came down and goblin raiders overwhelmed them all.

Flying birds cast brief, tattered shadows over processions of villagers in wagons and on foot, who were making their way along a blossomy country lane in Narngalis, not far from the Eldroth Fields. Two of these refugees seemed to have lost their way and become separated from their families, for they hobbled along all by themselves, following a meandering sheep track through a meadow. Evidently trying to rejoin their kindred, they were making for the lane.

Strange-looking women they were, with lopsided breasts and voluminous bonnets, and scarves tied about their faces. They struggled in their long dresses, tripping over every so often. As they passed a thicket of elderberries a couple of hulking shapes leaped out and stopped them in their tracks, whereupon they emitted rasping, falsetto screeches.

'Ho, what have we here?' said one of the Marauders, eying the women up and down. 'These are buxom wenches! Better than the Spawn Mother, at any rate.'

'Aye,' said the other. 'Hey, my pretty, give us a kiss!'

The swarmsmen made to grab hold of their prizes but instead they found themselves crashing to the ground, half stunned under the heavy rain of blows inflicted on them by the women's swinging fists. A moment later the wenches picked up their skirts and ran away, full tilt. As they departed they hurled rags and various other objects into the air, lightening their loads to make them fleeter of foot. Their outer clothing was later discovered lying in a ditch, along with four lumpy turnips of assorted sizes.

Weepers had begun their doleful chorus as soon as the Narngalish troops arrived at Ironstone. By now the men were accustomed to the sound, and though it still sent shivers through their flesh they did not let it lower their spirits. 'It is for our foes they weep!' they insisted. 'Their sobs are a promise of our victory!' Over four days the armies of Slievmordhu and Ashqalêth beleaguered the northern troops, hunting them through the steeps to the east and west of the pass. It was no easy task for the invaders; unless they were as sure-footed as mountain ponies they slipped down the sheer walls and were broken on the rocks. Whenever one fell, another took his place; purely by dint of numbers, the southerners still had the advantage. Those of Warwick's soldiers who had elected to remain outside the fortress sustained heavy losses, but deep inside Ironstone Keep the King of Narngalis was well ensconced and could not be prised from his sanctuary. They held the pass - for the time being, at least. Uabhar was aware, however, that Thorgild's Grïmnørslander battalions must be drawing nigh. Day and night he exhorted his officers with threats, bribes and punishments, ordering them to flush out the Narngalish, clear the pass and overthrow Warwick before reinforcements arrived.

An unexpected factor had upset his calculations. Since rumours of unseelie hordes had begun to send tentacles of fear twinging about men's hearts, the troops of both Slievmordhu and Ashqalêth had lost something of their lust for the spoils of war. They had grown uneasy and flighty. Morale was low, dampened by pessimistic speculation. Despite the ban on talk that might lead to sedition, gossip was rife. Like most mountainous areas the Black Crags had a reputation for being haunted, though in fact they were not – except by harmless weepers, warners and dunters - and human travellers had passed safely through them for years. Spurred by apprehension, the soldiers conjectured wildly. They began seeing things. There were claims of grotesque faces leering from crevices; of scrawny limbs erupting without warning out of fissures, tripping up passing soldiers; of clawed hands pushing unwary men over precipitous bluffs. It was whispered amongst the troops that bands of deadly wights such as gwyllion, kobolds and even goblin outriders roved the Black Crags.

The spirits of the invading armies had ebbed to a new nadir. Not only were they plagued by visions from nightmare, but lately the Desert Paladins and the regular Ashqalêthan troops had grown impatient with their king's feebleness and his constant deputising of leadership to Uabhar. They chafed at being - as they perceived with greater frequency - under the yoke of a foreign king whose greed and ambition threatened to engulf their realm. As for the Slievmordhuan forces - amongst themselves the Knights of the Brand unreservedly aired their discontent. They were increasingly suspicious that Uabhar had ordered the weathermasters to be slain, and that he had allowed Marauders to raid undefended villages and murder families in their homes so that he could wring higher protection taxes from his subjects. The knights' doubts filtered through to Uabhar's soldiers, who, already disturbed by the hauntings in the heights, began to lose heart for battle. They muttered – softly, so as not to be hanged for sedition – censorious comments about their king, and many longed to return to their homes to guard their families from the unseelie threat. The tide of public opinion was rapidly turning against the King of Slievmordhu, though he himself was too deeply immersed in his schemes, and so insulated by his own ruthlessness towards those who would reveal ugly truths, to notice.

King Chohrab, too, was proving to be a thorn in Uabhar's side once again. Even from his sickbed the desert king occasionally roused himself sufficiently to vex his ally over matters of strategy, maintaining that it was better to split off several battalions and send some of them across the Black Crags the long way around, through a distant pass many leagues to the east. 'That way we could reach King's Winterbourne without having to wait until we seize Ironstone Pass,' he said. 'Once we have taken and garrisoned Winterbourne we will rule Narngalis. We must capture the city without delay.'

It was with difficulty that Uabhar prevented his veneer of good fellowship from cracking. 'My brother, your reasoning is, as usual, excellent,' he replied. 'Of course we must capture Wyverstone's seat as soon as possible, and that is why it is of greatest importance not to weaken our battalions by dividing them. You yourself have always impressed upon me, 'unity is our strength'! Your words of wisdom are constantly uppermost in my thoughts. It is necessary to concentrate our forces in one place, for after we cross the Crags we shall no doubt meet Torkilsalven's army. Let me pour you some wine.' Chohrab opened his mouth to argue but Uabhar, seemingly unaware of his intention, continued, 'Consider the joy of your people, when you have annexed Grïmnørsland. Consider the joy of the Grïmnørslanders themselves, who have struggled so long beneath Torkilsalven's yoke. Your name will be shouted in songs of praise. You will be showered with rose petals as you ride through the streets of Trøndelheim.'

'Ah yes,' said the desert king, smiling and picking up his goblet. 'I look forward to it.'

'Allow me to send you my own personal physicians and apothecaries,' Uabhar said solicitously. 'I would fain see you welcome victory in robust health!'

'Here's to vanquishing those who would vanquish us!' crowed King Chohrab, and he quaffed Uabhar's wine.

Having placated his ally, the King of Slievmordhu returned to his schemes. He wanted to finish off Warwick, then push through Ironstone Pass to intercept Thorgild before the army of Grïmnørsland had the chance to join the Narngalish. His forces, however, had not been able to conquer the slim defile. Each time they made an attempt they were thwarted. Showers of flaming arrows, rocks and hot oil descended on them from murder holes and embrasures in the battlements and walls of the fortress looming high above the road. Uabhar directed his patrols to locate the entrance to the siege tunnel, but snipers well practised in bowmanship picked off the scouts amongst the coal-black tors.

The king pinned his hopes on a certain spy, a stealthy nimble fellow, the same who had secretly watched the weathermasters in the Red Lodge. 'There will be a siege tunnel,' Uabhar said to his lackey. here is always a siege tunnel, and the existence of this one is common knowledge. And I will make you the lord of as much land as you can ride on a long Summer's day, if only you can discover its location.'

'Majesty, I will not disappoint you,' the servant said, and he slipped away amongst the shadows.

Prince Ronin, fully armed and accoutred as befitted a warlike knight, was ever amongst the vanguard of each fresh push to secure control of the pass. He seemed fearless, as if unconcerned with preserving his own life; his conduct was daring to the point of recklessness, and if he escaped serious injury it seemed more by fortune than forethought. Indeed, the young prince astounded everyone. The men under his command quickly came to admire and love him. He inspired them to heroic deeds. 'Prince Ronin is the bravest of us all,' they declared.

Uabhar heard them. 'Clothe yourself in armour,' he said to Crown Prince Kieran. 'Ride at my side, that the troops may see you bearing arms. Let them call out your name and celebrate your courage.'

'I can do more than put on a show. I will fight, if you wish it,' said Kieran. 'I would fain be lauded for my deeds, rather than for the gear I carry. I can battle as valiantly as Ronin.'

'Conserve yourself. You are next in line for my throne,' his father said curtly.

When Ronin came from the field he would visit his brother. Together in the privacy of Kieran's sparsely furnished pavilion the two princes, who enjoyed each other's confidence, spoke as candidly as they were able of their distress at the struggle against their erstwhile friends in Narngalis, the unconscionable way their father had dealt with the weathermasters, and the prospect of war with Grïmnørsland. Though they generally felt at ease with each other, their discourse was somewhat awkward; it went hard with them to criticise their father, even in private.

Seated on a leather-upholstered stool Kieran propped his elbows on his knees, supporting his chin in his hands and staring glumly at a small casket that rested on a stand. 'My heart is not in this conflict,' he confessed hesitantly.

'I am of the same mind.' Ronin shuddered. 'Especially now that the fate of the weathermasters has been revealed and the blame lies at the door of Slievmordhu.'

'My conscience is in turmoil, I admit,' Kieran said with a sigh. 'I am finding it difficult to reconcile myself to the fitness or necessity of destroying the good mages of Rowan Green.'

'Such an act cannot be reconciled,' Ronin said simply. At this obvious censure of their father Kieran spontaneously flashed a look of hurt and anger at his brother, which faded as quickly as it had appeared. He sighed again. 'Perhaps you are right,' he said sadly. 'I know not, any more. He means well, but sometimes...'

They both struggled for words.

'Yes,' Ronin said into the pause.

The topic was too raw, too hurtful to be probed, and they let it drop.

'How do we find ourselves at war with our neighbours?' Ronin mused, as if thinking aloud. 'Can it really be true that they intended to attack Ashqalêth and Slievmordhu?'

'It must be true,' Kieran said without much conviction. 'Our spies are utterly reliable. Father chooses them himself. Yet I cannot help but grieve,' he went on, 'that I must take up arms against the homeland of my betrothed and my best friend. What must they think of me, Solveig and Halvdan? I had envisioned we would grow old together in friendship, all of us. Now our bond is sundered, probably forever. I am become their enemy.'

Ronin replied, 'They will understand you are not at the root of this conflict. They will know it is the result of forces beyond your control.' Wearily he rubbed his hands across his face.

'But will they forgive me for the part I must play?'

'I have no doubt of it. They must play their parts also. Halvdan will fight for king and country.'

'But Solveig, Solveig,' Kieran murmured, rocking restlessly back and forth. He reached for the casket, took out a golden locket and snapped open the case. It parted like the wings of a yellow moth. He brought it to his mouth and kissed the miniature portrait inside, then gazed fondly at the image, the pretty face, her amber-gold braids wound around her head like a crown, a gentle smile curving her lips. The prince glanced up and noted Ronin watching him with a look he could not interpret. 'Here!' Kieran held out the locket, its golden chain dripping through his fingers like strings of liquid fire. Ronin accepted it reverentially, glanced at it, then handed it back. Carefully Kieran closed the keepsake and replaced it on the stand.

'She is sure of your feelings,' said Ronin.

From just outside the tent a tiny bell tinkled.

'Enter!' said Kieran.

A footman came in. He bowed to Kieran, saying, 'Your Royal Highness, His Majesty requests your presence.'

'I must go,' said the Crown Prince, and he left immediately.

Ronin stayed longer. He barely moved, except to make as if departing, only to change his mind. Once or twice he glanced across the silk-lined apartment to the casket containing the locket, then tore away his gaze. Clearly his sole desire was to spring across the floor, seize it, and feast his eyes on the contents but he never touched it; indeed he barely breathed, until with a long exhalation he turned his back on the image of Kieran's troth-plighted princess and departed from his brother's quarters.

An Near sunset on the fifteenth of Juyn, unheralded by fanfare, the first of the reinforcements from Grïmnørsland at last approached the northern slopes of the Black Crags. Without access to semaphore signals from the north of the mountain barrier, without sky-balloons to observe and report activity behind enemy lines, Uabhar remained ignorant of Thorgild's arrival.

Asrăthiel, accompanied in the gondola by Prince Halvdan and one of the Grïmnørslander flagmen, guided *Lightfast* in advance of the new arrivals. Keeping the balloon low to avoid being spotted by enemy sentinels, the weathermage stared at the long line of dark hills vanishing at each end into the misty distance, north-east and south-west, their western flanks glowing golden in the evening light. Her brí-senses were subject to the air pressures that flowed around the range in invisible tides, the clamminess of the clouds that slowly seethed through the peaks; yet she apprehended them with detachment. Her eyes gazed, but her mind saw only the faces of Ryence and Galiene, Baldulf and Engres, and the rest of her friends and kindred who had perished at the hands of the King of Slievmordhu. Even the thrill of flight was gone. All joy was gone; there was nothing left except anger and terrible sorrow, since she had learned the truth.

A cavalcade headed by King Thorgild proceeded along the road below the balloon. Spurred by urgency, Thorgild's Shield Champions and cavalry battalions had raced ahead of the plodding infantry troops who, still on the march, were catching up as swiftly as possible.

Looking ahead, Asrăthiel spied Warwick's watchmen high in the rocky steeples, distinctive in the murrey-hued uniform of Narngalis. They spotted her too and, in greeting, waved flags, sending a series of signals in code. 'Warwick safe in Keep. Enemy at bay,' the flagman translated. Halvdan instructed the signaller how to respond, whereafter the flagmen on the ground sent, 'Guides ride now to meet Thorgild and escort him to Warwick.'

Equipped with this information, the balloon flew back to rendezvous with the King of Grïmnørsland. Asrăthiel did not land, for Thorgild refused to halt, even for a moment. Due to his desire for haste, he had taken to holding conference on the move. A short distance ahead of the procession she hovered just above the rutted road, while Prince Halvdan jumped over the side of the gondola and ran back to the advancing horsemen. His well-trained steed allowed him to vault into the saddle without breaking stride. While *Lightfast* ascended, Asrăthiel was aware of Halvdan animatedly passing the tidings to his father and brothers as he rode alongside them, but it all seemed remote, like a play being enacted before her, rather than an event in the world. Her heart was breaking.

Thorgild left his heavy cavalry bivouacked amongst the low spurs on the north side of the pass, while he and his three sons, with the Shield Champions, followed King Warwick's guides along a devious, hidden path that led high amongst the Crags. Along precipitous cliff paths and through a jumble of tors, pikes and scars their steeds climbed, alternately lapped by chill shadows and diagonal rays of amber sunlight, until the riders found themselves before the great circular door of stone that guarded the mouth of the siege tunnel. All were so glad Thorgild had finally reached his destination that they slackened their vigilance by a fraction. It was only a modicum, but enough that the watchmen failed to observe Uabhar's favourite spy, that sly, evasive fellow who had peered at the weathermasters in the Red Lodge. Having tracked the newcomers on quiet feet, even managing to dodge the sharp eyes of Asrăthiel in her balloon, he discovered the hidden portal and watched the kings and princes enter on horseback, ducking beneath the arch. Armed with this intelligence he slunk away, as the door of Ironstone Keep rolled shut behind the newcomers.

When Uabhar heard the spy's report his fury reached new heights. 'We have lost our opportunity to waylay the fish-stinking barbarians before they reached Wyverstone!' he shouted at his officers. To Prince Ronin he said, 'Lead your troops to this tunnel's door. Post a guard around it. Let no man enter or leave. Watch it strenuously, so that no provisions may be smuggled within, and none of our foes may escape. At the very least, I shall starve them out.' The prince bent to kiss his father's hand and acknowledge his orders, while Uabhar added, 'Wait for me there.'

As Ronin set off with his men, following the spy to the hidden door, the weathermage on the opposite side of the pass summoned a swift breeze. She flew back with her signalman to deliver the latest tidings to the oncoming infantry. It was her last errand for Thorgild. Her work as message bearer and escort to the Grïmnørsland army was now finished. She was free to return to The Laurels at King's Winterbourne if she so desired, but the idea never occurred to her.

Her lodgings seemed empty and unwelcoming without the urisk; moreover, above all things she wished for Uabhar's defeat, so that he might be brought to justice for his crimes. Chohrab was not exempt from blame either, for in his greed he had chosen to ally himself with iniquity.

It was impossible for Asrăthiel to endure the raging emptiness where her heart used to be. That void had to be filled, and what better to fill it than a renewed zeal to overthrow the invaders, who were ravaging Tir with their hunger for power and weakening humankind's ability to defend itself against genocidal wights. A powerful weathermage would be a useful weapon to the northern allies. On the spur of the moment she decided to join them in Ironstone Keep. Briefly she hovered low to let the flagman alight at the bivouac amongst the foothills of the Crags, and then ascended at great speed, gliding in amidst the upstanding wedges of the dusky tors. The Grïmnørsland knights and cavalrymen, who had been sharpening their swords and oiling their armour, paused in their tasks. They looked up at the ethereal bubble, lustrous against the gloomy escarpments, sunlight-gilded. Their eyes followed it until it vanished. 'Good Fortune go with thee, Lady in the Moon,' they murmured.

Good fortune did not favour Asrăthiel, however. In the dying afternoon she flew *Lightfast* down the gasping throats of soaring chasms and across clefts brimming with darkness, towards the place she had seen the guides taking Thorgild. At length, arousing herself from brooding upon Uabhar's atrocities, she realised with sudden shock that the enemy might spy the balloon and follow her to the hidden entrance. She was about to retreat when it occurred to her that perhaps she could twist this handicap to advantage. By feigning a landing at some spot far from the tunnel's door she could mislead anyone who might be watching. When night fell she could rise again under cover of darkness and alight closer to her destination, before ditching the aircraft down a crevasse where it would be hard to find and proceeding the rest of the way on foot.

To avoid the place, first she had to know its position. As she searched for the entrance to Ironstone Keep, arrows began whizzing towards her from some rocky rampart and she knew enemy marksmen had already spied her. The barrage did not worry her at first, for she skilfully kept out of range, but as the sun finally slipped beyond view and she caught, at last, a glimpse of the location she sought, flaming bolts began to sizzle out of the dusk, close at hand. The weathermage tried to dodge them, but a fiery bolt lodged in the balloon's rigging and flames took hold of the fabric. As it sailed over a sharp ridge the balloon shuddered and collapsed inwards, releasing a storm of sparks.

There was to be no saving the aerostat. It would crash down to the rocks below. The enemy would be able to locate the brightly glowing wreckage easily, and the pilot did not wish to be discovered there too. *Lightfast* gently tumbled out of the night sky, blazing, and Asrăthiel fell with it. Or rather, she jumped.

Just before she let go the rope and threw herself into thin air, a primeval voice within her skull screamed in terror, and every particle of her mortal ancestry revolted against taking such a suicidal plunge. Deep-rooted instinct flashed vivid memories of joy through her mind; times spent with her cherished parents, Avalloc, William, Dristan, Albiona, Corisande and Cavalon and others; she remembered laughing until her sides ached; whirling on a crowded dance floor; drowsing by the fireside at night, listening to raindrops pattering on the roof ... and she hesitated. A sheet of flame blasted from the shrivelling envelope across her field of vision, and at that moment she saw instead the faces of her betrayed kindred, and felt the anguish of voiceless beasts doomed to enslavement, torment and death through the agency of humankind, and then eternity unrolled like a path before her feet, leading nowhere. At that instant nothing seemed to matter any more and she released her grip.

Even as she hurtled towards the ground with the wind booming in her ears she could hear the sound of *Lightfast's* priceless sun crystal being smashed to smithereens against some adamantine cliff.

In those few moments it took to fall three hundred feet her mind cleared and she became extraordinarily calm. Composedly she took note of her surroundings so that when she landed she would know where she was in relation to the secret and tortuous route to the door of Ironstone Keep. It came to her, too, that everything in fact mattered a great deal. Curiously, it was the urisk she thought of, though briefly; that immortal creature Crowthistle. He lived, and so must she.

He had lived forever.

And so would she, regardless.

On the rocky rampart, Ashqalêthan snipers watched the sky-balloon's demise and believed they had destroyed one of the weathermasters aiding Narngalis. 'The mage sprang from the stricken vessel to avoid the flames, and fell to his death down a crevasse,' they said, when reporting their success to Chohrab. The ailing King of Ashqalêth jubilantly and mistakenly told Uabhar that one of the last remaining weathermasters had been slain, and the King of Slievmordhu was gratified.

'It is most likely the Storm Lord's granddaughter who has fallen,' said he with a smirk. 'There was talk the chit had some shield of enchantment about her, but if she hurled herself from the basket to avoid being burned alive she must have been as perishable as the rest of us. Now the age-raddled Storm Lord is the only remaining threat.'

Contrary to Uabhar's deductions Asrăthiel had jumped from the balloon, fallen three hundred feet and landed safely. Not so much as a bruise marred her flawless skin; not so much as a fingernail was chipped. After her body slammed into a rocky outcrop at high speed she merely picked herself up and looked around, trying to get her bearings.

She had guessed it would be that way.

Never had she taken the testing of her invulnerability to such limits, but there was no reason to suppose that plummeting from a great height could cause her injury, any more than fire, or water, or disease, or any bane of mortalkind had ever touched her.

Having survived the fall unscathed the damsel found herself standing on a ledge above a whistling, echoing gorge, deeply cloven. Overhead the stars were coming out, and by their feeble light, combined with her heightened sense of the atmosphere, she was able to discern her surroundings. Along tiny ledges jutting only inches from sheer walls she made her way. If the shelves petered out she dropped fearlessly to footholds further down the cliff face in a manner that would have made the most intrepid mountaineer think twice. If she missed her purchase she slid out of control, only to be brought up on the next projection, bones unbroken, flesh intact. She swung from rocky arches, climbed scarps and leaped across gulfs that would have made mortal hearts quail, and her strength never failed, though her heart pounded with excitement.

In this way the weathermage came, at length, near the door of Ironstone Keep well before Prince Ronin's battalion. King Warwick's watchmen, who had seen the balloon destroyed, spied her. Recognising her immediately they first poised stock still, jaws agape - for, ignorant of her immortality, they had believed her to be dead, killed in the balloon crash. Overcoming their astonishment the men were filled with joy, and sent word to the two kings inside the fortress, who, greatly gladdened, dispatched mounted men-at-arms to escort the damsel to their inner sanctuary. By the time Ronin's troops appeared, Asrăthiel was safely within. The warriors of Slievmordhu surrounded the basalt portal, which was shut fast against them. The massive door was shaped like a gigantic wheel, and it could be rolled back and forth by use of heavy, geared machinery within, but could never be operated from outside; nor could it be burned like the wooden doors of the Red Lodge. Ironstone Keep was immune to fire.

On the south side of Ironstone Pass King Chohrab Shechem's health had deteriorated. He lay, fevered, on a velvet couch in his ostentatious pavilion at the Ashqalêthan encampment, and his physicians were unable to cure him.

That night, in the wake of Prince Ronin and his battalion, Uabhar rode up the steeply winding paths with princes Kieran, Cormac and Fergus, to join Ronin in the vigil at the stone door. Confident of victory and wishing to appear warlike the king carried his personal arms: his shield, 'Ocean', his knife, 'Victorious', his spear 'Slaughter', and his sword 'Gorm Glas'.

Wrapped in furs against the chill of the night Uabhar braced his feet upon the wide stone platform of the threshold. 'Narngalis! Grïmnørsland! You have no hope of triumph,' he shouted.

His blustering had deserted him, now that he knew himself the victor. He resumed his old facade; unruffled, persuasive, eloquent. Buffeted by erratic highland updraughts, blazing torches flickered all around him, gripped in the hands of the mighty crowd of armed warriors that thronged outside the door. The flames spat out droplets of hot pitch and resin, throwing weird shadows into chasm and cleft. Firelight splashed like honey against louring cliffs.

'You have walked into your own tomb! You will starve. Dead kings beneath the mountain are you!' Uabhar jeered. Silence answered him. 'Yet I am not unmerciful. If you come forth unarmed, I will treaty with you. Come forth and live!'

The wind careered through cavity and rift, keening with a disquieting dissonance that resembled mourning at a funeral and set on edge the teeth of the listeners. Their apprehension deepened when it came to them that they hearkened to the sound of actual sobbing. Here in the Black Crags, amongst the adamant slabs and sudden drops and sheer rock faces, the wailing sounded louder. Eerily it echoed and ricocheted. Weepers, the wights that heralded deaths amongst humankind, were once again broadcasting their portents of doom.

'It appears that Wyverstone and Torkilsalven give no credence to your good intentions, sir,' Prince Ronin said to his father. He was standing at a short distance from Uabhar, dressed in plate and mail, helmed and fully armed. Kieran, similarly equipped, waited close by.

Slievmordhu's monarch stepped back from the door, his spurs jingling. 'Bring in the quarriers,' he cried.

Several men ran forward, garbed in the stout leather jerkins and heavy boots of mine workers. Some rested ladders against the door and ascended them; others worked at the portal's base. All used augers to drill oblique holes, angled downwards, into the rock. They would fill these strategically positioned worm burrows with water, before plugging them securely. It was an old and effective mining technique. Overnight, when temperatures dropped below freezing point at these high altitudes, the water would turn to ice, expand, and crack open the stone.

'Stand back!' Uabhar ordered his troops. 'Give the diggers space to work!' The soldiers complied, gathering about the door's threshold in horseshoe formation.

Even as the miners worked the wind dropped, and clammy steams came coiling out of the hollows of the mountains. Eying those mists the men shuddered and drew closer together.

Within the yard-thick walls of Ironstone Keep the kings and princes of Narngalis and Grïmnørsland presided over a large gathering of their foremost advisors, including Asrăthiel. Sentinels, looking down upon the rocky platform in front of the door from spy-holes high in the outer walls, kept the assembly informed as to the movements and demands of those who besieged the fortress. The debate had been long and intense, though marked by solemn composure. They made a striking picture, the two royal families standing together beneath the high-vaulted ceilings; the dark-haired, grey-eyed Narngalish in porphyry and indigo, their tabards emblazoned with the emblem of a sword; the blonde, blue-eyed westerners in aquamarine and turquoise.

As pale as pearls was the beautiful face of the weathermage, and her aspect was bleak. The inner turmoil she had suffered since receiving the tidings of her kindred's fate was like a sickness. Often to be seen staring blankly into the distance, she spoke very little and kept to herself. She never smiled.

'Alas,' King Warwick was saying, 'my plans have come to naught.

I intended to hold the pass until you arrived, Thorgild, then abandon the fortress and let the enemy advance piecemeal through the defile so that my troops could pick them off with ease. Now the foe has discovered the door and I realise my mistake, for we find ourselves trapped in the Keep. I can only blame my lack of foresight on battle fatigue.'

Asrăthiel said, 'We ought to take advantage of the hours of darkness, and the chaos of the milling crowds before the door.'

'Indeed. We shall rush the enemy and overwhelm him!' said Warwick.

'Agreed!' Thorgild said, clasping the hand of the Narngalish king in a firm grip of friendship. 'And when we have broken free my trumpets will sound from the peaks, and my cavalry will come pouring through the pass, to our aid!'

Thorgild's youngest son, Gunnlaug, was particularly eager to fight. 'We have been too long on the road,' he said. 'Let us begin the butchery! There are heads to be broken, and plunder to be got. Father lend me your sword, that I might make you proud.'

'You shall not have it. This is no time to be playing at heroes,' his father said sharply.

'Then,' Gunnlaug replied, 'I plan to win myself the sword of Uabhar; Gorm Glas!' He drew out his own blade and brandished it defiantly.

'We must all work together, Gunnlaug,' said Thorgild. 'The purpose of this battle is not merely to win personal glory. Your bragging becomes tiresome.'

The prince's face congested with dark blood. He thrust out his jaw. 'I will prove myself braver than any man here,' he said.

Before he had finished his declaration a sentinel came running. 'They are drilling the door!' he exclaimed. 'By morning they will have broken it!'

Warwick gazed at the man in consternation. 'Then there is no time to be lost!' he cried.

'To arms!' shouted Thorgild.

Prince Gunnlaug had departed even before the order was issued. He raced through the labyrinthine halls of the Keep, and climbed a steep stair. Halfway up he came to a halt and began to pull crumbling masonry from a window embrasure that had long ago been bricked up. On first entering the Keep he had explored it, found this potential breach and kept the information to himself. When the aperture was clear he squeezed through, dropped to the ground and stole away into the night mists. After creeping around the outside of the walls to the siege-tunnel door he drew his sword and sprang amongst the miners who drilled at the stone door, bewildering them, kicking aside their cressets and lanterns, slaying four with his initial onslaught and striking terror into their hearts with his savage war cry.

Uabhar peered into the murk, unable to glimpse anything save for a swift-swirling glimmer of lamplight upon the silhouette of a warrior. Even in the confusion, the king's cunning did not desert him. He commanded his men to be silent. They obeyed immediately, whereupon he shouted into the gloom at the door, 'Who is this champion that wreaks havoc amongst my men?'

The chest of the lone combatant inflated with pride.

'I am Gunnlaug, son of Thorgild Torkilsalven,' he crowed, yet he kept out of sight, in the places where the vapours curdled thickest and the shadows were darkest.

'Ah, Gunnlaug,' Uabhar said into the blinding haze, and his tone now was sweet. 'You and I have never argued. There is no dispute between you and me. I count you amongst the mightiest warriors that ever lived. If you cease your attacks upon my men and come over to me I will bestow magnificent gifts upon you – ten thousand acres of land, a seat beside me at my table and my authority to support you. How do you like my offer?'

The son of Thorgild, unseen, wavered.

Uabhar's instincts, however, were keen. In the silence he sensed not denial, but imminent success. 'Gunnlaug,' he went on, 'being the youngest son you will not inherit much land. You are well aware that your father is trapped in an awkward corner, with no hope of victory.'

For months Gunnlaug had been hearkening to the whispers of certain sly druids in Grïmnørsland who - on the instructions of Primoris Virosus - had been talking of Uabhar's growing might, and speculating that he might one day become High King of Tir. He thought, Better the generosity of the winning side than the good favour of the losing side, and he recalled, too, with anger, his father's reprimands. In that instant he made his decision. 'I'm with you,' he said to Uabhar, emerging from darkness into the light. And Uabhar in front of his fighting men welcomed the prince, grinning with glee in the knowledge he had acquired a warrior of great skill and strength, while depriving Thorgild of the same, and his son besides.

Such was the perfidy of Gunnlaug, last-born son of Thorgild Torkilsalven.

But Halvdan, suspicious of his brother's lone departure, had noted that he headed for the side stair. Subsequently he stationed himself with the sentinels at the arrow loops and shot holes above the siege tunnel door, peering through the vapours, watching for any sign that the miners had broken the stone. From that vantage point he witnessed the entire scene. When he saw Gunnlaug change sides so easily his wrath overmastered him and he could no longer rein himself in.

A helm of Narngalish steel lay at hand, a conical barbute with a reinforced nasal. Halvdan jammed it upon his head, then seized his father's sword and shield. He raced in his brother's footsteps, taking the treads two at a time and when he saw the ruined embrasure he knew it had been Gunnlaug's exit and jumped out. It was not long before he too had circumnavigated the walls and reached the mist-shrouded stone sill of the round door, where Uabhar's troops were gathered.

Shouting, 'While I breathe, I never shall forsake my country!' he sprang to the attack. Like a spinning-top he whirled with such rapidness and dexterity that none of the men he encountered could stand against him. He hewed this way and that, making a bloody circuit of his foes. Brilliant sparks showered from his sword's edge when steel bit steel.

The watchers above the portal of the keep saw this, and one hastened downstairs to take the news to the two kings, shouting it aloud as he ran. Men ran hither and thither seeking the exit through which the princes had passed, so that soldiers could be sent to Halvdan's aid, but no one had seen Thorgild's sons depart and it was not known which direction they had taken in that maze of stone.

Witnessing Halvdan's massacre from amidst a phalanx of bodyguards, Uabhar smiled. He murmured to one of his captains, 'Another misguided hero, and a superb fighter like the first. Challenge him. He will be as venal as the one before him.' To his soldiers he shouted, 'Fall back!' and they withdrew.

Uabhar had misguided notions of this second warrior's character. His captain offered generous terms to him if he would change sides, but Halvdan would not even deign to listen. He was patriotic in the extreme, and above all, loyal to the people he loved. Having carved a lonely place for himself in the dimness before the stone door, surrounded by the bodies of the fallen, it came to him that there remained one way of saving his household and his kingdom from certain defeat. Hoarsely, panting for breath after his exertions, he called out, 'I invoke my entitlement to a duel on behalf of Thorgild of Grïmnørsland. According to custom, this quarrel between kingdoms can be settled by single combat. I hold Uabhar Ó Maoldúin bound to answer to me with his body for this belligerence towards the kingdoms of the west and north. Let him stand against me!'

Uabhar strained his eyes, squinting into the gloom. 'Who is it that offers this challenge?' he asked Gunnlaug.

'By his voice, it is Halvdan, my brother. And methinks he brandishes my father's sword and shield, which were never offered to me.'

'Halvdan? He who is friend to my son Kieran?'

'The very same.'

Uabhar called back, 'Your challenge to the house of Ó Maoldúin is accepted.' He summoned the Crown Prince to his side, cutting short the prince's outburst of surprise and distress that his father would risk his own life. 'Let me speak first, Kieran,' Uabhar said. 'It is Halvdan Torkilsalven who makes the challenge of single combat to our household. You and he were born on the same night, if I remember correctly, or so your mother forever harps.'

'That is so, Father.'

'And by the rules of single combat I have the right to choose someone else to fight in my stead. One man from the household of Ó Maoldúin must stand against him, and I deem you the best of us.'

The prince stood stock still, speechless with a new kind of dread.

'This night,' said Uabhar, 'Halvdan wields his father's sword. As the two of you share a birth night, so you shall share the honour of bearing your father's arms. Here is my shield, my knife, and my sword Gorm Glas. Conduct yourself courageously in contest against the son of Torkilsalven. If you do not vanquish him the house of Ó Maoldúin will lose the throne of Slievmordhu.'

Uabhar's captain proffered the shield and weapons to the Crown Prince, but Kieran ignored him. He stared incredulously at his father. All around them the pinnacles of the mountains rose out of the brume, their summits outlined against star-filled skies. From somewhere beyond the vapours came the muffled sobbing of unseen weepers.

'Father,' said Kieran, 'do you mean that I should go in combat against Halvdan?'

'The Fates have laid their benison upon these weapons, and that will surely preserve you.'

'My lord, since our earliest years, Halvdan and I have been the best of comrades!'

'I daresay the son of Torkilsalven does believe himself to be fond of you,' said Uabhar, articulating his words with exactness. 'That is, of course, the beauty of the scheme.'

As his father's intimation sank in the prince took on a look of horror, as if he was awakening from a pleasant slumber, to discover all that he had believed was true and upright had been no more than a dream.

'Tarry no longer,' said Uabhar, turning his attention to a thread on his own sleeve and picking assiduously at it. 'It gives you a semblance of cowardice.'

'But I cannot - '

Uabhar cut him off. 'Show your brother the true meaning of filial obedience.'

Glancing to one side Kieran took in the stricken countenance of Ronin, who, lingering close at hand, had overheard all. No word passed between the two siblings, but their gazes were filled with anguish, misunderstood on both sides.

Abruptly, Kieran took – almost snatched – the sword and shield from the captain's hands. He spoke no further word, but girded himself for battle, squared his shoulders, and strode to meet his adversary on the stone threshold.

As he did so the great door roared and rolled open. Uabhar's warriors faced it, brandishing their weapons and readying them-selves to fight, but it was King Thorgild alone who stood in the entrance, his copper-red hair shining in the radiance of the torch he held aloft. He called to Halvdan in tones of despair, 'There are many amongst us who wish you had never made that challenge.'

His son replied, 'I can win this war by spilling the blood of one man, and in this manner also I shall compensate for the black disloyalty of Gunnlaug, who this night has brought shame upon the name of Torkilsalven.'

Then Thorgild perceived that there was nothing he could do or say to alter Halvdan's course, and a harrowing agony laid hold of his spirit.

Thus it came about that the two lifelong friends met in battle.

Through the haze and gloom Kieran sought the son of Thorgild, and when they found each other not a single word passed between them, for they understood one another so well that it was as if their thoughts were exchanged without the need for speech. Those who looked on, aghast that two such fine young men should engage in a fight to the death, felt that they could read what passed between them as easily as it had been shouted to the starry peaks.

So it is you who takes arms against me, Halvdan's eyes sorrowfully transmitted.

Kieran nodded, as if to say, yes it is I. His expression of torment added, I love you as I love my closest kin. That which I am about to do wounds me to the very quick of my being. I do it only because I am obliged to obey my father's direction. Would that he had asked me to carry out any task but this.

Halvdan, in his turn, briefly dipped his head. I comprehend how it is for you. Of all men it is I, your truest friend, who best understands. You are the obedient son. Your very loyalty is one of the virtues I esteem most in you. I would have given my life to save yours, but now I must make myself the instrument of your death. Halvdan lifted his father's sword.

Likewise, in reversed mirror image, Kieran raised Gorm Glas.

Fleetingly the two young men held each other's gaze. Then a signal seemed to leap between them; If this pitiable farce must be played out to the end, let us go to it.

Then Kieran and Halvdan clashed against each other in battle, bounding to and fro, balancing on their feet although the ground was slippery with the blood of the fallen; changing positions as each attempted to get under the other's guard, but from many of the observers who surrounded them there arose moans of sadness and regret, that this pair of brave warriors should be doomed to such a terrible undertaking. The clamour of their efforts and the jarring blows of sword smiting upon shield rebounded from cliff face and monolith, from tor and scarp, scattering down cleft and chasm.

At that same moment, unknown to anyone, a rider was approaching, ascending the high cliff paths. Conall Gearnach, chief of the Knights of the Burning Brand, had ridden long and hard from the South Eastern Moors where Uabhar had sent him on a wild goose chase. On returning to Cathair Rua he had petitioned Queen Saibh for news.

She had informed him that Uabhar had tricked the weather-masters to their deaths and declared war, that her sons had gone with Slievmordu's troops to capture King's Winterbourne, and that unseelie throngs, reputedly goblins, were swooping down from the north, cutting swathes of destruction.

The knight did not stay to ask for details, but at once called for a fresh horse, and after leaping upon its back he galloped along the highway towards Narngalis. His physical endurance was extraordinary; on the way he neither rested nor paused, except to change horses. When he reached Ironstone Pass he encountered mounted sentries of Slievmordhu, to whom his person was well known. They told him about the siege of the Keep and readily showed him the route to the door, leading him by lantern glow through the murk.

As the riders climbed the dark and tortuous paths amongst the crags, clouds folded their soft draperies across the constellations overhead. The night darkened, but the closer Gearnach drew to the portal the more clearly he heard the sorrowful murmurs of the throng at the threshold and the chime and clatter of arms, and he said to himself, I know that sound. It is the sound made by the king's shield, Ocean, which tolls like a great bell when struck. The king himself is in danger. is policies disgust me to the point where I am torn between loyalty and moral principles, but in the end I must abide by my oath. It is my clear duty to defend him.

Guided by the noise of combat, Conall Gearnach closed in on the scene, threw himself from his mount and ran forward.

In front of the door Halvdan had gained the upper hand. Perhaps Kieran was sick to the heart, and perhaps this sickness debilitated him, for he showed no evidence of any ardency for the duel. With one powerful flat-bladed thwack of his father's sword, Halvdan knocked down his opponent. Kieran measured his length upon the platform, the heavy shield, Ocean, falling on top of him and the momentum of the onslaught causing his body to skid along the stones.

In the very instant that Kieran hit the ground Conall Gearnach appeared at the forefront of the watching crowd, his spear in his hand. In normal circumstances the champion could sense anomalies by intuition. This night, however, he was weary from his long ride and his senses were dulled.

Under the hidden stars the basalt doorsill was lit only by erratically flickering torchlight diffused by drifting veils of haze. As Gearnach set eyes upon the spectacle of the duel it seemed clear to him that it was Uabhar who lay in peril beneath his shield. The fallen man's helmed adversary was commencing a savage charge and Gearnach's military reflexes told him he must act immediately.

Without hesitation he hurled his spear at the unknown opponent, using all his strength and skill. The weapon struck the warrior between the shoulder blades and pierced deep into his back. A shout of disapproval and dismay arose from the throats of the onlookers, when they witnessed this fatal blow. The young man collapsed to the ground, and fell upon his side in a fast-spreading pool of blood. Gearnach strode up to him and wrenched off the helmet. Halvdan's face was clearly illumined in a patch of torch-light and Gearnach recognised him at once, but stared upon him in dumbfounded disbelief.

Halvdan looked up. Struggling for breath he cried, 'Was it you, Conall?' A spasm of agony took him and he writhed. When the convulsions waned he muttered, 'Great wickedness you've wrought, my friend, for by this duel I meant to put an end to Ó Maoldúin's bloodshed.'

The face of Gearnach took on a livid hue. It was then that he perceived also that the opponent beneath the shield, who was struggling to regain his feet, was not Uabhar but Kieran, bearing his father's weapons. The knight looked down at Halvdan Torkilsalven, the prince who had saved his life and vowed eternal friendship, the brave young man dying from a blow given by his own hand. Uttermost rage filled him. It was as if every drop in his veins had been distilled to the essence of madness, and rushed upwards through his spine to explode in his brain. All rational thought deserted him.

'This is some game of Uabhar's!' Gearnach screamed, ripping his sword from its scabbard. Made sightless by mist, sweat, rage and despair, he failed to perceive the King of Slievmordhu watching from the shadows. The old, berserk frenzy boiled up in Gearnach, that same irrational impulse that had once driven him to kill his own racehorse for upsetting the running of another steed. His sole desire was to take revenge on Uabhar, and that vengeance proved close at hand. 'I'll give him fair payment. For this night's chicanery he shall lose his own son!'

And with a single, violent blow of his sword he struck Kieran's head from his body.

Halvdan's father and elder brother ran from the gateway, converging upon the fading prince of Grïmnørsland, but Gearnach was there before them, kneeling at his side, drenched in his young friend's blood. With one last supreme effort Halvdan called out the name of his dead friend, cast his father's sword in the direction of Ironstone Keep and perished before the stone door.

Deranged by unbearable sorrow and anger Gearnach jumped up. Abandoning his weapons he charged at tremendous speed from that place, and no man found it within himself to obstruct him. Fleeing far from the door he bellowed in a terrible voice, 'Spread the word! Uabhar Ó Maoldúin has betrayed the weathermasters, and the Knights of the Brand, yea, he has even betrayed his own kindred. All of humankind is forfeit to his schemes!'

None dared oppose him, and many hearkened.

During the ensuing day and night, driven by blind grief and ferocity of spirit, the knight behaved as if he had taken leave of his senses, recklessly reporting Uabhar's treachery far and wide and broadcasting the news of the advance of the unseelie hordes every-where he rode.

But at the threshold of Ironstone Keep Prince Ronin knelt by the body of his brother Kieran, while King Thorgild lifted his dead son Halvdan in his arms. Most who looked upon that prospect were deeply moved, and riddled with doubt, for it seemed to them, standing there amongst the profound abysms and steep escarpments of the wight-haunted highlands, that it was hard to comprehend whether they fought on behalf of justice or wickedness.

A cold breeze swirled the vapours and swept away the clouds. Behind the peaks of Black Crags stars glimmered intermittently. Their light heralded the appearance of a damsel at the mouth of the siege tunnel.

Dressed in garments of pure white linen, the weathermage Asrăthiel Maelstronnar poised like a pale flame before the portal. Her hair streamed loose along the rising wind, and her eyes glowed with the intensity of blue fire. She was like a diamond, brilliant-cut with mathematical precision, each facet gleaming in perfect symmetry. So radiant, so delicate and almost ethereal was she, that some of the onlookers felt their hearts clench in pain, and could not turn their eyes towards her.

As the bloody corpses of the two young princes were borne away Asrăthiel spoke to the captains of the warriors gathered there on the wide ledge, endeavouring to drive home to them the truth about the impending arrival of the goblins and the need for immediate action. Summoning all her powers of eloquence she exhorted them to understand that every human inhabitant of Tir was at risk, and that the armies of every kingdom must join in alliance to fight the unseelie foe. She called for peace amongst humankind, but they would not listen.

It mattered nothing to King Uabhar how Asrăthiel had survived her fall from the sky, how she came to be inside the keep or what she was actually saying; his one desire, in his sudden panic at her reappearance, was to shout her down. She was one of the enemy, she wished to ruin his plans

and destroy him; therefore he must prevent his subjects from hearkening to any of her words. He thrust himself forward, shouting, 'The hussy is false. Do not trust her. She panders to Wyverstone and his sons. 'Tis clear she will go to any lengths to secure herself a royal husband. er ploy is to lull us into unwariness, so that Narngalis and Grimnørsland may destroy us all.'

Next moment Prince Fergus sprang out in front of his father, his face crimson with ire. 'By all the Powers,' he bellowed, biting off every word, 'it is you who has wrought this entire tragedy. It is you!'

Uabhar gaped blankly at his youngest son, as if uncomprehend-ing. His hands fell to his sides and dangled limply.

'Did you hear me?' screamed Fergus. 'This war was propa-gated by your foul and lying tongue. Slievmordhu bleeds for you. Your own son, you slew! The blame for every calamity in the Four Kingdoms lies at your door. You make me sick to the guts, you marble-hearted deceiver! Did you hear me?'

For an instant Uabhar seemed frozen, completely at a loss, as if this was so far beyond his experience that it belonged in another dimension. Then, impulsively, he turned away and flung a gesture in the direction of his foes, yelling, 'Slay them!'

But Asrăthiel stepped forward in a whirlwind, blasting her foes with strong gusts, while from the high-vaulted tunnel at her back King Warwick and his sons, on horseback, charged to the attack at the head of their troops, and Thorgild galloped forth with Prince Hrosskel, the knights of Grimnørsland following in their wake. The soldiers of Slievmordhu and Ashqalêth, confounded by all they had witnessed, scattered in disarray, fleeing down the mountain tracks. In the melee, some fell off the vertiginous pathways to their deaths. The Narngalish and Grimnørslanders who had been trapped in the Keep pursued them down the northern slopes, aiming to join the bivouacked army of King Thorgild.

Soon afterwards, while the confusion and fighting still rampaged in the heights, on the highway below the troops of Slievmordu and Ashqalêth broke through Ironstone Pass and flooded across the gap to the northern side. Grimnørsland's battalions had been awaiting them, and by nightfall another furious conflict was under way.

For three days the battle of Ironstone Pass continued. The south-ern forces pushed the northerners further and further back until the front line was less than ten miles from King's Winterbourne. It was then that the tide began to turn, but not as anyone had foreseen.

The countryside was swarming with refugees from northern Narngalis; from Mountain Ash and Silver End, from Silverdale and Silverburn, from Trow Green, Fairyhill and Cold Ash - all the old districts named for the mines, or for the faerie creatures that haunted them, or for the goblin wars - and from numerous other locations besides. The soldiers of the southern kingdoms could not avoid seeing the frightened villagers, and hearing their tales of wholesale slaughter in the eldritch mists. The truth was driven home when their own scouts and patrols verified these reports.

At last they comprehended.

The weathermage at the stone door had spoken no falsehood; the widespread rumours were not fabrications, but truths. Unseelie hordes were on their way to mow down the human race, and the leaders of the southern kingdoms had destroyed mankind's most powerful defenders, the weathermasters. Every man, woman and child of Tir was in the direst peril.

When the whole world was threatened, patriotism suddenly seemed petty and meaningless. Suddenly, the course of events began to change as quickly and violently as an avalanche. The wild proclamations of the breakaway Conall Gearnach, a knight so widely esteemed, carried immense authority, and his messages had been spreading rapidly. Combined with the rising swell of discontent already demoralising the invading forces, his revelations about Uabhar had shattered the last illusions of the populace and finally tipped the balance, turning opinion against the King of Slievmordhu and any who allied with him, especially the Marauders.

It was the elite warriors of Slievmordhu, the Knights of the Brand – deprived of their beloved Commander - who first rebelled against Uabhar and Chohrab. Almost simultaneously, the Desert Paladins, who had chafed under Uabhar's yoke since their own king abandoned them, joined their ranks. Risteárd Mac Brádaigh, High Commander of the Slievmordhuan armed forces, was slain in battle. Thereafter the other captains of Slievmordhu's army, perceiving the self-destructive folly of Uabhar's campaign, executed a military coup to deprive their sovereign of power. Uabhar was seized, and bound in iron chains. On witnessing the success of the coup the Ashqalêthan captains decided to overthrow their own monarch. Two squadrons were sent to the outlandish pavilion at the base of the pass, and the ailing Chohrab Shechem, too, was taken prisoner.

The precepts of hierarchy and the entitlements of hereditary authority run deep. Not one of the revolutionary officers was prepared to issue an order for outright regicide. After forcing both kings to publicly abdicate they took them away and locked them, in chains, within the ancient dungeon near the granite Obelisk that stood alone in the wilderness at the corner of the Four Kingdoms. A handful of warders tended them, keeping them alive on bread and water.

To Prince Ronin, heir apparent, the lords of Slievmordhu offered fealty; he, however, stubbornly refused to succeed to the throne, declaring, 'While my father lives, I shall not take the crown.' His grief and regret ran deep. He put aside his armour and vowed he would never again take up arms. When not attending to his most essential duties, he spent his time consoling his mother, or lighting candles to Lady Destiny, and it was only after his advisors had pressed him hard that he agreed to accept, temporarily, the title of Prince Regent.

The conflict between kingdoms was over, but a new war was just beginning. Terrified of imminent invasion by hosts of unseelie slaughterers, hundreds of townsfolk and country folk hammered at the doors of sanctorums across the four kingdoms, begging the druids to ask the Fates to protect them. In response the druids declared that they were indeed intervening on behalf of the commonalty, but they emphasized that should the Fates decide not to rescue them from the goblins, it would be the people's own fault. Of late, the public had been neglecting to donate sufficient goods and services to the hard-working servants of the Fates. If the populace displeased the Fates, then naturally those divine Lords and Ladies – Ádh, Lord Luck; Míchinniúint, Lord Doom; Mí-Ádh, Lady Ill-Fortune and Cinniúint, Lady Destiny - would hardly be disposed to help them. Coin and treasure began pouring into the coffers of the sanctorums in every kingdom, donated by folk from all ranks and trades, in the hope of salvation from the wicked goblins.

Now that their monarch had been deposed and the country was under military rule the captains of Slievmordhu unanimously turned to Conall Gearnach, seasoned warrior and leader of men, for direction. The fever of madness had left him. He became as cool and hard as tempered steel, proving himself a brilliant tactician and, after they made him Supreme Commander, a proficient warlord.

By contrast the captains of Ashqalêth had no desire to form a military dictatorship. Chohrab Shechem had no male heirs and no woman had ever ruled that realm, so with all due speed Shechem's brother-in-law, Duke Rahim, was sworn in as Regent until such time as the governance of the country could be debated at greater length.

The armies of the four kingdoms being now united, their leaders hastily met in conference so that they might formulate a stratagem for the forthcoming encounter with the unseelie hordes. Gearnach's first meeting with Thorgild was fraught with tension; these two statesmen, however, being true leaders of men, refused, for the time being, to allow personal antagonism to interfere with cooperation. In his heart Thorgild fervently wished Gearnach dead, and privately vowed to seek him out and slay him, eventually, no matter whether the war was lost or won.

The princes Cormac and Fergus accompanied Gearnach, though both stood apart from him, loathing him for his deeds before the door of Ironstone Keep. Like Ronin, they were also devastated and humiliated by their father's loss of face. They struggled to believe the truth while simultaneously attempting to justify Uabhar's actions, for his seeming-persona was the very foundation of their self-perception, and if that had crumbled away like rotted masonry, then all that ad sprung therefrom must be shored up, or fall apart.

It was the first time Asrathiel had seen Avalloc since his collapse at the news of the weathermasters' fate – which had left him, for a time, bedridden. He arrived by balloon, and after he climbed woodenly down the short stepladder the crew had propped against the outside of the basket he turned to greet his waiting grand-daughter. To her he seemed shrunken. He leaned on a staff and his

skin and hair looked paler, as if the colour had ben scoured away
by the harsh blasts of a desert sandstorm. The tragedy had taken
its toll. Gently the damsel embraced him, kissing the papery cheek
just above the soft fall of his beard.

'Grandfather,' she whispered, and he answered with a smile like
sunrise that warmed her heart.

'My dear child,' he said, 'I am glad to see you!'

She took his arm and accompanied him from the landing-apron.

Later, in front of that assembly King Warwick asked, 'Lord Avalloc, in your opinion, what chance have we of victory?'

'Small chance,' Avalloc replied sombrely. 'Gold is our chief
weapon, but I doubt whether we have enough of it. It is written that goblins can be destroyed by gold, but only by prolonged
contact with large quantities thereof. This is comparable with
the way mortal creatures react to, say, arsenic poisoning, or any
number of other potentially fatal influences which, in small doses,
cause harm but do not kill.'

'They can be destroyed?' cried Duke Rahim. 'But wights are
immortal!'

'Immortal, yes,' said Asrăthiel. 'Age cannot conquer them, nor
sickness. Weapons, however, can inflict upon them a harsh fate;
one might call it a version of death. They cannot truly die, but they
can be changed. Their original form can be broken and their power
nullified. In some insignificant shape they continue to live forever,
powerless and perhaps also mindless.'

Her grandfather said, 'It would take more gold than exists in
the Four Kingdoms to annihilate such vast hordes.'

'Then, without the aid of the other weathermasters,' Thorgild
stated bluntly, 'it will be impossible for our armies to vanquish them.'

Avalloc nodded.

Duke Rahim said dispiritedly, 'We have two choices; to fight
and be wiped out - or flee and be wiped out.'

'We must fight!' Conall Gearnach declared in a voice of frozen
steel. 'If we fight, we shall diminish their numbers, even if only
by a modicum, for there is always the possibility of striking down
a few if we hurl enough gold. But if we simply turn and flee the

foe's numbers will remain the same. Furthermore if we fight we temporarily hold back their advance, seizing a little extra time for the people to escape southwards and find places to hide. Should our armies withdraw, we will soon find the enemy hard on our heels, mowing us down from the rear and cutting deadly swathes through the territory we have abandoned.'

'Aye,' said Thorgild. 'We fight. We stand our ground. If we are to die – barring some miraculous intervention from the Fates – we shall die not like cowards but with honour!'

'When the hounds corner the fox,' Gearnach added quietly, 'the fox always puts up a fight, despite knowing that death is certain.'

Rahim, who had been pondering deeply, roused himself and said, 'Lord Avalloc, the weathermasters captured the goblins by trickery once before. Why not again?' He looked around animatedly, his face alight with new hope. 'Could the goblins be lured back into the golden caves, as previously, then sealed in with rockfalls started by lightning blasts?'

'There is small probability,' said Avalloc, 'of tricking them into entrapment a second time, because now they know of the caves' existence. Yet methinks you are on the right path, good sir. Our only real chance lies in devising some plan to thwart them with cunning, since we lack adequate force.'

'Let our best strategists be put to the task at once,' said Warwick.

'Even the greatest thinkers will need time to invent such a plan,' said Asrăthiel, 'and time is what we lack.'

'Then,' said Warwick, 'our forces must hold the goblins at bay for as long as possible. We fight. Are we agreed?' A chorus of affirmations greeted his proposal, and thus it was that the council of war decided that the Four Kingdoms would take a stand against the hordes, no matter how bleak the outlook, no matter how futile the attempt might seem, no matter how inevitable the defeat.

While the united armies of Tir marched northwards to confront the unseelie threat, in south-eastern Narngalis an odd-looking, uncoordinated cow limped across the landscape.

Evidently it had swallowed two men who remained alive, because two arguing voices could be heard, issuing from inside its stomach.

'Oi tell ya, this is unnecessary. Them goblins will not slay us!'

''ow can you be sure?'

'Because they won't think we look 'uman. It's only 'umankind they prey on.'

'We moight look 'uman enough for 'em to stick a sword in us.'

'Have ya looked in a glass recently? You're uglier than a goblin.'

'Better safe than sorry.'

'But 'ow d'ya know they don't slay cows?'

'Of course they don't slay cows. Nobody's ever 'eard of 'em slayin' cows.'

'Just because nobody's ever 'eard of it doesn't mean they don't do it. Everybody else I know of slays cows. What if the goblins get 'ungry and feel loike a nice 'aunch of beef?'

'Then they won't bother with us, ya idiot. You're too stringy to give anyone a decent meal.'

'Oi am not!'

'You are so!'

Still arguing with itself, the misshapen cow loped off across a field.

Inexorably the goblin forces gained ground by night, passing without haste across the fair hills and meadows of Narngalis, drawing their eldritch mists like veils as they came. They met no opposition from the allied armies of humankind, who were mustering their troops for one last courageous stand along the southern borders of the Wuthering Moors.

Within the castle at King's Winterbourne, Asrăthiel met in conference with Warwick and his sons.

'The goblins are coming,' the king said in a voice filled with pain. 'Upon the advice of the Storm Lord all kingdoms are gathering their gold, from pantry, jewel casket, mine, mint and treasury; gold to bombard goblinkind.'

'The Storm Lord told us,' said William, 'that in olden times, kobolds of the mountains hurled many hundredweight of gold into the legendary Inglefire, so that it should no longer plague their masters. Sorely do we now need that metal. 'Tis a great pity the werefire is now untraceable and we have lost those resources.'

Asrăthiel said, 'It is time for me to send for the instrument of our final hope.'

'What might that be?' asked Prince William, although he knew already and dreaded the answer.

'That which they once called 'Sioctíne', she replied. 'That which is sometimes named 'Frostfire', because it burns like both ice and flame, and its colour is of the sun. The golden sword,' she said adding, as if suddenly breathless, 'Fallowblade.'

4
FALLOWBLADE

Ye knights awake, for valour's sake. Hark now, the war-horns sound!
We've foes to kill, their blood to spill upon the battleground.
From gold-bright halls with lofty walls we'll ride, their heads to hew,
Though they be countless thousands and our numbers be but few!

Knowing they were on the verge of desperate combat, the soldiers of Narngalis were singing battle songs to fire their blood. Midsummer's Day had passed without celebration. It was the beginning of Jule, middle month of Summer, twelve days since the Battle of Ironstone Pass, and throughout the Four Kingdoms of Tir, tension had risen to an intolerable level. The goblins' lethal advance proved inexplicably slow.

Without doubt, either the malicious creatures had discovered some formidable power beneath the mountains, or else the old stories of their ineptness were spurious. They seemed unconquerable. Clearly, if the whim had moved them, they might have swept down through Narngalis with excruciating speed, killing every human being they found. Yet they dallied. It was as if the wights, in their wickedness, were toying with their prey in the same way that fell-cats cruelly toyed with birds, allowing them to believe there is some chance of escape only to continue the torment, repeatedly dashing hope.

Displaced inhabitants of the northern villages were flooding through the streets of King's Winterbourne. Moved to pity at their plight, Asrăthiel offered shelter at The Laurels to large groups of refugees, gave them food and sympathised with them about the hardship they had to endure, leaving their homes. Terror hollowed their eyes; the weary men and women, the children clinging to their mothers and fathers, crying, or – worse – in blank silence. The children's faces crumpled with bewilderment as their young minds struggled to comprehend the enormity of what was happening. Innocent and helpless were they, their unfledged frames too weak for them to defend themselves. The vulnerability of the little ones touched Asrăthiel's compassion and wounded her to the quick. The damsel forced her own pain aside so that she might bring consolation to others. It angered her to see how the contentment of good people had been ruined, their lives thrown into chaos by war.

The beggar's tale of the slaying of Asrăthiel's kindred became well known, and bit by bit – with the help of Queen Saibh - the truth about Uabhar's plot against them was pieced together. Bitterly the people of Cathair Rua repented the accusations they had levelled at the weathermasters. They sent apologies and gifts of atonement to the Mountain Ring, and aldermen composed contrite retractions to be read aloud in every city square.

Avalloc Maelstronnar, still frail and not fully recuperated from his recent illness, arrived at Wyverstone Castle in the sky-balloon Windweapon. Two prentices from Rowan Green crewed for him, and five others arrived in Greygoose and *Icemoon*, the two latest additions to the Rowan Green fleet. Great was Asrăthiel's joy at greeting her grandfather. The Storm Lord brought Fallowblade with him, in the care of the Swordmaster of High Darioneth, Desmond Brooks.

'You must not use the golden sword immediately,' the Storm Lord warned his granddaughter. Gravely he watched her from his deep-hooded eyes of jade. His mane of silvery hair appeared sparser, and he looked gaunt, yet his cheeks were ruddy.

'Why not?' she asked. 'It is imperative that we defend ourselves against the goblins with every means at our disposal!'

'You have not yet wielded Fallowblade in training, let alone in real combat.'

'Only because I have never been presented with the opportunity. Besides, I promised you I would not do so until Swordmaster Brooks judged me to be of sufficient merit. He is here with us now, and I daresay he is pleased with me.' She exchanged glances with Brooks, whose expression remained diplomatically noncommittal.

'Dear child,' said Avalloc, 'it has been long ere you rehearsed even your everyday sword drills. I would have you practise well with the golden blade, before you go into combat. Fallowblade is perilous to wield.'

'History tells us that Aglaval Stormbringer offered Fallowblade to the brothers A'Connacht. I do not recall hearing that they had ever been trained to wield it, or even that the brí flowed in their blood!'

'Oh, but they had been trained. In their earlier years Aglaval was great friends with their father, and he taught them the ways of the golden sword. Besides, their grandmother was a brí-child in her youth, though she never became a mage.'

'But how can Fallowblade scathe me? I have never understood your stance on this matter. I am invulnerable!'

'The blade is extraordinary,' said the Storm Lord. 'It is like no other in Tir. Do not for one instant consider it a mundane thing. This is no mere tempered and honed edge of metal. Gramarye and weathermastery are bound up in it, in the very essence of its making. Fallowblade possesses properties of which even I know very little. I suspect -' he broke off.

'You suspect?' the damsel prompted.

'Well, I may have been bedridden of late but I have not been idle. I have been propped on pillows, poring over tomes from the libraries of Rowan Green. According to the lore books, one of the reasons goblinkind is lethal is their uncanny ability to literally move as fast as lightning. I have long wondered whether the golden sword perhaps allows whoever wields it to shift rapidly through time itself, in order to match the supernatural fighting speed of the wights.'

'An intriguing premise!' Asrăthiel said. 'Yet, how could such a property harm me?'

'I cannot say my dear, for the manner whereby it works is a mystery, but it would be wise to take no chances. If 'tis true that the sword affects time, there is no way of knowing whether the wielder might, for example, risk becoming ensnared in some never-ending loop, or maybe trapped in the past, or the future.'

'This is all conjecture, Grandfather. Alfardēne Stormbringer handled the sword, of course, for he fashioned it; and Avolundar Stormbringer used it to defeat the goblins long ago. Both mages lived to a ripe age, if accounts are accurate.'

'Avolundar used it, but he had learned all about the sword from the teachings of Alfardēne. If any intimately understood the sword's properties, it was Alfardēne and Avolundar. They wrote down what they knew, but over the years some of the records have gone astray. Much of their knowledge is lost to us. 'Twould be sleeveless for you to attempt to use the sword in haste, only to have it destroy you. You must not ply Fallowblade until Master Brooks is satisfied that you have attained perfect control over the weapon.'

Disappointed, the damsel bowed. 'I submit to your wisdom, Grandfather,' she said, adding with a flash of her blue eyes, 'despite that it thwarts my wishes.'

The corners of Avalloc's own eyes crinkled in amusement. 'I am glad to be in your company again, dear child,' he said.

'Without Fallowblade,' Asrăthiel subjoined, smiling, 'I am better placed at wielding weather than sword-fighting. In any case, William has begged me not to take up weapons other than wind and fire and water. In his view it is unseemly and dangerous for women to engage in battle.'

'And what is your view?'

'For my part, if I am to destroy living creatures, I must drive myself to it. I cannot imagine getting any joy of such an exercise. My natural inclination is to heal and nurture; causing injury or death is the antithesis of that. If I am to fight, I must first be convinced that my actions will protect those whom I love. Only then could I go to it with a vengeance – but what a vengeance!'

'I have always understood that you abhor the unmaking of life, dear child, but our fight now is against unseelie wights. Eldritch creatures are not mortal. Their lives cannot be unmade.'

'Truly. Nonetheless, the nature of eldritch immortality is that they may be forced to transmute to some lesser shape, which is their equivalent of death.'

Avalloc said thoughtfully, 'That semblance of life's end is the reason why, once in every few centuries, a new immortal entity is born. Were there to be no endings, there could be no beginnings.'

'I do not know whether it is comforting or terrifying.'

'Of what do you speak?'

'The knowledge that, in some measure, even immortal life can be terminated,' said Asrăthiel.

One night Asrăthiel dreamed that she found herself amongst the armies of Tir as they fought against goblinkind. In her dream she heard Prince William cry 'Beware!' but she heeded him not, and drawing her sword of Narngalish steel she ran headlong into the fray. Surrounded by a churning mass of dwarfish monsters she hacked at them with all her might. They howled and screeched, raking her with their claws, slashing at her with their knives, and swinging axes to chop her limbs, but nothing could touch her, and her sword sang, and pitchy ichor spurted from eldritch flesh.

The fight lasted for a heartbeat or a millennium, but ultimately the imps rushed her and leaped upon her, without regard to her energetic blows. They fastened their teeth and talons upon her limbs, weighing her down until she could no longer lift the weapon, and she toppled beneath the weight of her assailants, falling upon her sword, which broke asunder and turned out to be a blade of birch-lath, after all.

The wights tried to crush her with their bodies, and smother her, and gnaw her; but they laboured in vain for she would not be scathed. She was rendered powerless, however, and could do them no more harm. She was outnumbered, pinned down.

Then Prince William and a company of Narngalish knights, Companions of the Cup, came battling through the turmoil. They attacked her assailants, skewering them and throwing them off, until eventually they released the weathermage.

'Come!' shouted William, taking her by the elbow. 'Quickly! There are too many of them, too many goblins. We must flee from the field of battle!'

It was then that she awoke, dazed and alarmed. Stars shone in at her window, and a cyanic breeze stirred the curtains.

The goblins were coming.

The Storm Lord had given his granddaughter the choice of any sky-balloon at Rowan Green to replace *Lightfast*. Most of the great aerostats lay idle, now that the majority of the weathermages were gone - the old ones used by Asrăthiel's father; *Windweapon, Northmoth, Snowship* and *Mistmoor* - the newer ones; *Autumnleaf, Featherflight* and *Soapbubble; Silverpenny, Dragon-fly* and *Icemoon; Greygoose, Farhover* and *Sparkapple.* Asrăthiel selected *Icemoon,* its spidersilk envelope replaced with the heavier vegetable-fibre cloth she preferred on ideological grounds.

Two days later she joined the united armies of the Four King-doms as the commanders dispersed their troops along the southern borders of the Wuthering Moors in readiness for the inevitable as-sault. A thick and resilient carpet of heather covered large tracts of the open land. At this season it was beginning to bloom, its spikes of mauve flowers jumping with bees and perfuming the air. Heath, with its pink bell-shaped flowers, thrived in clumps amongst the heather, while common violet and scarlet pimpernel hid in the shade of the shrubs, and harebells sprang in the open grassy spaces. Spiny-stemmed gorse sprouted in the corners and crevices of de-caying stonework - the antique remnants of buildings - its golden, sweet-scented blossoms furled tightly in their buds. Low bushes of bilberry had finished flowering, and small green fruit were begin-ning to set on the stems. Crisp tufts of hardy crowthistle bristled here and there, the dark green of scalloped leaves contrasting with the vivid purple of the inflorescence. Soon, most of these wildflowers would be crushed into the soil.

The choice of site had been thrust upon the armies of Tir by necessity; the hordes-in-the-mist were beating a path directly south from the Harrowgate Fells. It was estimated they would reach the moorlands that very afternoon, for they no longer travelled only during the sunless hours but by day, wrapping themselves in darkling mists. In favour of the setting an ancient city had long ago stood on the Wuthering Moors, and the broad acres were criss-crossed with remnants of old fortifications such as low stone walls and the shells of ruined towers. The defenders wasted no time in putting these barricades to good use. Furthermore the southern edge of the moors was slightly higher than the northern, which gave the mortal armies a small but significant advantage over the foe.

The Narngalish were particularly determined to try to save King's Winterbourne from capture. After the Storm Lord's revelations about the power of the goblins Prince William had admitted to Asrăthiel, 'In slumber I am tormented by visions. If the royal city falls, the gutters will run with blood. Goblins will empty the streets and buildings, making of it a hollow place inhabited only by beetles and rodents and spectres on the wind.'

'Do not dwell on visions,' she had replied, banishing the echoes of her own dream. 'It may never come to that.'

Yet she, too, was frightened.

The goblin wars of olden times were legendary. Avalloc had told her that long ago, those death-dealing wights had almost overrun the lands of men but ultimately their king, Zaravaz, was overthrown. Then they were vanquished by the weathermasters, led by Avolundar Stormbringer wielding Fallowblade, who forced them underground, sealing them into gold-lined mountain caverns, in a prison whose walls were thousands of tons of rock. There the immortals had remained incarcerated, until now. The wights' extended confinement would have provided them with plenty of leisure to ponder retribution. If they had been hostile before their long punishment, certainly their aggression must have increased a hundredfold. Released by some inexplicable means, they intended – it was clear - to take revenge for their defeat and prolonged imprisonment by destroying humanity, inch by inch.

In their vengeance they would be aided by their kobold slaves, those monstrous little creatures which, unable to penetrate the golden shell in which their masters were imprisoned, had been wont to lurk in underground places and poison mortal miners with their toxic presence.

It was written in the surviving records that iron could not injure goblins, nor fire nor stone, nor any mundane weapon. By the efforts they went to in avoiding daylight it was conjectured that the sun's rays, also, might be their bane. One thing was certain - they could not abide the touch of gold. The war councils of the Four Kingdoms used this knowledge to formulate strategies for the forthcoming confrontation. Quantities of gold had been hastily collected from the treasuries of kings and noblemen, then melted and rolled out to the thinnest leaf, or cast into shot. Laden wagons rolled up to the Wuthering Moors; from these vehicles treasury stewards unloaded huge chests and coffers filled with costly ammunition. At Avalloc's command the containers were set out in rows, some forty feet from the knoll on which he and Asrăthiel would take their battle positions. The lids were unclosed and the bullion lay ready, open and gleaming under the skies.

At this mellow time of year the day's eye lingered long overhead, but even Summer days must eventually end and night must rule again. A sense of foreboding seized the waiting battalions. No man doubted that when darkness fell on the Wuthering Moors the goblins would come.

The mournful cries of curlews sounded across the open land, and the calling of snipe and teal and lapwings, and the sobbing of weepers that few mortals ever glimpsed. King Warwick rode amongst his troops talking to his men, giving words of encouragement, boosting their spirits; calling all his officers by name. Thousands of soldiers waited, rank after glittering rank ranged along the southern marches of the moors, staring out across the sea of wildflowers. Their hearts hammered in their chests and their palms sweated as they gripped their weapons tightly in their fists, for the season of doom was nigh, and ultimately there could be no avoiding it.

They were coming; the goblins.

All of Tir's soldiers stood in readiness. Sunset emblazoned the west with rich cinnabar and dripping ruby glazes, before twilight altered the firmament to softest cornflower blue, deepening to perse. High in the ceiling of the world a scattering of silver points began to appear, increasing to a twinkling ocean of spangles. Not a single cloud obscured the sparkling splendour of the stars. It was to be a fine evening for death.

Shadowy swathes of mist began unfurling from east to west, along the opposite side of the moors. Amidst those vapours a hint of gargoyle faces, a green shimmer of tossing manes, a flash of gleaming metal.

Atop a low knoll on the southern border, Avalloc and Asrăthiel waited, clad in shirts of glimmering chain mail and cloaks of weathermaster grey. Statuesque and unbent stood the Storm Lord, despite his recent agues and advancing years. As for his grand-daughter she was a flower stem, slim and pliant; her eyes like the blue wings of evening, mesmerizing. Both were murmuring phrases of power and drawing shapes in the air with quick, graceful move-ments. The two weathermages had been busy. As soon as they had learned where and when they were to encounter the horde, they had commenced to manipulate local and distant weather patterns. Now they were quietly raising a southerly breeze in an attempt to blow away the fog. Even though Asrăthiel's sorcerous blood and unique birthright amplified her powers of weathermastery, she and Avalloc knew they would not be capable of defeating this scourge unaided; yet their kindred who would have supported them had been murdered, and those who lived must do their best alone. Their grief at the loss of their loved ones still harrowed them fiercely, and they were distracted by thoughts of what might have been: Baldulf should have been leading the calling of the wind; Galiene should have been standing at my shoulder; if only Ryence were here we would conjure a storm the like of which has never been seen, a true weapon of accuracy and power; ruled as straitly as man has ever ruled the lashing elements. Their sorrowful conjectures impaired their abilities, and thereby the power of both was diminished.

Close around the mages, precisely arranged in concentric circles six rings deep, stood their defenders, the Companions of the Cup. Tall and straight as javelins they stood, their plate and weapons gleaming in starlight. Some forty feet from their position stood the array of open chests and coffers filled with heaps of shining material. At the Storm Lord's orders, all men gave the arks of gold a wide berth; soon they would become perilous.

Darkness deepened.

By night the goblins came, silently.

The mages' brí-summoned wind swept over the heather; the mists swirled and dispersed, the last glimmer of afterglow faded from the west and a great arch of constellations, glinting hard and sharp as sparks of white metal, was flung across the heavens from horizon to horizon.

One moment the moors were empty; in the next they were there across the heath, motionless, mounted on their daemon horses; some twenty-five thousand, rank upon rank, with their kobold slaves thronging at their sides. No mist obscured them.

And they were beautiful.

Tall, pale, and handsome, with the appearance of human men, the goblin knights – for that is what they must be – could it really be so? - wore fabulous battle harness evidently fashioned of polished jet, writhing with glittering intaglio. Their mail looked to be made of linked lizards' scales, and their accoutrements of black leather were decorated with silver. Some had helms adorned with curving horns, branched or smooth. The knights' hair cascaded past their shoulders, and it was darker than the night. Their long tresses rose and fell, buoyed by the breeze, and the stars of the firmament seemed snagged therein. Dark were their eyes and lashes, as if they had been pencilled with kohl; even from many hundred yards' distance this could be discerned through the glassy clarity of the night air. Swords they bore, but no shields. One knight was positioned a little forward of all the rest, and he was the most comely of all, yet there was some quality about his demeanour which made him appear dissolute and depraved.

Long-legged and graceful as greyhounds were their daemon horses, the trollhästen, caparisoned in silver. Fey also were these steeds, with a kind of ghastly knowingness about them, and terrifying; utterly unlike their inoffensive mortal counterparts. Their manes and tails gushed like founts of green fire. High above the great tide of riders, shadowy birds hovered in jagged waves. Down amongst the horses' fetlocks swarmed the foot soldiers; bluish-skinned kobolds, as high as eight-year-old children yet ferocious, and clad in brick-red armour marked with an equal-armed cross. Gold-coloured paint decorated their faces and harness. They were ugly, stunted creatures with long tails, pointed ears, malicious grins, wide, flat noses and long slits of eyes – the epitome of traditional goblin descriptions. Yet there was no dilemma in the minds of any of the mortal observers as to which were goblinkind and which were their gnomish slaves. Patently, the nursery tales had erred again; history had been twisted out of recognition, or lied.

Stunned, the armies of Tir stirred not. Indeed, the shock was so great that some scarcely breathed. Was it some form of glamour? Had a net of enchantment been cast over their mortal senses? Many soldiers carried objects that allowed the bearer to see through the disguises of eldritch glamour. They stared at the oncoming spectacle through holes in the centres of rare river-worn pebbles, or touched the dry sprigs of four-leafed clover stitched into their shirts. The terrible, beautiful riders passed every test. What they charm-wearers saw differed not one jot from what their neighbours beheld. By these means it was confirmed that the goblin knights had cast no illusion to give themselves a semblance of fair shape, but were really as marvellous in form as they appeared.

At last, one man roused himself from stupefaction. The Companions of the Cup made way for him as he passed through their ranks and strode out to the forefront of the human armies; to the very head of that armed mass of mortal men. It was Avalloc Maelstronnar. In a voice augmented by the power of the wind he called out, 'Will you parley with us?'

Then to the ears of the human audience, there came the clamour of rushing water and beating wings. Mingling within that great sigh, harsh voices seemed to be saying words in an unknown tongue; *Glashtinsluight ny beealeraght lesh sheelnaue.*

What this meant, nobody could tell, but to the listeners it felt like a negation, a denial. There would be no parley.

Overhead, sullen clouds seethed and shadowy birds hovered menacingly. Then, as one, the goblin riders flung aside their cloaks, which seemed to merge with the night as they fluttered away. It was a gesture that patently indicated they were ready to fight.

Avalloc returned to Asrăthiel's side. With all speed the two mages resumed their muttering of commands and sketching of arcane gestures. They drew together unseen threads, tipped invisible balances, and caused particular forces to build while others decayed. Local eddies swirled around them; their hair whipped across their faces, their cloaks billowed. They were calling a storm to batter the goblin knights, and it was no normal atmospheric disturbance. A furious gale exploded, whisking golden flakes out of the open coffers in ascending spirals. Boiling clouds unleashed sudden sheets of vigorous rain. Tiny fragments as thin as snow, and spherules as hard as hail hurtled out of the skies, yet they were not snow or hail but flakes of gold leaf and golden beads; a precipitation of bullion. When these fragments smote the goblin knights they flinched as if burned by white-hot iron, and some cried out, and their armour and flesh smoked where the gold touched them. Their daemon horses reared on long, graceful legs. Kobolds tossed their own shields to their comely masters, which the riders threw up for protection. In spite of this setback the knights charged into the teeth of the aureate fusillade; the manes of the galloping trollhästen trailing like tongues of emerald gas, and the kobold infantry leaping eagerly to the attack brandishing pitchfork, fang and talon.

Trumpets rang out, clear and bright as glass. King Warwick and his battalions led the charge as the armies of humankind thundered across the moors to meet the unseelie hordes.

War's cacophony roared like the eruption of a volcano. Artificially produced winds wailed, crashes of thunder jolted the roots of the hills; men yelled their battle cries and weapons clashed. From their vantage atop the knoll, the mages were able to survey the battlefield, judging where best to send their biting levin bolts and their vicious squalls, where to fling their barrages of Autumnal gold. Dodging the mages' golden artillery, the goblin knights fought with calm precision. Their speed, as Avalloc had predicted, was abnormal, and their power extraordinary. So swiftly did they move that to the human eye they appeared blurred - almost invisible, like the rapid-beating wings of a hummingbird, making it nigh impossible to target them. Against such opposition mortal men had little chance.

The arrant skill of the wicked wights was uncanny enough, but more disturbing still was the fact that many of them sang as they went about their gory work, in raw, rough tones, as if they joyed in what they did and celebrated it. Not in unison did they vocalise, but their individual voices blended in electric harmonies; a wild, unsettling music, exultant with bloody triumph yet, as with their visible aspects, strangely beautiful. With their singing they seemed to be boasting that they felt so carefree, so lightly pressed and so scornful of their foes, that they had leisure to use their breath on divertissements. If it was a tactic to demoralise, it was a brilliant one. By contrast, their mortal adversaries could only gasp and grunt and pant under their exertions.

Despite all the efforts of the weatherlords and the clever strategies of the battle commanders, despite the skill and experience of the knights of all four kingdoms, and the strength and courage of the troops, and even in spite of their outnumbering the foe four to one, the soldiers of Tir were being mown down in vast numbers. Their counterattack was driven back, and the singing hordes followed up. Appalling slaughter was done on the Wuthering Moors, and the weathermages witnessed it all. As Avalloc Maelstronnar stood at the eye of the storm working the winds, tears flowed down his furrowed cheeks.

It seemed inevitable that the night would end in red ruin, and dawn would bring only the terrible stillness of mass extinction, but unexpectedly there came relief. All of a sudden, when complete victory was in their grasp, the goblin knights withdrew from the field and vanished northwards. Once again it was as if the wights, in their vindictiveness, were trifling with their adversaries, luring humankind to suppose they had some chance of escaping harm, merely to later excruciate them anew. There was no doubt these lords of wickedness could overwhelm the troops at any time, but they restrained themselves from dealing the deathblow, as if enjoying the moment, amused by prolonging the torment of their helpless victims.

Dawn mists rose from the battlefield like a spectral ocean, submerging stonework, crushed flowers and fallen men. Weary and sick at heart, the soldiers of Tir retreated, bearing the wounded, the dying and the dead.

The dandelion petals of morning unfolded.

'Goblinkind cannot abide daylight,' everyone was saying, clinging to all vestiges of hope. 'We shall, at least, be safe until nightfall.' They avoided mentioning the eldritch mists of daytime.

Goblin lore had become the burning topic, and no one knew more about the wights than Avalloc Maelstronnar - save perhaps for Asrăthiel, for he had taught her a great deal during the moments they had stolen together for private discourse. There was much he had discovered in Rowan Green's history books; past generations of weathermasters had had numerous dealings with goblinkind in days gone by, and the elderly mage took it upon himself to disseminate the truth.

'Storm Lord,' many soldiers asked as Avalloc moved through the tents helping tend to the injured, 'why is it that the goblin knights look like human men? We believed them to be ugly creatures, small in stature, something like spriggans, or bogles, or the blue kobolds.'

'After the passing of the goblins, men told stories to diminish the vanquished enemy,' the weathermage patiently explained afresh. 'Our tales made out the enemy to be stunted, repulsive monsters. Humankind considered it comforting to ridicule the danger after it had passed.'

To stave off the weariness of the troops the carlin Lidoine Galenrithar had mixed barrelsful of invigorating herbal potions. She saluted the Storm Lord as she hurried by, on her way to distribute the remedy, accompanied by three other carlins and an apothecary. He nodded acknowledgement, noting the anguish graven into her features. The carlin seemed hunched, as if her shoulders were bowed beneath the burden of mortality. The battle had been waged at a terrible cost – thousands had fallen and countless numbers had been wounded. .

The Storm Lord was more skilled in healing than his granddaughter, for, being unable to feel physical pain Asräthiel found it difficult to empathise with sufferers. Therefore, while the old man went about his doctoring amongst the tents with the apothecaries and carlins, the damsel attended meetings with the military commanders of the united kingdoms. They asked her to repeat all known facts about the goblins, and as she did so, she was reminded of a time when she had sat with William in the gardens of Wyverstone Castle. They had seen a black and white bird; William had called it a magpie, but she had another name for it. The prince had commented, 'I have heard my old tutor say that in some cases the same name is applied to entirely different birds in different parts of the country, and thus confusion reigns.'

Ruefully she thought: *How true! We gave these human-seeming warriors the same label as the beastly little woodland imps who hawk enchanted fruit to unwary buyers…*

'By what means were the goblins imprisoned, Lady Asrăthiel? How is it that they have returned?' she was asked.

'Long ago, after the overthrow of the Goblin King, Lord Avolundar drove the wights under the mountains, sealing them in with rock falls veined with gold and lined with gold leaf. As for how they escaped,' the damsel shook her head, 'we do not know.'

'Is it true they cannot abide daylight?'

'It is thought they might be able to endure the rays of the sun,' Asrăthiel replied, 'but they prefer moonlight and starlight. When the sun is in the sky they seek cloud cover, or conjure their mists as a shield.'

'In that case, might they attack by day?'

'Perhaps not, but remain vigilant.'

Later, in the presence of his granddaughter, the Storm Lord confided, 'There is no need for the hordes to put themselves to the trouble of a daytime assault. They have the upper hand, and may defeat us at their leisure.'

'Tir's greatest tacticians have as yet failed to produce any design for victory,' said Asrăthiel. 'Grandfather, Fallowblade is our one remaining hope. We must purchase more time; stave off the foe for as long as possible. I am determined to wield the sword, whether or not Desmond Brooks deems me sufficiently expert.'

Reluctantly, Avalloc nodded, 'Very well, my dear. You may do so. Yet it is only in our hour of most desperate need that I acquiesce.'

The king's private museum at Wyverstone Castle housed seven antique panoplies plated with gold, which were now quickly conveyed to the moorland encampment. These armours had been made long ago, during the goblin wars, after it was discovered that the supernatural weapons of the goblins could not scathe the yellow metal. The royal armourers offered this war harness to Asrăthiel but, recognising that the craftsmen were unaware of her immunity to damage, she confessed to them, 'I do not need this protection.'

As it turned out, none of the segments fitted her in any case, because her form was too slender. Avalloc, too, refused the harness, whereupon King Warwick, his sons and the Knight-Commander of the Companions put it on, encasing themselves within the warm lustre of ancient gold, like fantastic shell creatures abducted from ocean crypts. The rest they sent to Thorgild, as a gift.

News from the bleak and lonely dungeons of the Obelisk arrived, by way of the encampment of Warlord Conall Gearnach. The overthrown king of Ashqalêth had grown sicker than ever, ultimately expiring from his maladies. The body of Chohrab Shechem II had been borne away to his desert kingdom for burial. Subsequently Prince Ronin, acting on behalf of himself and his brothers, had petitioned Gearnach to free their disgraced father from the humiliation of imprisonment in such ignominious circumstances.

Most people could not understand why the prince seemed so intent on leniency. They did not know how long and earnestly he had confided in Queen Saibh, before taking this step.

'I have renounced anger, Mother,' he said to her. 'I can take no delight in vengeance. And my father has done unpardonable wrongs but I cannot, overnight as it were, alter my lifetime's habit of revering him.'

Her eyes brimming with tears, the queen mutely signalled her sympathy.

'In some strange manner,' Ronin continued, speaking hesitantly, as if striving to decipher his own thoughts, 'it is as if I have two fathers - one who exists in my mind's eye, whom I regard with deference and devotion, and around whom all my circumstances are built...'

'The man you wished him to be, and in whom you tried so hard to have faith,' Saibh said.

'Even so, Mother. Then there is the real man, who is beyond redemption, and that is the man I no longer wish to set eyes on. Yet he represents the fleshly embodiment of the ideal father in my mind. And absurdly, I find it hard to separate the two.'

'It is confusing,' his mother concurred, 'when one's inmost beliefs are so utterly challenged. I know. It will take much time for the truth to really smite you, and even then you will long for the father you wanted. You will yearn so desperately that you will always be rebuilding that image in your mind and trying to make the real man fit the dream, no matter what evidence to the contrary presents itself.' Tears trembled on her lower lids. 'I am considered compassionate by all who know me well, yet even I can find in myself no mercy for Uabhar. But my son, though your heart is at war with your head, you must do as you see fit. If you wish to plead clemency for him with that hateful Gearnach – may the Fates curse him - I will not gainsay you.'

Displaying enormous fortitude and charity of spirit, at Ronin's request Conall Gearnach ordered Uabhar's release. The abdicator was brought to King's Winterbourne, where he was placed under house arrest in well-appointed apartments within the heavily forti-fied walls of Essington Tower.

Asrăthiel could not help but be irked at the knowledge that the tyrant who had ordered the destruction of her kindred should be quartered in comfort; yet she knew, also, that it must be so. Uabhar was no longer king but he was of royal blood, and would always be treated as royalty. Kings and once-kings were privileged by birth, no matter how heinous their crimes. More than anyone else it was their equals who recognised this, for they knew that if one who had ruled from a throne could be shackled and cast into a dank cell, then the highest rank of all was subject to the same fate as the lowest, and royal mystery would be cast to the winds. A king must be imprisoned with propriety. Even a king's execution must proceed with dignity. Throughout history no sovereign had ever dangled from a public scaffold - royal heads were lopped, in ceremonies of relative privacy, by the finest steel blades.

Lacking the ability or impulse to organise themselves into a unified force under a single leader, the Marauders had taken to roaming the countryside. Reports poured in from the field of battle near at hand: swarmsmen were crawling across the Wuthering

Moors, plundering every fallen speck of gold they could find amongst the blood and flies, the mire and the corpses. They were also seeking goblin swords, which had been seen to pierce steel armour as if it were as soft as tallow, but by all accounts none were to be found. Disgusted by this opportunistic behaviour, archers from all kingdoms were shooting at the pillagers. Now that Uabhar had been displaced, swarmsmen were considered fair game. Whatever clandestine treaty had once existed between them and Slievmordhu was deemed null.

Asrăthiel paid little heed to the reports. The goblins' wholesale slaughter made her sick at heart and she longed to defend the people of Tir from catastrophe. Distressed by having witnessed such butchery on the previous night and still aching with grief for her slain kindred, she made use of the peaceful interlude not to rest, but to rehearse with the great sword, Fallowblade.

She and Avalloc were accommodated, along with the king and princes of Narngalis, in a stately chastel on the edge of the moors, where the heathlands verged upon the slopes of a straggling, windswept pine forest. Hundred House, turreted and ivy-webbed, was one of King Warwick's country estates. Soon after dawn the damsel took herself to the ballroom to rehearse her sword drill. She would not be trading blows with the swordmaster – Fallowblade was too lethal for practice games – but she knew it was necessary to accustom herself to the weapon's weight and balance and distinctive characteristics before bearing the powerful heirloom into battle.

At one end of the chamber a small conclave, unable to find repose after the night of ruin and terror, had gathered to watch from the sidelines. The king and his sons were present, as well as Avalloc Maelstronnar, Desmond Brooks the Swordmaster from High Darioneth, the swordmaster's apprentice, Knight-Commander of the Companions of the Cup Sir Huelin Lath-allan, and several officers of the king's household guard. They were wide awake; not invigorated, but shocked. Tension and astonishment kept them alert. The world had suddenly become a different place; it could no longer be trusted, when goblins turned out to be disarmingly beautiful, and weapons of steel lost their potency, and the long-enduring human race glimpsed its own annihilation fast approaching.

Asrăthiel was to practice with the golden sword under the astute gaze of the swordmaster. As she awaited his signal, letting the scabbard rest across the palms of her outstretched hands the young mage mused: *Only someone who wields the brí of weathermastery can employ Fallowblade to fullest advantage. And of all full-fledged weathermages now living, only I have rehearsed with this weapon. How strange it is, that I once wished to wish to handle this sword of gold and electrum purely as a pastime, because it intrigued me - and now the burden has been laid upon my shoulders, that I must brandish it in the face of absolute wickedness. To defend humankind, to slay goblin knights; for this purpose Fallowblade was wrought.*

She gripped the scabbard. The spectators' posture altered elusively, and a tremor ran through them. They had been keeping a perfunctory eye on the proceedings while discussing important military matters amongst themselves; now they focused their attention.

As sword slid from sheath the watchers sighed.

Fallowblade gleamed. Sun motes swarmed up and down its length. Asrăthiel held the weapon in a steady grip, staring in renewed wonder at the fluted blade engraved with its runes of gramarye. The words of the old song chimed though her mind: '*And all along the keen and dreadful blade he wrote the words in flowing script for all to find: Mé maraigh bo diabhlaíocht – I am the Bane of Goblinkind.*'

'*Mé maraigh bo diabhlaíocht,*' she whispered. The sword seemed to be giving off luscious twinkles of white-gold glitter, while attracting them at the same time. The entire weapon was a smooth seethe of glimmers. Other famous swords might be fair, but had they not been compared with Fallowblade they would have seemed fairer.

Experimentally, the damsel weighed the hilt in her hand. She sliced the air. Swoop sang the blade, like a gust passing through tight-strung wires, or through ship's rigging; but behind the hair-raising threnody another note breathed, as of bright, untame voices singing without language. This sound was accompanied by the eerie sensation that the world, for an instant, had slowed. Wild and strange the melody, Asrăthiel whispered to herself, the blood-song played by winds against the leading edge. She had felt and heard these phenomena before, when holding the sword, but never so forcefully, so immediately. Perhaps the runes of gramarye written along the blade were wakening, now that goblins were in the vicinity. *Mé maraigh bo diabhlaíocht – I am the Bane of Goblin-kind.*

The swordmaster's usual advice floated through Asrăthiel's mind.

Remember - to make a thrust truly effective you must use your shoulders, hip and thigh to give impetus to the blow. To deliver the thrust with maximum force, push your body weight through behind the weapon.

'Wrapcut!' she cried, aiming at an invisible opponent with a thrust at head level. When she judged that the blade's fulcrum had passed the adversary's spine she flipped her wrist, turning the blade perpendicular to his body, and behind his neck. Abruptly she leaned backwards, as if dodging her opponent's swing, bringing her own blade towards her. An imaginary head flew off a set of fictitious shoulders, and crashed silently to the floor.

Asrăthiel returned to her balanced stance, holding the shimmering weapon pointing outwards like a horizontal streak of living sunlight. The observers uttered not a single word. She wondered if she had erred in some manner; until the swordmaster suddenly applauded, and it came to her that her audience was dumbfounded. They were regarding her with looks of astonishment.

'A pretty decapitation,' Desmond Brooks said admiringly. ''Twas a shame I barely saw it. I commend you. Never have I witnessed such speed! That is to say,' he amended, in an undertone, 'never until last night.' He brightened. 'Perhaps it is true, what they say about Sioctíne.'

'I believe it is true,' said Asrăthiel, lavishing her gaze on the creamy loveliness of the blade in her hand. 'It alters time. Methinks it slices between time's very particles. That is how it feels to me.'

The swordmaster stepped close to the damsel and adopted a more serious tone. 'A heavier and stronger fighter has a huge advantage,' he said. 'So does one with a longer reach, or one who is faster. Therefore, you must be faster. Do not depend on the enchanted blade. You must have quicker reflexes, be better balanced, possess greater endurance. Naturally your tolerance of pain is greater than that of any mortal creature, but you must be more cunning than your opponent, better trained, defter.'

'Luckier,' added Asrăthiel.

'If your adversary is a lot bigger than you, you cannot afford to let him close with you. He would just push your sword out of the way and mow you down. And be sure, those unseelie warriors we saw last night are no dwarfs.'

'Pushing Fallowblade away would be no easy task,' said the damsel. 'This blade is so sharp that I'll warrant it could sever your shadow from the soles of your feet. Some compare broadsword fighting to killing an opponent by degrees, because one is more likely to maim a limb than succeed in driving a thrust to a vital organ. I sense that Fallowblade, on the other hand, would kill instantly, with the slightest touch.'

'Perhaps,' said Brooks pragmatically, 'but it is always a mistake to rely on one's weapon rather than one's training. Eventually it all comes down to practiced reflexes - you cannot actually think through a fight because it happens too fast. Once a serious exchange of blows starts, a bout is usually over in a very short time. Your body reacts, and you are either defeated or triumphant. Now practice!'

Needing no further encouragement the damsel rehearsed swordplay all morning. Her audience gradually dispersed. Many urgent tasks awaited them; they could not afford to spend time idling. All must prepare for nightfall – a night that might prove to be their last. Asrăthiel was their greatest hope - perhaps their only hope - but they must take every measure to aid the cause.

Patrolling troops reported no sign of goblin riders returning on the northern horizon, so after partaking of refreshment when the sun reached its zenith, Asrăthiel resumed her sword drill, staying at it throughout the afternoon.

As the shadows were lengthening Avalloc entered the ballroom. 'Cease your exertions, dear child!' he exhorted. 'Take your ease. You will need all your strength if they come back tonight.' He said 'if', to indicate hopefulness, but he meant 'when'.

Asrăthiel was reluctant to desist, but eventually she sheathed the golden sword and tried to obey her grandfather. Relaxation, however, eluded her. She felt keyed up with excitement. If the goblin knights reappeared after sunset and battle started afresh, then she would be severely tested for the first time in her life. With Fallowblade in her hands, she would confront the unseelie horde. It would be her part to strike down beings that resembled human men.

Hitherto, the closest she had approached to doing such a deed was smiting Desmond Brooks with a sword of birch-lath, or plunging a rapier into the heart of a straw-stuffed scarecrow. The notion of extinguishing life, even the life of a creature that would continue to exist in some altered, confounded state, filled her with revulsion. Yet there would be no avoiding it.

To work herself into a killing mood she called to mind the faces of the refugees on the streets of King's Winterbourne, and her memories of butchered copses in the cellars of Silverton. It seemed sufficient to summon determination, but she could not know whether she would pass the test until the circumstance eventuated. When confronted by a magnificent warrior, strong and vigorous, eyes flashing with intelligence and vitality, could she bring herself to skewer him through the heart? Or would she drop her sword and run away? Would the prospect of such a morally confusing deed be too dreadful to bear?

After dinner, restless and fidgety, the damsel set out for a walk in the forest park behind the chastel. Alone she went, shunning company, for she wished to contemplate in silence, with no distractions. There could be no danger; vigilant sentries surrounded the parklands, and the entire area had been scoured for signs of anything untoward. King Warwick and his household were well-guarded, and the sun was still in the sky.

She wore no cloak but a gown with layered skirts in weather-master hues; dove-grey, blue-grey, ash, steel and slate, all stitched with silver thread. Strapped at her side, the golden sword in its scabbard slapped her thigh with each step she took. Since morning, she had not allowed Fallowblade out of her sight. Even as she strolled beneath the wind-sculpted pines, deep in thought, her fingers found their way to the hilt and she caressed the intricate embellishments on the elemental ores. It was in her mind to practice fighting moves alone, one final time before battle.

No weeds grew underfoot in the springy carpet of fallen needles. Pine fragrance sharpened the air. The dark green boughs were fruiting with pendant bunches of cones. Asrăthiel glimpsed, between their rough-rinded boles, a glimmer of water in a hollow, and directed her steps toward the pool. Overhead, cirrus wisps dry-brushed into watercolour blue. The sun's lower rim was almost grazing the distant hills, burnishing the west to copper. Twilight was prolonged at this time of day, in this season, at this latitude. Indeed, to Asrăthiel, Summer evenings evoked a long moment of timelessness, when the world paused as the sun kissed the horizon and let forth a spill of radiance with the glow of honey mead.

Narrowing her eyes the wanderer looked up through the fret-work of nodding branches. Long streaks of cloud were taking on the colours of sunset. She was aware they were forming along the upper edge of a front, at such a high altitude that they were wholly composed of ice crystals. Her mage-senses informed her of the onset of a depression; back at Hundred House her grandfather and the prentices were wielding the brí, to ensure that there would soon be a major change in the weather.

A south-westerly breeze shivered through the forest.

'Yes, we are the deathless ones,' said a familiar voice, 'but when it comes down to it, all other things have a beginning and an end.'

Beside the pool the urisk was seated, amongst the gnarled roots of one of the most ancient trees. Something within Asrăthiel leapt for joy.

The wight's penetrating eyes were directed upon her with a curious look; whether joy or anger, tenderness, predacity or something else, the damsel could not discern. 'And in millennia of millennia,' he continued, without offering any form of greeting, 'five billion years to be fairly precise, when the sun has exploded and this world is nothing, not even a ball of seared stone rolling through the firmament, what shall we be then? Shall we exist as conscious particles of dust lost in that chaos, knowing, being, watching the long, slow death of tortured stars, until frozen darkness is all that remains, and we hang there, changeless motes, in night eternal...'

Still water held the wight's reflection, dark-veiled, and mirrored the venerable tree also. He turned his head to stare down at it. 'You are the only human creature ever to be born immortal,' he said, 'which means you are one of a kind. You have no true kindred. Even your father, who gave you the gift of eternal life, was not born with it, but acquired it. You are unique. You are alone.'

The damsel nodded. She was accustomed to the creature's unpredictable ways. His melancholy mood could not dampen her delight at seeing her companion again. 'That is so,' she agreed. 'It is hard to endure, but it is so.'

'I too am alone. There is no one like me. We are not so different from each other, you and I.' Again he fixed his gaze on her.

'You have come to me,' she said, acknowledging that he had kept his promise, 'in my most bitter hour. After tonight I might see you nevermore. I am invulnerable but my kindred are not, and if I fail to protect them, there will be nobody left to guard me from eternal captivity. Glad am I that you came, for it is my chance to bid you a last farewell. If I never set eyes on you again, be assured that I will - ' suddenly she found herself stammering - 'I will miss you.'

As she spoke, she found herself unable to look the wight in the eye. She was forcing herself to proclaim her inner sentiments because it seemed right to do so, but unaccountably she felt embarrassed and discomfited, especially by her last four words. She felt her face grow hot, and suddenly wished herself far away. The battlefield seemed like a simpler challenge than dealing with this wayward and subversive creature.

Seeking a way to deflect the topic she cast about in her mind for some token of friendship she might give. Her fingers closed around the jewel at her neck, and she thought, why not? Unclasping the chain she held out the dazzling stone on its necklace, offering it to the wight. Not lightly did she do this. Had the urisk not been a kind of family heirloom, like the jewel, she would not have acted thus. She told herself that it seemed fit that two things that had been passed down through the generations should reside together.

The urisk sighed and rolled his eyes. 'You certainly persevere with these acts of bestowal. Very well, if you insist.'

Rising to stand upon his hoofs, the little wight approached her. She leaned down to pass the ornament to him. The jewel sparkled in the urisk's hand.

'Will you not wish me luck in battle?' Asrăthiel asked, straightening up.

'I never asked for your gifts, nor did I comprehend they came with an obligation to compensate you with good wishes in return.' The urisk slipped the jewel into a pocket of his shabby clothing.

'Well, there is no obligation.' Asrăthiel frowned. She felt foolish, and somewhat vexed, until it came to her that this prickle of annoyance was a sting she would feel the loss of, if she never saw the urisk again. 'It is true you do not ask for gifts,' she said penitently. 'You have never asked me for anything at all.'

'And would you prefer it if I had?'

'Yes.'

'As it happens,' the wight said casually, folding his arms and leaning against a tree bole, 'it was my intention this evening to make a request of you.'

At this revelation, Asrăthiel could not help but feel intrigued and surprised. It seemed out of character.

'Anything,' she said. 'Anything you ask of me, if it is within my power, I shall grant it.'

'Oh, it is within your power all right,' said the urisk, and there was something about the way he uttered those words that gave Asrăthiel the feeling that her she ought not to have responded so unthinkingly. A foreboding squeezed her heart. *Why did I just now promise him anything he desired? I have made an unspecified vow to a wight! What a fool I am. Such oaths cannot be broken without dire consequences, if at all!*

In trepidation she enquired, 'What would you have of me?'

'Do me one last favour.'

She nodded.

He said, 'Draw your sword and strike off my head.'

Twenty-one crows flew across the sky, silhouetted against a backdrop of tawny vapour trails. Their cries jarred against the sough of the breeze through the evergreens.

'I will not!' Asrăthiel exclaimed, shocked and horrified.

'You gave me your word.'

'But why?' the damsel burst out in anguish, backing away from the wight as though he were a plague carrier.

'I asked you to perform a simple deed, not to pepper me with questions!' the urisk said coldly. 'Is it so hard to oblige me?'

'It is! Why do you want to be forever changed into a fly, or an ant, or - ' she searched for words - 'or a nameless speck scuttling in compost?'

'Do you think I enjoy sentient existence? Do you know how long I have lived? Can you comprehend the tedium of enduring the sluggish pace of millennia?'

'You must not ask this thing of me.'

'I have asked it.'

They argued, beneath the whispering trees, while the gloaming deepened and the sun slipped further down, ready to vanish behind the world's shoulder. At length, after much debate, the urisk persuaded Asrăthiel that she must accept this duty she had brought upon herself. She was bound by her word, and must resign herself to it.

'If you are so determined on this course,' she said sadly, 'I wish you had asked someone else to give you the stroke. Cruel wight, your death will cast an eternal shadow on my spirit.'

The urisk offered no response.

'I will do it tomorrow,' she said, vainly grasping at excuses and making as if to depart.

'You will do it now.'

Asrăthiel clapped her hands to her head, slapped her palm against a tree trunk, then paced back and forth in extreme perturbation. 'This is the most onerous demand that has ever been asked of me!' she cried. 'This is indeed my most bitter hour, for you have made it so!'

'Do it, and it will be over.'

'If I could weep, urisk, I would be drowning in tears.'

'Draw your sword.'

Asrăthiel grasped the hilt of Fallowblade, but hesitated.

Meeting his eyes unwaveringly she pleaded in a low voice, 'If I must slay you, I ask only that you do not look me in the eye.'

For one last instant he held her gaze, then turned aside.

She pulled Fallowblade from its scabbard. Spangles effervesced along its length, chiming a silent music of bells. The wight half closed his eyes, as if the golden brightness caused him pain, but stood unflinching before the weathermage. His curly hair was short enough that it did not cover his neck; nor did he wear any collar. The stroke would not be obstructed. It raced through Asrăthiel's mind that prisoners who faced beheading by axe were made to rest their heads on a chopping block, to provide resistance to the blow. It would be too appalling, however, to be forced to search for some fallen tree trunk - she and the urisk, seeking a wooden platform for butchery. If she were to endure this unspeakable trial, it was best to do get it over and done with as swiftly as possible. Besides, the golden blade had the sharpest edge of anything she had ever encountered. She could believe it was acute enough to sever one instant of time from the next. It would pass through the small neck as if the urisk had never existed. As these pragmatic thoughts churned in her head she could hardly believe they were her own, so profoundly did they shock and disgust her.

Gripping the sword in both hands she lined up her mark. After drawing a deep breath and focussing her concentration to give her courage she drew back the weapon, then swung it in a wide and whistling arc.

Wild and strange the melody, the blood-song played by winds against the leading edge.

The urisk's horned head toppled from his body.

At the same instant, the sun disappeared behind the horizon. Sick with horror, Asrăthiel ran from the scene without a backward glance.

As she took part in last-minute preparations for the night ahead, thoughts of the urisk churned and pounded in Asrăthiel's head. She despised herself for making the promise, hated him for asking it, for forcing her to become the agent of his suicide; was seared by guilt, devastated by bereavement, hot and cold in waves, replaying the event in her mind, asking herself what if I had refused outright? What if? What if? Although weighed down with grief and trouble, she did not speak to anyone at Hundred House about her travail. Her companions already had enough strife to contend with. Besides, there was no one she could really confide in about this matter; none of her friends had been acquainted with the wight. Hardly anyone had ever seen him, for that matter. Those who had glimpsed him, such as Albiona, had never viewed him in the light of friendship. Furthermore, the entire household at the chastel was preoccupied with making ready for the dark hours, and dread of what they might bring. No matter that they conversed in tones of optimism; no one harboured any illusions. It was a certainty that the night would usher in the return of the unseelie hordes and their death-dealing. In some remote corner of consciousness the damsel wondered what obscure and mindless form the urisk had dwindled to, whether a beetle or a gadfly, or even a live particle of some disease, such as the murrain or the pox.

The first stars were appearing as the depleted armies of human-kind readied themselves to face, for the second time, the unseelie onslaught. Though disheartened and terrified, they refused to yield to despair. Some even joked and sang, feigning confidence, in an attempt to bolster to spirits of their comrades. To the north, the Wuthering Moors stretched into darkness, empty and foreboding. The allies waited, effecting last-minute adjustments to the security of their positions.

During the greater part of the day Avalloc Maelstronnar had been directing his energies toward shepherding high and low pressure systems. A storm maturing south of the moors had changed direction and begun to roll northwards, gathering vehemence and momentum as it travelled.

The two weathermages and the handful of prentices who had accompanied Avalloc from Rowan Green planned to send the storm barrelling across the moors to meet the unseelie hordes before they could reach the defenders. It was hoped that their powers, combined, would be great enough to escalate the gale to the status of a hurricane. The force of such a blast could hurl chunks of hail the size of trebuchet ammunition, and drive winds strong enough to uproot trees and smash buildings. With luck it would pulverize the goblin knights, or at least scatter them.

Yet the Storm Lord was attempting a feat that demanded the skill and attention of many senior weathermages, rather than one alone, aided by a few students. He was weary, besides. Asrăthiel, engrossed with perfecting her sword technique and striving to overcome her abhorrence at what she had done to the urisk, could spare little time to participate in the summoning.

The clear skies dimmed and stars winked out as the weather change swept in from the south. Out on the Wuthering Moors raindrops began to fall sporadically. Asrăthiel waited atop a small bulwark of mouldering stone, flanked by King Warwick and Prince William. The king had banished Prince Walter from the fray, for he refused to jeopardise the lives of his two heirs simultaneously, though they both begged for a place on the battlefield. Mounted on their warhorses the Companions of the Cup bided in watchful silence, encircling the three upon the low rampart. The Knight-Commander had stationed himself closest to his sovereign, easily within earshot.

The weathermage wore no armour of chain or plate, but was clad in a loose-fitting tunic shirt of snowy cambric, and trousers of bleached linen tucked into knee-boots. Her hair was bound in tight braids about her head. Nor did she carry a shield. A small, gold-handled dirk nestled in a scabbard at her right side; she intended to keep it at hand in case the sword was wrested from her grasp. Clasping the hilt of Fallowblade she drew it forth with care approaching reverence, aware that many heads turned to watch. The golden blade flashed with its splendid inner light. Around it the falling rain sparkled like chains of diamonds.

Asrăthiel tentatively flourished the sword, sensing the point of balance, feeling the weight. As she did so the eerie wind-song played along its edges, and it seemed to her that the falling rain-drops slowed, as if the atmosphere through which they dropped had become as thick as honey. The appearance of the suspended drop-lets as they drifted gently down was quite astonishing. Contrary to her expectations they were not rounded at the base and pointed at the top, in the teardrop shape that artists traditionally attributed to them. Instead, the smaller ones appeared to be completely spherical, while those that were middle-sized exhibited a tiny indentation on their underside. The largest drops resembled the ear-muffs travellers wore on cold Winter's days – two blobs attached by a slender arch. Asrăthiel knew that she was witnessing the true shape of falling raindrops. As the sword moved, it was actually altering the rate of time's flow around her. When she held the weapon steady the rain seemed to speed up, and pattered down as before.

Keeping Fallowblade motionless, she gazed across the shadowy acres of heath land, into the north. There was no evidence of the goblin knights or their minions, except perhaps for the merest hint of a low-level haze. She sheathed the sword.

The storm never reached its full potential. It petered out before midnight. Avalloc had reached the point of exhaustion and the prentices were too inexperienced to keep the vast, unstable systems within their control. Asrăthiel recognised that even if she had contributed all her energies to weatherworking, a storm as great as that which was required could never have been brewed and mastered without the cooperation of all the Councillors of Ellenhall. As the atmospheric disturbances abated the skies cleared; starglow coolly illuminated the countryside, and the moon gleamed, a pale opal.

It was not until moonrise that it occurred to Asrăthiel she had left her mother's white jewel with the decapitated corpse of the urisk beneath the pines - or with the bloated spider, or crawling ant, whatever he had become. Somehow the forfeiture of the treasure meant nothing compared to the loss of her eldritch companion, he who had identified himself with the odd name of Crowthistle.

At midnight they came.

First a mist arose, winding in and out of the stumps of the forgotten city on the moors, making phantoms of the vestigial towers and walls. Then came a low, distant rumble, which grew louder. The rumble expanded to a roar; the thunder of one hundred thousand powerful hooves shaking the ground. Men peered through the haze until their eyes ached. Dimly they descried shapes hurtling in the murk. The shapes solidified, becoming silhouettes, vespertine blue against the pale grey of the vapours; terrible outlines, horned and antlered, brandishing a forest of spears; row upon serried row of apocalyptic horsemen from nightmare.

Towards the united front of the mortal armies the goblin horsemen galloped, their fantastic garments trailing like scalloped kelp strands, their lawless hair flying, their kobold slaves bounding maniacally alongside. Tatters of shredded mist streamed from their limbs. Daemon horse and fell rider, both were both accoutred with jingling silver and pale jewels. Exquisite were those sinister steeds, the trollhästen, with their smooth, resilient stride and their high-set necks. Their ghostly tails and manes streamed out along the wind of their swiftness, green as burning copper-salts. To those mortals who dared to stare, or who, like prey fascinated by the hunter, could not look away, it appeared that the bizarre battle harness of the unseelie knights included trimmings of sable fur, sprays of sooty feathers and claws, and trappings of ivory, horn or bleached bone.

The human troops braced themselves for a frontal assault. Archers drew their bowstrings to their ears and poised, ready for the command; foot soldiers lowered their pikes; cavalrymen pulled sword from sheath. Asrăthiel's hand rested on Fallowblade's hilt, ready to draw the swift blade.

Only a few hundred yards separated the horde from the battalions of Tir. Just as it seemed certain they would hurtle headlong into the front lines, their pace abated. They slowed to a canter, then to a walk, causing their overwrought adversaries great confusion and perplexity. No one knew what to expect. Argent and crystalline dazzles flashed from the unseelie knights' ebony harness, and from the sombre fabric of their garments.

'A bizarre manoeuvre,' muttered Warwick, grimacing at the riders who approached so leisurely. 'What are they at?'

'It is to unnerve us,' said the Knight-Commander of the Cup during this enforced interlude. 'They mean to show they need no advantage of impetus to destroy us, and that they may do so when they please.' Ever the tactician, he added, 'But it baffles me how their leader signals his commands to such a mighty throng. They have no flagmen, no trumpeters.'

'It may be that they speak the language of those uncanny birds that follow them,' said the king. 'Perhaps the birds relay messages.'

William, at Asrăthiel's side, scrutinized the shadowy winged shapes gliding above the goblin cavalry. 'Those are carrion crows that attend upon their masters.'

'Look more closely. They are owls,' said Asrăthiel. 'Horned eagle owls, sooty-feathered.'

'The goblins clothe themselves in black,' murmured the prince, 'symbolic of their wickedness.'

And of their power and beauty, thought the damsel, although the notion was unwelcome, and she refrained from saying it aloud.

The spectacle of the unseelie warriors moved her to a disquieting degree. She resented the effect of their incredible comeliness upon her senses, for it thrilled her as nothing she had ever known before. Such excitement was inappropriate, and she did her utmost to banish it. This reaction of hers irked her, for she had always considered it unfair that people had a tendency to favour the beautiful. Beauty was too often forgiven for deeds for which plainness would have been condemned. Beauty was accorded privilege, attention, advantage. Beauty was invested with traits of virtue, wisdom, authority and even goodness. Asrăthiel had prided herself on esteeming others for their personal worth without being influenced by their looks, and now here she was, falling into the common trap like some simpleton. Goblins were everything she despised – cruel, ruthless and immoral. Whether ugly or fair, they ought only to be hated and reviled.

But as the invaders approached in leisurely fashion, she spied the rider presumed to be the leader of the goblin hordes; he who last night had been positioned a little forward of all the rest, the especially well-favoured, dissolute one.

Then she turned her gaze slightly to the left and saw someone else…

… a stranger, a supernatural knight whose unbound hair, falling to his waist, was like the evening wind. Strands of that torn-shadow hair were blowing across a lean and handsome countenance. When she saw that face she gasped; gasped at his beauty.

He was so beautiful it was like pain to look at him.

The damsel stared, her eyes fixed, her mouth open. In answer, the eyes of the marvelous stranger stared back. He rode near, and his daemon horse was the colour of despair. This new knight outshone the libertine leader of yester-eve as the moon compares to a silver shilling, or a star-blazing sky to a strewing of pins.

No mortal ever possessed that aspect; everything about this stranger was elemental, consummate and magnetic; extreme and maleficent. Watching him, Asrăthiel felt the strength of her sinews melt and drain away, as if the mere sight had the power to paralyse. And the thought struck her – might she have glimpsed that face somewhere once before . . .?

'That one is the mightiest of them all,' said one of the Companions of the Cup. 'There is something in the look of him.' His brothers-in-arms murmured in agreement.

'I'd say that is their leader, and not the other,' said King Warwick.

'On my word, there can be no doubt of it,' William said in a low voice.

'By the flames of bloody war!' shouted Avalloc, 'How could this come to pass? I'll wager that is none other than Zaravaz, King of the Silver Goblins!'

5

COVENANT

To forge the mighty Fallowblade upon the peak of bitter snows
The Storm Lord laboured long and hard. The heights rang
      with his hammer blows,
Hot sparks flew up like meteors. A lord of fire was Alfardēne;
With power terrible he filled the sword. And all along the keen
And dreadful blade he wrote the words in flowing script for
      all to find:
Mé maraigh bo diabhlaíocht – 'I am the Bane of Goblinkind'.
Upon a dark time long ago.

A VERSE FROM THE SONG 'FALLOWBLADE'

With no signal or forewarning, the unseelie knights attacked.

Clearly, the Goblin King was the most wicked and lethal of them all. He fought skilfully, competently, as if revelling in bloodshed. It was dreadful to watch him; a hewer of limbs was he, a striker of sparks from weapon edge, his swordplay neat and efficient, economical, ruthless. Though many of his brethren voiced their spine-chilling battle-song, or jeeringly yelled, '*Paag dty uillin!*' he fought in silence. He could always be found where the fighting was fiercest – if fighting it could be called – it was more akin to a massacre, being so one-sided; mortal men could not stand against goblins, and if any lived awhile out there on the moors it was only at the pleasure of the cruel wights, for their sport. Force of steel delayed the goblin knights but never threatened them. Only the deluge of gold affected them, for it scathed them severely. Behind the lines Avalloc and the prentice weathermasters kept up the gold-laden breezes as best they could.

As the battle intensified, Asrăthiel shook off her initial curious lethargy. Hard-pressed were the armies of Tir. The bodyguard surrounding King Warwick, Prince William and herself had dwindled, for the king had ordered his knights to join the action. The weathermage felt the burden of her duty intensely. All of Tir now looked to her. Fallowblade's renown had increased a thousandfold as the history of the goblin wars spread throughout the populace; Sioctine, the Singing Blade, the Great Golden Beacon of Tir. And only one had been trained to wield it.

Mortal soldiers shouted Asrăthiel's name; they clashed swords against shields and brandished spears on high. 'Asrăthiel! Asrăthiel! All hail the Lady of the Sword! Asrăthiel for fair Narngalis!' they yelled. 'Tir salutes you!' and 'Fallowblade! Fallowblade! Ádh for Narngalis and the king!' Everyone looked to her. She had become the symbol of their hope.

William, however, placed a hand on the damsel's elbow, and made a last ditch attempt to dissuade her from going into battle. His efforts were in vain, for she would not heed his entreaties.

'Would you have me sacrifice our people?' she asked. 'Besides, if I lose you all, what will become of me?' The prince acquiesced, but she could see it went ill with him to do so. He was plainly devastated; his face looked ashen and haggard beneath his golden helm.

The bodyguards stepped aside for Asrăthiel, forming an impromptu avenue of honour. She gathered her strength and courage; then, with William by her side, leaped down from the rampart and launched herself into the thick of the fray. Fallowblade glittered like the heart of a newborn sun as a goblin knight who had leaped from his trollhäst's back sprang forward to challenge the one who brandished it.

From that moment onwards it was thrust, cut, punch-block; fall back and check for imminent danger; then whale, parry, wrapcut, fall back and seek a new contender; swing, hack, chop, fall back. Asrăthiel's focus closed down to a narrow sphere that was all motion and impact, the clash of weapons, the jarring of a blocked blow, the song of the sword, the liquid pressure of a thrust driven home. She sweated, gasping for breath. It was hard work, but there was some virtue about Fallowblade that made the sword seem to lift itself, to fling itself through the air, to guide and sustain her limbs, instead of weighing them down.

The goblin knights were taller than Asrăthiel, and well muscled as opposed to her slightness. She, however, possessed a weapon that could injure them with the slightest touch and destroy them utterly with a well-placed stroke. She was naturally fast and flexible, and she fought them within their own accelerated time scale. Moreover, nothing could wound her flesh. Even so it was always uppermost in her mind never to allow her opponents to close with her. They were so much larger than her; as Desmond Brooks had warned, they would merely knock Fallowblade out of the way with their own weapons, and mow her down.

Even though she had learned well from her swordmaster, she had never tried imitating his style. She was neither big nor heavy enough to carry off the techniques used by men. Instead, she adapted her techniques to suit her stature and abilities, relying on speed, skill and accuracy rather than strength and force. Using this strategy she was often able to slip past her adversaries' guard. It was a lot easier, faster and less tiring to dodge and avoid than it was to try to batter their weapons out of the way to create an opening. The goblins' black and silver armour was lightweight. She suspected it served less as a weapon-deflective covering and more as a display of rakish elegance; a show of contempt rather than protection. They wore it flamboyantly, with no regard for systematic body coverage; a gauntlet, perhaps, on the left hand but not the right; a cuirass here, a greave or vambrace there, asymmetrically but stylishly placed amongst the scales and fur, the feathers and claws, the silver and moonstones. Some wore nothing on one arm but a decorative band, while the other was encased in leather or armour from shoulder to wrist. Asrăthiel's blade of gold and iridium sliced through most of the goblin plate easily enough; she did not even have to look for chinks at the joints.

Fallowblade seemed to be the only weapon that could penetrate the flesh of the foe; all others could only hinder, by their impetus. Goblin flesh smoked at the edges of the hewn limbs, where the golden sword had carved through. The unseelie knights fell, and when they touched the ground their swarthy armour rolled like empty shells on the heathery sward, but huge black beetles flew away.

At whiles, a mounted knight rode against the weathermage. On the first occasion she hewed halfheartedly at the rider's thigh, hesitant to engage with him because she abhorred the idea of hurting the daemon horses. Accidentally she slashed the hide of the trollhäst and it lunged at her, swivelling its long neck like a serpent, its eyes bright with fury, pointed fangs snapping. The daemon steed managed to catch a hank of her hair in its teeth. It flung its head from side to side, trying to throw her off balance. She struggled to stay upright while the creature pulled on her tresses, hampering her efforts to smite the rider. At last, with a nimble twist she broke free, threw herself to the ground and rolled away, but the creature came after her, razored hooves stamping, trying to pound her into the ground, and she knew she was dealing with no gentle herbivore broken by a trainer and forced into battle against its nature. Patently, this savage steed revelled in the slaughter as thoroughly as its rider. After that the damsel knew she must equally treat with trollhäst and goblin, or be vanquished.

To force herself to harm living entities, Asrăthiel deliberately maintained her rage, quashing her instinct to protect the living. Again, in her mind, she shaped pictures of the frightened children in the streets of King's Winterbourne. She must brace herself and defy the menace, or the weak and the innocent would suffer. Her task of killing was made substantially more difficult by constant confrontation with her foes' physical perfection. It was impossible not to tremble with exhilaration at the close proximity of the goblin knights and had it not been for Fallowblade's almost sentient motivation the damsel might spontaneously have allowed her weapon to fall from nerveless fingers and submitted to defeat. She supposed this was some eldritch spell of fascination on the part of the artful wights, to disarm their opponents.

Ultimately, when it came home to her that the combat was in earnest and the foe was attacking her with sincere intent to overcome her, some primeval instinct took hold - for she was, after all, born of a mortal race - and she began to fight without qualm, as if for her life.

Positioning the golden blade at a precise angle, she parried an overhand blow from an unseelie warrior. The unexpected deflection of the stroke hurled the weight of her opponent's sword back at him, throwing him off balance. His weapon missed her body by a hair's breadth; contact would not have injured her, but it might have knocked her sideways and sent her sprawling. The frightening memory of her nightmare washed over her and briefly she shuddered at the thought of being taken captive by goblins. Death would indubitably be preferable to that fate – yet death was no option for her.

She ducked, smote, and fell back. Detachedly, as if she viewed the battle from a distance, she wondered why no stain of gore besmirched her. It was as if the eldritch knights did not bleed, or their blood was a colourless fluid that instantly vaporised. Remotely, too, as she wielded the enchanted blade she was aware that the mortal armies seemed to move with a curious, graceful slowness, as if they were struggling underwater. The goblin knights had ample opportunity to toy with the soldiers of Tir before ending their lives.

Like red-hot brands the cries of dying men seared into the flesh of the night. The battle was going badly for the defenders; many hundreds had fallen, and the mortal battalions were being driven back. Asrăthiel heard a clarion blast; the signal for the troops of

Slievmordhu to rally to their captains.

Shortly thereafter the horns of Ashqalêth blared a retreat, followed by the bass-voiced conches of Grïmnørsland, and the sweet-throated trumpets of Narngalis. Then she was flooded with dread, knowing for certain that all was lost.

The last battle for humankind was being waged on pathless moors beneath a glittering sky. Without the aid of the Councillors of Ellenhall, who might have slammed the foe with lightning and pelted them with ceaseless barrages of golden hail, the human race was doomed. The unseelie horde was fully capable of genocide, and seemed bent on it. In the hearts of leaders and troops alike, frustration and fury fused with despair. Loudly they railed against the Fates, cursing Lord Doom and his axe, Lord Luck and his vain talismans, Destiny's sharp shears, Ill-Fortune's malice. Knowing they must soon perish even if they surrendered, even if they fled, even if they tried to hide, men vowed anew that they would bid for glory and die fighting. Now remained only the postponement of the inevitable, the final hours between living and dying.

Refusing to surrender to her sense of futility, Asrăthiel struggled back to the embankment where King Warwick and his chivalric bodyguard were making their last stand. She had not glimpsed William since the battle began, and did not know whether he still lived, and burned passionately to have news of him, there at the doorstep of humanity's end. When at length she spied him in the midst of a company of Narngalish knights, blood-spattered but hale, a fleeting gladness shot through her; but her eyes continued to rove the moors, for it was another that she was seeking, without comprehending her own desires.

Until her gaze rested upon her unconscious objective, and she knew.

A terrible excitement gripped her when she looked again upon the Goblin King. With effortless grace he rode the daemon horse that was the colour of despair, and he was utterly breathtaking. Blacker than wickedness, his hair swirled about his shoulders like a cloak of shadow. Presently he seemed to glance in the direction of King Warwick, whereupon he held up his pale, long-fingered hand, commanding his legions to desist. The unseelie knights left off the assault. They drew back. The hubbub of battle waned, and a rift opened between mortal and immortal armies.

Into that gap rode the handsome Goblin King, with a kobold striding at his knee and the licentious knight advancing alongside him like his second-in-command. The latter was clad in close-fitting garments of interlocking scales, like lizard skin; a jewelled codpiece, and a horned helmet of strange design adorned with fantastic winglike patterns. His fur-lined demi-cloak, worn over one shoulder only, was tied with a heavy cord, and the cuffs of his gloves flared like the spathes of black arum lilies.

The garments of the Goblin King, on the other hand, were the plainest, the most austere, of all his kin. A sleeveless thigh-length doublet of black suede or leather clothed him, the pliable material being embossed with intricate designs, black on black. This was overlaid by a loose-knit asymmetrical hauberk of silvery chain mail that resembled several webs of filigree haphazardly knotted together by demented spiders.

The doublet was cinched around the middle by a belt of thicker leather, also embossed, and clasped with a buckle that was cast in the shape of a pair of unfurled wings, upswept at a narrow angle; silver-white metal plumage inlaid with palest blue vanes and swirls. His trousers were leather, the colour of midnight. About his neck hung a fine silver chain that dipped beneath the high collar of his black linen undershirt. Full and generous were the shirtsleeves, leaving plenty of room for movement when fencing or sparring. He rode with grace and dexterity. His daemon horse pranced proudly, exhibiting its points and paces like a mortal steed directed by the skill of a super equestrian.

Some of the soldiers muttered, 'Mayhap that Prince of Death is going to challenge one of our champions to single combat to decide the outcome of this contest!'

Others shook their heads. 'That one has no reason to parley or make covenants with us. He has the advantage. We are doomed for sure. In any case, what champion of Tir could stand against the likes of the Lord of Wickedness? Not even Two-Swords Gearnach would be a match.'

They did not for a moment consider mentioning Asrăthiel: to send a girl unaided against such a foe was contrary to their every instinct, despite the fact that they had witnessed her prowess amongst them in the field.

Two hundred yards distant the pair of unseelie riders stopped short. The Goblin King remained silent, while his deputy commenced to speak. The voice of the second-in-command rang out with amazing clarity, although his accent was foreign and his tone corrosive.

Into the battlefield hush he said, 'Know that you stand defeated, human *brouteraght.*' His smile was a sneer. 'You, who believe you are so special, so free-willed! You, in your ignorance that like all things your lives are governed by numbers, that the same mathematics that describe the fractal patterns of a fern leaf or a spiral seashell dictate the very code by which your bodies are fashioned. Learn that you are as slavish as a leaf that must fall from the tree. Learn that you have no importance. You are nothing. You shall become less than nothing.'

His voice carried across the entirety of the Wuthering Moors, whether projected by some spell or by some talent of his species. All those assembled could hear every word.

'Know me as Zauberin,' the goblin officer continued, '*aachionard;* first lieutenant of the Argenkindë. Defeated you are, but not yet extinct. My liege commander will offer you terms.'

A murmur of astonishment rippled through the ranks of the human listeners. Beyond all imagining a glimmer, perhaps, of hope? Something to postpone the end? More likely an eldritch trick. . .

It was King Warwick who, guiding his horse to the forefront of his troops, responded. Again, perhaps by some bewitchment, there was not one amongst those many thousands of soldiers, weary or wounded, hale or dying, young or old, who failed to catch his declaration.

'I, Warwick Wyverstone, King of Narngalis, take it upon myself to speak on behalf of the Four Kingdoms of Tir, for the nonce, whether it be my part or no. We await your terms.'

The king's voice was strong, yet Asrăthiel, with her acute vision, perceived that his hands were shaking. She too was shivering, but whether from shock, or anxiety, or sorrow, or something else entirely, she could not be sure.

'The Argenkindë will withdraw and leave your sties unmolested,' said the comely, malevolent knight Zauberin, 'if you'll comply.'

'Do you mean to assert you will leave the Four Kingdoms of Tir in peace?'

'Assuredly.'

The crowds gasped at the enormity of this declaration, and another murmur ran through their ranks, on this occasion louder, and on a rising note.

'It is some hateful prank,' several listeners whispered. 'They make sport of us. When they have victory in the palms of their hands, why should they offer us our heart's desire?'

'What would you have of us in return?' Warwick asked guardedly. Asrăthiel surmised that he was playing for time. Whatever the goblins demanded would certainly be too high a price; she could tell Warwick believed it was pointless even to enquire, but every moment of delay was another breath of life for humankind and, as the saying went, where life is, hope is. The king was gambling on the infinitesimal chance of a miracle.

'I demand,' said Zauberin, 'certain ransoms or hostages on behalf of Zaravaz, King and Knight-Commander of the Argenkindë.

'So it is indeed he!' muttered Avalloc, leaning on a bronze-tipped oaken staff and shaking his head in wonderment. During the dialogue between mortal and immortal, two knights of the Cup had conducted the elderly weathermage to Asrăthiel's side. 'Against all odds, that cruel tyrant has returned!'

It was the damsel's wish to ask her grandfather what he knew of this Goblin King, but she kept silent so that all might hear the words of the unseelie lieutenant.

'If they are handed over without argument or haggling,' said Zauberin, 'we will depart without striking another blow, unless humankind strike first.'

Asrăthiel guessed at once the names of those who would be claimed as prisoners, and she knew also, with a sinking feeling, that if the goblin knights made that demand it would never be granted.

'They will claim our monarchs and commanders, and maybe the pick of our princes also,' murmured the Narngalish officers nearby, echoing her thoughts. 'The most generous-spirited of our dignitaries will agree to be sacrificed for the salvation of the people, but there is no doubt they would be taken away to be humiliated and excruciated. In which case it is Tir's duty to refuse this offer of covenant. We simply cannot allow the best of us to suffer such a doom, no matter what the cost.'

'Whom would you take prisoner?' enquired Warwick calmly and boldly.

To Asrăthiel, Avalloc said in an undertone, 'Our sovereign knows that we have no choice but to comply with their demands, for now. If they named Uabhar, he would deserve whatever fate they had in store for him, but I'll warrant Warwick has no intention of handing over anyone of good renown.'

'Indeed,' Asrăthiel agreed. 'He is playing for time.'

'Time!' her grandfather muttered. 'Every extra breath is sweet!' They glanced up as the Goblin King's premier lieutenant spoke again.

'First,' he said, 'bring us the two kings of men that languish in the Prison of the Obelisk.'

The tremendous sigh of relief that swept through the masses was like a loud-whispering breeze. Their abatement of anxiety was short-lived, nonetheless, for as soon as people recalled that Chohrab Shechem II lay in his sepulchre beneath his sculpted effigy, they uneasily began to wonder who the wights would call for to replace him. Further, they were in dread as to who else would be named as human tributes, and what their number would be.

'Given that the enemy seems to know so much about the affairs of men,' Avalloc said in Asrăthiel's ear, 'I am surprised they were not aware of Ashqalêth's passing.'

'Perhaps they did know,' his granddaughter replied, 'and this is part of some abstruse game of theirs – for they toy with us like cats with mice.'

'King Chohrab is dead,' replied Warwick, 'and Uabhar is imprisoned within Essington Tower.'

'Oh, that pile still stands after all these years?' said the disdainful Zauberin. He tilted his head towards his liege lord to receive instructions inaudible to the human listeners, then proclaimed, 'Bring the living man here.'

'Do you pledge your word you will not harm him?'

The goblin first lieutenant laughed loudly, offering no other reply.

Then a clamorous chorus broke out on all sides, and a clashing of weapons beating against shields. The armies of Tir were calling for the blood of Uabhar, to pay for their lives. Prince Ronin's vehement protests were drowned out.

'It will take at least three days to fetch him,' Warwick said coolly. 'I ask that you give us time.'

Zauberin turned aside and again consulted with his sovereign, employing the harshly musical language of the goblins. Presently he readdressed the mortal king with as much discourtesy as before. '*Slane vie*,' he said, apparently careless whether or not his words were understood. 'Send away your clockwork battalions and vow that Calaldor, that you call Tir will prosecute war against us no more. Unless,' he added snidely, 'you would like to provide us with a little sport to while away the decades. No? Then Zaravaz of the Argenkindë will give you time, and you will deem him magnanimous. Meet us again at this place, not in three days but three weeks. You must bring with you the living king from Essington

Tower and every human spawn of consequence in Calaldor; the druids, the weathermasters, every member of every royal family, every carlin. Bring no gold!'

'What? Would you take all of us away?' cried Warwick disbelievingly. 'All the notables in the Four Kingdoms?'

'No. Merely, we will make a selection.'

'How many - '

Zauberin cut him short. 'If you value your short and inconsequential lives you will obey. Do not disappoint us. Should you fail to act precisely as we describe, your breed's extinction will be unavoidable, for we do not love your race. And we will know if anyone is missing from the gathering - oh yes, we will know.'

The Goblin King softly spoke into the knight's ear.

'Yet in the end there is one we shall except,' said Zauberin. 'The wife of the Storm Lord's son slumbers wakelessly in the Mountain Ring and can be of no use to us. Other than Jewel Maelstronnar, none are granted exemption. Scheme not to hide anyone from us, *cloie yn ommidan*.'

'It shall be done,' Warwick said diplomatically, though fury blazed in his visage, and the other listeners muttered of their amazement that the wights knew such a great deal about the affairs of Tir.

'Meanwhile,' continued the goblin lieutenant, 'no human being may cross north of the Wuthering Moors. This territory is the property of Zaravaz, King and Overlord of Calaldor, *Cooilleeneyder, as Ard-veoir Armyn*. Furthermore, you must render to us the *Corlaig Keylley*, which you call the Sylvan Comb, for it is a thing of goblin make and should be returned to its owners. Go now, and do as your indulgent overlord bids.' With a supercilious smile, Zauberin added a parting caveat: 'Travel by day, for the night is ours.'

In that moment Asrăthiel's every conceit and conviction crashed to an end, and for an ageless instant it was as if the mechanism of her pulse had jammed.

For the Goblin King had smiled also.

It was a knowing smile, a sudden flash of white heat, after which he and his first lieutenant exchanged glances. They rode away, those two exceptional knights, followed by their stunted bluish-skinned familiars; and the horde of eldritch chivalry parted to let them through, then closed in at their backs and melted into the gloom.

Avalloc and Asrăthiel found themselves at the centre of a flurry of activity. Three weeks seemed all too brief. It would have taken months for all the luminaries of Tir to travel by road from every capital city, so the weathermages and their prentices had to work speedily, ferrying notables by sky-balloon to King's Winterbourne. Obstacles both foreseeable and unexpected cropped up; the poor health of some elderly dignitaries, the inexperience of the prentices at piloting aerostats, problems with sending and receiving messages, and various other setbacks. Some, terrified out of their wits, refused to cooperate. If persuasion and cajolery failed, they had to be brought to the city by force. 'The wicked ones will know if any are missing!' they were warned. 'Their retribution would be swift and terrible!'

Loud and long were the debates held in hall and house and castle, as to the merits of co-operating with goblinkind. Many spoke against it. In particular Prince Ronin was vociferous in his protestations. Supported by his brother Cormac he declared that while he lived he would never allow his father to be turned over to the unseelie hordes.

'I will stand in line with everyone else and take my chance as to whether the Wicked Ones will choose me as a tribute, but I will fight until my last breath to prevent this other wrongdoing!' he proclaimed. 'Why have they singled out my father above all others? Besides Shechem he is the only one they have named. I'll warrant they have some cruel plans for dealing with him! I cannot countenance that my own sire, the head of my house, should be surrendered to a horrendous fate without my so much as lifting a finger to save him!'

His peers endeavoured to convince him otherwise, bidding him bear in mind the falseness of Uabhar, the murderous compacts he had made with the Marauders, the trickery by which he had slain the weathermasters, the wiles with which he had ensnared submissive King Chohrab, the tyranny of his rule, the greed, now exposed, by which he had determined to subordinate all the lands of Tir and the extensive loss of life that had resulted. When Ronin appealed to his mother for abetment in his unpopular cause she refused to enter the argument, taking neither one side nor the other, but young Prince Fergus opposed his brothers' stance and pronounced that justice would truly be served, were their father to be sacrificed in the cause of preserving humanity.

'Were it you, Ronin, who was nominated for forfeiture,' Fergus rejoined, 'and our father who stood in your place, do you truly credit he would hesitate to throw you to the merciless wights? Recall how effortlessly he sacrificed Kieran! Recall how qualmlessly he made you prove your loyalty by sending you into battle time and time again. He would have no compunction, were he in your position. You are a fool if you believe otherwise.'

'I am aware of our father's shortcomings,' Ronin said sadly, 'and I would that he were a as good a man as idealism would prescribe. He has wrought unpardonable evil upon the four kingdoms. Yet it were faithless of me to condemn him to a fate of unspeakable wretchedness, such as would surely await him at the hands of the goblin knights. If he is to be judged let it be by human arbitration, if he is to be punished let it be by human laws, not by the spiteful sadism of an alien race.'

'He deserves all that they can inflict upon him,' Fergus said rancorously, 'and more. There is no honour in saving such a sire from the consequences of his own wrongdoing. He slew Kieran as surely as if he had struck the fatal blow, as he would have slain you or me if it had suited him. With his persuasions he blindfolded us, but in hindsight and free from his influence, I can see clearly. He deceived us all.'

'Yet he is our father,' said Ronin.

He made an impassioned plea to the Sanctorums, to the weathermasters, to Conall Gearnach and the Knights of the Brand, begging that they take his part. They refused. A few Slievmordhuan aristocrats hearkened, calling for bargaining and compromise, but in the end it was Avalloc who settled the matter once and for all.

Angry with the dissidents he said to them, 'Do you truly understand whom you are dealing with? By some unaccountable quirk of circumstance it is none other than Zaravaz, King of the Silver Goblins, whose coadjutant parleyed with us on the battlefield. It was my understanding that Zaravaz was rendered powerless forever at the conclusion of the goblin wars, but it is now clear I have overlooked some twist, some proviso or loophole in the intricacies of the matter, for he has risen again. The lore books have much to tell about his wickedness. He hates humanity with a vengeance. He would stop at nothing to destroy human life. A slayer of countless thousands is he; a ravager, an assassin, a hunter and killer of men. The atrocities he has wrought surpass belief. What more can I say? How better can I argue?

'Never in history has Zaravaz offered to negotiate with humankind. It is a miracle that we have been presented with any opportunity for reprieve whatsoever - despite endless hours of consultation and deliberation our best strategists have failed to come up with any feasible plan to save us. The goblins will honour their contract, for eldritch wights are bound to keep their word. Have you forgotten that since my kindred the Councillors of Ellenhall were destroyed, it is within the power of the hordes to erase humankind from the world? And that is precisely what you risk, if you presume to argue against their terms. I cannot fathom why they would give us any chance at all, when they despise us so. The fate of all people hangs upon a thread. Test that thread and it will snap, I guarantee.'

Prince Ronin said, 'We could fly from them. '

'Their steeds are swift!'

'We could hide out, in the deserts, in the Tangle - '

'Even if we survived the perils and privations of those wastelands they would find us out, eventually. They have powers we know little about, and they are deathless, Ronin. They would have all the time in the world to track us down.'

'But during that time - '

'During that time, if they gave us any, the pitiful remnants of our race would exist as terrified, scurrying mice, living from hand to mouth, our civilisation degenerating as we slipped into a pit of backwardness and ignorance.'

'The surviving prentices would come into their full power!'

'Do you imagine the goblins would wait that long? Are you suggesting we condemn entire kingdoms to death on that possibility?'

'They have not specified the number of prisoners they will take, Lord Avalloc. What if they demand dozens, or hundreds, or even thousands? What if they claim each and every one of Tir's greatest warriors and philosophers and mages and statesmen?'

'That is pure speculation.'

'But it might happen.'

'What would you have, Ronin?' Avalloc cried, his eyes flashing as if fireworks had kindled behind the panes of jade. 'Two paths only are open to us. We may choose the security of humankind, paid for by many lives or few, or we may choose the total annihilation of our race. Both choices are evil but, as I see it, they are our only options.'

Then at last Prince Ronin bowed his head.

'If that is so, then I must reconcile myself and let it be,' he said, his voice rasping with strangled grief. 'But I will ask the Fates to be merciful to my father.'

The Storm Lord's reasoning silenced the dissenters, whereupon the feverish undertakings continued with fresh zeal.

Throughout those weeks of hectic activity Asrăthiel was the object of effusive love and deference from all quarters. She had always been esteemed as a weathermage of surpassing skill, grandchild of the Storm Lord, heiress to the House of Maelstronnar and weathermage to the king of Narngalis. Since she had displayed her mettle in the field, however, the people adored her as their rescuer, praising her with such names as Queen of Swords, Tir's Champion, Heroine of the Four Kingdoms and Lady Conqueror. Some took to simply titling her Fallowblade, as if she and the sword were indivisible. Indeed, she carried it everywhere with her, buckling it on every morning and wearing it constantly at her side.

Such adulation, however, did not sit well with her. 'Give me no credit,' she begged, sincerely. 'It is not my doing, but a happy accident that I was born a brí-child and gifted with qualities that make me unafraid of the battlefield. Were anyone else possessed of these talents, they would have done the same.'

Despite her protests the encomiums continued unabated.

Another matter further contributed to the damsel's discomfort, though to a lesser extent: across the realms, tidings of the goblin encounters on the Wuthering Moors had spread like smoke along the wind, and everyone was talking about the shock of seeing the unseelie horde; surpassingly fair to look upon, when stories had described such surpassing ugliness! But the chief topic of conversation in certain circles was the Goblin King, Zaravaz.

Apart from the vast numbers who were consumed by grief for husbands, brothers, lovers, sons, and grandsons slain in battle against the goblins, women of all stations had taken to talking about him. It was not so much the fact that they discussed this epitome of wickedness, it was the frequency with which they discussed him that vexed Asrăthiel. The princesses Lecelina and Winona, for instance, could often be found in the castle solar with their ladies-in-waiting, interminably conjecturing about Zaravaz's clothing, his hair, the colour of his eyes. They discoursed upon his every action as reported from the battlefield - his horsemanship, his fighting prowess - with a kind of fascinated horror, like passers-by at the scene of an accident who cannot look away although their flesh crawls at the gruesome sight. Every scrap of information about Zaravaz was gleaned and examined minutely, every conceivable possibility was raised; the tales told of him, his history, the legends, the manner by which he and his unseelie hordes had been let loose upon Tir again, where they had been hidden since the goblin wars, where they disappeared to between battles.

'Rumour has it that Zaravaz was not buried with his knights in the golden caves,' the feminine newsmongers tattled. 'Some say he roamed free, but with his powers bound by some mighty enchantment.'

'We've heard he rules a stupendous palace made of ice, some-where in the heights of the north,' they prated. 'A charmed fastness guarded by deadly wights, where no man dares venture.'

Always the chatterers spoke in tones of disapproval, tut-tutting and shaking their heads, but they could not leave their theme alone, and an uninformed observer might have surmised that they could not wait to set eyes on the infamous Goblin King, though they avowed, vehemently and repeatedly, that they hated him and wished him wiped out of existence.

Asrăthiel could not brook such gossip, nor did she have time for it. Most of her waking hours were spent overseeing sky-balloon transport, piloted by inexperienced crewmembers, ferrying passengers who had never in their lives flown through the sky. When she had a spare moment to herself her thoughts would stray to grievous or disorienting matters; she felt the approach of doom; she longed for her sleeping mother to revive before the end so that at least she might embrace her and say farewell; she fretted for her father and ached with sorrow for the betrayed councillors of Ellenhall.

She bled, too, for little, wanton Crowthistle and the terrible deed he had obliged her to do. Why had he wearied of the world, when it was filled with endless wonder? How could she have missed any clues to his despair, she who had believed she knew him as well as any human being could hope to know an eldritch wight? Had she understood the depths of his despondency she would have tried everything possible to cheer him. Was it possible she had been at fault in some way, perhaps unwittingly contributing to his sadness? Now, none of these questions could ever be answered.

At whiles her musings did alight, too, on the subject of the women's gossip, but she never allowed them to remain there for long. *I dismiss ruffian losels from my scope. They are unworthy of attention.* Notwithstanding, she once asked Avalloc, in passing, if he knew aught about the reports of the Goblin King's enchantment.

'It is true he was not entombed in the golden caves,' he replied. 'His sentence was a different form of imprisonment. The weather-masters bound him with unimaginably potent chains of gramarye, rendering him harmless, unable to use his powers. That much I have learned, but if there is more it will have to wait. No doubt there will be ample record of it in the archives, somewhere, but I have not yet had sufficient leisure to delve amongst the tomes, and the scribes have been inundated with urgent matters.'

Happier than Asrăthiel was one of the lesser druids in the Sanctorum of Cathair Rua, he whose baffling task it was to engineer fresh – and increasingly bizarre - prophecies to be proclaimed by his seniors. On receiving the latest news from the battlefield he leapt about in glee, claiming to have accurately predicted the entire sequence of events; though when pressed he was forced to admit that if one put a finer point on the matter, there was only one truly apt phrase in the augury to which he referred: 'Thrice upon the moors will they gather.' Taken out of context it might have referred to the confrontation between unseeliekind and the race of men, but the phrases precedent and antecedent made that conclusion a moot point:

'When the flaccid vole drops off the old oak sundial,

Thrice upon the moors will they gather,

And the half-baked loaf will be downtrodden…'

It took enormous effort to meet the demands of the goblin knights, and on occasion Asrăthiel dreaded that they would not fulfil the conditions before the arrival of the deadline. Albeit, by the specified night the task was completed. For the third occasion – and, everyone understood, the final one no matter which way the dice fell – Asrăthiel waited with her companions at the southern edge of the Wuthering Moors while twilight gathered.

It was a warm evening. Solemnly, with fast-beating hearts, the luminaries of Tir assembled, in the knowledge they faced possible sacrifice. No common soldiers escorted them; instead they were attended by a vast concourse of military officers, and courtiers, both men and women; the attendants of royalty. The dead had long since been carried from the field, and wonderfully, even in those few short weeks, the brutalised heather, the trampled gorse and bracken had begun to spring afresh, sprinkling the heath lands with a haze of palest green. Purple tufts of crowthistle daubed the leafy carpet. Pale pink and white moths fluttered like petals of apple blossom through the Summer dusk, and the firmament glimmered a luminous shade of sapphire, darkening to foundered amethyst.

Upon the steps of a decayed and roofless Oratorium Prince Ronin knelt, surrounded by his closest companions and courtiers, whispering pleas to the Fates to be kind to his father. A handful of senior druids stood upon the raised floor of the ruin, enclosed by an open palisade of jagged pillars in varying heights. Led by Primoris Virosus, they were intoning a chant. As the sun's last radiance struck the sides of the columns, striping their rounded grooves with apricot and saffron, another noble company approached. It was the entourage of Princess Solveig Torkilsalven; she who had been betrothed to Ronin's brother Kieran. Side by side, prince and princess knelt on the corrupt stones in the posture of submission to higher powers, pleading with the Fates to be lenient with the people of Tir. Clouds of tiny wings, like flickering scraps of confetti, wove in and out of the stone palisade.

Watching that fair assembly illuminated by topaz light, amongst the mossy ruins and the pastel drifts of moths, Prince William said softly to Asrăthiel, 'Solveig and Ronin plead for help from an invention fabricated by the druids. But what else is there to do?'

'Aye,' said the damsel, tenderness in her glance as she gazed upon the scene. 'Ronin is aware of the Sanctorum's power plays, yet he has crossed the brink of desolation. The ritual gives them some comfort.' Meeting the eyes of the comely prince she murmured, 'My grandfather maintains, 'Even false hope is better than none'.'

Dragging a cloak of darkness behind it, the sun sank out of sight. The flying insects vanished like candle flames. Little watch-fires sprang up amongst the tents, and the first hours of darkness began to stretch agonisingly on the rack of apprehension.

From horizon to horizon the heavens arched above the open acreage of the moors; a bowl of black crystal encrusted with startling glints and meteor flashes.

Before midnight there was no sign of the goblin knights, and then quite suddenly between one blink of the eye and the next, they appeared in the distance. As before, nobody had actually witnessed or heard them approaching. As before, their trollhästen and kobolds attended them, and their inky owls soared above like leaf shadows; as before the numinous knights were arrayed in sable and silver, and glistening diamantes of pure frost. Their hair was almost silk-straight, though with the hint of a sweeping wave. Impossibly, they seemed more beautiful than ever, and those who had never set eyes on them gaped, thunderstruck, while those who had seen them earlier were awed afresh by their excellence.

He rode once more at the forefront of his cavalry, Zaravaz the Goblin King. Women sighed when they beheld him. So far beyond handsome was he, that they knew not what to do, and were rendered speechless. He was tall, perhaps six feet two inches in height, and strikingly well made. With utter poise and composure he sat his steed. Vitality and effortless grace imbued his every move-ment, and when once he turned to look back across the echelons of the knights who followed him, something glinted behind his head - a plain silver clip shaped like a pair of upswept wings clasping the profuse storm cloud of his hair.

As for the immense crowd who had gathered at the command of Zaravaz, they mounted their horses or boarded their chariots, from which all golden embellishment had been stripped, and went forth to meet him with a great clatter and jingle but rarely a word. There were few other human folk who dared to stay and watch, if they had not been summoned. The goblins' reputation for piti-less savagery had fired their hearts with terror. Soldiers, peasants, ordinary folk; most had broken camp or abandoned their abodes to take flight far away from the moors, looking for a place to hide, in a desperate attempt to escape a tragic fate...

Tied with silken cords, Uabhar, worn out and sunken, sat astride a chestnut mare; to his left rode Conall Gearnach; to his right, Prince Ronin. With them went the two remaining kings in Tir, Warwick and Thorgild, with their sons and daughters and high-ranking office-bearers, and Queen Saibh, and Queen Halfrida of Grïmnørsland, and even Chohrab's widowed queen, Parvaneh; Duke Rahim and Shahzadeh, Princess Royal of Ashqalêth; Lord Avalloc and – on foot – Lady Asrăthiel Maelstronnar. Primoris Asper Virosus and all the most venerable druids of Tir were amongst that assembly, along with Cuiva Featherfern Stillwater, the White Lady of the Marsh; the carlin Lidoine Galenrithar and a company of her sisterhood; the Duke of Bucks Horn Oak; Lord Genan of Áth Midbine; the principal aristocrats and knights of all the realms, and numerous other influential persons besides.

And when they had all gathered before the Goblin King upon his pyrogenic steed, Prince Ronin dismounted, fell to his knees upon the wiry foliage blanketing the ground and bowed his head, saying, 'Lord, behold your humble petitioner,' at which the prince's loyal Slievmordhuan retinue seethed with repressed outrage to see their liege thus humiliate himself at the feet of anathema, their frustration exacerbated by being curbed from so much as stirring a finger to right the wrong. Most of them averted their eyes, unable to countenance the scene.

'I am the uncrowned king of Slievmordhu,' said Ronin, 'and therefore of political value to you. I beg of you, permit me to take my father's place as ransom.'

The maleficent leader said not a word in response to this entreaty, but Zauberin, insolent first lieutenant, replied, 'You try our tolerance. It was stipulated that ransoms must be surrendered to us without argument or haggling. One more word in this vein will put an end to our patience and the covenant will be forfeit.'

At some negligent signal from the Goblin King one of Zauberin's unseelie brothers-in-arms came forward, saying, 'Know me as Zerstör, second in rank of the king's lieutenants. The terms have been set, Ronin Ó Maoldúin. Seek to argue again, and we shall communicate no more with words, but only with swords, and a far greater delight it shall be to me and my brethren, I assure you.'

Ronin's followers glowered and clenched their fists impotently, burning with wrath at this ill treatment, but the prince merely rose to his feet mutely and stood beside his horse.

Then Uabhar lifted his dishevelled head as if it were as heavy as a millstone and spoke, saying disparagingly to his son, 'You would try to make a hero of yourself at my expense. I would rather have perished in the dungeons than pander to your self-glorification.'

'Father - ' the prince's agony was piteous to witness. He struggled to convey his thoughts; clearly it was a tremendous effort. 'Father, you are too harsh on me,' he continued, 'for I have never been aught but a dutiful son. My intentions are honourable, though I acknowledge I have my faults. Perhaps you could value that in me and do likewise.'

It was the first time in his life he had come close to criticising his father.

Uabhar stared condescendingly at Ronin and made as if to speak, whereupon Fergus, who had been standing nearby, his chest heaving with fury, broke in, 'You old canker! You are so raddled with corruption you can no longer even recognise purity. My brother would give his flesh for king and country, yet all you can do is mouth insults.'

'Get away,' Uabhar spat, 'you are no son of mine.'

'Enough of these family squabbles,' Zauberin snapped, making a threatening gesture, but Uabhar managed to throw in one final barb for his ungrateful progeny.

'Much good may it do you to wear the crown of Slievmordhu,' he said bitterly to Ronin. 'You might as well fall on your sword. Virosus has cursed the royal lineage, father and son, for all time. You will never thrive, for all your swaggering and posing.'

After that, Prince Ronin withdrew into silence, but the look on his face was the look of a man pierced by a blade.

As for Asrăthiel, to her own dismay she found herself barely able to respond to the troubles of Ronin. Her attention was drawn inexorably to the Goblin King. Now that she was closer to him than ever before, she let her gaze linger upon him as long as she dared, capturing every detail.

His presence was mesmerizing. He looked to be aged somewhere between twenty and thirty-five Winters, yet he was immortal, of course, and must be thousands of years old. His hair, pouring down his back, was intensely black, shot through, here and there, with a sheen of blue iridescence, like the colour on a butterfly's wing or peacocks' feathers; not a pigment but an effect caused by the way light was reflected from each hair shaft.

And such eyes.

Their colour was, of all colours, deep violet, like a rage of storms. Dark were the lashes, and smudged with a fine black line along the roots; no cosmetic but a natural colouration, a contrast that only enhanced his arresting looks. He seemed fashioned of midnight and moonrise, flame and ice. So achingly beautiful was he that to look upon him for too long was to abandon hope.

Asrăthiel wrenched away her gaze.

'I will take three of you,' said the Goblin King, 'as tithes.' He had spoken for the first time, and the sound was thrilling. His voice was clear and penetrating, like the vital song of fast-flowing rivers; not as harsh as the tones of his brethren, but rich and velvety in timbre. By contrast, the words he pronounced were keys winding up the springs of human dread to their uttermost torsion, despite that he had just alleviated their fears that hundreds might be claimed as captives. Goblins had proved highly unpredictable. Each mortal listener wondered: Will it be me? Will it be someone I love?

'Three ransoms for four kingdoms,' said Zaravaz. 'You get one free. I can be generous.'

'The king of Slievmordhu is one of the three you asked for,' Avalloc said formally, indicating the scowling prisoner. 'The Sylvan Comb can be found within the purse at his belt.'

All attention turned again upon Uabhar, who glowered from his saddle.

'If 'twere I who was taking hostages I would as lief have second thoughts,' scoffed Zauberin. 'That one is as long-faced as a horse at a wake.'

As if prompted by its rider's intention alone, the daemon horse of the Goblin King walked lightsomely over to the chestnut mare on which the abdicator was seated.

'Uabhar Ó Maoldúin, have you any gold about you?' Zaravaz asked.

The object of unseelie scrutiny had lost the cool demeanour that had possessed him when he humiliated his son. The Lord of Wickedness addressed him now, and Uabhar quaked in his boots. He seemed too frightened to frame a reply, but Avalloc said, 'We divested him of all his gold, as requested; his rings, his buckles, his cloth-of-gold linings.'

'While I doubt not your word, Lord of Storms,' said Zaravaz. 'I wonder if you are mistaken. Uabhar, have your teeth ever rotted?'

'I have no gold in my mouth!' Ó Maoldúin blurted impetuously. 'Leave me alone, you profane thing, you creature of darkness!'

'Certes, man, I would like to verify your report.' Zaravas gave a sign to a nearby kobold, who sprang onto the back of Uabhar's mare like some enormous cat pouncing on its prey and pulled the rider to the ground. The imp was wielding a huge set of metal pincers. Uabhar howled with rage and fright as the grotesque creature forced his jaws apart and rummaged in his mouth, but the goblin knights burst into merry laughter.

'Since your tongue has proved so discourteous to me just now, Uabhar,' said the Goblin King, 'I should by rights ask gentle Nidhogg to tear it out and teach it a lesson.'

Pausing in its exertions the kobold looked inquiringly at its master while its victim writhed and moaned in its grip.

'But then we would be deprived of the sweet music of your pleadings, so perhaps later. Shut his head,' said Zaravaz to the kobold, who obeyed and jumped off Uabhar's chest. 'Any nasty surprises in there, Nidhogg? No? Then it is well for you, Uabhar, that your ivory champers are in fine fettle, else my little vassal would have been bound to loosen them.'

The humiliated wretch, once the perpetrator of deeds such as this and worse, shrank into himself. Towering over the fallen man on his trollhäst, Zaravaz looked him up and down, as if amused by some secret joke, and then said, with a slight smile, 'Let there be a test for those who would be permitted to enjoy goblin company. Answer me this question, Uabhar Ó Maoldúin. If you were running in a footrace, and you overtook the person running second, in what place would you find yourself?'

Targeted by such an unexpected inquiry, Uabhar flinched. For a while he said nothing; it was evident he was striving to overcome his terrified disconcertment and concentrate on solving the quiz.

'There is a time limit,' Zaravaz said mellifluously.

'I believe it to be a trick question,' Uabhar managed to gasp.

'Yet you must answer, now.'

'First!' the man shouted shrilly. 'I would be first!'

'Wrong,' said the Goblin King. Aiming one long, beringed finger at Uabhar he added, 'Therefore you must come with us, after all!'

A rasping sob escaped from Uabhar's throat. Whereupon two nuggetty kobolds came forward, hauled the cowed unfortunate to his feet and carried him off between them. Five others in red armour stripped saddle and bridle from the waiting mare, and turned her free to gallop away. As the kobold warriors frog-marched their prisoner into their own ranks he began to scream and beg for mercy, writhing in their grip, yowling and wailing like a fell-cat, promising to give anything in return - his wife, his sons, his treasure - if only he could be spared, but the wights gave no quarter. 'Beshrew you, caitiff! Be quiet!' one of the goblin knights said sternly, 'or soon your mother will not recognise you!'

The aristocrats of the Court of Slievmordhu averted their eyes from their quondam king and shuffled their feet uncomfortably, embarrassed by this display. Prince Ronin stood upright and motionless beside his steed, staring straight ahead, as if he were made of glass, and would shatter if he bent. Indeed, something like a glass bead glittered on his cheek.

When Uabhar had passed from sight and earshot, the singularly arresting Zaravaz bade his steed canter back and forth along the rows of human dignitaries watching in trepidation. As he rode he said,

'Now for our second guest. I might have also taken the other king, Chohrab Shechem, but in his current condition he would provide us with little amusement.'

His trollhäst slowed to a halt.

'Being dead, I mean.'

Some of the goblin chevaliers laughed. Amongst the human audience, no one spoke.

In the starlit distance, a misshapen cow loped toward the pine forest at the rim of the moors. Cocking his head to one side the sharp-eyed Sovereign of Goblins watched the beast speculatively, over the heads of his captive audience. 'Instead of the unfortunate Shechem I might take that cow,' he murmured.

People looked over their shoulders to discover what he was looking at. Every man and woman held their breath and crossed their fingers. There were to be three tributes, no more. Eldritch wights were bound to honour their word. If the goblins took the cow, they would choose only one further ransom.

Then Zaravaz said, 'But I think not,' and immediately the human listeners felt as if the blood had been drained from their veins and soaked into the moors.

They watched apprehensively as the Goblin King returned his consideration to the assembly. Raising his voice, he spoke to a well-dressed old man whom nobody else had noticed lurking at the back of the crowd. 'I might take you!'

Emitting a shriek, the old man collapsed. A squire ran to his aid.

Prince William could contain himself no longer. 'I pray you sir, do not take that greybeard,' he said to Zaravaz, momentarily forgetting the prohibition on protest, in his haste to ease the old man's panic. 'He is but a harmless vagrant who has been of great service to us, and who is under the protection of Narngalis.'

The Goblin King sighed. He began to drum his fingers against the sword belted at his side.

A hush fell.

In that moment William realised what a grave mistake he had made by giving argument, and all others realised it too, and they paused, and felt their hearts freeze in their bodies. First Lieutenant

Zauberin had warned, 'One more word of haggling will put an end to our patience and the covenant will be forfeit.' And Zerstör, second of the king's lieutenants had reinforced this edict, saying, 'Seek to argue again, and we shall communicate no more with words, but only with swords.'

Handsome Zaravaz shook his head regretfully, like a patient tutor whose student had forgotten a lesson after repeated attempts to memorise it.

'Well, *aachionard*,' he said to his first lieutenant in conversational tones, 'what do you think - should we finish them now?'

'*T'eh lhien, y hiarn*,' answered Zauberin. 'They attempt to dicker, treating us as if we are naught but wood-goblins or market vendors. They insult us and they are forsworn.'

'I crave pardon for my fault,' William protested swiftly. 'Do as you will with me, but prithee, do not punish all, for the error of one!'

'You fail to understand,' said Zauberin, curling one corner of his upper lip, 'in many ways all men are alike to us. I can scarcely tell you apart. You say you are to blame, but it might have been the man next to you who gave us insult just now. Since we cannot be sure we must chastise you all, so as to be certain to afflict the culprit.'

William scowled in shame and rage, and Asrăthiel stepped closer to him so that she might stretch up and place her hand upon his arm, to give him comfort. Before she could reach him, her way was blocked by three grinning kobolds. Their tails thrashed back and forth like furious serpents. Recoiling in shock, she proceeded no further; but, on an instinctive reflex, her hand had flown to the hilt of her sword.

She had brought Fallowblade with her. The mistake had been unintentional. Though she knew the goblins had required that humankind 'Bring no gold,' she never thought of Fallowblade as gold - as ordinary gold, at any rate. The weapon was obviously - glaringly - the Golden Sword, but the damsel had come to view it not as metal of any kind, but as an heirloom and symbol; a fine, rare and precious object. In fact she had buckled it on as usual that morning without thinking, and it was not until that instant that she recalled, with a cold feeling, that the goblin ban on gold must necessarily include her sword. Even as she realised her error, it came to her that she had somehow managed to get away with it. The goblins must have overlooked the sword in its scabbard.

'*Brouteraght*,' said second lieutenant Zerstör, gorgeous in black mail and etiolated jewels, directing his words to the human assembly at large, 'we never asked the princes and leaders of humankind to meet us unarmed. Do you know why? It is because we have no fear of your iron and steel. Your weapons avail you naught.'

Intensely aware of the reassuring weight of Fallowblade hanging at her side, beneath her hand, Asrǎthiel thought, *except for one.*

'Except for one,' said the Goblin King, as if reading her mind. He was suddenly right next to her, stooping from his steed. His sword point had already slashed through the loop at her belt, and Fallowblade in its scabbard was soaring, spinning as it flew. In its wake the king's sword of goblin design arced aloft, spitting and hissing as it dissolved. The golden weapon landed with a thump amongst sprigs of heather, but the goblin blade evaporated, a smear of sooty smoke on the breeze. Zaravaz was gone as swiftly as he had appeared; when the damsel looked again, he was thirty feet away.

The goblins had not overlooked Fallowblade after all.

'Do not harass my lady!' William cried in anger, while he, his father, Avalloc and many others hastened to converge around the young weathermage. 'Are you hale?' the prince said softly into her ear.

'He never touched me.'

'How many more indignities shall we be forced to suffer?' King William growled, although he kept his voice low as a precaution.

'I cannot endure any more of their games,' Thorgild said wrathfully. 'How I long to put an end to their wickedness!'

'We bade you bring no gold!' Lieutenant Zauberin cried. His indignation appeared to be mingled with joy at the fact his foes had given him an excuse to punish them.

His liege lord, however, gestured as if batting away a fly, saying, 'The butter knife is a mere trifle.'

Prince Walter leaped from his saddle and ran to retrieve the fallen sword, but a fierce band of kobolds confronted him and he drew back.

'Leave Sioctíne where he lies,' the most beautiful goblin warrior called out impatiently. 'We have more business to do.'

Asrăthiel could not help but note that the hair of he who spoke – so fascinating that surely it must be interwoven with some spell – was the utter absence of light, yet when the evening wind combed through it, liquid glimmers ran up and down each strand as if black fire flowed there. She felt detached from reality. The dreadful circumstances that threatened her entire species, the upheavals of the past and the probable future, the uncertainty as to what the mercurial Zaravaz would do next; all this seemed remote and dreamlike by comparison to the immediacy – nay, the urgency of the Goblin King's presence, which overcame her senses like some potent apothecary's brew and left little awareness of anything else.

For a long instant the Lord of Wickedness paused, as if irresolute, while the human watchers wondered when he would take revenge for William's outburst and whether this evening would be the last they would ever see. Asrăthiel flexed her sword hand, yearning to retrieve the weapon, their only defence, yet simultaneously distracted. Zaravaz pondered, then presently seemed to reach a conclusion. A slow smile illuminated his exceptional features as he said, 'Very well. I acquiesce to your wishes, William Wyverstone. I will not destroy humankind because of your error. Know that I can be twice merciful, as well as generous.'

This wry comment evidently amused the goblin chivalry, for many of them grinned and exchanged comments, while some laughed loud and uncouthly, as if entertained by some obscene joke beyond the ken of their foes. Nonetheless, at this unexpected reprieve, tides of incredulity and relief swept through the human concourse. They could hardly believe their good fortune, and many gave silent thanks to the Fates for another few minutes of life.

'Merciful to be sure, y Hiarn,' concurred the second lieutenant, pressing the backs of his fingers against his lips to stifle a smile. His eyes unfocussed, and he looked as if he were recalling some past act of unspeakable cruelty. 'My lord's mercy can be boundless.'

'For example,' said Second Lieutenant Zerstör, as if sharing the joke and elaborating on the charade, 'if my lord can find no tributes to satisfy him he might decide not to rinse clean the lands of Calaldor-Tir with human tears.'

'Even so,' concurred the Goblin King in a tone of utmost reasonableness.

To this ambiguous declaration his audience reacted with uncertainty, while the unseelie knights laughed softly.

Briskly Zaravaz subjoined, 'Because I'd prefer to rinse them with human blood. However, at this point I am still selecting living pledges and so far we are two short. In which case,' he continued, 'I must choose another in place of Shechem. Let me ask a question of you.' As he uttered the final word his steed caracoled. The unseelie lord directly confronted Primoris Virosus, who gagged with terror and turned pale.

The old druid had been loitering in the wings, as it were; staying in the background, succoured by a galaxy of attendants. His mount was an ambling palfrey, and by the way he slumped in the saddle, he was obviously unaccustomed to perching upon its back. Armchairs, couches and carriages were his preferred seating arrangements. Now that the Tongue of the Fates had been singled out by the Goblin King, his attendants recoiled as if the druid had just announced he was infected with the Black Death. Amongst the goblin knights one was heard to comment, 'This looks a corrupt old piece without a doubt; another craven wretch.'

Prince Ronin stepped forward once more and bent his knee. He wore the look of a man who valued his life no longer and was merely continuing to exist in order to do his duty. 'Sir Goblin,' he said to Zaravaz, 'if you are to subtract this venerable servant of the Fates, pray allow me to make a request of him before he goes.'

'Well, Ronin, you are a bold one and no mistake,' Zaravaz observed somewhat coldly. 'To test me a second time takes courage. Do as you will, for you have shown yourself to be brave on the battlefield and have provided my *graihyn* with some lively exercise. But be quick. I begin to grow jaded with human company.'

The prince turned to the druid. 'I beg you, Lord Primoris,' he said, 'to lift the curse you placed upon the House of Ó Maoldúin.'

'No,' came the sour and simple reply.

Visibly upset, the prince acknowledged the judgement of the Tongue of the Fates with a low obeisance and made to withdraw, but the trollhäst of Zaravaz unexpectedly barred his way. 'Give no credit to their superstitions, Ronin,' said the Goblin King. 'His curse is naught but claptrap.'

'I believe in the Sanctorum's malediction, Sir Goblin,' said the prince. 'What the Tongue of the Fates says is so, must be so.'

'Then more fool you,' said Zaravaz. 'He who gives credit to a curse becomes cursed. Asper, tell this bonny bold believer your so-called hex is null.'

The Primoris, seizing on an opportunity to ingratiate himself with the powerful, immediately began to mutter an incantation, rolling his eyes and raising his hands to the skies for added effect. This went on until First Lieutenant Zauberin, unable to forbear, snapped, 'The night is not endless!' At the same time Zaravaz suddenly shouted into the sage's ear, 'I trust we are not keeping you from anything important,' whereupon Virosus jumped to a considerable height for such an antiquity and instantly ceased his exhibition, stating, 'It is done.'

'I am grateful, Lord Primoris,' Ronin replied, giving the druid a low reverence. His face shone with joy and wonder. He bowed also to the Goblin King, who nodded in recognition before redirecting his attention the sage and saying sternly, 'Now, Asper, say, "Ádh bless the Argenkindë."'

'No, no, I cannot!' shrieked the Tongue of the Fates, 'it were blasphemy to call for the benediction of the Fates upon unseelie wights!'

Said the unseelie lieutenant, 'Say as my liege commands, or have your liver scorched with heated pitchforks.'

Moaning and wringing his hands the druid forced out the words.

'Louder,' Zauberin said, and the sage screamed, 'Ádh bless the Argenkindë!'

'Good!' approved Zaravaz. 'Behold, people of Calaldor, denizens of Tir, you may henceforth believe the Starred One has conferred wellbeing and prosperity on my bloodthirsty *graihyn*. The Tongue of the Fates has said it is so; therefore to you it must be so. Asper, have you any gold on you?'

Asper Virosus shouted, 'No, Your Lordship! None at all!' The druid's fawning servility conferred further public disgrace upon him.

'And have you any rotten grinders in that decaying skull of yours?'

Quick as a flea, even before the Goblin King had finished speaking, the aged druid had whipped out his porcelain false teeth and was holding them up for all to behold, whereupon the unseelie knights went into further fits of laughter.

'It is well that you are eager to please me, old trout,' Zaravaz said amusedly. 'My *graihyn* have not been so properly entertained this many a long year. Though that,' he added, 'is not much of a recommendation, given that they have been buried underground for centuries.' He lifted a finger, at which the kobold Nidhogg lashed out with a whip, deftly flicking the dentures out of the druid's grasp. The prosthesis flew into the human crowd.

Virosus took on a woeful aspect, his caved-in face resembling a stitched-up leather bag. 'Have mercy on me, proud sir, for I am old and weak. It would be unworthy for noble knights such as yourselves to destroy me. It is an ungallant deed to crush a beetle.'

'In sooth you are old for a member of your race,' observed Zaravaz. 'All the more shame to those who let you live so long.'

'Ah, valiant sir, you and your kind do your best to humiliate us,' mumbled the druid. Hard-boiled and resentful by nature, and by virtue of his long exposure to universal deference, he had managed to summon a smidgin of bravado. 'To persecute us is your delight.'

Zaravaz scorned to reply.

'And rightly so,' replied his lieutenant, taking up the discourse, ' for your race is held to be accursed by all the Glashtinsluight, and we cannot endure your presence in the world. We count it our duty to dip our swords in human blood.'

'Burn no more starlight at this business,' said the Goblin King, re-entering the conversation. 'I would make an end of it this night.' In something of an offhand manner he threw the druid a question, 'Asper, if you were participating in a race and overtook the last runner, what position would you be running in?'

A crafty look crept across the desiccated visage of the Primoris, replacing his erstwhile expression of horror. He hesitated as if mentally confirming his reply, licked his flapping lips, then said, 'Worthy Sir, the similar question you asked of the execrable Uabhar had no catch. The answer to that was 'second place'. This, however, is a trick question, because if one is running in any race, it is impossible to overtake the last person!' As he finished the declaration his baggy mouth elongated in a type of grimace of triumph.

The Goblin King said, 'Correct!' and, indicating Virosus with his index finger he continued, 'Therefore, you must come with us!'

'But I answered the question accurately!' screeched the panic-stricken druid.

Zaravaz replied severely, 'You did so, in very deed, Asper. How very clever of you. So clever that you must come with us.'

The druid screeched and wailed as kobolds bundled him off his steed and dragged him away, crying, 'What do you mean to do with me?' but none of his human acquaintance moved or made any attempt to soothe him. Foremost in the minds of most was the unpleasant notion, Two taken, one yet to be taken. Whom shall it be?

Again Zaravaz paused and scrutinised the faces of his adversaries. 'Now we come to it,' he said. 'The last tribute. Dismount, all of you.'

Aghast and bemused at what this new instruction might indicate, the leaders of Tir obeyed, but in a dignified manner, and without haste. 'What can be the reason for this?' they muttered to each other. 'At best 'twill be some fresh slight, at worst a cruel joke.'

Some alleged, 'It is trickery for sure. We'll not escape so easily. The goblins sport with us.'

'Now take the gear from the backs of the horses. Throw it down and let the steeds go,' commanded Zaravaz. 'If you cannot support yourselves on your own two feet, you will have to be carried or dragged.'

'Will you take all of us, then?' Avalloc Maelstronnar challenged as the horses were unsaddled. 'All, instead of only one more, as you promised?'

The crowd shuddered at the weathermage's display of daring, but the Goblin King raised one eyebrow and quietly responded, 'I said I would take three, Storm Lord, and three I shall take. The rest shall walk home, perforce.'

Conall Gearnach could restrain his ire no longer, and boldly cried, 'Do you mean to humiliate us?' He stood upon the ground, feet braced apart, hands on hips.

Alarmed at his outburst, bystanders tried to hush him. 'Two-Swords, do not let pride be our undoing!' Warwick warned.

Musingly, Zaravaz regarded the famed warrior who had called him to question. 'Be wary how you speak to me, soldier of Slievmordhu,' he said. Turning his back, he directed curt instructions to another of his officers, who proceeded to deal with Gearnach's challenge.

'I, who you may denominate as Zwist,' this lieutenant said coolly, 'say to you, Conall Gearnach: Be careful not to anger my lord Zaravaz, or you will come to regret it with every beat of your overweening heart. Now, regarding the unbinding of the animals on whom you have so lately been pressing your buttocks: Examine your principles. Do you truly believe it is estimable to batten upon the spine of a beast, to make slaves of freeborn creatures? Is it admirable for a grown man or woman to behave like an infant who is carried on its mother's shoulders because it is too feeble to walk on its own hind legs?'

It struck Asrăthiel that these opinions were surprisingly close to her own. The appearance of kindness in these unseelie wights seemed strangely at odds with their demonstrable cruelty. She realised, too, that no war horse had been harmed in battle.

'So it is a moral issue, is it?' Gearnach shot back. 'If riding horseback is so degrading, why do you?'

The goblins Zwist and Zerstör flanked the warlord in an invisible instant, their daemon horses sniffing at him with their red nostrils, and baring their pointed teeth, but Slievmordhu's foremost knight did not quail or betray any sign of fear.

'The trollhästen,' explained the unseelie knight called Zwist, obviously at pains to restrain himself from executing Gearnach on the spot, 'unlike the horses of Calaldor, have a symbiotic relationship with goblinkind. Do you know what that means, O unkilled brave?'

Gruffly, Gearnach shook his head.

'Believe me, we would hesitate to waste our breath explaining,' said Zwist, his pale fingers caressing the haft of his dagger, 'only that our lord has requested it of us. Symbiosis signifies a relationship of mutual benefit or dependence.'

'The trollhästen, in fact, love goblinkind,' said Second Lieutenant Zerstör. His steed tossed its emerald mane. 'They draw nourishment from the power that resonates from our life force, we of the Glashtinsluight. When they are not near to us, they begin to fade and waste away. Their obsession is to bear us upon their backs. They are our contracted companions, never our slaves. Do you understand?'

Gearnach sucked his teeth as if debating within himself. 'Convenient,' he risked brazenly.

Gripping his sword hilt Zerstör directed an impassioned plea to his king, which was denied.

'Leave Conall Two-Swords to his dilemmas of principle,' Zaravaz said in bored tones, waving a hand dismissively. Like his opponents, he had dismounted. His lieutenants reluctantly withdrew from Gearnach's inflammatory presence, casting longing looks over their shoulders, like wolves whose pack leader has forbidden them to devour a fresh kill. The ground reverberated with the hammering of hooves as the last of the unsaddled horses galloped away.

'Let me think,' the Goblin King said loudly and theatrically. 'One more ransom. Whom shall I choose?' Dangerous, sardonic, vigorous, Zaravaz strolled unhurriedly up and down the lines of the human assembly, absent-mindedly tapping his fingers against his black-clad thigh as if deep in thought. All at once he came to an abrupt stop.

Steeped in resentment, fear and ire yet standing as straight and proud as their dignity required, his audience waited. Although they were racked with misgivings, they were beginning to believe that they were escaping their predicament relatively lightly. So far, the Lord of Wickedness, true to the unpredictable nature of wights in general, had chosen hostages – or victims – who were hated or feared by much of the populace, and in fact most people considered that the four kingdoms were well rid of the two scheming tyrants.

Zaravaz spoke again, so suddenly he surprised them all. 'I believe I shall take - ' he spun around on his heel, his cloak flying, and flung out one arm - 'this one.'

He spoke Asrăthiel's name.

The damsel started. She stared, wide eyed, but there could be no mistaking that it was she the unseelie slayer had addressed. 'What?' she cried in disbelief. 'He jests!' she remonstrated, looking wildly around, seeking confirmation of her diagnosis from her companions. When she perceived by their stunned expressions that none would be forthcoming, a stringent iciness seemed to douse her slowly from head to foot. Her heart began to race as countless possible scenarios flashed through her mind, and she struggled for breath, as if she were drowning. In that agonised moment, she almost wished for instant death. 'Save me,' she whispered, so softly that no one heard but herself.

Hubbub broke out on all sides. William rushed forward to position himself between Asrăthiel and the Goblin King. 'I forbid it!' he shouted, while Avalloc and Warwick and every human voice joined in clamour to express their displeasure.

'A covenant has been made!' exclaimed Zaravaz. 'You must honour your word!'

'We will not give her up,' they vowed, and the swords of men chimed like silver bells as they slid from their scabbards.

'You may take the first two tithes, Zaravaz,' roared Avalloc, 'but not the third.'

'On my oath, it is like chopping stone necks with a blunt axe!' the Goblin King cried indignantly. 'Will we ever get through?'

As he spoke, hundreds of flashing eldritch blades appeared in the hands of the extraordinary knights, the kobolds extended their talons and brandished their pitchforks, and the trollhästen neighed, rearing up and scraping the air with barbaric hoofs, their satin coats gleaming with a metallic lustre, their manes and tails streaming like green torchlight. The horde drew together in a dark mass of antlered helms and gleaming swords, from which their silver embellishments and pale jewels glimmered like stars in a sable sky. The assembled multitude, who had raised an uproarious shout of condemnation, hesitated. They gazed silently on the formidable and experienced corps they had spontaneously defied, and recoiled from their forward line.

The lieutenants of Zaravaz petitioned their king in the language of Tir, so that their foes might comprehend, 'Merely say the word, lord, and we shall tear them socket from socket. We shall rend their flesh and pluck out their eyes; mince them and scatter their steaming meat across the moors to feed the crows.' Aroused by desire to attack, the goblin knights trembled with choked back truculence and pent yearning.

Not for nothing, thought Asrăthiel, are they feared. But I must be strong. And indeed, after the first instant of immoderate panic she had quickly recovered her equilibrium. Relegating fear, she faced her prospects with as much calmness and rationality as she could muster.

She glanced around, sensing the thirst for blood ripe in the air, and noting the look of intense anticipation on the faces of the unseelie warriors. What she chose to do at this fraught moment would prove to be a pivot point. If the terms were refused, the entire human race would be in utmost peril. It was an inconceivable responsibility, but the right path was unquestionable. Wights speak the truth, and honour their promises.

Besides; against almost all evidence she was beginning to formulate the odd notion that Zaravaz might not intend to deal harshly with her. His impromptu display of what might, at a precarious stretch of the imagination, be termed kindness towards Ronin, though it was inconsistent and entailed browbeating the decrepit druid, had sown that seed. Goblinkind's incongruously merciful philosophies regarding animals reinforced this impression.

Stepping around William she faced the Goblin King and said, 'Since you have given your word of peace, I will go with you.'

Uproar broke out again.

Cuiva Stillwater and Shahzadeh of Ashqalêth took hold of Asrăthiel and pulled her back within the mortal fold. Everyone in that company vowed they would never allow her to become hostage to the wights.

'There is no choice to be made,' Avalloc said wrathfully. 'You shall not go. How could you make such a foolish declaration!'

It was the first time in her life Asrăthiel had ever seen her grandfather angry with her.

'There will be no talk of yielding to this demand,' said King Warwick, scanning the battle-primed goblin ranks in a last-ditch effort to take measure of their strengths and weaknesses. 'When we perish we will take as many of them with us as possible.'

Thorgild said darkly, 'The day the House of Torkilsalven gives a girl to the Lords of Unseelie is the day the world is engulfed by the sun.'

Flourishing his sword high in the air, Conall Gearnach cried, 'Let us put an end to these unscrupulous stealers of women, these ravishers!' and Prince Ronin said, 'Asrăthiel, you are Storm Lady, heir to Rowan Green. What should we do without you?' The reply that sprang to her tongue, although she did not utter it, was Exist.

'I pledge my kingdom's army to your protection,' said Princess Shahzadeh, 'should the goblins try to take you by force. Come, let us away from here, you and me! Let us find horses and ride for Ashqalêth!'

But Asrăthiel shook her head. 'That is a dream,' she answered.

Cuiva Stillwater, White Lady of the Marsh, whispered, with tears in her eyes, 'As you loved your mother, and love her still Asrăthiel, forbear from lunacy. Think of her lying in her glass bower amongst the roses. Would you abandon her? Would you abandon us all? Jewel would never have let you go.'

This, of all appeals, touched Asrăthiel most, yet it could not blind her to circumstance.

'With respect, Mistress Cuiva,' she said presently, 'I believe you are mistaken. My mother would wish me to do as I judge fit, and my father also.'

William Wyverstone gazed at the damsel; at the swan-curve of her waist and her eyes bluer than the distance. He was being eaten out with passion; consumed with the heartfelt desire to keep her secure. Taking her aside he said, 'Asrăthiel, I beg you not to even consider such an act of sacrifice.'

From afar came the ringing voice of Zaravaz; 'Some time this century would be convenient.'

'My lord is not to be kept waiting!' warned Second Lieutenant Zerstör.

'William,' the damsel said gently, 'I am invulnerable.'

'Upon my life, Asrăthiel, that hardly matters! There are a thousand atrocities they might devise for you!'

The Goblin King stood watching, a little way off, leaning against the flank of his daemon horse as though afflicted with ennui. Asrăthiel looked up at him and called out, 'If I should go with you as your prisoner, will you work me harm or disgrace?'

'If you ask us politely,' he replied, giving a sarcastic bow.

The weathermage turned back to William, who muttered furiously, 'What kind of answer is that? 'Tis, at best, prevarication, at worst a dire threat! You know how clever all wights are at equivocating, since they are incapable of lying!'

'I believe they cannot seriously harm me, even if they try.'

There was no way to explain, even to herself, her unfounded and probably invalid premonition that the wights would not work ill upon her. 'I am willing to take the risk.'

William took the damsel's hand without speaking, and gazed at her mournfully. Shortly she added, choking on the words, 'I must. For all that I hold dear.'

The prince kissed her fingers and released her.

'No gold,' cautioned Lieutenant Zauberin, and Asrăthiel unclasped her sword belt, giving Fallowblade's scabbard to her grandfather, along with a swift embrace. She moved to the forefront of the mortal crowds, where she addressed her people.

'My decision is made,' she cried loudly, so that as many as possible might hear. 'If you respect me you will not hinder me. Sheath your weapons. You might grieve for me awhile, but then put aside sadness, for now begins the season to restore order to the four kingdoms. Mankind is saved. Rejoice. Farewell, friends. I go of my free will alongside Ó Maoldúin, and Virosus.'

With that, and with the shouted entreaties and blessings and lamentations of the multitude filling her ears, the damsel turned and walked towards the unseelie hordes.

Bitter was the anguish of those she left behind. There was not a dry eye amongst them, and many called out her name, extending their arms as if to reach out and retrieve her. Prince William flamed with grief and wrath. Like many, he was unable hold himself back as Asrăthiel departed, and made to dash after her, and had to be forcibly restrained by his own men.

With a jolt of surprise Asrăthiel felt herself being swung through air as if she were a wisp of straw, and next moment she was seated sideways upon the back of a fluidly moving daemon horse, in the midst of a sea of fell riders as alluring as lovers. The swords of the goblin knights had been returned to their scabbards, their conditions for the cessation of hostilities having been fulfilled. The miserable captives Uabhar and Virosus had been hoisted on the shoulders of hefty kobold warriors. They were being unceremoniously carried pick-a-back, jolting up and down as their eldritch bearers trotted along on muscular legs. As the cavalry began to move northwards, the king's lieutenant flung a last retort over his shoulder, 'We depart, but we leave behind our Watch to enforce the law.' No one was quite sure what that meant, but it was too late to enquire.

Asrăthiel fancied she spied something moving in the new-sprung herbage; a small figure, a wight maybe. Against reason she watched from the corner of her eye, half expecting the urisk Crowthistle to make some rash move to rescue her, from which she would, naturally, try to save him. But she saw him not.

Of course not! Anxiety and lack of sleep must have impaired her memory - she had dispatched him with the golden sword.

She moved off with the eldritch chivalry, but her compliance was not to be the final interaction between humankind and goblin-kind that night.

As the unseelie knights withdrew, a band of mortal warriors attacked them from the rear.

Even as Asrăthiel had been speaking earnestly with William for the last time, Conall Gearnach was holding a separate discussion with Prince Cormac Ó Maoldúin, who had, after much inner striving, managed to find it in his heart to set aside his hatred of his brother's slayer in the cause of military cooperation.

'The Lady Asrăthiel is immortal and invulnerable,' said the warlord, his eyes sparking with anger, 'but those unseelie libertines will not scruple to invade her honour with the most unbridled licence. I will die before I allow that to happen.'

'I am of like mind with you,' said the prince, somewhat aloofly, 'but she has chosen. It is her will. What can we do?'

'There is one chance left, sir. Mindful of wights' skill with equivocation I have studied their words closely, and it dawned on me that while the wights indicated that if we met their king's terms our race would be spared, they have never precisely stated that he would authorise genocide if we did not. It is a slim hope, but worth clinging to.'

'Why should they not carry out their threat?' Cormac asked.

Gearnach shrugged. 'The reasoning of wights is as convolute as a nautilus shell and not readily laid out to the light, but I'll vouchsafe they would be pleased to have a few human toys to trifle with during the idle hours of their immortality, and that they cannot do if we are all gone. If mankind's death can be postponed, it might later, somehow, be avoided.'

'What is your intention?'

'I have committed a crime for which I have not yet compensated,' Gearnach declared bleakly. 'I have still to pay for my folly before the gate of Ironstone Keep.'

'A crime of passion, yes,' answered Cormac, 'nonetheless the blood tax is already paid. You have served Slievmordhu like no other soldier in the annals of our realm.' Magnanimously he appended, 'Be at peace, Conall.'

'It was an offence committed in haste and error,' said the Knight of the Brand, 'but with unbearable, unpardonable consequences. Kieran and Halvdan were as my own sons. No,' Gearnach continued, 'justice is not yet balanced, and I cannot live with debt overshadowing me. I cannot - live.'

Silence followed his words.

Said Cormac, comprehending Gearnach's full meaning by the words he had not spoken, 'I believe it is worth the attempt. Ronin would stop you if he knew.'

'Of that I am certain,' said Conall Gearnach. He added, 'Yet Ronin will rule our country well. Better than he that went before.'

In painful understanding the two men gazed upon one another, and for an instant the warrior made as if to reach out his hand for the clasp of friendly parting, but let his arm drop by his side instead.

And that was how Gearnach came to lead the desperate charge against the departing goblin knights.

The delegates of Tir saw him running to the attack. It was all that the warlike ones amongst them required; for too long had they been keeping their rage in check. Without delay they rushed forward in his wake, brandishing their swords.

'Madness!' shrieked Queen Halfrida, wringing her hands. 'They must be stopped ere they drag us all down to ruin!'

Yet it was too late to stop them.

'At least Gearnach had the wisdom not to try to pick up Fallow-blade,' said Cuiva Featherfern sadly, peering at the streak of sunlight that lay on the heath under the stars.

Queen Saibh of Slievmordhu closed her eyes, so that she might not witness her three surviving sons plunging into this insane and unwinnable conflict.

'Fall back! Fall back!' courtiers were shouting in panic, and the queens, with their retinues, were shepherded to safety, away from the site of the skirmish. Men were turning on each other, some endeavouring to join Gearnach, others fighting to restrain their comrades from such recklessness. Furore held sway. They were armed, the dignitaries of Tir, and armed to the teeth. In preparation for their final encounter with the perfidious goblins, several had put on hauberks or brigandines beneath their outer garments. Accoutred were they, but their efforts were far from being coordinated. There was no military discipline. Furthermore, some were getting old, a few were not in the best of health, and many had led lives of indolence; they had not the strong thews of trained soldiers. Each fought his own battle.

The four royal leaders were all of the same purpose – to stem further bloodshed. Warwick, Thorgild, Ronin and Rahim hastened away from the field with their standard-bearers, gathering subjects and followers with their rallying cries; 'To Narngalis!' and 'To the Brand!'

Meanwhile the Goblin King had again vaulted down from his trollhäst and was despatching adversaries with speed, skill and evident delight. He jumped, leaped and flung his body exuberantly through the air as if there were no such tyrant as gravity. By comparison, even the fittest of the human combatants moved as if wooden; laboured, laden, arthritic and ancient. Whirling, dodging and smiting with preternatural precision, his hair and cloak flying, Zaravaz once more showed himself to be as utterly ruthless as legend described. He even took the time to be sarcastic as he fought, mocking his opponents as he joyously spilled their life's blood.

People were dashing hither and thither. 'This time there can be no reprieve,' someone shrieked. 'The wicked ones swore to kill us all if we struck a blow against them! They will fulfil their oath! We are lost! We are lost!'

Asrăthiel attempted to slide from her eldritch steed, but its hide became as sticky as the coat of a waterhorse, and it would not let her escape. She had, however, been careful not to place her hands upon the trollhäst, and in a limited way she was free to act. She watched in anguish as reckless Conall Gearnach doubled back on foot, eluding a swarm of ravening kobolds. A trio of goblin knights was in hot pursuit of him; amongst them Asrăthiel recognised one of the lieutenants he had antagonized. The imps scattered before the onslaught of the eldritch warriors, and as the knights rushed at Gearnach he dodged, threw himself to the ground and rolled over. When he stood up, with one smooth movement, he was, after all, holding Fallowblade, which had been under him - but holding the sword awkwardly, like a man who has no control over a lightning bolt he suddenly discovers he has grasped. He sliced one adversary and slashed another; before the third closed with him. Together they fell, but Gearnach had managed to interpose the unruly weapon between himself and his opponent and, as they toppled, its double edges sawed them both to the spine.

Man and goblin perished in the same instant.

Shortly thereafter, three huge staghorn beetles lumberingly flew away with a heavy droning of wings, leaving the mortal soldier's lifeless form prone on the heather, the golden sword lying athwart him, wrapped in a red, spreading mantle.

So ended the deeds of Conall Gearnach, Commander-in-Chief of the Knights of the Brand, a valiant man, Slievmordhu's foremost warrior.

When Asrăthiel saw the sons of Tir hard-pressed by kobolds with pitchforks and knights with eldritch blades, she screamed aloud, to anyone that might hearken, 'Avaunt! Stay thy hand!' but she doubted whether anyone heard over the cacophony of battle.

Perhaps they heard not, but they felt the blast of the freezing wind that came rushing out of the north, smiting them all like the breath of absolute Winter. It quelled their hot battle rage. Then the conflict ceased, for the warriors of goblinkind left off their battering and the kobolds followed suit. Fighters both mortal and immortal drew apart – the former carrying their wounded with them - leaving the ground littered with the fallen.

Asrăthiel let the summoned wind go barrelling away, and as the roar of it died, she sighted the Goblin King. He looked at her steadily for an instant. Meeting his cruel violet gaze without unflinching she cried passionately, 'Let them be. You have done enough!'

She said it with some confidence, for, during the brief conflict she had been thinking quickly, and had arrived at the same conclusion as Conall Gearnach; namely, that there was a chance that even if their human foes broke the terms of the covenant the wights would not revenge themselves as drastically as they had implied.

Then came another hiatus when nothing moved except the wind-stirred heather and a meteor sizzling across the black heavens. Even the piteous groans of the stricken seemed to grow fainter. At the third and possibly the final juncture, the representatives of humankind and the prosecutors of unseelie wickedness waited upon the verdict of Zaravaz.

He made no comment in answer to Asrăthiel's plea, but instead swung himself upon the back of his daemon horse and rode up to her.

'Spare them,' she repeated.

'Will you go or will you stay?' he enquired.

'I will go with you. I have promised.'

He smiled.

At this, the urgency of the situation unaccountably fled from Asrăthiel's consciousness. 'But have you,' she said, growing dizzy and unable to think with clarity, 'no quiz for your third guest?' as soon as she uttered the words she wished she could unsay them. She thought, I am raving like some discomposed flirt, like some infatuated idiot! And on a bloody theatre of war, and to this unpardonable avenger!

Leaning from his trollhäst, Zaravaz stroked her hair. A stab of unspeakable intensity speared through her, and whether she had spoken foolishly or not ceased to matter. This close, his breath was so fragrant that the winds must be in love with it.

'Yes,' he said. 'I have just asked it.'

Then his steed, and hers, wheeled and sprang forward, and the unseelie horde followed, and without causing any further harm the Silver Goblins with their living booty passed from the view of humankind into the shadow of night.

After their departure, William and his comrades hastened back to their fortresses and armouries. They prepared in secret to ride in pursuit of the goblin contingent, their purpose being to rescue Asrăthiel. Much of the populace mourned the fallen, while others celebrated with wild delight, for the unseelie threat had apparently vanished, and the Marauders had dispersed to their remote caverns, and a fragile peace seemed ready to settle upon the four kingdoms at long last.

But Zaravaz the Goblin King, whose hair was blacker than calumny, led the unseelie hordes northwards at preternatural speed; past the dim marches of the Wuthering Moors, across the river Clearwater at the ancient stone bridge, through the town of Paper Mill, and over the Harrowgate Fells to the foothills of the Northern Ramparts.

Ahead of them the mountains; great, strong, enduring bones of the land, were flung up against the sky. So high they loomed that the clouds settled about their shoulders and their snowy peaks were lost to view. Further that cavalcade pressed onward into the bitter north, for they passed beneath the shadows of the mountains and climbed beyond, and ultimately Zaravaz led them high into the icy fastnesses of the high latitudes; to the fabled halls where he reigned as Mountain King.

6
MOUNTAIN HALLS

Glisten of the argent river where the frozen rushes shiver,
Glitter of the moon in Winter, shining like an icy splinter,
Lambent leaves of birch and willow; gleam of foam on stormy billow;
Starlight from the heavens spilling; polish on a mint-new shilling;
Crucible of precious sterling, glassy fish in cistern swirling,
Hoarfrost glinting on the clover, tinsel filigree all over.
Dewy web like pearly cable, lustrous ware upon the table;
Chalice, tankard, spoon and platter. Candle-flames like diamonds shatter.
Thread and needle for the tailor; guiding beacons for the sailor.
Shadow in a burnished mirror, sharp as crystal, brighter, clearer.
Elemental, clever metal, snowy as an almond petal.
Shimmer on nocturnal water, heart-enslaver, shining; silver.

THE LOVE OF SILVER:
TRANSLATED FROM THE LANGUAGE OF THE TROWS.

A cross the entire sky constellations, heart-piercingly pure, glittered against a ceiling of hyacinthine mystery, as if caught in some intricate mesh. The stars silently radiating their splendour sparkled as brilliantly at the zenith as at the outer fences of the world. Presently a glow opened on the horizon behind the ranges, like the radiance from a city lit with white-flamed torches. Soon it brightened, impossibly, as if an argentine bonfire of gigantic dimensions had been kindled. A tiny arc of silver ascended, growing to become a semicircular disc. The moon had risen. Outlined against its pure luminosity, frozen mountain peaks raked the night sky, jagged as smashed crystal.

The journey across many leagues seemed hardly to take any time at all. Asrăthiel was aware only of a billion sidereal lamps wheeling above her head, while all else moved slowly, as if the world fell gently through a syrup of dark wine spiced with scintillants. She slept or dozed, at whiles, fastened by gramarye upon the back of the daemon horse, lapped by the cool aquamarine lambency of its mane, rocked like a child in a cradle. She had never imagined such refined movement; fluid, elegant and mellifluous, gentle as a breeze caressing blossom, but nimble as light. All the momentous events that had recently occurred and that currently unfolded seemed distant in time and place. As before, a type of detachment over-whelmed her. Temporarily, at least, inquisitiveness seemed to have drained from her conscious mind. The effects of the past anxiety-fraught weeks - the nights of scant sleep, the conflicts, the responsi-bilities, the urgency - had caught up with her. Now it was all over. Behind her lay places to which she no longer belonged, and people she had lost; before her lay places and beings unknown, but she was numb to all that. Her exhaustion of spirit was such that she must succumb to the opium of drowsiness. Lulled by the rhythmic gait of her steed, she accepted the ride amongst the eldritch chiv-alry, without any urge to ask where they were going or what would happen when they arrived. Let the future wait – it was out of her hands, in any event.

They had reached the Northern Ramparts. Supernaturally sure-footed, the trollhästen galloped thousands of feet up the steep and pathless mountain slopes as if they negotiated a level plain, finding purchase where no purchase could possibly be, climbing slopes at impossible angles; surely their hooves must be as adhesive as their hides. Slender and fine were they in build, but their eldritch energy seemed inexhaustible.

Amidst soaring crags the goblin knights rode in procession across a level terrace that gave onto an extraordinary bridge. Slender and transparent, it seemed fashioned of glass. Asrăthiel wondered how such a fine, attenuated structure, whose stanchions resembled icicles dripping from a twig, could hold the weight of such a considerable cavalcade. Beneath the bridge a crevasse plunged to unthinkable depths: there cloud-spectres twined with entombed shadows in valleys never touched by sunlight. A ravening gale blasted out of that chasm, so powerful and swift that any mortal horse would have been blown aside like thistledown.

She looked up.

High amongst the gables of icy Storth Cynros - the tallest and most central of all the mountains - a fabulous semi-subterranean city concealed its marvels from the world. Built in ages past, this citadel of the Silver Goblins was all spires and starlight, eyries and lofty halls, glittering with ancient jewels delved from beneath the mountains. Its turrets were wrapped in mists, its roofs spangled with snow; its gorgeous walls hewn from sparkling basalt. Its galleries broke through the heights where the views were most breathtaking. To this remote and secluded fastness the goblin horde and their haughty chieftain were bringing their three human tributes.

Ahead of them loomed a pointed archway as high as a fully-grown poplar tree; a grand entrance into the hillside.

'What is this place?' asked Asrăthiel.

'Sølvetårn,' said a voice nearby, although she could not tell to whom it belonged. 'Though mankind's legends name it Minith Ariannath, the Silver Mountain.'

Halfway across the bridge, the knight Zauberin, who was riding beside the kobold that bore Uabhar on its back, tore something from the dethroned king's belt and tossed it into the abyss. Asrăthiel watched a leather purse go hurtling down, to be quickly swallowed in the steaming cauldron.

'That was the Sylvan Comb!' she murmured, half aware.

Zaravaz rode a short distance ahead of her. 'I daresay 'twill lie in some forgotten niche until the end of time,' he said over his shoulder, 'or else some human fool will find it, and cause more mischief. Either way, I care little.'

It seemed an ignominious fate for such an improbable thing.

Their road passed beneath the archway and on into the mountain's interior. As they travelled deeper into the citadel, Asrăthiel, roused by wonder, stared about. The ingenious engineering, the delicacy of architecture, the spectacular ornamentation, the grace and vastness and cold splendour of Sølvetårn astounded her. Never had she imagined such a sight. Stairs of hailstone spiralled to lofty pinnacles. Glittering cobwebs draped pointed archways, apses and traceried windows. Fire and water adorned the caverns: columns of flaming gases flaring up to ceilings too high to be descried; cascades of chthonian water streaming down to the many levelled floors, their tumult echoing from wall to wall. Deep dived the caverns of Sølvetårn, yet they were airy and elegant, upheld by fluted columns, traversed by airy, suspended ways and seemingly fragile spans and stairs. Cleverly positioned mirrors conveyed reflections of moonlight therein, and torches flamed like luteous flowers. It was an architecture of translucent glass and ice, pale limestone and stalactites, flashing diamonds and crystal, laced through with waterfalls, lakes and underground rivers.

Presently the weathermage's attention was drawn to the two other human captives, who were being carried away down a glistening vaulted corridor in another direction, their wails ignored.

'Where are they going?' she asked Zaravaz.

'To a place of sighs.'

Envisioning her fellow hostages suffering some appalling torment she said, 'I ask you, sir, to grant them clemency.'

'Daughter of Rowan Green,' said her host, concentrating his violet gaze upon her, 'it is twice that I have shown extraordinary mercy, of recent times; thrice if you count my asking ransom for your kingdoms. Once when the man William Wyverstone, perhaps blinded by an excess of philanthropy, attempted to negotiate terms against my express wishes. Again when the man Conall Gearnach, perhaps blinded by a misguided sense of honour, assailed my *graihyn* as we departed. It has not been easy for me to show such unwonted tolerance. Do not ask it of me a third time.' He smiled dazzlingly at her. 'Besides, how can you know what fate I have in store for you? Would you not rather make a hoard of your clemency pleas? You yourself might soon need to beg for my leniency.'

Staggered by his inferences, Asrăthiel struggled to speak but failed. She felt as if she had been winded.

'Yet fear not, I will not deal hard with you. We shall hold a banquet in your honour,' announced the goblin king.

Before the damsel could say anything further, a brushing sound, like the swishing of leaves, or ragged hems sweeping the floor, heralded the arrival of trow-folk in great numbers. From the shadowy radiance of inner halls they emerged; small, grey-clad figures gliding toward the incoming cavalcade, uttering soft hoots and cries of gladness.

Asrăthiel recovered her composure and put on a brave face. 'So this is where the trows were bound!' she exclaimed.

First Lieutenant Zauberin's sprightly trollhäst trotted up, its rider shrugging back his fur-lined demi-cloak. He said, 'They clamour to be our servants.'

'Of course,' said Asrăthiel. 'How could they not? The trows would be attracted to your kindred.'

'They are attracted by silver,' said Zauberin. He glanced sideways at the weathermage, allowing one eyelid to droop - a trick that exaggerated his habitual air of dissolution. As he rode away, the hooves of his trollhäst clattered on the flagstones.

'Go with the Grey Neighbours,' bade the goblin king and, since her steed followed the trows, the damsel must go too.

After dismounting from the daemon horse that had brought her to Sølvetårn, Asrăthiel found herself bustled away by a gaggle of trow-wives; wights who looked like little women, half her height, in grey headscarves and tattered frocks, bedizened with silver bangles. These dames took her to a suite of exquisite rooms hollowed out of stone, where she bathed in a solid silver tub beneath a cascade of hot, scented water pouring from a wall spout, arcing through the air like a swag of pearl necklaces. The overflow splashed into a pool hewn in the rocky floor, from whence it gradually drained away through some unseen conduit.

Invigorated by the water, Asrăthiel woke fully from her somnolence and took stock of her situation. Here she was, alone amongst enemies; no ordinary enemies, but the sworn foes of humanity. What was it that the lieutenant Zauberin had said? '*Your race is held to be accursed by all the Glashtinsluight, and we cannot endure your presence in the world. We count it our duty to dip our swords in human blood.*' These wights were utterly antipathetic to the human race. Being anathema to her people, they were anathema to her also. She hated them with outraged passion, for all their arbitrary bloodshed and decimation. Yet she would receive as much profit by demanding that they treat her according to her rank, or haranguing them, or summoning storms against them, or refusing to cooperate, as a wave receives when dashing itself against a cliff of adamant. They held all advantage. Come what may her fate was in their hands, and if she were to exist in relative comfort it was in her best interests, at least for now, to appear compliant.

Eerie music was chiming faintly through the apartments. Asrăthiel looked about. The sounds appeared to be generated by airs wafting through shrewdly positioned interstices in the architecture. The ceilings, with their pointed-arch vaulting, were supported on slim pillars whose ornate plinths and capitals were carved with intricate, flowing designs, such as intertwining stems or roots, each stalk terminating in long, tapered leaves or fantastic tendrils. Silver shone everywhere, lustrous and pure as milk; untarnished silver, wrought in ways that enhanced its loveliness; cast, chased, filigree and repoussé, etched, engraved, carved, stamped and embossed. A separate chamber housed a splendid couch suspended on argent chains from the ceiling. By its fragrance, the mattress was stuffed with dry sprigs of lavender, poppies, hemlock and chamomile.

As Asrăthiel took in her surroundings the trow-wives dressed her in an ankle-length shift – which they called a sark - of white cambric bordered with lace, and proceeded to coif her hair.

While this was going on, the damsel plagued the wights with questions.

'What will happen to the two other prisoners? What will happen to me?'

All the little goodies said by way of reply was, 'We dinnae ken! Nae bothy kens!'

'Am I permitted to send a letter to my family? Where are the women of goblinkind? Will you please refrain from pulling my hair?' When she made this protest they shrieked and gibbered, instantly becoming much gentler with their handling. They peered at her earnestly from mournful eyes, over their long, drooping noses, giving the impression of being as dim-witted as they were quaint. Asrăthiel, however, had learned never to underestimate eldritch wights.

Numerous tall, star-filled windows pierced the walls, over-looking sharp valleys, and glittering precipices, and cupped mountain tarns.

'It is night once again,' the damsel said to herself in perplexity. 'How long did it take to reach here from the Wuthering Moors? Only a few hours? Or was it a whole day, and now night has fallen once more? Yet I do not recall the sun being in the sky during our journey. Perhaps the goblins enveloped us in their mist and blocked it out.' Her eldritch handmaidens could offer no solution to the mystery, though they were able to explain other matters.

'What happens during the day, when the sun shines fiercely?' she asked of them. 'Do its golden rays not shine through the glass? Does it not scald your masters?'

'An the briggit days, dem draps is closet,' the trow-wives said, 'aber sin oor maisters wisht dem draps kit open o'er the day, dem draw mist.'

Which Asrăthiel took to mean that on sunny days the window curtains – of finest silver mesh, with black lining - were drawn across the panes, but if the goblins wanted the curtains open in daytime, they would conjure mists to dilute the sun's radiance.

'Are they weathermasters, then, your masters?' she demanded inquisitively.

'Nay, ainly dem can draw mist.'

Which she understood to indicate that the goblins possessed the power to summon water vapours such as clouds, mists, fog, brume and haze, to diffuse the light of the sun, but they did not wield the brí.

'Does the touch of sunlight destroy them?'

'Nay. Dem can dure't, aber dem liken it not.'

'They can tolerate it, but they do not love it?'

'Aye, Guidlady.'

Some of the wights fluttered nimbly around their charge, weaving tiny gems through her hair; moonstones of shimmering iridescence, amethysts, and rock crystals. Others lurked in the shadows of these singular apartments, snooping, poking their long noses around corners, or nursing trow-babies wrapped in fringed shawls. They gave her nothing to eat, perhaps anticipating the promised banquet; but she felt no hunger and was content to drink water from the spout in the wall.

At length they brought a sumptuous gown of foam and cerulean moonlight to sheath the damsel in, but she had grown impatient with their skulking and fussing, and bade them go away and leave her in peace.

'Mun make thysel' fit for t'feast, Guidlady,' they twittered anxiously as she saw them off.

Ignoring their instructions she put aside the dress. She wondered how she could bring herself to dress up in finery and go to a party after the horrors she had witnessed so lately, the slaying of Conall Gearnach, good men falling beneath goblin swords while trying to save her. Again she puzzled, how was she to traffic with this enemy? And how would they traffic with her?

The cambric shift was flimsy, yet she did not feel at all cold in these airy chambers. As usual, her mother's gift of invulnerability kept her warm. Alone with her thoughts she took time to ponder whether Zaravaz had been giving veiled threats when he told her to hoard her pleas, but at length she concluded it was more of his banter and dismissed the notion. He had said, '*Fear not, I will not deal hard with you,*' but then again, goblin conceptions of gentle treatment might be quite at variance with human ideas. Yet, if they were going to do mischief to her, they would hardly be sending handmaidens to look after her, would they? Unless, of course, she were in some way being 'primed for the kill' like hand-fed livestock. Her opinions veered back and forth. If she were to be insulted, then surely it was unlikely the trows would be concerned about pulling her hair. It seemed certain they had been ordered to treat her well. Indeed she seemed to have some sort of dominion over them, for they acquiesced to her requests. Should that be so, maybe she could ask her captors, when she next saw them, if they would let her send a note to Avalloc informing him that she was well. It gave her much distress, knowing how he and the rest of her household must be suffering since she had been taken by the goblins.

Having thrown off her fears and feeling much refreshed after her ablutions, she was afflicted with a desire to discover more about this fascinating citadel; to explore it on her own, without being accompanied and directed by scores of shuffling trow-wives. If ever she found herself directly threatened, it would be useful to know something of the layout. The intentions of the goblin king were unclear. That he was perilous was a certainty; perhaps she would locate some hidden escape route to save her in extremity, should William's worst fears be realised.

Additionally, she felt reluctant to attend this goblin feast. If it were such a banquet as promised they would all be in attendance, the unseelie knights, while she, their plunder, would be alone and friendless in the crowd. More than that, she wished to put off meeting with a certain member of that eldritch chivalry, one so unsettling she refused even to think of his name. The mental turmoil that his presence engendered in her was so overwhelming that she did not know how to deal with it, and she wished to postpone such an encounter until she could make better sense of its inevitable effects. To her chagrin, all ideology became suspended whenever she set eyes on him. Always haunting her thoughts, jostling against concern and longing for the loved ones she had left behind, was an image of that compelling face with the black-lashed, violet eyes. To convince herself she was not longing to behold him again as soon as possible, she decided to deliberately make herself inaccessible, and late for the goblin banquet.

Another, more wayward element also motivated her behaviour. It vexed her that the goblin king disturbed her so absolutely, by his mere existence. To vex him in return was a form of revenge; furthermore, although she was loathe to admit it, some inexplicable inner perversity made her wish to discover what might occur if she provoked him, even if it were to wrath.

After she was sure the trows had dispersed, she tiptoed from the room on her bare feet. Taking note of her bearings she left her apartments and headed off through the citadel, exploring halls and galleries illumined by torch and moon and mirror, and great floor-to-ceiling windows teeming with brilliant galaxies. Instinctively she extended her awareness beyond the walls, sensing the familiar weather patterns of high altitude country; extremely low pressure and temperature, strong winds, mist gathering in the valleys. Outside, the air temperature had dropped below its dew point, and was becoming saturated. Cold air was flowing downhill, to settle in hollows and depressions. Lower summits were wreathed in thick, white vapours. Above the Winter snowline, where the citadel was situated, the tallest peaks were interfering with wind and cloud patterns, forcing currents to ascend or descend as they streamed over their higher summits. Gales were screaming through the upper crags at high speeds. Asrǎthiel speculated that the alpine winds could gust at more than twice that rate, driven against such steep heights. Far off, lightning flashed on the summit of Storth Cynros.

But the slim knives of the fast, honed winds could not penetrate the fastness of the Silver Goblins. Not so much as a breath or a whisper found a chink.

The complex of caverns and halls was extensive; part natural rock formations, part eldritch design. Outflung branches and adjuncts conceivably went running throughout the northern ranges for miles, connected by such underground passages as the damsel now traversed, or such steep overground roads such as she sighted from the windows, or dizzying bridges like those she stepped across; some with parapets, some without, obviously all unsafe for mortalkind.

Winding stairs with diamond balustrades she ascended, and the centre of each tread was indented by a gentle curve, worn by the passage of pedestrians over an immense time span. She passed thin, pouring water-curtains veiling archways, and narrow waterfalls hissing with white noise enough to flood one's skull, and fenestrations jutting out over wild rocky gorges. Along chiming quadrangles and galleries with floors of polished morion she tiptoed on her bare feet, and amongst fluted colonnades whose stanchions culminated in extravagantly sculpted capitals and volutes. On still lakes floated tall-prowed silver boats or gondolas, carved with grotesqueries.

Her explorations took her further, through crystal-ceilinged atria ornamented by masks with jewelled orbits. She sighed with wonder at pergolas and arbours entwined by silver metal serpents, whose eyes were perfect shards of white jade, royal azel and transparent topaz.

At length her wanderings led her to an elongated cavern, low-roofed and tubelike or cylindrical in shape, which looked to have been hollowed out by the natural action of water. Concave walls, floor and ceiling were lined with veins of silver and copper, and encrusted with gems. From her schoolroom studies the damsel knew that this was a pipe vein; a mineral-lined cavern left behind after the ebbing and draining of some ancient subterranean stream.

Near at hand, a cresset flamed in an ornate silver sconce. After taking possession of it she held it up and drew it near the wall to inspect the polished stones more closely. They flashed with the colours of rubies and sapphires, but were probably garnets and clusters of assorted spinels; there was the rose-red of balas ruby spinel, the purple-red of almandine spinel, the orange of rubicelle and the blue of sapphire spinel, as well as the green of chlorspinel. The lore of the underground had always interested the weather-mage. It was pleasing to find these pretty gems lavishly embedded in their native matrix.

As she moved to examine another section the flicker of an unlikely shadow on the opposite wall startled her. Hearing a low moan she turned around quickly, raising the cresset high, expecting to behold some stooping, limping trow that had been stalking her.

A human man was standing there.

The man cringed from the torchlight, squinting as if unaccustomed to brightness. Asrăthiel's sudden indrawn breath was a hiss that echoed in the tunnel's quietude.

'Who are you? What are you doing here?'

This was indeed an unexpected meeting. Aside from the two miserable hostages of Zaravaz, the damsel had presumed she was the only other human being in the citadel. This man was fair-haired, with watery eyes the bluish hue of diluted milk. Stringy was his visage, gaunt his slouching frame. His short-cropped hair was flaccid, greasy, and wispy. He might have lived through forty Winters, perhaps, but they must all have been exceptionally hard. Beneath the ingrained filth his flesh was as pale as the tentacles of a deep-sea cephalopod. He was dressed in dirty rags, and his hands – his hands! Those appendages were no longer anything partly human. Hard and blackened, they looked like charred hen's feet.

'Who are you?' Asrăthiel questioned again, somewhat in alarm.

'The light, the light,' murmured the man, lifting his elbow as if to ward off an attack. He stepped backwards.

Likewise Asrăthiel retreated with the torch, so that a veil of twilight shifted and settled around the fellow. 'Is that better? Tell me who you are.'

After a few abortive attempts to form words the man mumbled, 'I am hardly recalling my name.' He drooled, speaking disconnectedly as if he were half-asleep, or as if his tongue had thickened in his mouth, or he had forgotten how to talk. Asrăthiel thought his accent sounded familiar.

'Are you a captive of the goblins? Do they keep you imprisoned?'

'I cannot find the way out.'

The fellow's whining, unctuous tone made Asrăthiel's skin crawl. He was less a man than some horrid wormlike monster, a sham of a human being slithering in the nethermost regions of the underworld. She thought he might be partially blind; his eyes had a burned and weeping look. Stains of old blood dribbled down his cheeks.

'Are you human?' It was wise to make sure.

'Once I was.'

'If you once were, so you must still be, for it is not possible to change that.' At least, the damsel thought, I have always believed that it is not possible. Am I still human?

'I have not seen the sky for many years,' mumbled the creature with the hands of an aged corpse.

'Who brought you here? Was it the goblins?'

'No, a man. A vile man. He buried me alive.'

'But you survived!'

'Yes I survived,' said the pale fellow. 'And I delved. And I found something.'

He might be deluded. He might have dreamed he found some item of importance, though alighting on a stone. Still, in a place like this there must be plenty of secrets to stumble upon.

'What did you find? Bones? Jewels?'

'I found them.' Wrapping his skinny arms about his chest the man whimpered 'Cold. My ribs be a-cold.'

'Come near the flames. They will warm you.'

The fellow stole closer, timidly, and Asrăthiel extended the cresset towards him, but he made a sudden lunge and she threw it at his feet, recoiling in disgust. A pool of burning pitch spilled. The man squatted on the floor, warming his mummified hands at the guttering fires.

'If you try to harm me,' said the weathermage, 'I will hurl you along this tunnel and outside, right through one of the windows. Then you will feel the cold. I can do that - never doubt it, for I am powerful.' Dispensing threats was a form of self-defence. Ironically, Asrăthiel felt supremely vulnerable, alone with this creature in the jewelled pipe-tunnel, in the heart of an eldritch fastness.

The fellow moaned. 'What year is it?' he mewled.

She told him. Perhaps, she thought, he was simple-minded.

'How did you come to be in this pipe vein?' she asked. 'Have you been following me?'

'The hilltings came crowding from a doorway. Then you were coming after. Yes, I was following you. I have not seen you here before.' He added vaguely, 'You look like someone I once knew..'

Between pity and revulsion, the damsel was burning with curiosity. 'How came you here to this citadel? Tell me your story,' she invited, seating herself on the floor at a cautious distance. 'Tell me. Maybe I will be able to help you.'

The wretch's teeth chattered, he shuddered, he rocked back and forth and spoke syllables of nonsense. Despite all that, gradually he revealed his tale.

After the 'vile man', his persecutor, had buried him alive beneath the mountains, he had been faced with a choice; either stay where he was, alone in the darkness, or start moving and try to find something better. He chose to become a burrower. He told Asrăthiel that he had spent years digging in the ground and shifting rocks, breaking through from cavern to cavern, traversing from tunnel to tunnel, trying to find a way out of his lonely dungeon.

Years? she wondered, sceptically. What is there to eat down there in the darkness? Did you dine entirely on cave lice? Or is your story all delusion? But she nodded, and said nothing to interrupt his fascinating narrative.

He was lost, he said, for he did not know how to find an exit to the outer world. As he delved and blundered through the underground, he unintentionally disturbed certain manifestations that had been lying dormant. Some began to waken.

Working his way blindly along beneath the mountains, miraculously unscathed by their sudden flares of volcanic fires, improbably clinging to life despite lack of proper nourishment, the man with dead hands had accidentally tunnelled his way into a remote region where, unbeknownst to him, twenty-five thousand deadly and immortal warriors were entombed within a shell of bullion; a great cavern meticulously lined with gold leaf, and thickly veined with the precious ore.

'You found the Golden Caves!' exclaimed the damsel. 'Weathermasters imprisoned the wicked ones there when the Goblin Wars ended. They sealed them in for all time, that they might nevermore cause mischief to the human race.' Open-mouthed with incredulity she stared at the cowering creature. 'And you set them free!'

'Forgive me, lady!' snivelled the misery, grovelling. 'How could I be knowing? I was digging. I sought only my own freedom.'

'Go on with your recital,' Asrăthiel said. She found it difficult to tolerate this woeful toady, yet at the same time she sympathised with his plight.

'It was the Silver Goblins there, but the knowledge was not at me,' repeated the fellow self-pityingly. 'I was only pushing big rocks, and scraping gravel, and hand-scratching. And then I shifted a stone, and punched a hole, and the terrible light was spearing through.'

'What light?'

'A shining of silver - the power of the goblins maybe, caged all those centuries. And I was being drawn to the source of it, and I squeezed right into the cave. Then they seized hold of me.' The man squeezed shut his eyes, as if trying to shut out a sight too horrific to behold. He refused to continue his tale until Asrăthiel persuaded him with much coaxing. Eventually, little by little, it was revealed in incoherent fragments, which the damsel pieced together.

It had been impossible for the captive goblins to slide themselves through the narrow aperture created by the man they had lured to their aid. They would necessarily have come into contact with the gold in the surrounding matrix. Persuading the burrower with threats, they forced him to move the gold-veined rocks that they themselves and their kobolds could not touch. In terror, he obeyed. Being a weakling, he was only able to widen the gap by degrees, while the imprisoned horde chafed impatiently, unable to hasten the process but tormenting their thrall whenever he slowed. It took the labourer weeks to widen the breach enough for goblins to pass through without brushing against the gold that would have seared them.

In the meantime hosts of kobolds began to converge on the golden dungeons from the deepest mines of the mountains where they had bided quiescent; some eldritch sense had informed them the instant their masters gained their liberty, and they swarmed in their thousands to greet them.

The fair-haired man had been unable to find his way in the underworld, but the goblins knew their location exactly. Swiftly they passed through the passageways that honeycombed the Northern Ramparts, dragging the burrower with them, until they came to the extensive network of underground chambers where their daemon horses were housed. The steeds languished in a kind of torpid trance, deprived of their symbiotic partners; there had been no need to gild the trollhäst caves, for once the knights were locked away the creatures had no will to escape.

As his captors blasted the rock with jolts of unseelie energy to get at their steeds, the burrower, never permitted to rest, was put to work clearing away rubble. After the trollhästen had been freed, the unseelie warriors ordered their kobold slaves to unlock and set to rights their long-abandoned mountain halls, for at that time few trows, or 'hilltings' as the storyteller called them - the willing servants of goblins - haunted the Northern Ramparts. While order was being restored in Sølvetårn, Zauberin presided over a goblin moot.

'Zauberin, the first lieutenant?' Asrăthiel broke in. 'What of the goblin king? Why did he not conduct the moot?'

'That one was not with them then,' the pallid man replied. 'He was never enclosed in the cavern of gold. It was later that he came.' He hugged his knees to his scrawny chest as if recollecting an old terror.

'Then where was he?'

'The knowledge is not at me.'

That particular phrase, the knowledge is not at me, kept jolting a distant memory. Someone Asrăthiel had once known had occasionally employed that expression, but she could not call to mind who it had been. 'Go on,' she prompted her informant, whereupon he told her that initially, the goblins sent kobold spies into the world, to find out what had been happening since they had been incarcerated. While biding their time they began to conduct incursions into the northern villages - Silverton and surrounds – commencing their spate of nocturnal assassinations. Ultimately they set forth on the path of war. After their first full-scale assault on the human armies at the Wuthering Moors their triumph reached a new peak when their king returned.

The fair-haired man knew little else.

'That is the end of my tale,' he said. 'They have no further use for me, and have discarded me, but I am in their power now.' He began to babble. 'The blue gnomes cut off my hair when I was captured. Why should they do such a thing? I cannot understand it! Fain would I be escaping from this place but I cannot leave through their portals, for I fear the kobold sentinels. All I do is go wandering through their halls, avoiding them whenever I can.'

And a wasted, pallid terrified thing you are, thought Asrăthiel, not without compassion, as she endured his plaints. She found several as aspects of his narrative perplexing, and quizzed him to find answers.

'How could you dig amongst rocks without any mining equipment? You would have torn your own flesh apart and cracked your bones.'

'I heal again and again.'

But you heal awry, she thought.

'How long is it since you were buried alive?'

'Many years.'

'Methinks you have lost track of time! It is impossible for mortal men to survive for years without sunlight and nourishment. Under durance, time seems to stretch; perhaps that is what has happened. You are mistaken.' Just then, it came to Asrăthiel that her own mother had sometimes used that unusual phrase, 'the knowledge is not at me' - an expression favoured by subjects of Slievmordhu. Indeed, his accent was of the southern realm.

'I am not mistaken, lady. The knowledge is at me of how long it has been. It was the year 3472 when that base weathermaster entombed me.'

'Weathermaster? What weathermaster?' Asrăthiel shot back.

A silent bell was ringing.

'The one who tried to cheat me of my dues. He never succeeded, you know.'

'What was his name?'

'That is one thing I shall never be forgetting. His name was Stormbringer.' The knave peered at the damsel from rheumy optics. 'Your eyes are blue,' he said. 'Very blue.'

Asrăthiel felt a throb of heat surging to her temples as she stood up. 'By rain and deadly thunder,' she said enunciating every word slowly and clearly, 'I know who you are. Your name, may it be blasted to oblivion, is Fionnbar Aonarán.'

As a child at her father's knee she had learned the history of this person. The greatest calamities that had fallen upon her family were the fault of him and his murderous half-sister. He had drunk of the water of immortality, just as her own father had done; yet he had stolen the draught. His vindictive sister, Fionnuala, had tried to slay Asrăthiel's mother and almost succeeded. That attempt had resulted in Jewel's sleep without waking.

This wasted, pallid, terrified thing was in fact the bane of her parents. Knowing this, the damsel despised him with indescribable rancour, her revulsion even now mingling with pity. One thing was certain; she could not endure his presence.

'Ah yes, that is my name, enlightened lady!' he cried. 'Prithee do not be vexed with me, for you are the first mortal woman I have set eyes on this many a year! Besides myself, the only other human creature I have seen inside this place is - '

But already Asrăthiel was walking away, leaving the detested Aonarán kneeling alone on the floor beside the half-extinguished cresset. He rose and began to trail after her, but at that moment a covey of trow-wives, some sniffing at the floor like bloodhounds, entered the pipe vein and spied their wayward charge. They fluttered to surround her, uttering bird-like cries. Descending on her like a flock of grey doves, they began to shepherd her back to her chambers, and she was glad enough to go. Scorn and rage warred in her breast. Aonarán stumbled in her wake, calling out incoherently. Without pausing in her step the damsel snapped at the wights, 'Get rid of that man!' Whereupon some of them produced twig brooms and commenced to advance on him, sweeping vigorously and ferociously with shouts of 'Shoo! Shoo!' until he slunk away.

'Dat's name is Toadstone,' the trow-wives told her.

'If I hold any sway in this place,' declared Asrăthiel, shaking with shock and indignation. 'which possibly I do, judging by the finery you are showering upon me, I'll not have him near me.'

The small womenlike creatures nodded their unlovely heads and gazed dismally up at the damsel. At that moment she longed for a close friend in whom she could confide. These little wights were gentle and nurturing, in their way, but their culture was alien to her own; there was much about their eldritch mores she could not fathom. She missed her parents and her grandfather, her aunt Galiene, Ryence Darglistel, and the wise weathermasters whose lives had been so treacherously cut short by the contemptible Uabhar. She missed William, her maid Linnet, Giles the butler, and even Mistress Draycott Parslow. Sorely she missed the companionship of the wilful Crowthistle, who could unravel mysteries, and provoke laughter, and make her forget she was set apart. Pining for those whom she loved, cursing her exile, she descended into a melancholy mood. To be divided from all of them was heartbreaking. It would be her priority to try to send a message to family and friends as soon as possible, reassuring them that she was secure and well. While the little trow-wives dressed her, she wept as immortal human beings must weep; without shedding tears.

A mirror revealed her reflection; her dress of cerulean moonlight was trimmed with sapphires and transparent tourmalines. The boned bodice closely fitted her waist. Voluminous sleeves dripped with a lather of lace, and traceries of blue zircons echoed the colour of her eyes.

The curtains of Asrăthiel's rooms had been drawn shut, obscuring any glimpse of the outside world. Briefly, the damsel allowed her weather senses to probe past the walls. They informed her that the outside temperature was rising, by which she deduced that a new day had dawned.

A new day! Asrăthiel fell to wondering what doom this dawn would bring her, which led her to speculate on what was in store for her fellow captives, Uabhar and Virosus. They had been borne off by kobolds – and she had learned enough about the bluish skinned imps to know they were as merciless as machines. Her instinctive sympathy for the two men vaporised as soon as she recalled their crimes, as witnessed and recounted by the beggar Cat Soup. Between them the king and the druid had slain her weathermaster kindred. Pity gave way to antipathy.

Why did the goblins choose the three of us as their tithe? She pondered. What are the similarities between a weathermage, a druid and a king? We are all persons of influence, to be sure; but there the resemblances end, or at least I hope so. I trust I have nothing else in common with those power-mad, barbarous, loveless betrayers.

As she brooded, the final words of Aonarán suddenly registered in her consciousness: Besides myself, the only other human creature inside this place... Her curiosity greatly piqued, she wondered who the other human being could be. Had Aonarán perhaps spied the wretched king, or the druid? Or was he talking about someone else, possibly someone who had existed for longer in this citadel? I had believed myself to be unique in this eldritch haunt, but it is evidently crawling with people! In any event, at last count, five, including Uabhar and the druid.

'Who is the other mortal being in this citadel?' she asked the trow-wives but they adjusted her gown or swept the floor with besom brooms, and some continued rocking their babies. One murmured, 'Dere be many mortal creatures here. Dey be meeylen an worms an sneeuane ushtey and creeping crooagen.'

'I was not referring to insects.' Placing her hand on the bony, bulbous elbow of the wight who had spoken Asrăthiel said, 'What is your name?'

'I hight Hulda,' said the trow-wife.

'Hulda, tell me what mortal man dwells here, besides Toad-stone and the two new prisoners.' *If they are still alive*, she amended privately.

'Dat's Fehlimy macDall,' said the wight.

Asrăthiel had never heard the name. 'How came he here?'

'Trows stole dem.'

Stealing people or other animals was one traditional practice of trow-folk that Asrăthiel's kindred abhorred. In many other ways the wights were innocuous enough, but on rare occasions they would abduct human beings or farm animals, leaving a crude effigy, or trow-stock in place of the victim. Stolen humans would become servants to the trows, caught in their twilight realm and unable to return home.

'It is wrong to steal people,' Asrăthiel said, appreciating that such a statement, while it would seem a glaring truism amongst her own kindred, would be unlikely to dent the moral code of the Grey Neighbours. 'You must release this macDall immediately and let him go back to his family.'

'Guidlady, he'm be our servant noo.'

Before Asrăthiel could begin an argument, Hulda cried, 'Da banquet!' and the wights gathered around, mildly urging Asrăthiel to hurry to the feast.

'M'lady'm tarrying too lang!' they squeaked to each other. Vowing to herself that she would not let the matter rest, the damsel allowed them to guide her through the exquisite corridors and lofty caverns, then along a majestic enfilade. A shimmering water curtain drew back and she passed through an archway, entering the great hall.

Vast was this refectory; it seemed the size of a palace. So remote were its boundaries that they were lost to sight. Composed of a series of interlocking chambers, it accommodated seats for many thousands. The ceilings soared more than sixty feet high, criss-crossed by ribbed fan vaults, as if supported on the wings of stone dragons. Hundreds of silver chandeliers depended from the rafters on long chains, each a bonfire of candles. Thin columns of sapphire flame blazed up from flagstones of polished schorl, reaching as high as the roof; slender spirals of water spilled down quartz poles from ceiling to floor. The walls were adorned with carvings of stars and moons, tapestries depicting vistas of fiery mountains, marble reliefs portraying racing herds of trollhästen, flocks of owls, crows, ravens and other beasts, and banners broidered with sinuous inter-weavings of leaves, vines, and trees. In alcoves and porticoes, free-standing sculptures represented eldritch knights with bows and arrows, swords, and spears, or kobolds wielding picks and shovels. No repeated, balanced or geometric patterns were to be found; the lopsidedness the goblins favoured in their costume was also evident in their decoration. Asrăthiel suspected that they preferred skewedness of design because it was a novelty, the physical features of their own bodies being so flawlessly proportioned, so exactly symmetrical.

Long tables ran down the length of the main chamber, arrayed with gleaming vessels and cutlery all made of solid silver; cups, spoons, knives, ladles, wine vessels, tureens, jugs, platters, candle-sticks, and centrepieces. Each piece was decoratively chased, engraved, granulated or filigreed. The chairs pulled up to these boards were fashioned from pale driftwood and inlaid with a form of volcanic glass known as snowflake, or flowering obsidian, black with white inclusions. To one side of the chamber's upper end the floor was clear of furniture, conceivably for dancing, or wrestling, or other entertainments.

Goblin knights in outlandish attire crowded the hall. It came to Asrăthiel yet again that they were like no race she had ever seen before; always brilliant, beguiling and deceptive, perhaps in some ways ludicrous in the eyes of mankind, somewhat insane, yet possessing such ineffable beauty, grace and style that to set eyes on them was to be both tormented and transported. Trows, both male and female were serving food and drinks, but there was no sign of any goblin women. Transiently, the damsel wondered where they were – but for now there was too much to see, too much to try to understand, to puzzle over it.

The arch-necked trollhästen wandered about freely, nimbly, with no hint of clumsiness, never leaving muck or jostling the furniture; apparently they were guests also. Their hides resembled rippling metallic pewter, their manes and tails were the colour of sunlight pouring through green stained glass. Knights and daemon horses mingled companionably, at times sharing the same wide-bowled cup. Horned eagle owls perched high upon the chandeliers and candelabra, or on architraves, projecting sconces or banner poles, or the parapets of overhanging galleries.

All eyes turned upon Asrăthiel as she entered; she could feel it without needing to look. What were they thinking, the warriors of unseelie? Did they judge her a lamb in a flock of wolves? A leprous weed in a flower garden? The trow-wives' panic had proved unnecessary; the dining had not yet commenced, though savoury fragrances hinted of delicious fare undergoing preparation somewhere in the wings. Asrăthiel was reminded that she had eaten nothing since twilight the previous day, but she felt no weakness or hunger. For immortal beings, as she had learned, food was a pleasure rather than a necessity.

Fleetingly she recalled the ancient tale of her ancestor, Tierney A'Connacht, who had ventured into a sorcerer's domain to rescue his sweetheart. A prohibition had been laid upon him before this undertaking: He who wishes to succeed must neither eat nor drink of anything he finds in those domains, no matter what his hunger or thirst may be – for if he does, he will fall under the power of the sorcerer and maybe forfeit his life. The damsel had heard stories, too, of otherworldly realms in which it was perilous for mortal beings to partake of the fare, lest they be trapped there forever.

'If I eat your food, will some enchantment befall me?' she asked the nearest trow.

'Nae, my lady,' replied the creature, and Asrăthiel was satisfied with this answer.

A riot of kobolds could be glimpsed through a portal, occupying their own side-chamber, which was smoky and reeked of garlic. They were capering about and swallowing beer in great quantity, their bluish faces painted with simple geometric designs, in gold-coloured or orange pigment. Broken drinking vessels lay here and there. Segregation was clearly the solution to their boisterousness; serious trouble must undoubtedly have broken out had the heedless and smelly imps begun cavorting amongst the elegantly disposed tables of the goblins. On closer acquaintance Asrăthiel noted that there were two breeds of kobold – a larger variety, and a lesser. Both types wore peasant-style garments, marked here and there with an equal-armed cross.

As a covey of waist-high trows ushered Asrăthiel to her chair at the high table, she scanned the surrounds. They were all present, she judged; all the most eminent goblin knights, save for one. She seated herself, arranging the shimmering folds of her dress, pretending not to wonder where he might be. Other knights attended her, and her gaze wandered over their fantastic costumes, beginning with one who introduced himself as Fifth Lieutenant Zaldivar, whose baldric and belt hung with softly ringing wafer-thin discs of beaten silver engraved with signs or runes. His comely visage was framed by the upstanding, thick furry collar of his cloak, and partially obscured by a half-mask of gleaming silver, modelled like face of a horned eagle owl. Fourth Lieutenant Zande wore garments of dull and glimmering scales, made from the naturally sloughed skins of snakes which, he explained, had been toughened by certain processes invented by the lesser kobolds. His baldric was decorated with teeth, or fangs, and a thin band of chased silver encircled his head.

They conversed with one another in their own tongue, but courteously addressed their human visitor in her own language; still, it was daunting to be amongst them. Asrăthiel felt nervous, unsure of how to behave or what to say – was she a guest, part of a valuable ransom or a despised outsider? - and she was constantly on the lookout for him, jumping at the entrance of every newcomer to the hall. Her eyes darted every which way in an effort to spy him, though she tried to appear as if indifferent to the matter of whomsoever presented themselves or abstained from the banquet.

After a while it became apparent that the goblin knights were treating her like any invited dinner guest, and she supposed, therefore, that they expected her to act like one.

To ease the tension and feign confidence she decided to attempt conversation. Turning to Zaldivar she said, 'You wear much leather. Does it come from the hide of trolls?'

'To your eyes, Lady Sioctíne,' the knight replied, 'it may seem that we cover ourselves with fur, feathers, the scales of reptiles and what have you, yet they are not actual hides and plumage. Those ornaments are invented by kobolds, from coal tar synthetics, or else they are dried plants and fungi and fossils that resemble the wrappings of animals. What you imagine to be leather is in fact *svartlap,* a fungus common in these regions. Only creatures of your own race wrap themselves in the slowly rotting remains of deceased creatures, and the siofra also, who bedeck themselves in the sloughed carapaces of beetles and the deserted cocoons of moths. We scorn the practice.'

'In that respect I am entirely in accord with you!' cried Asrăthiel.

The culture of goblinkind was baffling. On one hand they revelled in killing and torment, on the other they eschewed, apparently on ethical grounds, the use of materials derived from the suffering and extermination of animals.

'Alas, the coat I wore on the battlefield is as riddled with holes as a sea sponge,' said Zaldivar. 'The kobolds made me a new one this very night, for your rain of gold leaf made a ruin of the old.'

He did not seem resentful. Asrăthiel took courage from that.

'Strange that a toadstool-flap should be dissolved by the touch of that metal,' she observed.

'Only when we wear it,' he answered. 'Gold burns right through the stuff, to our flesh.'

'Then you are injured,' the damsel said warily. Surely this knight must carry a grudge against her for her part in his wounding.

'I was burned, but not injured.' At her enquiring glance Zaldivar explained, 'You are perhaps thinking we heal quickly, Lady Sioctíne. Not so, for we are never scathed in the first instance. The touch of gold fragments affords us matchless agony and burns our garments, but does not actually mar our flesh. It is only if we come into contact with great quantity of the metal, or for a prolonged period, that it is lethal to us.' After a moment's pondering he subjoined, 'As is the ensorcelled gold of your blade, Lady Sioctíne.'

A troupe of grey-robed wights rushed past bearing flagons, and Asrăthiel seized on the distraction as an excuse to change the subject.

'These trows and kobolds about the place,' said the damsel, 'they are servants and slaves to you of their own will, are they not?'

Zande said, 'Even so. It is not necessary for us to exert so much as a finger.'

'If humankind were waited upon so zealously,' commented Asrăthiel, who had marked the sedulous solicitude of the attendants, 'they would scarcely need to move, except to chew their food and breathe.'

'But human things,' said Zaldivar, 'would wither, their sinews turning to paper, if they ceased activity; whereas my kind remain in perfect fettle whether we move about or spend our days and nights in uttermost sloth.'

'The Grey Neighbours are permitted to wait upon you, yet you separate yourselves from the kobolds,' the weathermage observed.

'We do not permit the garlic-stinking beer-swillers to be near us when we dine,' Zande replied. 'It is as much for their benefit as for ours. They are allergic to salt as well as gold. We enjoy our food salted.'

'But I have seen them wear gold war paint into battle!' said the damsel.

'Their traditional daubings are not gold, Lady Sioctíne. They use arsenic trisulphide, which artists call 'orpiment', or 'golden paint'. Greater kobolds, the bigger, more fearsome kind who fight beside us as common foot soldiers, originally began brushing it on their bodies in an attempt to bluff their foes into thinking they could tolerate the touch of gold. We do not brook orpiment, ourselves, for it is a disagreeable colour, and blackens any other paint laid over it.'

'Greater kobolds, you call them?' Asrăthiel said. 'What of the others, those who are smaller in stature and paint themselves orange?'

'Of the two species, the greater and the lesser, there is more arsenic in the constituents of the greater. They are the warrior caste, who wear erythrite armour and decorate themselves with orpiment. Lesser kobolds, diligent metalworkers and skilled craftsmen, are not so ferocious. They are inquisitive about all things. Indeed, I am told they snipped some hairs from the man called Aonarán, so that they might perform experiments on human tissue. On occasion they splash themselves with the pigment called realgar, arsenic monosulphide, which occurs in crystals, crusts and earths of that vivid orange shade. Both orpiment and realgar are highly poisonous to mortalkind. I would earlier have recommended that you keep your distance from them if you valued your existence, except that it appears you are not as perishable as your kindred.'

How much do they know about me? Asrăthiel wondered. *Are they aware of the ways in which I am unlike other human beings? Or does this Zande merely refer to my skill as a swordswoman? King Thorgild was certain that the trollhästen never permitted mortal persons to ride them, yet a daemon steed bore me to Sølvetårn on its back. Is it possible that the daemon horses sense my immunity to death? If so, have they passed this knowledge to the goblins?*

'Your assistants are numerous,' she said aloud.

'Even so! For every goblin there exist at least three hundred kobold thralls. They are our principal labourers and foot soldiers. Our retainers and entertainers include mining wights and spinners, whose skills are highly specialised, and water-girls, whose talents lie in other directions entirely, but whose chief accomplishments are luring human beings to death by drowning. Would you like some *peearen ayns lavander*, or crystallized *ooyl villish?*' Zande indicated a dish piled with glittering pinkish-orange crescents.

As she declined the offer, Asrăthiel could hardly believe that these knights should be making small talk with her without a trace of rancour, as if they were all attending a most genteel garden party at some stately mansion, when not so long ago they had been trying to batter each other's brains out. The unpredictability of eldritch beings was unnerving, to anyone accustomed to the ways of humankind.

'You are most instructive, sir.' Surveying the range of pre-dinner delicacies on the table, Asrăthiel added, 'Where does all this food come from? Do you steal it?'

'Fie, noble guest!' said Zaldivar, with such an appearance of affront that the damsel had to stifle a smile, struck by the contrasts in the lawlessness of goblinkind. 'It is impossible to steal from someone who owns nothing,' the knight expounded. 'Human beings delude themselves, claiming that land belongs to them and that things that grow thereon are theirs, but like all creatures they have no right to possess anything, save for their own bodies. We do not steal. Sometimes, however, we take. And at other times we obtain fruits and salads for our gustatory pleasure from our gardens here in the mountains, revived since we arose from the golden tombs.'

'How can crops grow in the mountains?'

Asrăthiel's dinner companion speared a piece of glazed fruit with the point of a quaint-handled knife. 'There is no lack of nourishing soil here, Lady Sioctíne; after all, this is a volcanic region, rich with nutrients from beneath the world's crust. Nor is there any shortage of sunlight or water. There is only a dearth of heat and protection from the wind, both of which our gardens require. When first Sølvetårn was built, our kobold workers constructed huge edifices of fine, strong crystal in certain locations. They are sturdy enough to withstand wind and snow and hail, reinforced with gramarye, and heated by thermal springs that well from plutonic sources many miles below. Much of our fare grows in those hothouses.'

The damsel sipped wine from a silver goblet delicately engraved with stems of ivy, but she scarcely tasted the liquor. Expecting every moment that Zaravaz might walk into the hall, she found it hard to sit still. Her ploy to needle him had fallen in ruins; it was he who was late for the banquet. He was the one for whom they all waited; the feast would not begin without him.

At long last he appeared, clothed in the splendour of night, and of course he was beautiful beyond all measure. The goblin knights, the trows, the kobolds, all rose to their feet and bowed. Their king entered, striding with a slight swagger, while the trollhästen tossed their gaseous manes and dipped their narrow heads.

When Zaravaz sat down beside her, Asrăthiel lost any vestige of appetite.

'Good morning,' he said. The look he gave her was measuring, interested, predatory. It was a glance of pure desire.

She stammered a reply, her composure in ruins, every premeditated thought flying apart like splinters from a smashed pane.

Then the banquet began in earnest, as hobbling processions of trows, bent double, began to carry in on their shoulders huge platters covered with high domes of silver.

'What do you suppose goblins eat?' Zaravaz asked, leaning back in his chair. 'Worms? Beetles? Bark?'

All around them, knights were turning their attention to their viands, falling to their repast. At whiles they talked or laughed amongst themselves for, as Asrăthiel had observed, they were a blithesome lot, as ready to laugh as to kill.

'I had not considered,' Asrăthiel said feebly.

'Allow me to introduce you to some goblin dishes. This one,' said Zaravaz, indicating a fusion of spices and dainties freshly uncovered before them, is called 'The Druid Fainted'. It is named because of what happened when the dish was first served to a sage of the Sanctorum, who swooned with delight at the deliciousness of it.'

'O, fortunate druid,' said Asrăthiel politely, 'to taste the food of the goblins.'

'Not really,' said Zaravaz. 'Later, Skagi cut off his hands and feet.'

'Permit me to pass over that dish.'

'Do not be too hasty! You should try it, it will please you.'

'Gramercie, but I shall forbear. What is this next one called?'

"As if to Celebrate, I Discovered a Mountain Blooming with Red Flowers'.'

'Inventive titles, to be sure.'

'Our cooks are as ingenious with their recipes as they are with the appellations.' The goblin king scooped up a silver spoonful. 'May I tempt you?'

He showed no sign of handing over the spoon so, hesitantly, Asrăthiel opened her mouth a little. With utmost gentleness he placed the morsel on her tongue. The food was indeed agreeable to the senses in every way, but Asrăthiel would have enjoyed it more had the network of her nerves not lately disintegrated. After swallowing the mouthful she said, 'Luscious, to be sure. I have never tasted anything so palatable.' A sudden concern struck her, and she added, 'Was it made from the flesh of some creature?'

'We eat no flesh.'

This statement further surprised the damsel. The goblins were warlike, and all the mortal soldiers she had ever known relished flesh, gorging themselves on roasted haunches; she had assumed that all warriors were fond of meat.

'We eat no corpse material, nor do we clothe ourselves in it,' Zaravaz continued.

Trow servitors placed more salvers before the goblin king, bowed, and backed away.

'This rich medley,' he said courteously, waving a hand at the provender, 'is known as 'Here is a Lush Situation'. Over there, a tray of rapturous confections called 'So You Think I'm Crazy'. For sweetness, I recommend this blancmange, 'Milking Roses for Honey', while if you crave heat, I would advocate 'The Passion for Pepper Burns Like a Flame of Love'.' As he described the latter dish, he bestowed a contemplative glance upon his dining partner. Soft, cascading tendrils of darkness framed the taut lines of his face and swung across his shoulders.

Asrăthiel tried to eat, but the action seemed extraordinarily difficult and she soon faltered.

The meal proceeded, twenty-seven courses being offered. The guest of honour, as she was deemed, could not eat more than a few bites, and as for the flavours, she could scarcely recall them, though she estimated they had probably been superb. Zaravaz, too, ate sparingly. After most of the dishes had been cleared away the knights remained in their seats drinking, laughing and jesting in the greatest conviviality.

Invariably jittery in the presence of the goblin king, the weathermage improvised, with awkward formality, 'Two of your captains introduced themselves to me just now. I would fain meet the rest.'

That was true, because the lieutenants with whom she had spoken had proved informative, and she wished to learn as much as possible about Sølvetårn and the Silver Goblins. Not to mention their leader. . .

'I seek only to please, of course,' Zaravaz said with exaggerated politeness. (What colour was madness? Perhaps violet, like his eyes.) Beckoning his ten most eminent lieutenants one by one, the goblin king bade them identify themselves to Asrăthiel.

Aachionard Zauberin was already known to her; he was the knight with the debouched air, who often mixed goblin language into his speech.

'No doubt, Lady Sword, you heard us sing out our battle cry when we stooped to slay,' said Zauberin, bowing ostentatiously.

'A jeering cry it seemed to me,' Asrăthiel replied steadily, refusing to be intimidated by references to battlefield carnage, so fresh and harrowing in her mind.

'*Paag dty uillin!*' the knight repeated. 'Indeed it is a jeering cry as you guess, Sioctíne, and we say it to your brethren as they die. It means 'kiss your elbow', which a human being can only do if dismembered or decapitated. Notably, '*uillin*' also signifies 'angle', so the phrase carries a cruder meaning of 'kiss your -''

'Enough,' said Zaravaz, holding up his hand in a warning gesture. He added something in the goblin language, after which Zauberin bowed his liege, murmured, 'Your pardon,' in Asrăthiel's direction, and moved away. The damsel knew him for a truly hostile enemy.

She recognised the next knight, Zwist, from the battlefield. He was wearing an ornamental cuirass and vambraces of black and silver armour, over resilient gear of swarthy eukaryotic material, sheared and stitched by kobold slaves. His velvet cap was decorated with flamboyant plumes.

'Second Lieutenant Zwist, at your service Lady,' said the tall warrior, bowing over her hand.

'I recall you tried to kill me recently,' she said sweetly.

'Ah, I was but bandying blows,' he replied with disarming amiability.

'I thought Zerstör was Second Lieutenant.'

'Conall Gearnach slew him yestereve.'

Yestereve! It seemed years ago. Or was 'yestereve' just a broad term goblins used to indicate the past? She wondered whether the knights grieved for their fallen comrade. Evidently not. Yet again, she felt perplexed by their moral attitudes.

The black bell sleeves of one named Third Lieutenant Zaillian were slashed to show the silver lining, yet he looked not at all the dandy. His belt was a chain of heavy silver links, and about his neck he wore a string of curved thorns, or fake claws. Like his comrades, he had on boots that flared from the top of the knee, reaching almost to mid-thigh. Other officers presented themselves in order of rank: Zuleide and Zamakh, Zinke, Zähe and Tenth Lieutenant Zangezur.

All the while Asrǎthiel sensed Zaravaz observing her, and indeed she was watching him, though feigning indifference. When his deputies had dispersed she turned ostentatiously to the goblin king, as if suddenly reminded of his presence.

'Zerstör was slain by Fallowblade,' she said. 'The golden sword is powerful indeed, despite having been wrought by mere human-kind.' Her statement was something of a challenge, of this she was aware. His proximity made her so restless that she felt inclined to goad him a little, as a form of retribution.

Her dinner companion said, continuing to look at her while toying with a half-empty chalice that stood on the table, 'You are hard to beat when you are wielding him, I admit.'

'Perhaps,' she said, daring to push the challenge a step further, 'I might defeat even you, with Fallowblade. Do you think it would be possible for me to slay you in battle?'

Zaravaz studied her amusedly. 'I doubt it.' Then, glancing down at the chalice he added with an intriguing smile, 'Although I have no doubt at all that you would gift me with the little death, were we to tangle.'

'What is 'the little death'?' she inquired, but he merely called for more wine. His hair and garments moved as if lifted by a breeze, even when the air was still, such was the play of eldritch forces about him.

Deep notes of music commenced to resonate from the walls. Upon a balcony, seventeen kobolds were plucking the strings of a giant earth-harp whose vertical cords, thirty-five yards long, passed through scissions in floor and ceiling, their bases rooted in the level below, their tips fastened in the storey above.

'I have a boon to ask of you,' said Asrăthiel as the melody, low and harmonious, pervaded the hall.

'Ask away,' said Zaravaz, resting an elbow on the table and idly flicking cherries into a bowl. 'I cannot guarantee it will be granted.'

'I would fain send a message to my kindred, assuring them that I am safe and well.'

He raised an eyebrow. 'You have my consent. Hulda shall arrange it.'

'I am grateful. And a second petition.'

'Entreat me.'

'The trows of this citadel have a human servant named Fedl-amid macDall. Will you give him freedom?'

'I care not whether he stays or goes. There is one who cares greatly – that is Queen Saibh, who dwells in Cathair Rua. He was once her servant. Perhaps more.'

'Since you care not, prithee tell the trows to release him.'

'If it pleases you, I shall do it. Hold still!' Zaravaz emphasized his unexpected instruction with a raised index finger. Asrăthiel complied, though baffled. He extended his arm and lightly plucked a stray owl's feather from her hair, where it had lodged and become entangled. After showing it to her, he cast it away.

'Gramercie,' she murmured, wondering why the hall was all at once so stiflingly hot. Presently she took courage and said, 'And another request.'

'Another!' You presume on my good nature.' Zaravaz smiled enigmatically.

'The other man who dwells here, Fionnbar Aonarán, whom the trows call 'Toadstone'. Why do you keep him?'

'We do not. He has served his purpose but lingers of his own device. He was useful, once. For months before their release my *graihyn* in the golden tombs had been detecting his slow approach, hearing it through thicknesses of rock. His noises had disturbed them from their prolonged ennui, so they commenced calling to him. He answered. Having made him their prisoner, they used him to effect their escape. If he is here still it is because he chooses to tarry, or has not found a way to leave.'

'I hardly think he would choose to remain amongst you. Your knights tormented him, I believe. In any case, I wish I might never again encounter him.'

'Have you met him? Has he vexed you?'

'Both.'

'I shall give him over to my kobolds to play with as they wish. Skagi keeps a very pliant whip for just such a purpose. Her name is Lady Thrash, and with her barbed cords she does make men sing.'

'You are cruel! He is a detestable man but I abhor the torment of any helpless creature.'

'Then we concur, for my lieutenants and I prefer to meet adversaries in clean battle, and they bearing weapons, or at the chase, and they running free. We are not interested in flogging unarmed men in fetters. That is more the kobold way.'

'Do not give him to the kobolds.'

'Now, Daughter of Rowan Green, will you make us quarrel on this matter? I would let my flaieen pursue their interests.'

Noting her expression of dismay, he relented. 'But if you insist, the wretch shall be thrown out of the citadel. Behold how I indulge you!'

'Indulge me again,' she said, realising it was a flirtatious remark but unable to stop herself.

Zaravaz sat up and left off his leisurely employment with the cherries.

'What else would you have of me?' he said softly, 'now that you have rid my halls of human men?'

After a moment she said, 'Will you give me my own freedom?'

'You are free.'

'Freedom to leave Sølvetårn.'

A bleak dreariness, like the tolling of a heavy bell, seemed to blast through the hall. The music paused, a hush settled on the crowd, and the goblin knights looked up, paying heed to their king.

Zaravaz said silkily, 'Sweet damsel, naturally you have my leave to depart at any time. Never have I sought to hold you against your will. Only bear in mind the terms of our withdrawal from the four kingdoms. Should you sunder your part of the contract and return to your kindred, the covenant will be rendered invalid. We shall ride down from the mountains and sweep through your realms like scythes through a cornfield, cutting down every man, woman and child.'

Inwardly, Asrǎthiel railed against the barbarity of goblinkind. Zaravaz waited, while she strove to conceal her vexation. She was unsuccessful. 'You would slay innocent children?' she burst out. 'Then I name you wicked beyond redemption.'

'Perhaps you are naive enough to think your mortal kindred are too virtuous to do the same, or perhaps you wish to enjoy your rosy delusions. Women, children, the sick, the aged, the helpless – those would merely find themselves enveloped in mists which caused them to fall asleep; there would be no pain, they would know naught about it. 'Twould be a better fate than many of your own kind have been wont to apportion, who batter wives and brats, or expose unwanted infants to die on open hillsides. There is nothing we would stoop to, that humanity would not stoop lower.'

At the mention of death in the mists a gut-wrenching vision of the councillors of Ellenhall falling asleep amidst the smoke of the druid's fires formed for an instant in Asrăthiel's mind. Nevertheless she had to concede that this, at least, showed a glimmer of mercy on the part of the goblins.

'It has apparently escaped you,' said Zaravaz, 'the history of the men my *graihyn* have so far slain. All your dead northern villagers were wagoners, butchers, fishers, hunters, fur trappers, tanners, saddlers, farriers, young bullies whose delight it was to catch black-birds in the hedges, innkeepers who served up hot mutton pasties, and similar exploiters.'

'As you see it,' the damsel interjected.

'All those we killed in battle were armed and set against the horde.'

Angry sarcasm rose to the damsel's lips. 'You are excessively meticulous.'

'We are thorough, into the bargain,' said the goblin king. 'If you depart, we will destroy every human being. None shall be hidden from us; we shall seek them all out. The choice is yours.'

Presently Asrăthiel said, 'That is quite a ransom. So be it. I remain your hostage.'

Frustrated at her feeling of helplessness in the face of such over-whelming odds, infuriated that the goblins would be prepared to go to such excessive lengths, hating their ruthlessness, the damsel was yet inebriated by sheer fascination with the extraordinary company she found herself keeping; her senses confounded by eldritch beauty and mystery, the intimation of pent up power, the keen edge of peril, the feeling of being precariously balanced on the brink of madness or ecstasy. So discrepant were her passions that she scarcely knew what she was thinking, but tried to conceal her confusion with a mask of calm self-possession and indifference. She drank from her cup in the hope that the wine might soothe her, or at least furnish some numbness.

The music started up again, and the hall reawakened with conversation and activity. The damsel brooded a moment.

Under the hubbub she asked, 'How long will you keep me with you?'

'Indefinitely.'

'Will you let me go back after you've had enough of me?'

Zaravaz looked away, evidently distracted by the skylarking of some of his knights. He observed them for a moment, laughing at their daring escapades. When he returned his attention to his guest he said, 'Frowning does not become you.'

Taking a deep breath, Asrăthiel fought a sudden urge to wrench a handful of his marvellous hair and blemish his insufferable arrogance with discomfort. It was pointless to pursue questions he chose to disregard.

'You have two other hostages,' she said. 'I have not entirely rid your halls of human men.'

'Even so.' The goblin king's tone was light, perhaps over-casual.

To gain a moment to marshal her thoughts the damsel drank deeply from her cup. 'Last night I asked you to grant them clemency. Since then I have had some leisure to dwell upon the beggar's eyewitness description of the demise of my beloved kindred at the hands of Uabhar, and to recall the complicity of Virosus. Do you know the history?'

'I do. Trows are newsmongers.'

'My wrath is kindled when I picture my innocent friends lying drugged by the druid's fumes while Uabhar's executioner hacked them to pieces. I tell you now; I care not what your minions do with Uabhar and Virosus. I do not relish the torment of any living thing but neither would I lift a finger or utter one word to assist those two.'

'It seems even you, gentle damsel, can be flint-hearted. I shall ponder upon the matter. Perhaps, after my kobolds have finished examining them, they might be hung in chains upon the face of the highest peak, fastened to fetters driven into the rock, there to perish, and their bones to rattle in the winds.'

Asrăthiel shuddered, and swallowed more wine. The strong draught served to deaden her vexation and her shocked senses, but also to make her blurt queries with scant regard to prudence. Abruptly she asked, 'Why do you not treat me as callously as you treat the other hostages?'

'Why, because you are pretty.'

She spluttered, almost choked, recovered. 'Is that all?'

'What would you like me to say?' Zaravaz smiled in a provoking way. He had been mellow, indulgent. Next instant, capriciously, his mood darkened. 'Is your vanity such that you would entreat me to catalogue your qualities?' he said, and now there was some iron in his tone. 'Would that gratify you?' The damsel followed his gaze, which might have lingered a moment upon the fastenings of her gown. 'Shall I examine you with the same close attention to detail my mispickels are devoting to your friends, though with more gentleness, and for the purpose of listing each charming aspect of your design?'

Weathermages were not accustomed to being thus spoken to. Between being incensed at his presumptuousness, annoyed at his having deliberately misinterpreted her comment and used it exasperatingly, and baffled as to his true meaning, Asrăthiel experienced a kind of delightful paralysis, as if transfixed by the stare of a basilisk, mingled with consternation that there could be any trace of delight at all in her response to such an address. She could not look at him, could not speak; nor did he seem to require a reply. She sensed, too, the element of anger behind his mockery, but could not account for it, unless she had some power over him of which she was unaware, which meant it irked him, despot that he was, to be thwarted.

He left off his teasing and remained silent awhile. At length the damsel became intensely aware that the very attractive incarnation of wickedness was seated very close beside her, and that his arm, in the soft, loose fold of a black sleeve, rested along the back of her chair, behind her head.

Together, earth-harp and trow-drums had been a rousing combination of sounds, but when uncanny violoncellos awoke, waves of fibrillation sawed up and down Asrăthiel's spine as if she were the instrument being played. The lyrics of a simple yet expressive ditty she had heard once or twice flashed arbitrarily though her memory:

'If it's going to rain, it'll rain,
And if it's going to shine, it's going to shine,
And if you're going insane, you'll go insane.
Now you've lost your mind.'

Upon an exalted platform a group of four beautiful knights – three cellists and a bass violist – was creating stirring music, swaying to and fro with the passion of their outpourings, their calf-length coats and long hair flying. Another accompanied them on drums, tubular bells and tambourine. The pouring hair of the musicians curtained the left side of their faces as they bent to their bows – for, all were left-handed; indeed, their hair, being so long, must have become entangled with the strings, though this never interrupted their performance; conceivably, part of the reason their music was so thrilling was because it was played upon the living strands of their eldritch hair.

Back and forth they swept the bows, with the deftness of artists executing precise brushstrokes, but their performance was utterly unlike that of some dignified human chamber quartet with heads solemnly bent, peering short-sightedly at pages of written score propped on a one-legged stand, motionless save for the fingers of one hand spidering up and down the instrument's fingerboard and the elbow of the other sailing in and out like a pompous barque.

Quite the contrary.

The goblin musicians seemed to be lifted up with the sheer energy of the performance, tossing their extravagant hair in time to the beat, feet pounding the rhythm; vigorous, fully alive. Their instruments seemed as alive as they - as if fused, an extension of the musicians' bodies - so that nerves linked them in one neural entirety, impulses flowing in a circuit through fingers, arms and bows, hair and strings, across the shoulders, up and down the spine, up and down the fingerboard, from head to bridge to base, engendering all the exultation that wild music can convey. Nor did the cellists remain glued to their seats, for from time to time they leapt up spiritedly, instrument and all, still playing, wielding the weight and cumber of the cello as easily as if it were a violin; jumping or spinning before flinging themselves back into their places to incite their dark, raw melodies with redoubled zeal.

Asrăthiel had no recollection of joining the dance. Across the floor she whirled in the arms of a partner who was thrilling to look upon, and she became lost in a darkness that held a scent of lightning and thunderclouds, and she thought some honeyed corrosive had excoriated her immortal spirit, and she must perish of the wounds.

7

STRANGE LOVE

There stands a fastness, hard against the stars
On bitter crags of mountains bleak and grim,
Where icy gales careen 'twixt jagged scars
And waters tumble into fathoms dim;
Where foot tracks wind through wild magnificence
Surmounting airy chasms, bridging o'er
Profoundest gorges, river-carved; from thence
'Midst pinnacles where foaming torrents roar.

Fair Minith Ariannath's slender spires
And lofty pointed arches pierce the sky.
Her roots are plunged in deep volcanic fires
Which sluggish streams of molten rock supply.
Palatial citadel of precious ores,
With silver ceilings, diamond balustrades,
Jade columns, crystal walls, carnelian floors
And polished porticos of sable shades!

Great Silver Mountain of which legend tells,
Entwined with veils of mist and cloud and snow,
Wrapped up in weird enchantment, laced with spells;
Your strangest secrets, man may never know.

THE SONG OF SILVER MOUNTAIN

Yet the dance came to an end, and Asrăthiel was soon sitting beside the goblin king once more while a trow-gaffer served beverages. The minstrels put away their eerie strings and bows, trows commenced a soft background tootling on breathy pipes, and the knights of unseelie fell to drinking, laughing and playing a confusing dice game.

Zaravaz took up his chalice and swallowed a draught of wine. 'I will expound further on the reason I treat the other hostages differently from you,' he said gravely, regarding Asrăthiel over the vessel's rim. 'It is because of what they are, and what you are not.'

Is it possible he knows that I am immortal? Despite their long incarceration, the goblins seem to know all about everyone in Tir - the trows and other wights must be industrious informers indeed. Can my immortality be the reason for his indulgence?

'Since you seem unaware, I will make clear to you,' he continued, 'why my kindred do not love yours.'

'Prithee,' the damsel said, thinking, Surely humankind must have done more to offend the goblins than simply being subject to death, whilst they are not! 'Prithee, tell on. Your words will fascinate me, sir, for I can imagine no offence that justifies such terrible revenge as you have proposed to exact on my race. You have waged war on us simply for being human.'

'Our aversion stems from humanity's belief,' said Zaravaz, placing the chalice on the table and reclining against the padded arms and back of his chair, 'that by virtue of their species they are superior to all others. Each one considers himself so special, yet in truth he might equally have been born a chicken or a cow. This mistaken conviction leads your people to commit atrocities most horrific against any beings that do not resemble themselves. You say we waged war on your kind, but what we did was nothing by comparison to what humanity has done. Every day, hundreds of thousands of nonhumans are victims of the longest-running, largest-scale war in history. They are robbed of their land, their freedom, their children, their lives, simply because your kind are capable of doing it. Within the culture of the Argenkindë and indeed of all the Glashtinsluight, such abuse is considered an utmost crime. For centuries we strove to open the eyes, the minds and the hearts of humankind – to no avail. Ultimately, your people have not the humility to accept that they are one of many different animal nations, dwelling beneath the same stars, all struggling to stay alive, to avoid pain and to experience joy.' Musingly, the handsome knight let his fingers trace the rich ornamentation on the sides of the silver cup. 'Having observed that human beings could not be taught to behave otherwise,' he said, 'we judged that they had forfeited the right to be part of the world. Our solution was to wipe out the human race.'

'Genocide is as much a crime as any of the offences you so detest!' Asrǎthiel exclaimed feelingly.

'When you submitted to being my hostage,' said he, 'was it not because you believed that the sacrifice of one person is worthwhile, for the greater good of many?'

She nodded.

'Similarly, the sacrifice of one species may be beneficial to the rest.'

'Who are you to judge?' Asrǎthiel found herself instinctively shrinking from her host, repelled by his emphatic affirmation of misanthropic intent. The goblins were manifestly devoid of moral principles, yet they justified their fiendishness in the name of righteousness. The sharp eyes of Zaravaz missed nothing, she knew; but other than a twitch at one corner of his mouth that might have indicated wry contempt, he gave no sign that he noted her recoiling.

'We are immortal beings,' he said, 'who have existed since the world was young. We have seen it grow sad and dim since the rise of humanity. You yourself have lived for only a handful of years. You cannot know how it used to be. Yet you are different from most, because you are no persecutor, like the rest.'

Asrăthiel's voice trembled. 'If you wipe out humanity, you destroy the goodness as well as the iniquity.'

'What goodness? Tell me about the great beneficence of humankind.'

'There is love, for a start – love and compassion.'

'Bitches love their pups, and guard them with their very lives. Adult elephants will take pity on an orphaned rhinoceros and protect it as if it were their own child. Elephants grieve for loved ones too, and weep tears at the death of family members. A bereaved lioness may nurture a motherless gazelle. Whales live in harmony with one another and never wage war. If you speak of love and compassion, plainly it exists in greater abundance amongst nonhumans.'

'You name creatures I have never heard of – but then, you have lived long and travelled far. What of the other virtues and achievements of humanity – music, literature, art? Do you mean to be rid of them too?'

'Amongst their own species, birds and dolphins teach songs to one another. With regard to art, what more wondrous work of art can there be than the world itself – a bird in flight, a tree in blossom, a stormy sky? And as for literature, well, what advantage does that bestow on the world at large? It entertains and informs human beings, no more, no less. Being a toy and instrument of the human race, it is rendered redundant if there are no human creatures alive to consume it.'

'This, then, is the paradox of your race,' said Asrăthiel in wonder, 'that you are cruel because you oppose cruelty. Truly, I cannot fathom your ethos. There is an unbridgeable chasm between your culture and mine.'

Was it a flash of pain, or of anger she glimpsed in those dark-fringed pools of violet?

'A scission exists indeed,' her companion said darkly. 'Goblin-kind is far more highly principled than humankind.'

Asrăthiel wanted to shout, 'What nonsense!' But the awareness of being surrounded by a horde of unseelie wights some twenty-five thousand strong clamped her tongue.

'How can you say so?' she cried, managing to remain relatively composed despite her indignation.

'To put it plainly, goblins slay men, but men do exactly the same to each other. One difference of consequence is that goblins do not wage war on one another. Humanity never seems to leave off making war on itself.'

'We have enjoyed generations of peace in Tir - '

'While your fellow humanimals, the Marauders, preyed upon you, despite that they are of your race, slaughtering and pillaging, as your travelling armies slaughter each other and pillage the villages of peasants who never lifted so much as an eyelid in rage against them. The very term 'humane', rather than denoting 'distinguished by kindness mercy and compassion', should mean 'characterised by exploitation, cruelty, sadism and ruthlessness'. Not content with harming their own kind, your people also enslave, exploit and torment innocent and defenceless creatures of other species.'

'Goblins torment the defenceless too!'

'Usually we allow the mispickels to indulge in such pastimes. And when we punish we are exacting penance for wrongdoing. Any divertissement it happens to afford us is an added benefit.'

'That alibi holds no water with me.' The weathermage seethed with frustration, unable to adequately express all the arguments that chased each other through her head. The wine of Sølvetårn was potent; its effects muffled clear thinking, and she knew she must eventually retire from the debate defeated but unconvinced. 'Goblinkind used to hunt human beings for sport,' she said, 'before the weathermasters imprisoned you.'

'After humankind was declared vermin we merely wanted to have some fun with them, to combine entertainment with just retribution before we dealt the final stroke, which, as it turned out, regrettably, was not to fall.'

'Not to fall because you would now give up your virtuous quest for a better world, so readily, in return for my company! Flattering to me, but unflattering to you. Is it so easy for you to forsake your ideals at a whim?'

'Sweetness,' Zaravaz said icily, 'you seem to presume that I act without forethought. Believe me, nothing is further from the truth. My views about your race have changed somewhat since days of yore. Unfortunately, due to recent exasperating circumstances, some of my previous convictions have been undermined.'

'Unfortunately?'

'I dislike vacillation.'

'Do you mean you are no longer certain whether or not human-kind ought to be obliterated?'

'Make of it what you will.'

'You say I am different from the rest,' Asrăthiel went on. 'How have you learned so much about me?'

'Are you truly so ignorant on that matter?' Zaravaz demanded. When she replied in the affirmative he said, 'Methinks I overestimated your shrewdness.' In a moment he added, 'Perhaps it is better this way.'

'If I am blind to anything that ought to be obvious,' she said, 'It is because you have enchanted and bewitched me, and I can no longer think on a straight course, if ever I could.'

After the damsel uttered those words the goblin king appeared to reflect upon them, but otherwise his expression was unreadable. For Asrăthiel that very impenetrability was somehow profoundly stirring, for she sensed beneath it an explosive impetuosity; vehemence at war with itself, locked behind a barricade of steely resolution.

A trow-girl started playing a merry jig on a whistle, and the cleared floor in the refectory became filled with stamping, jumping trows, while the goblin knights looked on, entertained at their antics.

'Your knights can be cruel to your kobold slaves,' persisted the weathermage. 'I have seen Zauberin holding them up by one ear, and Zande pulling their tails. You enslave another species and tease them – are you not hypocrites?'

'Goblins made kobolds,' Zaravaz replied testily. 'Kobolds are arsenic-based, artificially engendered entities, not really alive at all.

To animate them we initially employed a form of spirit or essence that flickers, half sentient, in the deeper strata of the mountains. They are more like organic machines than living creatures, though very cunning at manufacture.'

'Not alive maybe, but sadistic.' Asrăthiel's lids felt heavy. It had been a long time since she had slept deeply. Even the immortal must visit the land of dreams, or so it seemed.

'Call it what you will. They experience no empathy, only inquisitiveness. It stimulates their nodes of enquiry, to view the reactions of men goaded by the prod of agony. The trollhästen, on the other hand, are true living wights. They have a relationship of mutual benefit with us, as you have learned.'

'The trollhästen are delightful,' Asrăthiel mumbled, retreating from argument. 'Well, I have discovered much, this day.' The liquor that dulled her wits had made her somnolent.

Three goblin knights approached. After bowing to his lord, Aachionard Zauberin murmured, '*Y chiarn ard-ree, cloie shiu?*'

Glancing at Asrăthiel, Zaravaz said, 'I will play. I will make such music as will soothe this lady like a lullaby to her slumber, for she is about to start yawning.'

He rose from his chair, his wrist lightly brushing Asrăthiel's shoulder as he withdrew it from behind her head. A sparkle like voluptuous fireworks went through her at the contact, and she gave a start, but already he had strode away.

'What does it mean, 'the little death'?' Asrăthiel asked a passing trow, but the wight had no idea. She asked the goblin knights lounging near her chair, 'What is the little death?' but they merely laughed in a suggestive manner, while Zauberin winked insolently. Nettled, and suspecting she had been mocked for naivety, she let the matter drop.

Zaillian handed his lord a violin and bow, and all the other minstrels ceased their efforts, scattering like leaves. Silence reigned. The goblin king rested the foot of the instrument against his shoulder, instead of tucking it beneath his chin like a human violinist. He turned the pegs to tune the strings, drawing out long, poignant notes under the bow's caress. Then, with effortless grace he sprang onto the musicians' platform and commenced to invoke music.

Conjured from the strings by his art, the music caught fire. The hairs stood up on the back of Asrăthiel's neck, and an extraordinary feeling pulsed through her – one she could not express. It was as if she had bee asleep all her life and the music had woken her, or as if she were hearing music for the first time. Three in one was the melody – the Dance, the Lullaby and the Lament, and its frequencies sawed thrillingly at her bones, resonating with the rhythms of breath and blood.

As his fingers danced along the scrolled fingerboard and the bow glided back and forth, he moved subtly, shifting his balance, keeping pace with intricate counterpoints. He was part of those rhythms; more than that, the essence of the music sprang from the nature of his existence. Watching him was like witnessing someone else's dream. Between passages he transferred the bow to the hand holding the violin, swung across to a plinth by way of a nearby cantilever, and dropped down to the floor with great elegance before seamlessly resuming the performance. It seemed he could not remain still. He passed amongst the audience, cajoling the most moving melodies from the instrument as he went, and they turned their heads to follow him. The single strand of notes began to be interwoven with the sweet, mild voices of violas, the sumptuous tones of cellos and the low rumble of basses, forming harmonies as soothing as cream, as sweet as syrup, and as narcotic as hemlock. Yet no other musician was playing. Zaravaz was a solo performer, a virtuoso who could entice the sounds of many instruments from the strings of one.

Sedated by the lullaby, the wine, and the overwhelming sum of recent experiences, Asrăthiel fell asleep with her head in her arms, which rested upon the table. Her own dreams were extravagant; a comely goblin knight was falling through dappled fathoms of water, locked in the embrace of a luscious siren, a drowner; Prince William was burning in a heatless fire; the urisk Crowthistle was sitting on a stump beside a dark pool, and her mother, Jewel, opened her eyes inside a cage made of glass roses that shattered, leaving the roses to bleed.

The damsel awoke at eventide upon a canopied bed in her own silver suite. A couple of trow wives were sitting by the fireplace rocking their swaddled prune-faced infants and crooning a soft cradlesong. Asrăthiel's mage-intuition informed her that outside, the wind was hurtling through the heights of the Northern Ramparts, thunderclouds were rolling across the darkening sky, and the temperature was dropping. Standing at a traceried oriel window, still in her rumpled banquet gown, she watched the sun disappearing behind the mountains, a glistening slash of scarlet, as if the hearts of the clouds had been sliced open. Homesickness stabbed her. What might be happening to her family and friends in the world beyond the walls?

The gale roared and sang like hosts of spectres rushing by, and suddenly the weathermage longed for the touch of open air, the tingle of escalating thunderstorm charges. A door in the wall gave on to a balcony; she opened it, pushing hard against the force of the gusts, and stepped out. It was like plunging into ice water. Air currents slammed against her, blasting up from the valley below. Her tresses streamed back, scattering jewellery, while her gown flapped and billowed as if it would snatch her up like some great bird with blue satin pinions, and carry her off. The howl of rushing air blanketed all other sounds. Gripping the stone balustrade she narrowed her eyes against the invisible onslaught and looked down across the shadow-drowned valley. A few glowing coals trapped in notches along the horizon were all that remained of the sun. On the opposite escarpment, swathed in twilight, a line of horsemen was charging up the crest of a ridge; marvellous knights riding graceful trollhästen, racing the wind.

It was a perpendicular world that Asrăthiel beheld; all verticals and steep angles and razor-edged shadows. Clean-cut and glistening the basalt bastions towered, barren of any vegetation more sophisticated or less hardy than mosses and lichens. The Northern Ramparts made the aged, weathered heights of High Darioneth, clothed in soft greenery, seem mild and nurturing by comparison. These mountains were young, honed and vigorous; their corners not yet smoothed by the eroding actions of wind and water, still uttering an epochal gasp from the shock of their violent birth from pools of magma bubbling at their foundations. The weather-mage was conscious, by way of her brí-senses, of volcanic activity rumbling thousands of feet below.

The roots of her hair stood up. She became sensible of the enormous negative charge that had accumulated on the bellies of the thunderheads above the peaks. As the clouds moved they attracted a positive charge from the ground, which travelled along beneath them. Faint glows of corona discharge danced about the sharpest pinnacles, and a low, crackling hum began to emanate from the entire landscape. Most people would have been terrified by such an ominous buzzing sound, but the imminent lightning strike could not harm Asrăthiel and she remained serene.

The more she gazed at her surroundings, the more details she noted. Slender, exceedingly precipitous stairways twisted hither and thither up and down the precipices, none with banister or balustrade. They resembled goat tracks more than rights-of-way for two-legged creatures. Incandescent eyes in pinched faces peered from burrows and clefts in the rocks. The Northern Ramparts were not so uninhabited, after all; it was little wonder that men shunned them.

From the balcony on which she stood, a steep and narrow stair wound its way down the face of the cliff. The weathermage took a few steps down the flight of cramped treads. Gusts shoved her sideways, beating at her like powerful wings. Momentarily losing balance she teetered above the abyss, flung out a hand to steady herself, and fell back against the rock wall. If she tumbled to the floor of the valley she would not be harmed, but it would take a full day or more for her to reclimb that tremendous height. In the mean time if her absence were discovered, the goblin knights might believe she had absconded and set forth on their quest to scrape humankind from the world's rind. Bearing this in mind Asrăthiel retreated to the balcony, glanced one last time at the crimson ruins of the sun and returned to her chamber, leaving the door open.

Beyond the windows, inky clouds drowned the last of the after-glow. The electrical storm had begun; thunderous crashes tumbled from one end of the world to the other, and sheet lightning blinked like the broken light of a silver sun. The trow-wives squeaked and shrieked, and one scurried to close the door.

As her handmaidens attended her Asrăthiel asked, 'What am I to do here? How long am I to stay?' but of course they knew nothing, or would not say, or failed to grasp the question, or pretended to. They brought writing materials for her, whereupon she sat at an escritoire of white marble and inscribed a long and loving message to her grandfather, telling him everything that had happened, and all she had learned since arriving in Sølvetårn. Finally she made a list of names and asked Avalloc to pass on her tidings to them. After she had sealed the letter with red wax, a trow messenger came and took it away, promising to deliver it rapidly.

The damsel left her apartments and wandered through the aerial halls and galleries of Sølvetårn encountering, as she travelled, dozens of grey-clad, limping trows, ten greater kobolds marching in pairs, seventeen lesser kobolds carrying monstrous contrap-tions, a clutch of scuttling, diminutive, unidentifiable wights that resembled a crowd of little gentlefolk richly dressed in dandelion leaves and other garden weeds, three unseelie gwyllion hags who bared pointed fangs and slunk into the shadows, numerous patient, wary spiders and twenty-one horned eagle owls shaking out their plumage as they woke from slumber. But no tall, handsome lord with spellbinding black hair that wafted on an illusory breeze.

Evenings passed, and none could tell her where he might be.

After four nights – so quickly! How was it possible? – Asrăthiel received a letter from Avalloc, who told her how he had fallen to his knees and wept with joy upon receiving her communication that she was unharmed and still within Tir, though on the outermost borders.

Albiona found your letter lying on my pillow, he wrote in the correspondence. *How it came there I cannot tell, but I had not been to my bedchamber that night, for I have found little rest, my* dear, since you have been gone. Alighting on it, your aunt screamed louder than you would have believed possible. She would speak to no one, not even Dristan, but dashed through the house at break-neck speed, to the room where I sat alone, despairing, and seized me by the hand, and she was crying. Then everyone else rushed in, thinking that there had been some disastrous accident, and when the situation was made clear the whole house exploded with jubilation. All began jumping and yelling, embracing and kissing, servants and family alike.

The news spread swiftly through Rowan Green, and thence across High Darioneth and the length and breadth of Tir, in a wave of euphoria. My dear child, there is dancing in the streets and blowing of horns and ringing of bells as the people celebrate the tidings that their beloved Lady Asrăthiel, wielder of Fallowblade, is hale, and being treated well, and that their worst fears are unfounded - she has not been entombed in some dungeon with no access to the outside world, or insulted, or spirited away to some distant land, never to be heard of again. Since your departure we have experienced the full gamut of emotions - from initial shock, distress and disbelief when you were taken, to this new elation. I can hardly begin to describe how we feel; it is utter relief.

The people of Tir, strong though they be, have suffered greatly from war's legacy of grief and loss. To add to our woes, since the goblin horde departed, kobolds big and small steal across the king-doms like a blue plague, as enforcers of their masters' law. They are increasingly seen, especially by night, heralded by a stink of garlic, wielding whips or three-pronged forks. As they travel they inflict severe retribution upon human beings they consider guilty of cruelty and neglect and the confinement of animals. Our trades and craft guilds are in turmoil. What's more, now that the people are largely deprived of weathermasters' assistance they are forced to accept that the elements may now destroy their property and crops at whim, that seasons may be too wet or too dry, that flood or fire may overwhelm them, and there is nought to be done about it, for we weatherlords are too few. To discover that their Queen of

*Swords, Tir's Champion and Heroine of the Four Kingdoms has
not paid some unspeakable price on their behalf has buoyed the
spirits of our worthy citizens as nothing else could.*

The letter closed with these words:

*I wonder what final fate awaits the goblins' other two captives.
It seems from your description that they are being treated as
ungently as they have to often treated their fellow men. Our ambassador in Cathair Rua has discovered the secret burial place where Ó
Maoldúin laid the bodies of our Councillors. The mortal remains
of our beloved kindred have been disinterred, and are on their way,
in state, to Rowan Green. Here in our cemetery they will be
entombed with full honours. May rain fall around and upon them.*

The Storm Lord had included letters from Asrăthiel's friends,
begging to know if there was any chance the goblins might change
their terms and release her. She responded in writing, informing
everyone that she believed it was highly unlikely she would be liber-
ated, at least in the immediate future. Even Avalloc's house-guest
Agnellus had penned a note, but to Asrăthiel's surprise, there had
been no message from William.

The letters filled her with delight, nonetheless after she had sent
off her replies and found herself purposeless again, she began to fall
once more into a restless despondency. To counter this she filled
the hours by continuing her exploration of the fantastic stronghold
under the mountains, discovering a myriad wonders. There seemed
no end to the labyrinth. Having fallen into the rhythm favoured by
the nocturnal inhabitants, she took to sleeping during the day and
waking at sunset.

Letters flooded in from the outside world, however as
the populace began to realise that there was no chance of her
returning their rejoicing subsided and the flood dwindled.
Most people, especially the denizens of Rowan Green and High
Darioneth, vowed they would never give up hope that one day
Asrăthiel might be rescued.

Time seemed measureless. Nights elapsed bringing no sign
of Zaravaz, and the hostage languished amid the surreal elegance

of the goblin fastness. Every day her handmaidens brought her voguish clothes to wear, delicacies to nibble, and trowish bards to provide entertainment. She dwelled in idle luxury, while her heart was being eaten empty with a hunger such as she had never known.

I would never have believed, she told herself, that the yearnings of homesickness could be so overwhelming. What does the future hold for me? Am I to be forever lonely?

One evening, Asrăthiel rose from her couch and put on a new gown that appeared to be fashioned from plum-coloured orchid petals stitched with the delicate green skeletons of leaves. Soon afterwards, Second Lieutenant Zwist arrived at her door, carrying a lighted lantern of silver filigree. 'Condescend to honour me with your company, Lady Sioctíne,' he said with charming gallantry, bowing in courtly fashion. 'Tonight you are to visit the mines of Sølvetårn.'

This knight had always shown himself to be agreeable and ready to engage in conversation. Readily Asrăthiel accompanied him, thirsty for knowledge, yet also wanting to understand how such a courtly gallant could be part of the notorious goblin horde. She recalled the vehemence with which he had swung his sword at her on the Wuthering Moors, and his savage attacks on the soldiers who fought alongside her, mowing his way amongst them, striking left and right, glorying in the slaughter with a ferocity almost as terrible as that of his lord. It was difficult to reconcile these conflicting aspects.

They proceeded along a corridor whose walls were mottled, every inch, with the fossil imprints of dragonflies, sea spiders and horseshoe crabs, faithfully rendered in stone. As they walked, the weathermage quizzed her guide. 'Lieutenant Zwist, do you hate humanity as passionately as does your lord?'

'Like all of the Glashtinsluight, I detest your kindred.'

'It must be difficult for you to be civil to me.'

'Not at all. You have proved yourself to be different - in contrast to, for example, the Primoris Virosus - who, incidentally, currently decorates a mountain steeple in the skies above our heads.'

Of all the institutions maintained by humanity the Sanctorum is the worst, for it publishes a fabrication that the Fates decree the human race is entitled to oppress all other races.'

'Oh, the Primoris! Is that what they have done to him?'

'It is. To the other also.'

'Then, they are dead?'

'By now, undoubtedly.'

An image flashed before Asrăthiel's eyes; sickened, she banished it instantly. There had been too many atrocities; first the slaughter of the weathermasters, then the bloodshed on the fields of war, and now this. Since the demise of her kindred she had found it hard to sleep, and the sleep to which exhaustion of spirit eventually drove her was troubled by ill dreams. It was clear she must either exile horror to a remote corner of her mind, or be overwhelmed and succumb to madness. She chose the former.

Knight and damsel passed beneath archways built of limestone embedded with exotic treasures of the underground; graceful whorls of petrified ammonites and nautilus. Asrăthiel began to speak again, hoping to distract herself from the appalling vision conjured by Zwist's revelation. 'I am sorrowful, knowing that you hold my people in such low esteem. I wish I could convince you otherwise.'

'Even your people's use of language demonstrates their selfishness,' said the knight. 'Human beings will say, 'Thousands were slain' when they mean that thousands of human beings were slain. It's as if no other species exists. They say, 'It was a threat to the world' when they mean something was a threat to the human race. Ironically, a threat to the human race is likely to be a blessing to the rest of the world - bird and beast, leaf and tree, all would be better off without *sheelnaue*.'

Perceiving that nothing she could say would alter his opinion, Asrăthiel let the subject drop. 'Tell me of these mines,' she said, as they travelled together along passageways whose ceilings were so high they were lost to view, and down vast staircases whose exaggerated dimensions seemed better suited to giants.

Obligingly her escort said, 'The mines of Sølvetårn are ancient and extensive, a huge network of passages and stopes, caverns, drives and galleries, far below the halls where we dwell. Knockers dug the tunnels and now work them anew; you will soon see them chipping away at the lode. Kobolds toil down there too, but it is the knockers who do the actual digging and delving; that has ever been their trade and obsession, aided by blue-caps, who load ore, shovel gangue, and generally fetch and carry.'

'I saw no such wights at your banquet.'

'They miners never attend our junkets, for they will not leave off their digging. They are at it night and day. Mispickels, on the other hand, never miss a feast. They are great beer-drinkers.'

'So,' said Asrăthiel, 'you are taking me to see your kobolds at work! I am glad. They are curious beings. Your lord informed me that goblinkind engineered them so that they might be your slaves.'

'Even so,' said Zwist.

'How did you create such creatures?' the damsel wondered.

The knight smiled. 'Mispickels are the spawn of arsenic and cobalt and the gramarye of the Glashtinsluight,' he expounded. 'They were begotten in the silver mines, long ago, in the deeps of time. Cobalt often coexists with silver, as vein deposits with silver minerals. Indeed, humankind's word 'cobalt' is derived from an archaic term that ironically meant 'goblin' - did you know? When human silver miners work near cobalt, they are frequently plagued with maladies of the lungs, distempers of the feet and disorders of the brain such as delusions of persecution or grandeur. In days of yore their superstitious panic led them to believe that malicious, unseen wights associated with cobalt brought this mischief on them, and they named their imaginary oppressors 'kobolts', or 'goblins'.'

'I do not understand why the miners supposed it was the ore that gave them trouble,' said Asrăthiel. 'Cobalt is not toxic. My people use it to make invisible inks, because it changes colour if heated. When paper that is apparently blank is held near a flame, it turns green where messages have been inscribed in cobalt ink.'

'In sooth, the element itself is not toxic,' Zwist explained, 'but by nature it attracts arsenic. The human miners' madness and sickness were symptoms of arsenic poisoning. Coincidentally, and even more ironically, if kobolds had been skulking nearby, their presence would indeed have been toxic to the miners. Fortunately our rough imps will not affect you that way, Lady Sioctíne.'

So they do know I am invulnerable!

They walked away from another stair and along a broad promenade whose walls were curtained with falling water.

'Kobolds' blood was spilled on the battlefield,' said Asrăthiel. 'It was silver-white.'

'The colour of arsenic.'

'I heard they abhor salt.'

'Salt and iron, both. When in the mines, both varieties must avoid naturally occurring rock salt, iron ore, haematite, and iron oxides.'

'It is commonly known, salt and iron are anathema to many wights.'

'Of course,' said the knight, 'iron is also an element carried in human blood, which can prove troublesome to the mispickels in battle. Their armour must be blood-proof.'

'It is strange, their battle harness.'

'The greater kobolds make their red armour from erythrite, also called 'cobalt bloom'. It is a crust that coats the surface of skutterudite, a cobalt arsenite.'

Having crossed a wide landing they began to descend yet another spiral stairway hewn into basalt. Damp patches glistened on the walls, which contained fossilized bats and archaeopteryx, exquisitely detailed.

'Your slaves wear a curious insignia, a cross with arms of equal length,' Asrăthiel said questioningly.

'It is their emblem,' Zwist said, 'because sometimes arsenic occurs as a mineral called mispickel, or arsenopyrite, and this is often discovered in crystals that form crosslike shapes. When struck with a hammer, mispickel gives off a garlic odour, the characteristic smell of kobolds. Our own term for our slaves is flaieen, although at whiles, as you have heard, we call them 'mispickels'.'

Reaching the foot of a stair embossed with precious minerals, they walked through an arched portal carved with leering faces.

'The skin of both kobold races seems dyed with woad,' Asrăthiel commented, fleetingly admiring the exquisite precision of the carvings even as she paid close attention to the lecture.

'It is neither dyed nor painted,' said her informant. 'Cobalt is used to make blue tinting for porcelain and tile glazes and stained glass. To make blue glass, one must mix cobalt oxide with silicon. Cobalt is therefore an ingredient of smalt, an artists' pigment made of ground-up blue glass. Pigments made from pure cobalt tend towards violet in colour. Thus mispickels are blue-skinned.'

'Your lore is vast, Lieutenant Zwist! I cannot help but be intrigued by the secrets of the underground. The jewels, the ores and their strange properties - it is like opening a treasure chest of knowledge! In my pursuit of weathermastery I have studied fire, air and water, but never have I learned much about what lies beneath the ground.'

'That is quite natural, since weathermasters can interweave their senses with only three of the four elements,' replied the goblin lieutenant. 'You might find, Lady Sioctíne, that scientific inquiry into of the structure of this ball of rock and iron we call the world is a topic of endless fascination.' He ushered her across a crystal-studded bridge that spanned an abyss so deep that its floor could barely be seen. The movement of dots of light indicated that wights were working at the bottom. Towers of steam rose from below, along with the far-off clamour of drills, picks, shovels and splitters biting at the rock face. As they watched, a huge kibble, or bucket, came rushing at them from somewhere above and slid rapidly into the deeps. Asrăthiel ducked. It was only then that she noticed the thick steel cable strung above their heads. A moment later another bucket came banging up out of the depths, swinging from the constantly moving cable, travelling apparently of its own volition. With a metallic squeal it disappeared into the gloomy vaults above.

They crossed another flying bridge and went down a winding ramp, entering a torch-lit underground forest of wrought silver trees with argent leaves. Draughts, entering from cleverly placed vents, played pure, ringing music on pendant crystals. Asrăthiel marvelled at this splendour of light and sound. Her companion barely seemed to notice the triumphs of silversmithery beneath whose glimmering boughs they were passing. 'Did kobolds fashion these wondrous forests?' Asrăthiel wanted to know.

Laughing, Zwist answered, 'Mispickels smelt and forge most useful ores, and they are clever engineers, who don protective armour and work with iron. But for the main part we, the Argen-kindë, are the silversmiths. Artistic work is to our taste, and we are geniuses in the craft.'

'This I know well, from my experience of the Sylvan Comb,' said Asrăthiel.

'Ah yes, that object,' said her companion. 'We are pleased to have taken it back.'

'But after you demanded the comb from us with such insistence you merely threw it away! Why did you want it if you care so little about it? Did you have some purpose in casting it aside? Is there some consequence you want to prevent, or did you simply want to stop it from falling into human hands again?'

'The latter,' said Zwist. 'You see, Lady Sioctíne, we prefer to possess what is ours. Furthermore, we do not like our things to be sullied by humankind. Even if we have no use for one of our artefacts, we would rather keep it from mortal men. Besides, we own hundreds of similar items – hand-mirrors that appear to turn into lakes when flung to the ground, candle-sticks that become towers, shoes that become ships, belts that become rivers … items that humankind would perhaps find useful to throw off pursuit, or to amaze their foes in battle, but which for us are merely toys.'

'Toys to tantalise men, perhaps?' Asrăthiel suggested.

'Perhaps!' Zwist said lightly.

Asrăthiel dropped the subject.

'Where do the kobolds dwell when they are not toiling in the service of their masters?'

'They frequent their own levels, which stink of garlic as they do: the Slyving, for example; and the Kingswood Toad; the Dundgy Drift and the Nine Rivets. They have their own breweries down there.'

'Such curious names! What do you call this place where we walk?'

'This particular gallery is called Chloride Street; it gives onto the open mountainside at both ends; one at Quartz Gate, the other at Upper Gate. We are now in the Main Silver.' The knight gestured extravagantly. 'In that direction lies the Great Course. Up there is the Middle Course, and the Little Course is far away to the west, beyond Fountain Hall and Firestone. The levels stretch for miles in every direction, joining with other diggings such as Castle Mine, Old Mine, and Fershull Pit.'

Puffs of white vapour were whistling and hissing through the levels, and the air thickened with humidity. They arrived at the base of a tapered, four-sided tower of crisscrossed struts and girders, a sight familiar to Asrăthiel, for many such skeletal structures loomed over mineshafts near the villages around Silverton. It was a poppet head. A huge revolving gin wheel at the top, driven by chugging, panting machinery, wound steel cable to hoist lifts and buckets in and out of the shaft.

'How are your engines powered?' Asrăthiel asked. The winding engines she had seen aboveground were driven by draught horses, which had to plod in endless circles around a drum, a practice she deplored, and against which she often spoke out.

'Steam gushes freely from the volcanic regions far below our feet. It drives the ore-crushing batteries, the traction engines, the cable-ways and all.'

'I perceive how this can be, for I understand the forces of fire and water. In the four kingdoms, most people would wonder how steam could have such strength, it being so fragile and evanescent that the slightest whisper of wind blows it away. No human being has ever used this method to harness the power at the planet's heart. You speak of wondrous things. I am glad my people know nothing of this, for they would leave no forest unrazed, no fuel source untapped, to generate steam power, and the skies would be blackened with their smoke. Where do your chimneys vent?'

'On the upper peaks, amongst the clouds,' said Zwist. 'They are thousands of feet high, driven through the rock above our heads. Their crowns issue amongst the lofty peaks so that the lead-poisoned fume from our smelters may blow away on high-altitude gales without hurt to mortal creatures. Some of our chimneys are wight-fashioned, but others are simply natural fumaroles. Unlike humankind, the Glashtinsluight do not hew trees for fuel, destroying the world's lungs and the dwelling places of wild creatures. Our steam engines and furnaces are all volcanically fired. We burn neither wood nor fossil.'

Together they entered a metal cage bestraddled by the tower. From overhead, high up in a small cabin, a kobold peered at them. It threw a lever and the cage dropped thousands of feet in the blink of an eye, or so it seemed. Asrăthiel instinctively clutched at the mesh, feeling as if her stomach must fly out the top of her head. She was not afraid, but exhilarated and charmed by this new adventure. When the contraption came to rest Zwist courteously took her arm and they stepped out onto a dim platform, from which opened the masonry mouths of tunnels diverging towards various subterranean levels. The rumble of approaching wheels heralded the dark shapes of laden ore trucks rattling along their rails towards the platform. Shadowy, malformed shapes of kobolds moved in the gloom. Here and there a lantern shone like a yellow eye.

'Now we have come to dangerous ground,' said the goblin knight.

'What travels in those carts?' Asrăthiel asked, her curiosity whetted.

Zwist grabbed handfuls of small rocks from a passing truck and showed them to the damsel by the light of his silver lantern. 'These ores were not gouged from any underground vein,' he said with interest, examining the misshapen lumps. 'By the look of them, these have been lying about on the surface in some distant part of the mountains where mispickels are prospecting.'

'How can you tell?'

'They are sunburned. Ah, but it looks as if the mispickels have struck more rich silver country!'

'I see no glint amongst those dull stones.'

'Some of these are crystals of native silver,' said the knight, 'tarnished blackish grey by the sun's light.' When he scraped one crystal with the edge of another stone, it shone with a serene, chaste whiteness. 'Now you will recognise it. That is almost pure silver,' he said, patently fascinated by the metal. He placed one of the gleaming hexoctahedrons into Asrăthiel's palm; it weighed heavy. 'Sweet native silver occurs naturally, but seldom by comparison to more common silver ores such as these.' The damsel relinquished the fragment, whereupon Zwist proceeded to hand her a succession of mineral nuggets, pellets, scales and plates, identifying them with increasingly outlandish names; soapy nodules like greenish-grey wax, which he called horn silver; lustrous slugs of silver glance; richly hued ruby silvers; silver bromides, some vivid green antimonial silvers, oxides and iodides, stephanites and embolites, acanthites and sulphur-yellow iodyrites.

His pupil brushed away the veneer of dirt on each sample and studied them with interest.

'None of these have the look of silver, save for that which you call 'native'.'

'Silver must be purified by smelting before its true beauty can be seen.'

'Why silver? Why such a cherishing of silver?'

'Silver has a special relationship with electricity,' said Zwist, caressing the nuggets where the glimmered brightest – 'of all the elements, it is the best conductor. It is also sensitive to light, as you have just seen; a useful virtue. Your own kind use its compounds to create mirrors, those playthings of light and almost-windows onto another world. Human beings dye their hair with silver. Your apothecaries and surgeons use silver nitrate as a cautery and a cleanser of infection, and your royal treasuries mint coins of it. The freshness of water, wine and vinegar is better preserved in silver containers. You make of it tableware, jewellery, vases, pins brooches buckles and all the rest, you embellish with it by way of chasing, repoussé, filigree and inlaying, for you love it almost as much as we do, though you love gold better. Silver is the colour of star-shine and moonshine, of mirrors, and ice crystals, and reflections on shining water.'

'Silver is fair, but my people do indeed esteem gold more highly,' said Asrăthiel. 'Gold is the sun's colour, and the sun gives life. Aristocrats drink wines spiced with flakes of gold leaf, and wear cloth-of-gold, and gild the edges of their most important documents. Gold is kind, for it does not rust or tarnish.'

'Neither does silver, in the hands of the Glashtinsluight,' said Zwist with a stiff bow.

'I have heard tell,' said Asrăthiel, 'that gold and silver some-times combine naturally, beneath the ground.'

The knight might have shuddered. 'Speak not to me of tellu-rides,' he said. 'Sylvanite is an obscenity amongst ores. Electrum is a disgrace amongst alloys.' Holding a bizarrely lovely specimen up to the light, he murmured reflectively, 'I do admire the elegance of crystallized dyscrasite in calcite,' before gently replacing the ore in the next car that rolled by.

Leaving the railway they walked down a long drive shored up by stout columns of dressed basalt, the tight-fitting beams holding back huge forces of gravity. In places, water dripped through the ceiling. Asrăthiel could not help but quail for an instant when she pictured the enormous weight of rock pressing down from above. 'Miles of drives like this weave through every level,' said her guide, 'but fear not, for all are supported by baulks of petrified forests or other stone, set squarely and securely.'

The sound of tramping feet approached, and a band of grim-faced mining-wights carrying tools over their shoulders came around a corner, four abreast, looking to neither right nor left. They paused, did homage to the goblin knight, and then marched on their way.

An efficient system of water-curtains served to curb the spread of any fires that might ignite in the underground gases. Sometimes, as they walked down a damp and gloomy tunnel, the damsel and her escort would arrive at a screen formed from trickles of falling water, gleaming in the light. They would walk right through without getting wet, by some twist of goblin gramarye.

The basalt walls of the lower caverns were not dressed, but rough-hewn. Here, the floors were uneven and the design austere, displaying no ornamentation. Spitting oil lamps depending from hooks illuminated their way. Asrăthiel became aware of a background noise, a clashing and booming from the deeps toward which they were headed.

She had heard stories of the knockers; stunted manlike wights who wore clothes resembling the traditional garb of their human counterparts. Constant was their labour, yet they were not doomed to it, nor did they work for payment. It was simply that they were compulsive excavators, and could as easily stop mining as the wind could cease to blow. The blue-caps who assisted them were in similar circumstance.

'How did the knockers while away the centuries while the Argenkindë were imprisoned, Lieutenant Zwist?'

'Lady Sioctíne, I have never been peppered with so many questions. Yet I am bound to answer. They dug, as they always dig. Now they dig at our direction.'

'One matter has always puzzled me about those little diggers. None of the tales mention their having wives.'

'They have no wives. No wives, no lovers, no children. No parents, either, of course. Being deathless they have no need for procreation.'

'Trows, too, are immortal, yet they seem blessed with eternal domesticity.'

'Each race is different.'

Asrăthiel was about to ask, 'Where are the wives and lovers of the Silver Goblins?' At that moment, however, they entered a colonnaded gallery overlooking a vast cavern and the question withered before it passed her lips.

They had stepped outdoors, or so it appeared at first, after the close confines of the drive. An instant later the weathermage understood what she saw. The immense space that yawned before them, extending into the nebulous distance, seemed to have been ripped out of solid bedrock. Lamplight twinkled haphazardly in high places along the walls. Asrăthiel lifted her eyes to the remote ceiling. This enormous chamber was like a giant's treasure-trove of silver. Walls and ceiling glittered all over with pinpricks; multitudinous swarms of glistening silver motes.

'Stars have descended from the night skies to bedeck the underground darkness!' Asrăthiel exclaimed, enraptured.

'Nothing so romantic,' said Zwist with a laugh. 'Those are lead sulphides sparkling in the walls.'

Around every glowing lamp the silver flecks took on a misty appearance. Far up, close to the ceiling, upon long, narrow ledges hewn into the rock, dwarflike figures hugged the walls. In groups here and there they laboured, like insects out in the sombre remoteness. Motes of sapphire radiance indicated the presence of implike blue-caps. The great hollow was filled with lights and movement, yet as far as Asrăthiel was concerned, abruptly it all faded to a grey stasis. A rill of shock fired her nerves.

A masculine figure dressed in black was lounging at ease against a nearby wall of the gallery, his sunless hair sliding on his shoulders. She blinked, and he was beside her so swiftly she did not even realise he had moved.

His beauty was such that to gaze at him was like being wounded.

Lieutenant Zwist saluted his lord, who acknowledged him with a nod. Bowing to Asrăthiel with a flourish that hinted of satire Zaravaz said, 'I trust the Storm Lord's daughter is content with the hospitality of Sølvetårn.' As he bowed, his long locks swept through the air like black vanes, and she felt the caress of turbulence, as if a bird had flown by.

'Most content.' She uttered the words like an automaton, stealing an amazed glance at him during the instant his violaceous gaze was averted.

'Now I will show you the excavations that exist beneath this fast-ness.' Zaravaz offered her the crook of his elbow. 'Come with me.'

His sleeve appeared to be sable velvet stitched with seed-gems of morion; soft fabric covering smooth sinews as tempered and tensile as a sword blade. Asrăthiel's pulse hammered in her ears as she passed her own arm through his. Beset by a type of harrowing delirium she walked close beside him, linked in such a way that she must be in constant contact with his warm, living strength, unex-pectedly blind, deaf and disoriented. Sternly she told herself, It is some eldritch spell. I will not let it master me. But it was too late; already she had surrendered.

Lieutenant Zwist strolled in their wake as Zaravaz drew the damsel down to the deep caverns. Through limestone caves they went, where ancient stalactites and stalagmites had joined to form floor-to-ceiling columns, curtained with draperies of frozen calcium carbonate, and ornamented with fantastic natural sculptures, palely glimmering. They crossed subterranean lakes straddled by paths supported on stone arches, or spanned by suspension bridges on chains. Rickety catwalks swayed high above chasms. Causeways intersected shallow pools. The labyrinths teemed with eldritch wights; pint-sized knockers in their shirtsleeves, their quaint little faces black with dirt, busy at their digging, but not too busy to bow to the Mountain King as he went past; spinners, resembling elderly women working at their whirring wheels; the elusive fridean, mere shadows and gleaming optics in crevices; gorgeous drowners, their cascades of green hair dripping down upon their naked slender-ness as they rose from underworld waters to regard the passers-by, entreating the two knights with outstretched arms white-sheened as lilies. Strains of weird bagpipe music drifted subtly from myste-rious recesses.

Once, a huge cavern suddenly opened out at their feet and above their heads. They came to a halt, standing on a platform that jutted out over rarefied space. Chain-and-pulley lifts rattled up and down the chamber's sides, and buckets crossed it on cables, but Zaravaz ignored those contraptions. He seized Asrăthiel around the waist and pressed her close against him, while with his free hand he grasped a rope whose other end seemed anchored somewhere high in a distant ceiling.

'Hold tight,' he said, and she gasped. She clung to his shoulders as, gripping the rope, he swung in a sweeping arc out across the cavern. They landed on a matching platform that thrust from an aperture in the opposite wall, whereupon he let go of the rope and a lesser kobold materialised from a dusky corner to wind it around a wall hook. As they walked away she heard Zwist alight from a second swing, at their backs.

'You see how it would be difficult for you to navigate these warrens without assistance,' said Zaravaz.

'Oh,' his passenger said offhandedly, still catching her breath, 'I daresay I could manage the ropes on my own.'

'I was referring to finding your path,' he replied. 'I am sure you could manage the ropes on you own, but I enjoy it better this way.'

At last they arrived at an enormous void, the biggest cavern of all. 'Here is The Scatter,' said Zaravaz, 'where most of our misbegotten mispickels toil.'

Asrăthiel beheld a grim vastness hazed in smoke and steam, lashed by raw breezes. Gloomy little rivulets ran across the uneven floor, and glistening soakage trickled down the walls. Metal rails were hoisted high over this boggy surface, on viaducts across which wheeled steam engines puffed and wheezed, hauling furlongs of linked rolling stock that lumbered and bumped. Heavy-duty cableways stretched from one side to the other, cars swinging as they traversed through the acrid air. Somewhere, steam powered suction lift pumps could be heard rattling and thumping, draining water away from this foundered sink. The place was noisy, filthy and bleak.

'Mining wights thrive here,' Zwist commented, 'not only knockers but coblynau, cutty soams and bluecaps, buccas, gathorns and bockles. The Fridean also.'

And indeed, by the light of thousands of lamps it could be seen that the cavern was teeming with small figures who plied picks and axes, mallets and sledges, chains, ladders, winches, gears, scrapers and drills. They clung like bats up and down the walls, swarming to improbable heights.

'Enlighten the lady further,' suggested Zaravaz.

'The knockers have formed themselves into guilds,' Zwist expounded willingly, while Zaravaz leaned on a rough stone balustrade and observed the industry below, without relinquishing his grasp on Asrăthiel's arm, so that she must lean also. 'Over there the Stingelhammer Guild is working,' said Zwist, pointing to the left. 'On the other side are teams from the Three Brothers Guild.'

The untrammelled hair of Zaravaz, blacker than knavery and lifted on the updraughts, softly grazed the side of Asrăthiel's face. She closed her eyes.

'This is a natural cavern,' said Zwist, 'with ore veins running prolifically through it - chiefly galena, arsenopyrite, sphalerite, chalcopyrite, calcite and quartz. The thickness of the main ore veins varies from several inches up to one yard.

He might as well be speaking another language, Asrăthiel thought vaguely, for all it means to me at this moment.

'Those trolleys - ' Zwist pointed a finger – 'are taking freshly dug ore to be sorted. Worthless rock goes to the waste dump, for possible use as backfill. Low-grade ore is taken to the stockpile, for blending with high grade, or for later treatment. The run of mine, which is the valuable ore, goes to the millstock pile, to be put through crushers and sag mills, then to be cleansed and concentrated before proceeding to the smelters and thence to the refineries. '

Zaravaz stood up straight, drawing Asrăthiel with him. She opened her eyes, having barely absorbed anything she had been told.

'The smelters provide quite a spectacle,' said affable Zwist, behind her shoulder. 'No human being has ever seen them.'

'Is it your pleasure to view a silverworks, Lady Maelstronnar?' the goblin king invited, in his usual lightly mocking tone; part serious and gentle, part scoffing and ironic, part angry. So many elements of his manner seemed to be in conflict that Asrăthiel could not know what to make of him.

'I should like that,' she said.

A deep, inclined shaft blocked their path; they crossed it on a narrow plank. The ropes dangling down through the middle of the chasm were jiggling without apparent cause, and just as they stepped off the plank an empty bucket came tumbling down at their backs, banging and sliding. In exchange, a full container briefly illumined by Zwist's lantern shot out of the gloom below, vanishing upwards with startling rapidity. Had they remained on the plank a moment longer, Asrăthiel thought, they must certainly have been knocked into the shaft. The notion unnerved her, though her companions appeared oblivious of such dangers.

In a side cavern further along a vigorous fire was blazing against a rock face, tended by knockers in their shirtsleeves. The miners jumped back, while others brought up hoses. Jets of cold water spurted from the nozzles, dousing the flames, to the accompaniment of loud reports as the heat-expanded rock contracted and split into fragments. As soon as this was over, the little diggers attacked the rock face with zeal, gouging out the broken ore with wedges and picks. They paused only to salute the goblin king.

Asrăthiel and her two guides arrived at the foot of a spiral staircase cut into the rock. As they ascended the damsel could hear, through thicknesses of rock, the rhythmic thunder of the crushing battery's gigantic hammers. At the top of the stair they crossed the floor of a chamber occupied by enormous bins heaped with powdered ore that resembled mounds of ashes, sand or brick dust. Each bin was identified by a rune chalked on its side.

A cabbage-water stench wafted from a gaping tunnel. 'Down there lie the roasting furnaces,' Zwist informed Asrăthiel, 'tepid fires where mispickels rid the ore of sulphur.'

The goblin king steered a course in the opposite direction, and after a while the damsel found herself walking along a precarious footpath shallowly chipped into the side of a cliff. A slow-moving cable-way ran through the cavern below, which was as big as a tourney field. Laden skips traversed the cavern; as they did so, kobolds seized them with grappling hooks and tipped them up so that their powdery contents fell out onto the floor in lines. Hundreds more bluish-skinned imps were spreading the dusts in layers. Zwist said something about silver ores being mixed with fluxes of coke and limestone on bedding floors, but Asrăthiel hardly heard him.

The Silverstreet Smelter was situated in caverns abutting a volcanic vent. Washes of rich tangerine light flickering from pits of simmering lava illumined the whole place, and it was hotter than any ordinary mortal could endure - although the heat could not trouble Asrăthiel, who was by then suffering more severely from inner fires scalding her to the core.

'Here,' said Zwist, 'Is where the heat of the smelters drives off impurities such as sulphur dioxide and arsenic.'

Imps on high platforms threw the fluxed ore through the mouths of the blast furnaces. Molten metal, shimmering and smoking, streamed into wells on one side of the great ovens, and crews wielding long-handled pots ladled it into hundred pound moulds. Cooled bars of this base bullion were being stacked onto railway trucks and hauled away to be refined. The fume and steam was tremendous.

'Base bullion contains more lead than silver,' said Zwist. 'Mortal silverworkers, Lady Sioctíne, fall prey to the abundance of lead gases that blast furnaces pump out. Over the years they slowly choke to death on the poison.'

The weathermage felt obliged to be polite, in spite of her distractedness. 'You are most informative, lieutenant.'

She was whisked away to the underground refineries, where she observed bars of base bullion being melted in large crucibles, after which the kobolds lowered the temperature very slowly, skimming off the lead crystals as they formed on the surface. They repeated this process several times, using a succession of crucibles, until the metal's lead content was drastically reduced. This silver-rich residue was poured into cupellation hearths, from which blasts of fiery air raged through the caverns, hot enough to blister walls of stone.

'It is bruited that you are inviolable, Mistress Stormbringer,' said Zaravaz. 'How fortunate for you, here in this infernal pit.'

Had he placed some subtle, suggestive emphasis on the word 'inviolable'?

'I daresay you would fain be aboveground, weltering in your wind and rain,' he continued.

'On the contrary,' she said, darting a bold look at him. 'I like it here.'

Zwist took no part in this exchange. His attention was fixed fervently on the silver cupellation hearths. 'The heat converts the remaining lead to litharge,' he said, 'which assimilates any other lingering base metal constituents. Our mispickels drain off the litharge, leaving purified silver in the hearth.' The goblin knight stepped across the floor. With his bare hands he scooped up some of the cupelled metal, still hot, dripping and fluid as quicksilver. The watching weathermage could not help but cry out. Oblivious of her needless distress Zwist gazed long upon the molten silver before letting it trickle away through his fingers.

When he rejoined them a skin of shining metal was hardening on his hands. 'The slag is drained off on the other side of the furnaces,' he remarked, 'and trucked away to be dumped.'

'A wizardly trick,' Asrăthiel said, staring at his hands.

'Oh, I was in agony all right,' Zwist assured her. 'Silver has a low melting point compared to metals such as iron and iridium, but it sears goblin flesh indescribably. Pain but no damage.' Wincing, he peeled away pieces of the the thin film of silver; beneath, his skin remained unmarked.

'Are kobolds not as immune to the effects of heat as other wights?' asked Asrăthiel, noting that the imps wore thick gloves and attempted to keep away from the worst of the blasts.

'Watch,' said Zwist. He signalled to one of the workers, who ran up to him and bowed. The knight gave a command in the goblin language, whereupon the creature loped away and jumped into the mass of fiery slag spilling like syrup from the far side of the furnaces. A blue light flared and the kobold melted instantly.

Tendrils of indigo smoke corkscrewed into the air, then dissolved. 'You see,' said the lieutenant, 'they are not immune.'

Asrăthiel was horrified. 'You have no compunction!' she snapped, turning her back on him.

'The thing was unalive!' Zwist exclaimed, spreading his partially silvered hands palms upwards in a gesture of guiltlessness. 'The unalive cannot be killed.'

'Nevertheless,' said Asrăthiel.

'Short spans are standard fare for them,' the knight said in a somewhat conciliatory tone. 'This is perilous ground for mispickels. If they avoid falling into a furnace, they might be run over by a train or injured by direct contact with iron. Iron is prolific here, as you can see. Too, salts exist in these ores; sometimes in the form of sodium chloride, most damaging to them. Their existence is short, but fortunately more of them can be manufactured when necessary.'

'The lady disapproves of you, aachaptan,' said Zaravaz, evidently entertained by his lieutenant's attempts to vindicate himself.

Railway lines crisscrossed the floors of the refineries. A couple of kobolds whizzed by on a gangers' trolley, madly pumping the seesawing handles, their tapered ears blowing backwards or forwards with the speed of their passing. On a siding nearby waited long trains of linked freight trucks and other rolling stock. Workers were filling deep, open wagons with liquid slag, then hitching them to a moving cable that ran between the rails. Off they went, clanking up a steep incline that wound its way into a tunnel. When they reappeared on the far side of an underground hillock, they had climbed higher, mounting some distant scarp or embankment that resembled a dully-glowing waterfall in the dark. The heaped contents of each iron pot were incandescent, making the train resemble some mythical beast with long lines of moving eyes. At the top of the luminescent bank the monster halted and the eyes dimmed, but Asrăthiel could make out tiny figures with long pincers in their outstretched hands, with which they seized the lip of each wagon and slowly tipped them sideways, disgorging the entrails of the furnaces. Flaming meteors of red and orange fire sprayed the dim scarp, glimmering brilliant emerald and plunged in feverish amber, wheeling and splattering down the slag pile. Viscous fireballs tumbled, blazing, down over the dump, fanning out to become a surge that exploded over the scalded embankment in gouts of glittering froth.

It was like a vision from the world's birth.

Beneath the roar of blast furnaces kobold workers were belting out a song, keeping time with the twitching of their barbed tails:

'*T' fuill-yiarg er yiarn,*
T' glassoil er copuir
T' gormaghey er kobolt,
T' geayney er nickyl.'

'By Cleave and Lockridge, that song does so subtly unrhyme,' Zwist remarked, wincing.

'And so adeptly does the melody assail the hearing,' subjoined Zaravaz. 'Let us depart ere this rhapsody makes us swoon for joy.'

They returned to the upper levels where, at the bidding of his lord, Zwist left them alone.

At the midnight hour, when moonlight laved the heights, Asrăthiel stood with Zaravaz on a cliff-top balcony overhanging a precipitous ravine. The wind had subsided and, on the other side of the gorge grey-white vapours were pouring down the mountainsides like thin sheets of water. Near at hand a fountain gushed from a carved stone spout set into the rock, its droplets chiming like a wild music of bells. Somewhere amongst the rugged bluffs a lone flautist, some eldritch wight, was piping an ethereal melody that rebounded from every mineral facet, multiplying until it harmonised with its own echoes.

From the corners of sight the weathermage watched her companion. He had never been from her thoughts since first she set eyes on him. What was it about him that magnetized her so? Was it his demeanour – vital, untamed, unpredictable; or the look of him – tall and tapered, sculptured, the quintessence of masculinity;

was it the way he moved, with a predator's poised swiftness and a dancer's grace; swift, lithe and perfectly balanced, or was it those charismatic eyes, shards of dark amethyst rimmed by midnight lashes?

Or perhaps some kind of spell was woven into his hair. . .

. . .which flowed gently down, as black as hatred, to drape across his shoulders the way skeins of silk would caress cast steel. It might have been the contrast of the soft fluidity and the adamant, in such close juxtaposition; like water pouring over rock; like long plumes spilled over armour, or like a veil of shadow let fall upon an oaken beam that seized control of her senses. In that contrast was an allurement that gripped her heart and tore it out by the roots. And when the wind, the fortunate, lawless, imbecilic wind, dipped long fingers into the nightfall of his hair and lifted strands of it, at leisure, into the air while he remained motionless, unmoved, and more beautiful than heart's desire, she could have wept for jealousy and cursed the wanton air currents, and if she had possessed the power she might have grasped them in her hands and torn them and hurled them over the edges of the world, for daring to venture where she would trade her sanity to go.

It seemed the fixation was mutual, or else he had guessed her thoughts.

'*Eunyssagh. Aalin folt liauyr,*' murmured Zaravaz, catching up a wisp of Asrăthiel's hair as it blew in the breeze. Idly he stroked it. When he spoke, his breath had turned to ghosts.

She stood yielding. 'What is the meaning of those words?' she whispered presently, her own exhalations condensing to mist in the cold.

'Such lovely tresses.' He smiled down at her, then something caught his eye and, directing her attention to an outflung spur of basalt, clearly visible across the moonlit valley, he said, 'Look there!'

A daemon horse trotted into view, exquisite, fleet as cloud-shadows.

'Behold Tangwystil, who brought you here!' said the goblin king. 'She chose you on the battlefield, not being mine to give.'

'I am honoured,' said Asrăthiel.

'No human being ever rode a trollhäst, before you.'

Amongst so many eldritch beings, Asrăthiel was beginning to feel unhuman.

Zaravaz called out, his voice ringing clearly in the pure, cold air. The trollhäst named Tangwystil stamped and shook out her gaseous mane, then cantered away, sure-footed as a goat amongst the crags. She seemed limned by emerald pyres.

'Next time we ride out,' said Zaravaz, 'you shall come with us. Do you like the gifts I have sent, the gowns and other fripperies?'

'I do.'

'Then I will gift you with more pleasures.'

Taking Asrăthiel by the hand the goblin king led her through a doorway. They entered a large and high-vaulted chamber of gothic loveliness, circular in shape, its walls perforated almost all the way around by unglazed archways exposing the interior to the elements, its ceiling an intricate openwork lattice giving almost unrestricted view of the frozen peaks that towered against star-pitted skies. There was no sense of enclosure. This was a chamber that shut out neither landscape nor wind, neither cloud nor constellation.

In the centre stood a couch piled with sleek and glossy cushions, while to one side a table upheld a jewellery casket of embossed silver. Zaravaz lifted the lid from the casket and a diffuse illumination radiated out. He handed Asrăthiel a globe of light that reminded her of the jewel she had given to the urisk, Crowthistle, yet this sparkled palest blue whereas the other, at its core, had glittered virginal white.

'It is a frost-jewel,' said Zaravaz. 'They are enchanted baubles, quite rare, fashioned from frost, and hardened by gramarye so that they cannot melt, like the ice-fern traceries on some of your gowns.'

'Once I owned something like this,' she said.

'Now you own many,' said Zaravaz, gesturing towards the casket.

Asrăthiel picked up the jewels and admired them, one by one. Each was dazzling, yet subtly different in colour and lustre from the last. Carefully she let the brilliant ornaments fall back into their padded nest. Beholding them reminded her of her mother, asleep in her cupola of glass and roses. The white jewel had belonged once to Jewel, who was its namesake. Now she had given away that heirloom and it was lost to her, like her mother and father. It was gone, like the little urisk, as some day her grandfather would also be gone.

A sense of desolation and loneliness swept over Asrăthiel at this reminder of past grief, but even as she mourned, she thought a flame of midnight flared urgently at her side. Zaravaz was standing so close that her skin tingled in the dance of eldritch energies surrounding him. He placed a finger beneath her chin, gently tilting her head up so that he could look directly into her eyes. His gaze was calm, evaluative and acutely sensual. Adrift in the violent essence of his gaze Asrăthiel was, yet again, thunderstruck by the terrible beauty of the goblin king. His touch, his look, were erotic in the extreme. He was the most exciting eldritch being she could ever have imagined, yet violent beyond all limits. She utterly deplored his principles, or lack thereof, but was profoundly attracted, in a physical sense, against her better judgement.

It seemed he had divined the sadness that afflicted her when she looked at the jewels. 'It is time to celebrate life,' he said, and for once there was no trace of sarcasm in his tone, only tenderness. 'It is time to cease dwelling on the heartbeat that has stopped, and instead to rejoice in the heart that throbs with vitality, the pulse that quickens to the exuberance of song, the flight of dance, and the thrill of speed, and lovemaking, and power.'

For just an instant, she hesitated, shocked without fully comprehending why.

'An open book,' he said, 'is easily read.'

Understanding with a start of shame and outrage that he knew exactly what net she was caught in, she murmured some excuse, picked up her skirts and ran from the room.

The weathermage found her way back to her silver apartments; it was never difficult, for trow-wives tended to flock around, offering their services as guides. Dawn arrived, but sleep refused to accompany it. Asrăthiel rolled fretfully upon her couch, as if in the grip of pyrexia. She had never fallen ill in her life, but had witnessed other people suffering from fevers; noted the sweat pouring from their flesh, and seen the way they shivered and could not lie still. I have contracted some eldritch ague she said to herself, or been poisoned by arsenic, or bewitched. But they were all empty pretexts; she knew it was not so.

She thought it strange that this should happen. Asrăthiel despised everything the goblin king stood for; cruelty, pitilessness, exploitation, and war against humankind. For his part, he was arrogant and contemptuous of her well-loved people. Although her philosophies were identical to his in some aspects, in others they could not be more at variance. Genuine incompatibility existed between the two of them. Politically, they were worlds apart. On a completely different level, nonetheless, it was apparent that a fierce attraction existed between them. She had become obsessed with him, and it was obvious the obsession was reciprocated in full force.

So that, on the cloudy morning when Asrăthiel tried to sleep, racked by thoughts and desires, handsome Zaravaz, whose hair was blacker than wickedness, entered the twilit bedchamber where she was lying awake, and merely took a seat at the foot of her couch, nothing more.

She saw him through the gloom, sitting silently with his back turned, as if deep in thought, or as if waiting. At first she said to herself, I will fight this, but he continued to remain there without moving, and when she looked upon him once more all else vanished from sight and comprehension, leaving nothing but the intensity of his beauty, and she thought she must die of yearning. In spite of her misgivings she was no longer able to resist. She rose up from her pillows, reached out and touched him on the shoulder. He turned around.

After the swiftest of glances, which clearly told him all he needed to know, his reaction was as immediate as it was extreme. He took her in his arms, pushing her back down upon the pillows.

She felt his weight on her, his darkness pouring around them both like a canopy, his desire an ignition. Long and taut was his body, lean as a blade and hard. Through the spilling strands of her own hair, she stared with wide-open eyes at his handsome face, finely drawn against all that liquid shadow, and saw his look of fierce hunger. His mouth tasted as sweet as rain; his fragrance was myrrh and incense. A sweet and terrible heat spread from him to her like a delicious contagion, coursing through every pathway of her blood, and she lay transfixed with rapture beneath his touch. There could be no other embrace like this.

They spoke not a word to each other, but the consummation of their passion was single-minded, vehement and all devouring. It was a gale picking them up and dashing them against the midnight sky; more than a wind; a hurricane, a storm of ecstasy, but she clung to him as if she were drowning.

All she could do was try to breathe.

8
WATERGLASS TARN

What draws me to your flame, unseelie knight;
A moth to singe my wings with eldritch light?
What drives me mad to lie down at your side,
Reluctant, yet as eager as a bride?
You are some poison, yet a draught so sweet
I yearn to drink until I am replete.
You might destroy me with your wicked ways,
With pleasure's surfeit you could end my days.
Bring death or love – 'tis all the same to me.
In both I'm blind, in both I am set free.

A VERSE FROM 'CAITLIN GROVES',
A FOLK SONG ABOUT A DAMSEL BEWITCHED BY A GANCONER'S SPELL.

Then it happened that each day, while the goblin knights slumbered, or dozed, or lounged on cushioned couches idly pondering chess moves, or lingered in some trancelike state; and while the trows, who had retreated to their own niches, remained dormant until nightfall, and while the sun laved the Northern Ramparts with a pale radiance beyond Sølvetårn's black curtains, they lay together, Zaravaz and Asrăthiel; and each night, as if by mutual consent – although no such pact had been made between them - they behaved as though nothing had occurred. It was as if each of them had split between two different modes; the driven, silent, desperately sensual persona of Sølvetårn's sleeping hours, each devouring the other with need, and the cool, calculating, courteously aloof persona of the waking hours.

For matters had changed between them, necessarily.

All the ardency burned there in his hard and insistent touch, his look of fire, and she made no attempt to hide her own compulsion. When they were publicly in each other's company, however – at feasts, or when surveying some treasure store, or gliding in silver boats on mountain tarns, or riding through the wind-swept steeps - their conversations together held nothing of that. At nights they never spoke of their daily encounters, although the intensity of their fervour was conveyed with every glance and contact.

As for the actual encounters – never a word passed between them then, either. All took place in silence, for the language of the body was sufficient communication and more, and expressed what words could never, need never convey.

For Asrăthiel it was as if talking about what happened and acknowledging it would make it real; as if by never referring to it, she might make believe it was not taking place. Often, when alone, she would imagine she must have been bewitched. She could not conjure any legitimate excuse why she would lie with the very incarnation of wickedness. Every rational principle protested against it. He was not of her kind. He was iniquitous and fell. Indeed he was beautiful, but he was not for her, never for her, and she felt she ought to have held out against his allurement. And she would picture William, dear kind William, her friend and gentle companion who would have risked his life to save her. For years he had loved her without pressing his suit, because he comprehended she was not ready to love him in return. Patiently he waited, as her friend. Asrăthiel understood, now, how corrosively the waiting must have seared his spirit.

Sometimes she felt as if she were transfigured into another person entirely, every morning when her eldritch lover came to her, in her bedchamber. It could not possibly be Asrăthiel, Daughter of the

House of Maelstronnar, powerful weathermage, who had allowed herself to descend into such a predicament – bound by wanton passion to an unseelie lord. To lie with him was like coupling with the night itself; it was to be consumed in an inferno of bliss. She wondered – was she exceptional in his eyes, did she mean anything to him, or was he perhaps so amorous with all women? But there was no way of knowing, and ultimately it hardly mattered, since, of course, she cared nothing for him and was merely ensorcelled.

She mused, too, upon the histories of mortal men and women who had united with eldritch wights. Swanmaidens and lake damsels had been known to marry human men, for example. The men had prospered in their lives before losing their seelie, luck-bringing wives by carelessly violating some eldritch prohibition. Not so fortunate were human beings who transacted with unseelie incarnations - the seductive, deadly youths called ganconers satisfied their lust with unwary maidens then left their pining victims wasting away to their deaths. The baobhansith were sluttish beauties who slew their erstwhile lovers and, conceivably, drank their blood. Whether seelie or unseelie, every such alliance ended in tragedy. There was a saying in the Four Kingdoms of Tir: '*All love between mortal and immortal is doomed*'; but some quoted it as, '*All love between human being and eldritch wight is doomed.*'

However there was no love involved in their intrigue, Asrăthiel told herself, and no mortal, either. It was outside the bounds of anything that had been before, and subject to no rule except the natural law that dictated that the flame of desire must eventually flicker out, but might be enjoyed before its inevitable extinguishment.

At whiles she went out riding with the horde, and they would career across the mountains as if winged, leaping impossible gulfs, springing up to incredible heights, with the breath of chaos howling in their hair, in an ecstasy of exhilaration. Joy was hers, and pure elation. It came to Asrăthiel that she was in fact celebrating life to the fullest, for the very first time - rejoicing in the heart that throbbed with vitality, the pulse that quickened to the exuberance of song, the flight of dance, and the thrill of speed, and power, and lovemaking.

A verse from one of the urisk's old ribald ditties ran through her head and would not be got rid of:

'*...My arms reached upward. I was not to blame.*
For all my heart seemed hungering to feel
The strange delight that made my senses reel.
It seemed so strange that pleasure should be pain,
And yet I fain would suffer once again.'

Asrăthiel guessed the goblin king understood she was acting against her better judgment, being swayed by ungovernable impulses. Once, as they paused on an icy summit watching stars fall from the night sky, he said, as if commenting on the spectacle, 'We are all at the mercy of forces beyond our control. The world itself is subject to influences from alien reaches, such as this ceaseless rain of flaming meteors. From epoch to epoch, chunks of interstellar rock or ice the size of planetoids slam directly into the planet's surface, with far reaching effects on the environment. The sun's rays power the atmosphere, nourish life and propel the currents of the oceans. Solar flares influence auroras and the world's magnetic fields. The moon collaborates with the sun to create tides in the oceans, in the atmosphere and even in solid rock. When a mortal man is shut away from sunlight for a long period, as Toadstone was, the internal clock that tells him when to wake and when to sleep resets, synchronizing itself with the tides. Even the world's pathway around the sun is being gradually changed by the gravitational tug of other planets. Over a one hundred thousand year cycle, the shape of the orbit alters from a circle to an ellipse. What's more, the pull of other planets modifies the angle of our planet's axis, giving rise to profound climatic changes; the cycle of the ice ages. The inspiration of stars that died billions of years ago still lives on in ourselves, and in this globe of ore and stone veiled with water. Celestial bodies and otherworldly energies affect life forms and their habitats everywhere. If the very world is subject to unruly persuasions, what chance have such as we to dodge them?'

Asrăthiel made no reply and Zaravaz said no more on the topic.

Days and nights passed, throughout which she exchanged more letters with the outside world by way of trow messengers, thereby learning from her grandfather that William had been sending messages she never received. She presumed either the trows had lost them or, more likely, Zaravaz had intercepted and destroyed them. Her indignation had no recourse; if she accused the goblin king he might decide to cut off her every contact with the outside world, and that, she would not risk.

Avalloc's letters kept her abreast of the principal events unfolding in Tir. Across the four kingdoms the human population was striving to rebuild lives riven by warfare. Many nonhuman populations were also striving to recover, for there had been much slaughter and destruction done by the travelling armies; large numbers of wild birds and beasts had been slain by foragers. The kobold watch that the goblins had left behind was assiduous in its duty, zealously keeping an eye out for what they considered to be wrongdoing, and swooping in to chastise.

At High Darioneth there were few prentices who could wield the brí, but Aoust being a temperate month of long, sunny days and balmy nights, scant weathermastery was called for. Dristan oversaw such matters. Avalloc spent many hours in his library, deep in discussion with two of his oldest friends, who had accepted the Storm Lord's invitation to live out the rest of their days in the Maelstronnar household.

Following the goblins' startling and ominous removal of Primoris Asper Virosus the Sanctorum authorities, eager to undo Virosus's works and thereby prove themselves unallied with that offender of goblin sensibilities, had released the controversial sage Constanter Clementer from the sink of a cellar beneath a remote rural sanctorum, in which he had languished for years. Somewhat the worse for wear, but with his spirits unbroken and his notes for A Treatise on the Iron Tree; a Narrative Concerning the Tree, the Precious Stone Trapped Therein, and the Consequences of the Stone's Removal intact, Clementer and his colleague and life-long comrade Almus Agnellus were enjoying Avalloc's hospitality at Rowan Green. No longer was there any need for Agnellus to spend his days in hiding, travelling incognito, continually moving from place to place to elude discovery, living from hand to mouth. In their twilight years these two venerable gentlemen could take pleasure in bodily comforts, good company, and the leisure to write page after page in undisturbed contentment.

When not in conference or attending to his duties, Avalloc would compose long letters to Asrǎthiel. At nights he left the scrolls, tied up with thin red ribbon, next to his pillow. Come morning they would be gone, sometimes replaced by an epistle from his granddaughter locked away in the Halls of the Mountain King. He conjectured that the household brownie delivered the letters by way of a trow courier, but he could never be sure; though he seldom slept, his eyes were not quick enough to spy the doings of wights.

He told Asrǎthiel how there had been general rejoicing at the announcement of her news that Virosus and Ó Maoldúin had perished at the hands of the goblins. The druids of Slievmordhu's Sanctorum had disowned the actions of their old primoris, he who had aided Uabhar with the slaying of the weathermasters. Some obstinately continued tinkering at their 'weatherworking' apparatus, with limited success, while terrified others tried to dismantle the appliances in case they should somehow cause offence to the goblins. Much squabbling went on within the sanctorums.

The elderly mother of Uabhar died serenely in her sleep. Her ancient minstrel, Luchóg, composed a dirge for her that was widely complimented, to his own amazement. Great songs and ballads were also made to celebrate the name of Conall Gearnach, glorious champion of the Knights of the Brand, who had been slain while performing deeds of valour in battle.

After the downfall of Gearnach, the people of Slievmordhu turned to Prince Ronin, next in line for the throne now that his elder brother lay in his tomb. They begged him to receive the crown straightaway. There could be no internal dissension if the heir to this long-enduring dynasty assumed the throne - but almost as importantly, Ronin was a popular choice, since he had already proven his bravery and qualities of leadership. He was the one man who had the power to unite all parties in loyalty and obedience. Unhesitatingly, so as to restore order as swiftly as possible, the captains swore and oath of allegiance to him and King Ronin succeeded to the sovereignty of Slievmordhu.

'Let dissent never be confused with disloyalty,' he told his advisors and courtiers in his first address to them as their sovereign. 'Do not fear to speak your mind to me. To see what is right, and not to do it, shows want of courage.'

His first act as king was to abolish the Day of Heroes.

Though Ronin accepted the crown and throne of Slievmordhu, contentment eluded him, for he mourned his brother and father, and sometimes in the dead of night he woke wondering whether he had inherited the Sanctorum's punishment; whether the house of Ó Maoldúin was still cursed for all time in spite of Virosus's hasty recantation. But it was said of him by the sages that he was a great leader, for a good leader inspires others with confidence in him, while a great leader inspires them with confidence in themselves.

The anguish of Queen Saibh at the loss of her son Kieran was as harrowing as only a parent's grief can be. Fortunately for this meek woman, a dear and long-lost friend returned unexpectedly. It was her servant Fedlamid macDall, he who had been deemed slain while on an errand for his mistress. The reappearance of this loyal man in Cathair Rua brought great joy to the royal household and provided some solace to the grieving queen. He told of being trow-bound in a mountain fastness from which, unaccountably, he had been set free. When he learned that Lady Asrăthiel had been taken to Sølvetårn he became convinced that she had bargained for his freedom.

It was at this juncture that in the desert kingdom of Ashqalêth a previously unsuspected groundswell became evident – widespread popular support for deceased King Chohrab Shechem's eldest daughter, Princess Shahzadeh. Jhallavad's royal advisors and retainers held her in the highest esteem. It had long been whispered in court and throughout the land that she had turned out to be the cleverest and strongest member of the royal family, and for years many had bemoaned the fact she had not been born male.

In an unprecedented move, Shahzadeh was officially made queen uncrowned; monarch-in-waiting. Never before had a woman ruled Ashqalêth, but Avalloc Storm Lord sent his unqualified blessing, and the Sanctorum followed his lead soon afterwards – convinced, possibly, by the large sums of money the princess shrewdly bestowed upon that institution in token of her considerable respect for the druids. With the sanction of such powerful authorities so evident, the approval of the populace, already considerable, grew even stronger.

Grïmnørsland was in mourning for Prince Halvdan, and now for his youngest brother also. Thorgild had forgiven Gunnlaug for his tergiversation at Ironstone Keep and received him back into the royal household, but soon afterwards the rowdy prince had died in a brawl outside a tavern. Drunk and unsteady he threw a punch, slipped, and fell on the cobbled roadway, hitting his head. The injury proved lethal. Upon his untimely demise the people of the western realm grieved, but not for long. His untrustworthiness had made him exceedingly unpopular; nobody liked a man who changed direction with the wind. In contrast Halvdan had been well loved, and his death was lamented bitterly.

Elsewhere in Narngalis, to the shock and amazement of all who knew the history of the Iron Tree and the wells of everlasting life, the immortal Fionnbar Aonarán was found wandering and jabbering, half-witless amongst the abandoned mines at Silverton. Having roundly declared that he regretted his immortality and would continue to seek a way to end his life he had thrown himself off a cliff. This proving unsuccessful, he had leaped into a bonfire, then tried to throttle himself by means of a noose depending from the rafters of a hayshed. His alarming attempts, which all failed, were in danger of becoming farcical, but before he could take them any further a band of constables conducted him to the Asylum for Lunatics at King's Winterbourne.

This much Avalloc conveyed in his letters to Asrăthiel, but there were many affairs of which circumstances kept her in ignorance. In his earliest correspondence to her, for example, the Storm Lord had written, 'Ever since you rode away with the goblin knights, Prince William of Narngalis has hardly been seen to eat or sleep. He spends every waking moment planning your deliverance, and feverishly works towards that goal, aided in every way by Warwick and his household, myself, and throngs of willing supporters throughout the land.' Though ink had flowed from the nib of the Storm Lord's pen onto the paper, though he had sealed the letter with red wax, and though the wax had seemed unbroken when Asrăthiel received the billet in her hand, somehow, between the sending and the delivering, those phrases – and other remarks on the same topic – had been lost. Even more strangely no gap, no damage, no mark existed to show that they had ever stained the page.

There were also subjects upon which Avalloc rarely touched.

No matter how many other matters claimed his attention, the Storm Lord never failed to keep his customary vigil at the side of his sleeping daughter-in-law, in the rosy cupola atop his house. There, upon chatoyant satins and soft bolsters of crimson velvet, Jewel lay like a marble sculpture of a beautiful, dark-haired woman. Her living skin glowed like peach blossom and powdered carnations; her lids, lightly closed, were blue opal fishes.

'We will fetch her back, my dear Jewel, I promise,' Avalloc would murmur. 'They will never keep her.' Sometimes, dropping his grizzled brow into his hands he whispered to himself, distraught, 'I cannot lose them all!'

Then there were events and circumstances about which even the Storm Lord could know nothing.

In the Eastern Ranges two timid Marauders discovered they now had the run of the caves because most of their kin-swarmsmen had died in battle, so they rolled some great boulders and stopped up the tunnels leading to the lair of the Spawn Mother in case she pounced and devoured them while they were sleeping. There they lived out their lives in contentment.

In the north of the kingdom, atop the highest peak of Storth Cynros where clouds left pearly kisses on knives of rock, two misshapen bags sometimes flapped, sometimes hung motionless. Spikes had been driven into the rock face, and fetters clamped the flapping objects to the spikes. Clad in perished rags and desiccated hides, two sets of human bones swung and clashed in the wind.

Hundreds of feet below those blowing skeletons and unaware of them, within the icy mountain fastness of Sølvetårn, Asrăthiel was being schooled in many matters, amongst them the true history of Goblinkind.

She learned that in past millennia when Tir, which they called Calaldor, had been warmer, Goblinkind - the Glashtinsluight - had dwelled in a remote land to the northeast. Ellan Vannin, the Land of Mists, was a lush and verdant realm, swathed generously in glimmering vapours, but with the advent of a new Ice Age the whole world had grown cold, and Ellan Vannin changed. Then differences of opinion arose amongst the Glashtinsluight. Those who proclaimed they wanted to move away immediately in search of more temperate climes were at variance with a group who wished to stay forever, as lords of the approaching ice. Others wanted to emigrate, but preferred to wait a little longer before leaving their ancient homeland. These differences gave rise to no conflict; it was their way to trust their leaders, and ultimately to accept their choices.

Most of the *liannyn*, the alluring she-goblins of the Glashtinsluight, favoured the notion of remaining for a while in Ellan Vannin. Of their masculine counterparts, the *graihyn*, most split into three factions, or clans, and ventured forth - some travelling east, some west, some due south. When they had found a pleasing territory, they declared, they would return to fetch those of the Glashtinsluight who wished to follow them there. Asrăthiel wondered why the liannyn had wished to stay behind – she could only conjecture that perhaps they preferred a settled existence, or wanted a temporary separation from their consorts to spice up the tedium of eternal existence with the anticipation of rendezvous and the excitement of reunion. The workings of eldritch minds were baffling; maybe they could never be comprehended by human beings.

Notwithstanding their original intentions, as decades went by the three departed clans delayed their return and extended their travels, their attention continually caught by some new adventure. They forgot, temporarily, those they had left behind, (what cared they for time, the immortals? There would be time enough for everything); drawn on by the excitement of exploration and discovery.

As Ellan Vannin cooled, it became Ellan Istillkutl, the Land of Ice. Once, humid mists had blocked out the sun's light. Those vapours dried out and vanished but the land remained dim, now overcast by persistent cloud. The *graihyn* and *liannyn* who tarried said, 'We shall stay in our native land and become the Istillkindë, the Ice Goblins, taking this name to ourselves as a token of the choice we have made.'

Glaciers came creeping down from the north pole, and the trees dwindled. Increasing cold transformed the margins of the land into tundra, with permanently frozen subsoil, supporting only low-growing vegetation such as lichens, mosses and stunted shrubs. Ellan Istillkutl's heart froze over, but the Ice Goblins reigned in ice castles.

It was an inherent trait of the Glashtinsluight that they attracted clouds, mists, fog and all manner of steams and fumes. They did not relish daylight, although they could endure it if necessary. Overcast or misty days suited them best - and, of course, the night - therefore the clans who ventured forth sought territories where the sun's rays were weak. Those who became the Fire Goblins, the Ailekindë, went southeast, to dwell in volcanic lands darkened by smokes and ash-clouds and dusky gases. The Dorragskindë, the Midnight Goblins, travelled due south. At length they came upon an ancient forest of mighty pines, deep and vast, whose dense canopy harboured profound shadows, screening out the sun, and it was there they established themselves.

At whiles during this long-drawn era of their history, messengers passed between the clans. The Silver Goblins received some tidings, for a while, but eventually reports petered out and finally ceased. Last they heard, most of the she-goblins had departed from Ellan Vannin, setting an eastward course. Asrǎthiel supposed this had been some impulsive move on their part; she had learned enough about goblinkind to know they could be mercurial, unpredictable, spurred to action by a sudden whim and heedless of the consequences.

Those that had journeyed west, the Silver Goblins, happened upon sprawling acres of barren hills they named Cheer ny Yindyssyn; Land of Wonders. Humankind would have marvelled at this jewelled landscape, for though vegetation was sparse, beauty could be found everywhere. The knights of the Argenkindë lingered long amongst valleys carpeted with zircon sands and garnet gravels and walled with slabs of lapis lazuli - heavenly blue flecked with pyrite 'gold'. They delighted in the bijouterie hollows of this countryside, taking their daytime rest in caverns richly encrusted with precious stones. But ever and anon they would look south toward the great, notched peaks of the mountains, the Smuinaghtyn, or Northern Ramparts as they were called in the four kingdoms, and eventually they left Cheer ny Yindyssyn and travelled to this destination.

The Argenkindë discovered silver in abundance beneath the Northern Ramparts. Sølvetårn they built there, of starlight and jewels, its towers mist-enfolded and frost-silvered. While the primeval mining-wights continued their digging, the kobold slaves manufactured curious artefacts, and goblins wrought splendid ones. Content were they to remain there, for many years, because the mountains and the mines were good to them in all but one respect, and that single flaw - the werefire that continually raged in the depths - could easily be avoided.

Avalloc had taught Asrǎthiel about this phenomenon. The Inglefire, he had told her, was no common conflagration, but an ancient, everlasting blaze of gramarye that burned deep beneath Silver Mountain. Its name was a corruption of the old word,

'Aingealfyre'; 'Aingeal' meaning 'light'. The fire was enigmatic and no man understood it fully, the laws that governed it were not known, and even the weathermaster swordsmith could not plumb its deepest mysteries. One thing was known for sure, however; the blaze was anathema to unseelie things. The horde could not abide it; could not even go near it. Indeed, the phenomenon was perilous to all beings in some degree.

When at last they tired of metal-smithing and enhancing their wondrous fastness the Argenkindë looked south once more. It was then that they first mingled with the human race, and learned how mortal men, despite being wise enough to know better, treated other living beings.

To begin with, the Argenkindë sent ambassadors and teachers to persuade humankind to change its habits. When this approach did not succeed the horde, outraged, began to hunt and slay men as punishment for their offences, while declaring to humanity that these raids would cease if they renounced their exploitative ways. When threats also failed to have the desired effect, the *graihyn* decided to conquer the four kingdoms and make them a dwelling place only for goblinkind.

They would do so, nonetheless, at their leisure for, jaded as they had become, they meant to get some use out of the condemned race before they rendered them extinct. Instead of delivering one deadly stroke of annihilation the goblins, in order to amuse themselves and bring cheer to their eternal years, deliberately prolonged their sportive hounding of those who violated the rights of blameless creatures.

Like all the Glashtinsluight, the Argenkindë were hampered in their building and their delvings by one problem – the fact that gold was poison to them, and to their kobold slaves. Whenever the wightish miners struck veins of gold, they must order them to stop digging. So it came to pass that the goblins decided to capture some human slaves, who could handle gold on their behalf.

The Glashtinsluight, in the way of eldritch wights, were arrogant. They considered themselves stationed far above humankind, because goblins possessed powers such as mortal men could only envy and yearn for. Humanity was weak and vulnerable. After passing sentence upon them, the Argenkindë opined they had the right to use these criminals as slave labour. Therefore they stole the able-bodied men, and left the weaklings; the women and children and the elderly. They employed the men to dig out gold ore, and hurl it into the pit of werefire, so that it would no longer pollute the world with its yellow shining and its scalding pain.

This enslavement and brutal hunting continued for decades. The human population was powerless to stop it, and their anger and resentment grew, until men decided to move gold from their treasuries into their arsenals and the Goblin Wars began. Massive military offensives, punctuated by skirmishes, continued over a period of several years. The mortal forces were always defeated because they could not match the fighting speed of their foes, and besides, the four kingdoms, being divided by political arguments, would not unite against them. Moreover there was quarrelling over the valuable ammunition. The Argenkindë exacted severe revenge when any of their number was scorched by gold, thereby the wars escalated, and the unseelie forces always had the upper hand.

During the wars, lies and propaganda grew into tales of horror about goblinkind. It was true they slew men, but stories said they inflicted atrocious torments on the weak, which they never did. It was true their looks were exceptional, but human legend twisted their beauty into ugliness, the better to make the enemy worthy of defeat. Those who looked upon their beauty in the mists rarely lived to tell the tale; those who survived thought them monsters and described them accordingly, or confused them with the kobolds.

The Argenkindë failed to suspect that the great weathermage Alfardëne possessed the skill to fashion a weapon of gramarye; nor did they foresee that daring weathermasters would steal secretly, by day, into the goblin-shunned caverns beneath Silver Mountain where burned the werefire, there to forge Fallowblade. The unique virtues of that fire strengthened the blade's properties a millionfold, and the golden sword became pivotal to the downfall of the Silver

Goblins. Instead of conquering, the Argenkindë were conquered by the weathermasters, and imprisoned in caverns coated with gold.

Their defeat would not, however, have been possible without one deciding factor. It was a betrayal from within the ranks of the goblins themselves that ultimately clinched their downfall.

'Tell me,' said Asrăthiel to Zaravaz. Under snowy crags that glimmered pearly white against the midnight sky she and he glided in a high-prowed boat upon Waterglass Tarn, he standing, graceful and careless, resting one hand on the prow while he looked across the water; she seated, her gaze wandering down the black shower of his hair. 'Tell me of this betrayal that brought down your kindred.'

Star reflections meshed the shadowy water and the sky sparkled with sidereal light. It was like being enclosed within a sphere of obsidian studded with diamonds.

'It was I who was betrayed,' he said.

And he told her.

The hunting of men was amongst the favourite sports of the goblin king. He took great pleasure in that chase. Furthermore, he liked to capture large numbers of human slaves, because he was keen to ensure the unmaking of as much gold as possible.

His first lieutenant at that time, Aachionard Zorn, was of a different ilk. Zorn declared that humanity must be immediately wiped out if the goblins were ever to bring true justice to Calaldor. This would entail destroying all the slaves, and all the men so often pursued as game. Time and again, Zorn begged the goblin king to change his mind and commence wholesale slaughter. Zaravaz, however, would be ruled by no one.

While devoted to his sovereign, Zorn also believed he knew what was best for him, and for the Argenkindë. He was convinced that Zaravaz was blind to reason. To persuade his lord to come around to his way of thinking, the first lieutenant formulated a plan: he would betray Zaravaz to the weathermasters and allow them to capture him. He was confident that the tribulation of being imprisoned by those he despised would persuade the haughty goblin king to hate the human race so viscerally that he would perceive the wisdom of Zorn's advice. The first lieutenant expected that Zaravaz would employ his considerable powers - which he unhesitatingly used against kobolds and knights who disobeyed him - to escape, thereafter leading the Argenkindë in triumph to extinguish the human race once and for all.

As she listened to this tale of unseelie cruelty Asrăthiel withheld protest. Zaravaz was aware of her opinions; voicing them again would not change anything. 'How was it done, the betrayal?' she merely asked.

He replied, 'Zorn made a secret pact with your forefather, Avolundar Maelstronnar. My faithful first lieutenant avowed he would lure me into a snare, under the condition that Avolundar would let him, Zorn, go free after the event. Though Zorn could not lie, as none of us can lie, he was as adept at prevarication as anyone. He made out that he wanted to be king in my stead, and that once crowned, he would lead the Argenkindë out of Calaldor, leaving the human race to go about its cruel business unmolested. For my part, I was unaware of the clandestine discussions between Zorn and Avolundar. I knew Zorn was loyal to the core, like all of my proud *graihyn*, and I never questioned his motives. I fell for his dissembling, and accompanied him to the place he nominated. There the weathermasters trapped me in a golden cage.'

Zaravaz fell silent, as if brooding, and Asrăthiel pondered on the disastrous effects of gold upon goblinkind. To be caught in a golden cage would surely have caused him unimaginable anguish.

'And did you not respond as Zorn had estimated?'

'I did not, for I had not foreseen any of it, and your kinfolk were too swift for me. As I writhed in the prison of pain they summoned every ounce of their energy, bending it upon me in one awful curse. It needed all their combined strength to lay that enchantment on me, yet had I not been discomfited by the touch of gold, they could never have bound me with it. But bind me they did. They could not destroy me; they merely diminished me, warping my shape and stifling my power, until I became harmless to them. Then they set me free. It was by then too late for revenge, for I had been rendered ineffective. To the Argenkindë I was as if dead, for they knew not whither I had gone. Without the head the body is incapacitated. While they had been plotting to ensnare me, the weathermasters had been forging Fallowblade. After my downfall they assailed my brethren, led by Avolundar, their foremost warrior, who wielded the golden sword. My knights, in sudden disarray, were defeated.'

'It seems to me I have heard this tale before, or something like it,' Asrǎthiel mused. What of Zorn?'

'Tortured by regret for having brought about the ruin of his captain and kindred, that one plunged into the pit of the Skagnyaile, that men named the Aingealfyre, and perished.'

'The Aingealfyre! That is the furnace where Fallowblade was made; the Inglefire. Does it still exist?'

'It burns in its pit far below these ranges, even as we speak. Its whereabouts have passed out of human knowledge, and I would keep it secret, lest any more weapons like Sioctíne should ever be created.'

Asrǎthiel recalled hearing it said that the Inglefire burned out wickedness; that was why the sword was pure, and smote goblins so well. After the Goblin Wars no human being sought the Inglefire, for it was deemed there was no need to fashion more swords such as Fallowblade.

Little had they guessed, in those days.

An umbrageous breeze of night-time fanned the damsel's hair with its wings, and ruffled the surface of the tarn. 'I understand that the Inglefire is a flame of purification,' she said, riding in the high-prowed boat with the irresistible king of goblins. 'As a blast furnace refines silver, ridding it of base metals, so the Inglefire decontaminates unseelie visitations, burning away the badness.'

'Somewhat true, regrettably. More accurately, it destroys us,' said Zaravaz. He stood tall and straight, directing his lavender gaze across the water as if witnessing some occult circumstance she could never hope to comprehend. 'Unseeliekind do not perish immediately, but suffer extremes of agony as they wither, becoming a fragment of living ash that flies up to blow about in the atmosphere for eternity.'

'What is the way of the Fire of Gramarye with mortalkind,' asked Asrăthiel in horrified fascination, 'should anyone be so unfortunate as to accidentally topple in?'

'Mortal men do not perish immediately but fade slowly, without much pain, in some kind of trance. Those who are pure of spirit survive longer than those whose hearts are corrupt.'

'You are exact in your descriptions. It sounds to me as if you have seen such things happen.'

'That I have.'

The damsel refrained from asking whether the men he had observed perishing in the werefire had fallen in by chance or been thrown in by kobolds; the answer seemed obvious.

'A fire that burns out wickedness...' she said instead. 'Little wonder the Glashtinsluight avoid it.' This was close to an insult she knew, but dared it anyway, unable to resist allowing a small but stinging barb to escape from her pent-up arsenal of resentment against goblin savagery.

Her companion merely laughed. 'What is wickedness?' he said lazily. 'Humankind calls genocide 'wickedness'. We, too view the taking of lives as 'wrong' in the broad sense, though, like your kind, we believe that if it is 'in a good cause' it is justified. The Glashtinsluight are not bad or wrong – far from it – though if 'wickedness' refers to the propensity for killing; in particular the supernatural propensity for killing human beings, then yes, we are wicked.'

'And that is what we call 'unseelieness',' said Asrăthiel. 'If all the unseelieness were scoured out of the Glashtinsluight, what would remain?' Without waiting for an answer she went on, 'Ah, but the Inglefire is astonishing. It is the most incredible forge fire, for Fallowblade affects time itself, or appears to. When wielding him I felt as if I were labouring through some viscid substance instead of air; my surroundings seemed to move slowly. In battle this allowed me to pause for deliberation and enabled the swiftest action.'

'That weapon permits whoever holds it to enter the time stream of the Glashtinsluight,' said Zaravaz, bending his head to look at her, 'lending the swordsman the capacity to match our fighting speed. The gravity of Fallowblade is negative, and therefore it accelerates time.'

'I do not understand.'

'The stronger the gravity, the more slowly time passes. Gravity slows clocks of all kinds.'

'How curious!' said Asrăthiel. 'But Fallowblade is made of gold, platinum and iridium. They are ordinary metals, I daresay, with ordinary weight and gravity. The sword always felt heavy enough in my hand.'

'Only because you assumed the same gravity when you took hold of it,' replied the goblin king. He took a seat beside her - so close that she was instantly intoxicated – leaning back against the prow and negligently resting one booted foot upon the gunwale. 'In their normal form those three metals are in fact relatively weighty. As the estimable Zwist so often repeats, delighting as he does in numeracy, the specific gravity of gold is nineteen point three, of platinum twenty-one point five, and of iridium twenty-two point four. By comparison silver's gravity is ten point five and that of arsenic is only five point seven three. Part of the miracle of the accursed Skagnyaile is that it reversed the gravities of Sioctíne's component metals, making them preternaturally slight.'

'Fallowblade is wondrously fair to look upon,' said Asrăthiel, 'yet no doubt the Argenkindë would like him to be thrown into the werefire and destroyed.'

Zaravaz looked amused. Slightly cocking his head to one side he said, 'Do not presume, witchling, that we reason like mortal men. The thing is a fount of divertissement for us. The slight chance of being extinguished is an unfamiliar novelty, adding zest to life. We seek thrills through risk. Endless existence might otherwise threaten to pall, through monotony. Nothing presents much danger for the Glashtinsluight; your Fallowblade is one exception. Besides,' Zaravaz added with a smile characteristic of goblin haughtiness, 'there is scant need to fear some man-cobbled artefact that can only be employed by a rare few.'

As if unaffected by her lover's nearness Asrăthiel leaned over the side of the boat to watch her own image reflected in the lake, a wistful countenance framed by dark tresses, against a backdrop of stars. 'I cannot imagine what it must be like for you, to dwell always in a faster time stream.' She trailed her fingers in the water, vaguely hoping the chill might cool her unwanted ardency.

'Not always - we can move in and out of it at will. Antigravity capabilities are inherent in us; we can summon them or not, as human beings summon adrenalin when instinct tells them to fight or flee.'

'Gravity is the opposite of levity,' said Asrăthiel. 'The Argenkindë are inclined to levity, I have noticed.'

'Perhaps we do laugh longer and oftener than solemn human beings who, being destined for the grave, wax grave. Yet it seems,' Zaravaz said musingly, 'since my return from exile I have lost much of my former jocosity.' Glancing in Asrăthiel's direction he added cuttingly, 'Forgive me for wearying you with tedious exposition, Mistress Stormbringer. You cannot imagine how distraught one would feel, to have bored you.'

'On the contrary!' the damsel looked up quickly. She admired his cunning eloquence; that he, an eldritch wight unable to tell falsehoods, could juggle truth and sarcasm with obvious ease. 'You misread me. I find Glashtinsluight lore intriguing. There is much about your kindred I have yet to learn.'

His marvellous smile never failed to disorient her.

'I trust I may continue to lesson you,' he said, gathering himself out of his relaxed sprawl and turning towards her.

She had to look away again, lest she grow dizzy and fall out of the boat. 'Prithee, tell me more about goblinkind.'

'Of course, if it please you,' he said, very softly, his mouth right next to her ear. He stood up once more, fluidly, barely rocking the boat but leaving her forsaken. 'My kindred are intimately connected with the universe. When we look into the sky we can perceive distant quasars, supernovae and other astronomical phenomena that the human denizens of Tir will never know, though some might observe the nearest through their rude spyglasses.'

'I should like to see such wonders.'

'If you wish, a telescope will be built for you on one of the highest crags.'

'I do wish it.'

Zaravaz turned upon the damsel a look of desire so extreme it might melt basalt, like plutonic fires. Impetuously she reached out to touch him, but at that moment a group of horsemen passed by along the shores of the lake, and when she glanced down she saw the almond-eyed face of some lake-maiden peering up from beneath the water. Disconcerted by these intrusions Asrăthiel drew back.

Her lover smiled again, as if possessing some singular knowledge, and appeared to scrutinize the constellations. A breeze arose. As the boat skimmed across the water, behind him the silken length of his hair streamed like a cloud unravelled by the wind.

9
CROWTHISTLE

What is the wisdom of Queen Night,
Whom shining stars adorn?
She knows we yearn to reach those lights,
For of them we are born.

SUNG BY LAKE MAIDENS

Aoust the twenty-eighth was Asrăthiel's birthday. She had not mentioned the fact to anyone in Sølvetårn, yet apparently it was common knowledge. A party was got up, and the whole of the fastness seemed to be celebrating, or else using it as an excuse for revelry. As time passed the damsel had found ways to make herself more able to endure her yearnings for home, her straitened circumstances, the banishment from the company of family and friends. In her unseelie lover she saw what she desired most of all and least of all. He was with her every day. Before nightfall she would fall asleep, and when she opened her eyes he would always be gone. In the evening when he first set eyes on her, he would kiss her hair casually, but no more than that.

His thoughtfulness was constant, his generosity boundless. Often she would glance up, by chance, to see him watching her with that curious look of intense longing. He laughed and jested;

his witticisms could provoke uproarious hilarity; he could evoke the most moving music from the strings of a violin.

Occasionally, when they traversed the underworld together, she would place one hand upon the shoulder of Zaravaz and the other upon a rock of the living mountain, and then he would let her read the geological story of the mineral, and reaching deeper, the story of the making of the world. That way she learned of the ranges' birth; how they had begun beneath an ancient ocean as layers of pebbles and stones, sand and mud, mingled with the shells and skeletons of primeval creatures, and how the layers had built up until their weight had forced their particles together to become hard rock, one of the slowly moving dorsal plates on the world's restless reptilian hide. Two plates had collided, grinding together, and the lip of one slid over the edge of the other. Dragon's-breath heat from deep inside the world liquefied some of the lower plate's rock to magma, while huge forces produced by the spinning core of iron at the planet's heart began to lift the seabed. Great slabs of rock along the line of collision were forced upwards. Fiery magma jetted up through fragile spots, forming a row of volcanoes. As the two plates continued to slide together the buckling, twisting layers of rock were forced higher, while the volcanoes also grew, so that the range reared into the skies. The tremendous forces from beneath never ceased their slow violence, transforming the hard-pressed layers of seabed sediment into metamorphic or igneous rock, folding and cracking them to create faults, splitting the mountain range into blocks and grinding them against each other. Every year for millennia the Northern Ramparts grew a few inches taller.

As a weathermaster, Asrăthiel knew that even as the mountains were being born they were being worn away. Rainwater flowed into rocky crevices, turning to ice on the higher slopes. The ice's expansion thrust the cracks wider, eventually causing bits to break off with a sharp report and fall down the hillside. Broken fragments collected in piles at the foot of the slopes. Spores, too, took root in the hairline crevices that netted the moist rock faces. Lichens and mosses clung, their exploring roots making the rocks crumble.

Wind swept away the dislodged rocks. Rain and snowmelt washed them into streams. As they rolled down the streambeds they scraped away more of the mountain's flanks, while being ground down to lesser sizes. The rushing waters of rivers and streams excoriated deep furrows and valleys in the mountainsides. Rocks locked into glaciers abraded the land as they slid imperceptibly downhill towards the sea, where the ice would finally set them free to mix with other sands and muds to form new sediments. In the oceans the mountains began their saga and there they would ultimately return, to begin their cycle anew.

Asrăthiel was entranced by the life story of the planet as she received it through the influence of goblin gramarye, though no spell enthralled her like her lover. Unfailingly Zaravaz amazed the damsel. His eldritch gifts allowed him to move with a speed to outwit the eye, and with extraordinary precision. He could spring high and twirl four, five, six times before he landed. She had seen him catch hold of a rocky overhang and easily draw himself up on top of it by the pure strength of his arms. He could vault a high tor with no difficulty at all. While galloping at full speed on his incandescent daemon horse he could jump to his feet and ride standing up, or swing himself down beside the steed to cling sideways, along the length of its body, so that an observer might not know the trollhäst had a rider. Brazenly he flaunted himself before Asrăthiel; flaunted his beauty, his prowess.

Altogether he was appealing, confident and vivacious, yet in her life with him Asrăthiel was beset by doubt and loathing more often than not. She could not countenance the acts of cruelty he permitted to take place within his realm. To survive without losing her sanity she had to develop ways to push goblin atrocities from her mind before they overwhelmed her.

Zaravaz was not always at her side. Often he went away on business he would not give an account of, and she felt it best not to enquire in case it gave her nightmares; then she would walk alone on the mountains, for their strength and grandeur pleased her, and she could watch when goblin warriors went swooping on the virgin snow of the higher ridges, sending up plumes of ice-crystal powder as they plunged thousands of vertical feet in a controlled slide.

One windy night as clouds trailed like smoke across the moon, Asrăthiel was progressing along a narrow path when she spied, on the other side of a ravine, three human men in tattered clothing, lying beneath eaves of lichened rock. One was cowering and ranting, his comrade was coughing fit to burst, and the third was cradling his feet in his hands, whimpering as if they hurt him lamentably. Asrăthiel's first reaction was astonishment at beholding human beings in the environs of Sølvetårn; promptly she recognised the signs of arsenic poisoning; kobolds had lingered near those men, or had been handling them or mistreating them. The weathermage called out to the trio but they made no reply, perhaps not having heard over the bluster of the wind; perhaps being too wrapped in their private agonies. Wondering how they had arrived there and where they had come from she began to run towards the ice bridge that spanned the chasm, so that she might cross over and speak to them, but on the way she caught sight, through a gap between two boulders, of grinning kobolds riding on the backs of five more men, thrashing them with whips to make them go faster.

Bristling with indignation, Asrăthiel veered off her course in the wake of the kobolds. Translucent orange flames flared behind a bluff of rugged stone; rounding a corner she happened upon a group of goblin knights, amongst them Lieutenants Zauberin and Zwist. They had with them some mortal wretches in chains, who were hobbled, like sheep. Close at hand, kobolds were heating irons in a fire. From a distance, transfixed by horror, Asrăthiel watched as Zwist seized the men by the back of the neck and branded them on the shoulder, one by one.

'What are you doing?' she shouted.

Zauberin glanced sardonically in her direction. 'Killing time,' he called out.

With a cry of protest the damsel ran forward to help the suffering prisoners, but kobolds bundled them out of her sight. All she could do was engage in serious remonstration with the knights.

'You ride these men and brand them! Stop this torment!'

'Lady Sioctíne, these beishtyn were selected for our purpose,' Zwist politely responded, 'because they are strong and can run fast. And all have been chosen from amongst racehorse owners, horse-breakers, trainers, jockeys.'

'Not jockeys,' Zauberin interjected, smiling as he passed by.

'Nay, in sooth, for jockeys are too small to run swift, so they are, well -' Zwist said, 'how shall I put it delicately? I believe the euphemism used by humankind in horseracing is 'sold'.'

'Where did all these men come from?' Asrăthiel demanded.

Zauberin, returning, said, 'Some were recently captured, others were taken prisoner during the battles and have just now arrived here, having been herded across the land at their slug's pace. We allow them to roam the Northern Ramparts, for they are unable to break through eldritch barriers they cannot see - unable to return to the kingdoms of men. They are kept for divertisse-ment. We play with them, hunting the hunters from time to time, fishing for the fishers or letting the kobolds ride the horse-breakers. We keep some in a big glass bowl for entertainment, like gold-fish.' Plainly enjoying the damsel's reaction to his pronouncements Zauberin went on, 'Zwist is as enthusiastic about racing as any of us. We watch, we cheer, we bet on the outcomes. Often we give stimulants to the racers to make them run faster, for it adds to the excitement. And after the last race concludes we make men who once owned fighting cocks duel against each other with spurs on.'

But Asrăthiel turned away from Zauberin in cold rage and would listen to him no longer.

To Zwist she said, 'I had thought of you as polite, gallant, solicitous and helpful, utterly unlike any preconceptions of goblin hordes, and now I have seen you at this appalling work. You have shocked me back to reality. I was a fool. Never was there a truer saying, 'Be wary of wights. Be especially wary of unseelie wights."

'I vow, Lady Sioctíne,' said the knight, 'I will never harm you while you are under the protection of the horde. I vow the same for all the Glashtinsluight, and you must believe me, for we do not lie and we cannot help but honour our word as you know.'

'You mistake my meaning. It is not myself I am concerned for,' she said, and she took herself from their company.

Next night, in a tall barge draped with cloth-of-silver, Asrăthiel was floating with Zaravaz upon Ice Axe Tarn, mirrored and mist-twined. She brooded upon the situation of the horde's captives, and wondered how she could aid them. Her anguish was extreme. She was torn, unbearably, between hating her lover for authorizing - and probably encouraging - the savagery she had witnessed, and yearning only to cleave to him, excluding all others.

Some women, Asrăthiel knew, claimed to be attracted to 'bad' men, but she had never subscribed to that view or even come close to comprehending it. Cruelty could never compel her admiration – on the contrary she despised it with heart and mind. It violated everything she stood for. Her anger and confusion rose like a flood, drowning out coherency, and for some while she had been unable to bring herself to speak.

Clouds muffled the sky, and there was no breeze. Silver fili-gree lanterns hung at prow and stern, casting circular pools of clear white light around the boat, their radiance penetrating several yards into the walls of fog.

'Why have I not seen your human slaves before?' Asrăthiel asked suddenly.

'Oh, so you have found your tongue at last,' said Zaravaz, 'and the boddaghen also. They have been kept from your sight, lest their mewlings should distress you.'

'An ill secret, ill kept.' As she said this, Asrăthiel knew what look would flash into his eyes. She dared not glance up, but stared out across the water. 'Your harshness is beyond belief.'

The mists parted and she spied a group of bobbing lights, weak and yellow as withered dandelions. Ragged, emaciated men were straggling across the tarn in a flotilla of ramshackle boats, which they rowed with their hands. The damsel's heart went out to them in pity.

'They are starving!' she said indignantly to her companion, who turned his head to see what had caught her attention. 'Give them food and let them go.'

The goblin king did not reply, but a deeper stillness settled upon him. Asrăthiel recognised that stillness and her senses sharpened.

Small baskets woven of reeds plugged with clay came bobbing on the water. Some little fruitcakes nestled therein. Noticing these dainties, the men began to paddle eagerly towards them.

'It is clear to a blind man that this is some trap!' Asrăthiel cried. 'Those victuals are illusions created by glamour. I daresay they are nothing but pebbles, or wads of moss.' She shouted a warning to the men, but they took no notice. 'They are under some spell or curse!'

Zaravaz said coolly, 'Perhaps hunger is a curse.'

She called out again, but the goblin king gestured decisively with one hand. Their silver-draped barge tilted to one side and began to slew around to face the opposite direction. Before the men disappeared from view, however, the damsel saw them lean out of their vessels and grab the cakes, stuffing them into their mouths. Inclined lines, like bare willow withies, sketched themselves faintly against the mist...

The vapours closed in, muffling sounds, but through the thickness Asrăthiel heard a series of tremendous splashes. They were followed by spluttering and thrashing, as if paddles flailed in the water, interspersed with the sound of screaming. Waves fled across the surface, rocking the barge. Through the thinning mist Asrăthiel discerned a row of whip-like rods angling up from the shore, bending and bucking. The *graihyn* were winding in their catch.

'Stop this barbarity!' Asrăthiel shouted, but the goblin king spared her not so much as a glance, and the barge approached the land, bumping against the rocky shore. Zaravaz leaped onto dry land, but as he did so, a dirty human man ran up and prostrated himself at his feet.

'Lord, I beg for mercy,' said the man, too terrified to raise his eyes from the ground. 'Do not treat us like animals.'

'Are you not animals?' Zaravaz said in astonishment. 'Are you trees, or stones? You yourself, fisherman,' he continued in a voice of steel, 'have served other creatures worse than you are being served.'

'Great lord,' moaned the supplicant, 'we are not like dumb beasts and do not deserve to be treated thus. We have character, spirit, and speech. Beasts are not the equals of mankind!'

'Surprising news,' said Zaravaz. 'You are wrong.' He shot a quick look at Asrăthiel - who was climbing out of the barge - and added, with an air of sorely tried patience, 'Let me teach you, fisherman. Your prey is infused with social intelligence. They recognise individuals, and are mindful of complicated social relationships. Fish display consistent cultural traditions, and co-operate with one another to examine predators and gather food. Some wield tools, some construct houses, others tend underwater gardens. Their memories are exceedingly long. Their spatial memory is as good as that of your own kind; they can create complex cognitive maps by which to navigate. They feel agony as you do, for the pain centres in their brains match your own. You think they have no language? Their communication is not by speech but by pulses of electricity or by movement, or by altering their colours.'

Zaravaz stared haughtily down at the man, who had hoisted himself onto his knees. 'Fisher, is the way you view the world necessarily unbiased? Is it the only way? I will answer; no it is not, for like your fellow men your viewpoint is self-centred and narrower than a worm's gut. You, who have only ever seen fish contorting in the bottom of a boat or dead on your plate would not know any of the secrets of this remarkable race. So go you now, fisher, and flop about on a hook, that you may learn how they die, if not how they live.' He made a gesture as if flinging away a stone and the dirty man fell over backwards. Sobbing, he scrambled away. Zaravaz watched him depart, displaying no sign of emotion.

Asrăthiel approached the unseelie king. She was shaking from head to toe. 'You tell me,' she said, her voice trembling, 'that you wish to make me glad. Do so by ceasing at once your torment of these people. Release them!'

He turned his shoulder and began to walk off. 'It pleases me to please you when the whim strikes me,' he threw back, in wintry tones. 'But never delude yourself that you rule me.'

Zaravaz was well aware of Asrăthiel's hostility to his unkindness, but he made no alteration to accommodate her views other than, she surmised, generally separating her from scenes that would upset her. He could not be bothered with people who opposed him, and if she made a fuss he simply went away.

This, too, was difficult to bear.

To make matters worse, First Lieutenant Zauberin had taken to slyly winking at the damsel. She had overheard him, behind her back, derisively referring to her as 'the king's eager pupil' and 'his noonday dancer'. Recently that knight's every gesture, glance and word seemed filled with innuendo, so that she felt sullied in his presence, and she shunned him whenever she could. At such times Asrăthiel would say to herself, Once I was a powerful weathermage. Now I am reduced to being the doxy of a Lord of Wickedness, infatuated with a misanthropist who is rightly accursed and reviled by my race.

Zauberin always made certain his leader was out of earshot when he quipped. 'How merrily the water tumbles down yonder cliffs,' he said to Asrăthiel, pointing out the view through one of the windows. 'A pretty morning for a tumble, is it not?' and he pinned her with a meaningful smile, clearly tickled by her angry blushes.

'Pray, do not spurn me,' he would protest. 'Do not be discomfited! Your efforts are admirable.'

'Spare me your ridicule,' the damsel coldly retorted, walking away.

He pursued her. 'So quick you are to take offense, proud Sioctíne! I was about to compliment you, for you are a diplomat amongst us at this period of conflict, an ambassador for your people.'

Vexed and resentful, the damsel did not deign to give reply.

'In times of hostility,' the lieutenant persisted, 'when humankind takes issue with eldritchkind, it is only reasonable that the representatives of each nation should come together in congress to discuss their differences and grapple with the questions.'

Away she would hasten, but he'd locate her again, eventually, and lead her into some other eloquent snare.

The harasser went even further. Once, catching her off guard he whispered in her ear, 'Dwelling here must be a tedious struggle for you. Perhaps, if you become bored, you would like to struggle with someone new?'

On a night when Asrăthiel had again met Zauberin as if by chance, and been forced to bear his suggestive allusions, she made the wrenching decision to cease her liaison with Zaravaz. Her lover's harsh treatment of human beings had, since the beginning, been driving her to break the bond with him, coupled with ill defined qualms about whether there was some sort of moral wrongness to such a bizarre eldritch-human union. For certain, much of her uneasiness sprang from the fact that she had been raised to believe that all dalliances outside the covenant of wedlock were unethical. Against all these doubts she had been inwardly contending, day and night. The remarks of the lieutenant pushed her at last beyond the limits of endurance.

At the evening banquet she behaved coolly toward the goblin king, and would not look at him for fear she might change her mind, though they sat side by side.

'What troubles you?' he asked at last, when the feast was over and the music beginning. His voice was low, so that none might overhear. His black hair fell down, draping inside and outside the high svartlap collar that flared like the upright petals of a dark flower around his neck.

'I regret,' the damsel murmured stiffly, 'what happens between us in the mornings.'

'Why?'

There were so many reasons. 'For a start,' she replied, fixing her attention on an arrangement of jewellery fruit that adorned the table, 'amongst my people, such liaison should not be undertaken outside marriage.'

For a suspended moment, it was as if the air had frozen.

'Oh,' Zaravaz said loudly, 'you wish to be married? Why did you not say so?' He snapped his fingers.

With improbable swiftness, trow-wives placed a wedding veil on Asrăthiel's head, held in place by a silver chaplet decorated with tiny jewels. Before she could protest, or even move, they had wrapped her in a dress as white as new-fallen snow, covered with ice-fern traceries, festooned with filigree spider webs of silver thread, bordered with silver netting and silver lace, and beaded with seed pearls. Lieutenant Zauberin appeared before them all, solemn and pious in the white robes of a druid, while a band of trows struck up a wedding march on their squeaky fiddles.

The whole enterprise smacked of pantomime buffoonery. As Asrăthiel gaped at Zaravaz, who was suddenly dressed most dash-ingly in a long frockcoat and a top hat at a rakish angle, a squinting kobold thrust a bunch of crystal flowers into her hand. The goblin king clamped her arm under his elbow and said, 'Well, lady, are you ready to be wed?'

Asrăthiel wrenched herself free. 'No!' she cried, throwing down the bouquet, which smashed to pieces on the floor.

'Is it Zauberin you object to? We can always abduct a real druid…'

On impulse, Asrăthiel shouted, 'It is William that I love!'

This deliberate untruth seemed to have an effect. Zaravaz stared at her, and it was as if he wore a mask of iron. Then he strode away.

She did not see him again for three weeks.

During that time the damsel's attitudes were mixed indeed. She teetered between heartbreak and misery, loathing and longing, despair and anger. At her wit's end, she had no idea what course to take. Seated at her escritoire she wrote a flood of letters, but all incoming messages had ceased and she feared Zaravaz had blocked them, severing her only access to the outside world. Next it occurred to her that he probably scanned her outgoing messages, and wondered whether they were still delivered to her friends and family, or if it was a waste of time putting pen to paper. She asked the trows, but as usual they did not know, so she searched for Zwist, to beg him for information, but she could not find him or any of the knights. The feast hall was always empty, and the trows brought meals to her in her apartments, but she did not want to eat and left the food untouched on the trays, drinking only a little of the wine.

Some small comfort was to be found in allowing her brí-senses to wander out into the familiar circulation patterns of the atmosphere; tracing paths along the contours of cold fronts and cyclones, measuring the vectors of the winds, detecting the gath-erings and dispersals of humidity, apprehending storm cells and the fluctuations of temperature. From time to time great rolling outbreaks of rain and hail let down their mercurial chains across the mountain range, or snow stormed on the loftiest peaks. Eldritch mists and charmed clouds unfurled to drift caressingly along the slopes as gentle as phantasmic lovers.

She slept often, and when not sleeping she roved out alone, carrying food in case she stumbled upon any prisoners of war. None were to be found. The mountains were desolate. Only the wind moved amongst the crags. Even the minor wights seemed to have vanished; no wizened faces peeped from rock crevices. It was as if they had all turned their backs on her except the swift, aristocratic trollhästen, whose complex language of sound and movement she could not understand.

Unexpectedly, early one clear evening in late Sevember she encountered Zaravaz.

She discovered him on the high crag where stood the telescope the kobolds had made for her; a huge metal tube bolted to the rock and aimed like some weapon toward the stars. As was his wont, the goblin king was leaning on his elbows, resting them on a parapet that overlooked a sheer drop of more than a thousand feet. The breeze lifted his hair in glimmering strands that were black with the blackness of subterranean caverns never touched by sunlight, yet shot with blue opalescence. Asrăthiel fancied that if she touched that hair she'd get her fingers burnt.

On beholding him she experienced a spasm of relief, or hurt, and went to stand at his side. Without greeting her or acknowl-edging her presence in any other way he said, as they studied the night sky together, 'Telescopes are like time machines. To look into space is to look back in time. By the moment we see a celestial light, the event that caused it is long past.'

Asrăthiel regarded him quizzically. Had she once heard similar words in a dream?

He went on, 'From the stars come the elements from which this planet, and all things that live are made. If one views the life-time of Calaldor-Tir as a clock spanning twenty-four hours, the Glashtinsluight would have arisen two minutes before midnight, and the history of mankind would occupy only the last second. Yet in spite of differences we are all fashioned from star-dust.'

'Who told you that?' the damsel asked sharply, unsettled. She straightened, stepping back from the parapet.

He, too, stood up. 'Come hither,' he said.

Inquisitive yet wary, she obeyed. From his sleeve Zaravaz produced a velvety purse, and from that he extracted an object, which he showed to her. She drew a rapid breath. In the palm of his hand lay a point of convergence. It was as if moonlight was being sucked into this point and condensed to its purest essence, in the form of a mote of dazzling light the size of a cat's eye.

This concentrate of silver-white, this scintillant, gave off sparkles of reflected radiance, pure, yet flashing with every colour. There could be no doubt - it was the jewel, the heirloom of Asrăthiel's mother, which she had given to the urisk.

Asrăthiel felt a hand of iron clamp around her heart. 'What have you done,' she said slowly, 'to Crowthistle?'

And Zaravaz, more beautiful than starlight, answered gravely, 'Ah, Weatherwitch, I thought you would know. Your stroke, given in love not hatred, freed me. What I have done since then, I have done for you. You have my heart in thrall. Do you understand? I am Crowthistle.'

On hearing those words Asrăthiel disbelieved, but only for the space of a heartbeat. Next it was as if she had known all along, for it was so patently obvious. In wonder she stared at the goblin king, and a million questions and memories came crowding into her brain, and she must sit down at once, there on the edge of the world, on that ledge teetering above a thousand-foot drop scoured by blasting gales, so that she might absorb it all.

He rested beside her.

There was so much, then, to be told between them.

Zaravaz spoke again of the mighty curse cast upon him by the greatest of weathermasters. They caught him in a golden cage but they could not destroy him, he was too powerful for that, and there was no time to cast him into the Aingealfyre, for they must work quickly, before he could summon his gramarye; so they imposed upon him the shape and constraints of an urisk, intending that years spent as a domestic wight, mingling with mankind, might conceivably make him sympathetic to the human condition. All curses, nonetheless, no matter how dire, must have a cure. Zaravaz could be released from the enchantment only by the decollatory stroke of Fallowblade – then newly forged - wielded by a human being; a stroke given in freely bestowed love, not in enmity. These terms would seem impossible to fulfil. Indeed, Crowthistle had since waited long, without hope, for the curse – and his neck – to be broken.

Ironically, the same sword that had been forged to destroy goblins was the one object that could return him to his natural state. It was a property of the enchantment that the blade would not put an end to him, but instead free him – albeit, agonisingly. For he had suffered from that stroke, and suffered exquisitely.

When they crushed him into that urisk shape, the weathermasters also gifted Zaravaz with a gibing nickname; 'Crowthistle'. It was the weathermasters' joke on the defeated King of Goblins; the weed crowthistle being vulgar, hardy, difficult to be rid of, and despised by humankind, a plant that could not be eradicated; hated, prickly and hurtful, yet fair to look upon. Like goblinkind, crowthistle was one of the scourges of humanity. At first Zaravaz took perverse delight in the appellation. Later, it grew onerous.

It was a property of the curse that the urisk could not speak his true name; could not speak, either, of what had befallen him. Worse, he was unable to tell of the cure - not that it would have availed him. He had no reason to hope that any human creature would ever wield Fallowblade to strike the blow of freedom for him.

Having rendered him harmless the weathermasters let him go. They took care to make no song of their deed, nor to preserve it in records, in case human beings should take to harassing urisks. More pertinently, they wanted the Goblin King to simply fade into obscurity; they wished to wipe out memories of his name, his existence. They had no need to boast of their deed, not being braggarts. Besides, they surmised that if the story were known amongst unseelie wights, some would put forth great effort to bring about the liberation of the Goblin King.

As it happened, the few eldritch creatures who did encounter Crowthistle - such as the Maelstronnar brownie - sensed his latent powers regardless of the disguise; however there was nothing they could do to free him. In any case, he hated going amongst wights in that ignominious form, so he shunned them, mostly.

After wandering the four kingdoms in a frenzy of wrathful frustration the urisk eventually settled in the Great Marsh of Slievmordhu, because something in his urisk design was attracted to water. Eventually he decided to move on, but as the season of Spring sprinkled colours across the marshes Laoise Heronswood Swanreach married Tréan Connick, and the tale of Álainna Machnamh and Tierney A'Connacht came to the notice of Crowthistle. Tierney A'Connacht had once wielded Fallowblade, the only instrument that could free him. He felt impelled, then, to keep an eye on the family.

'I knew your mother,' Zaravaz said to Asrǎthiel, high on the windswept mountain crag beneath night's mantle. 'I knew her, and her mother Lilith, and her grandmother Liadan. I knew Laoise, the mother of Liadan. I was acquainted with them all, though perhaps they did not know me.'

'My mother!' whispered Asrăthiel, who had been listening in silent amazement.

'Once or twice Jewel saw the truth,' said Zaravaz. 'She witnessed my authentic image. She was the only one. Even such a unique curse as that which the weathermasters wrought with all their energies was insufficient to do more than barely overmaster me, and my own strength was still such that the glamour they imposed on me would not always extend to reflections. In water, or polished metal, or silvered glass, my genuine aspect was sometimes revealed, though such revelations were of no help to me. So intense were those images - powerful enough to push through the enchantment - that they often lingered on the surface after their subject, myself, had gone elsewhere. Once, Jewel saw a reflection of me in a pool near where I had been sitting. Another time she perceived my face mirrored in the back of her silver hairbrush, after I had stood for a moment close by.

'I could tolerate Jewel,' he said, 'more than I could bear others of your kind. She and Lilith, I found that I could endure them both.'

Asrăthiel knew this was a compliment of the highest order, from him.

He went on, 'Out of curiosity and perhaps an absurd shadow of hope - for what else was left to me? - I followed your mother when she migrated from the Marsh to High Darioneth, though she was not aware of my pursuit. In Rowan Green I stayed, despite my contempt for the lives and property of the weathermasters.'

'Did you ever speak to her, my mother?'

'We exchanged words.'

'I miss her so. She sleeps eternally in the house of my grandfather.'

'Yet if not for the intervention of Crowthistle she would now lie in her tomb.'

'What can you mean?' Asrăthiel stared at Zaravaz as if she had never seen him before.

'They believed she had died, after the mistletoe arrow of Fion-nuala Aonarán pierced her. They put her in the ground.'

'That I know already,' said the damsel. 'Agnellus saved her.'

'Before that,' said the goblin king, 'it was myself-as-urisk who, lingering by Jewel's grave, heard the long slow heartbeat beneath the ground, and knew she lived. I comprehended that this could only be because she had borne an immortal child. Thereafter I instructed a spriggan to steal some ink and take it to a swanmaiden, who took one of her discarded quill-feathers, and wrote down what I had discovered. At my direction a brownie stealthily placed the scroll amongst the papers of the scholar Agnellus.'

'So it was your doing! My family owes you gratitude indeed!'

The solemn mood of Zaravaz lifted a little, and he twitched an eyebrow, while examining his fingers. 'If that be so, you have already repaid the debt, Weatherwitch. Yet,' he appended, 'it is such a debt that it requires paying over and over.'

Confused about her own unspoken response, Asrăthiel made no immediate reply.

Presently she said softly, 'You guessed my mother still lived, although she was in her grave?'

'It was more than a guess,' said Zaravaz, 'it was certainty. Many amongst the Glashtinsluight are granted wisdom and insights, stemming from centuries of accumulated knowledge and experience, and from our intimacy with the cosmos.'

'Then, do you know how to waken her, too?'

Gently he said, 'Nay, ben drultagh, I do not,' and Asrăthiel's face fell. 'We understand much,' he continued, 'but not all.'

'But surely, as you say, your wisdom is as old as the ages…'

'Do you doubt me?' her lover's tone sharpened. 'We know of no balm for Jewel's ailment, for we have never had need to seek physic for humankind.' He did not add, Rather, the opposite, but the damsel could not prevent that phrase from flashing through her mind. 'Recall, I saved Lilith by leading Jarrod to her, and Jewel by letting the scholar know she still lived, so that she would be disinterred; now let Arran do his part and find a cure for Jewel, if one exists. If he cannot do that, he hardly deserves her.'

'Forgive me,' Asrăthiel murmured. 'I doubt you not.'

She sat quietly, her arms clasped about her knees, pondering on past meetings with the urisk Crowthistle. As she pictured an evening in the courtyard at Rowan Green, a revelation came to her like a burst of light. It had been during that discussion, when he had said to her; *No one is alone,* that, without being aware of it, she had fallen in love with him.

Then, he had worn the body of a goat-thing, or the illusion of it. There was never any chance of advancement of their association. They could be no more than friends. Now, on the other hand, matters were very different. Yet perhaps not so different, for although an alien shape no longer disunited them, now an alien mindset kept them apart. She loved him, yes; profoundly, but could never tell him so. His unseelieness was the stamp of doom on any furtherance of their connection.

Digressing to an earlier topic she said, 'In legend and lore, many shape-curses are ended by decapitation. After I felled you with the stroke of Fallowblade, what happened?'

'I do not know what occurred at first. Time passed, but I was not conscious of it. When I awoke, lying upon the ground, I inhabited my true form, but you were gone, leaving me with nothing other than some torn urisk weeds and your mother's jewel. I was not forsaken, however. Word had reached me, long before, that the knights of the Argenkindë had broken free of the golden caves. Already, I had travelled to Sølvetårn, where my *graihyn* welcomed me most fervently, but I was unable to lead them again unless I recovered my original estate. After you obliged me, I returned to them once more and assumed my rightful station.'

'Even as a humble urisk you never lost your kingly disposition,' said Asrăthiel. 'Crowthistle commanded a swanmaiden, a spriggan and a brownie! You were still giving orders, though deprived of capabilities!'

Zaravaz leaned lazily back against the parapet and stretched out his long legs. 'As I told you, eldritch wights could detect the echoes of high gramarye lingering ineffectively about me. It served to make them offer me more than the usual esteem.'

'Ah!' exclaimed Asrăthiel. 'I recall how our house brownie used to respect and fear you. You bullied him unconscionably.'

'At the time I could not resist frightening the squeamish doormat, but I regret it now,' her lover replied with the flicker of a wry grin. 'Such behaviour was beneath me. In my defence I can only declare how bitter it was to me, that the creature hung about your house, living under the same roof with you, able to be privy to your most intimate moments and with access to your personal belongings. In my jealousy, I would have hounded any mannish thing – eldritch or human - who had wormed his way so close to you though not a member of your family.'

'We had other servants.'

'But none who could disappear in the twinkling of an eye, or lurk unseen.'

'Of course!' Asrăthiel said, suddenly understanding. 'Knowing you now,' she added, 'I daresay it also enraged you to have been bundled into brotherhood with such a docile wight.'

'Even so. My pride took a beating, I admit. My enforced shape thwarted me at every turn, and I vented my anger on the nearest manlike creature that was neither your blood relation nor mortal.'

'Is that also why you threw out our belongings?' Recalling the pile of goods outside the front door of the Maelstronnar house the damsel could not help smiling. She turned aside, so that her companion should not see. In retrospect the event seemed quite hilarious.

'Well,' he said, and by his tone she could tell he was smiling too, 'I was a vexing house sprite, was I not? A troublesome imp. Small wonder you tried to banish me.'

'I never did!' she retorted, laughing aloud now.

'Some shirt you wished to give me,' he said playfully, 'or else my memory deals me tricks. You've made me crazy since I've known you, witch.'

Quite swiftly he put his hands on her shoulders and pressed her to the ground. Covering her body with his own, he lowered himself full length on her, and kissed her firmly on the mouth. His prosperous hair cascaded around them both in a dark tumble, shutting out the stars. She laughed, as a diversion, and teasingly pushed him. They rolled over and over like gambolling children, perilously close to the brink of the shelf, before he separated from her and they came to rest at last. With her back hard against the paving stones she lay beside the goblin king, looking up at the sky. She was burning for him, but determined to hide it. The deception had taken all the strength of her will.

'I understand now why you threw out some furnishings and not others,' she said, continuing the deflection. 'The library and kitchen disgusted you because the library accommodated parchments and vellum, while the kitchen contained dead flesh, organs, bones.'

'I despised your stables also, for all their leather saddles and tack,' he said. 'I loathed your wardrobes for their furs and leathers, the plumed hats. The dressing tables with their artefacts of ivory, and bone, tortoiseshell and horn, coral and pearl were utterly contemptible, and I spurned the use of quill pens made from live-plucked feathers.'

'So many articles of everyday use are derived from suffering,' Asrăthiel said sorrowfully. 'Dyes of cochineal and purple from mussels, beeswax candles, soap, lamp oil, eiderdowns, horsehair couches and bows, moleskins and glue; the list is appalling. In one respect,' she added, 'you and I could not be more alike. We share compassion for living things, and indignation at their persecution.'

'Save for the single species that is not blameless.'

'Having dwelled amongst us, do you still disdain us?'

It was a long time before he answered. 'Not quite as much.'

'You vowed you would slay every man, woman and child if I left Sølvetårn.'

'At the time, I meant it. The mood was on me. You understand, I am incapable of lying.'

His hair fanned out across the flagstones like the rays of a black sun. The damsel was aware her companion knew she was deceiving him, but was indulging her, allowing her to play the game. Such is his pride, she thought, that he nonchalantly waits, assured that I will return to his embrace, confident that no one can defy him.

Probably, also, he knew she was aware he knew. A small, hard object was digging into her left shoulder blade. She realised that her mother's jewel on its chain had swung around behind her back, and she was lying on it. Shifting her weight she reached over her shoulder and retrieved the ornament. Holding it aloft she watched the starlight seem to pour into its unwinking eye.

Her thoughts strayed to her relatives at Rowan Green and the companions she missed, and as she stared at the jewel she fell into a gloomy reverie, feeling as if she had betrayed them all with her misplaced passion. Presently she became aware that Zaravaz was watching her.

'You are unhappy here,' he observed.

Tucking away the scintillant inside the front of her bodice she made no reply. The silence lengthened. Eventually she said, 'How long will you keep me with you?'

'Until I tire of you.'

'You are impetuous. In your current disposition would you take such total vengeance on humanity, if I departed?'

'Weatherwitch,' said he, one moment lying down, the next seated upright, 'I have told you before - you ask too many questions.'

'And I shall continue to do so. Why do I receive no letters?'

'If it is letters you crave, I can write them aplenty.'

'From my friends and family!'

Zaravaz sighed and gave an exaggerated shrug. 'Well there it is,' he said. 'Your princely William has been encamped outside the gates of my halls almost since the night you arrived. Every hour he demands your release, but my knights, while assuring him that you're unharmed, tell him that you will not come forth, so he must go away. If it is traffic with him you want, you need only go to my front door and wave your hand.'

'William keeps vigil on your doorstep?' Asrăthiel started up, outraged. 'Why did you not advise me!'

'I am advising you now,' Zaravaz said formally.

Equally aloof the damsel said, 'Why was this information not conveyed in my grandfather's letters?'

'The wightish couriers might have been careless and dropped a line or two inadvertently as they carried the messages.'

'Oh yes, they might have been, but they were not, for how else can a line or two or an entire passage disappear except by deliberate trickery?'

The light-heartedness between them had vanished like morning mist. They both rose to their feet. Asrăthiel knew that her letters must have been tampered with, so that she had received no hint of William's proximity.

'One final question,' said Asrăthiel. 'As Crowthistle you always despised William. Why have you not killed him, if he vexes you so?'

'Perhaps you should run to save him,' Zaravaz said mockingly, and the steel in his voice was so sharp that a passing owl shrieked, and wheeled away in terror. 'Run away and save your poor little prince from the nasty goblins.'

10

BANQUET

A cruel chain, this mighty spell
That tames my strength with fetters fell
And warps the shape, and binds the tongue,
So secret sagas bide unsung.

Enchantment vile deceives the eyes
And tricks the brain with quaint disguise.
Fain would I crush this abject sham,
And trumpet who I really am!

LAMENT OF THE ACCURSED.

Straight away Asrăthiel hastened to the battlement walks over-looking the bridge of vitreous slenderness that crossed the crevasse at the front gate of Sølvetårn. On the far side of the span a burnished host was encamped on the terrace and up and down the nearby slopes, armour and weapons gleaming like pewter tableware in the starlight. It was not a large assembly – perhaps half a battalion. The damsel was sharp-eyed, yet the men were too distant for her to be able to make out individual faces. She descried, however, the flying banners of Narngalis and the Companions of the Cup, streaks of vivid colour on the wind, and amongst them the Royal Standard of Wyverstone.

William was down there.

What was he thinking? This was a rash move, which could easily incite the ire of the goblins. Conceivably the prince was counting, somewhat recklessly, on the battlefield promise of Zauberin, which could not possibly be false, but which might be worded equivocally, moulded by cunning subtlety. 'The Argenkindë will withdraw and leave the Four Kingdoms of Tir in peace,' the malevolent knight had said, 'if you'll comply.' That statement had been entirely open-ended, with no set time limit, and on close inspection, might have implied anything.

The weathermage watched the platoons for a while; the glint and stir of men moving amongst the tents. They had no horses with them. It would have been construed as an insulting gesture to bring beasts, caparisoned and tethered, before the Halls of the Mountain King; besides, the kobold watch would have prevented it. This challenge, a confrontation by human men, was insult enough. Dread dried out Asrăthiel's throat like astringent, and sapped her vitality. There could only be one outcome, if William were to provoke the anger of Zaravaz. She longed to go down to the encampment on the slope beyond the bridge; to see her dear friend again would make her glad. Yet the jealousy of Zaravaz would be lethal. Even as an urisk he had proclaimed his resentment of the prince. Crowthistle had disparaged William, apparently envious of his place in Asrăthiel's affections.

I counted Crowthistle amongst my comrades, mused the damsel. I believed he was fond of me. More likely, he only culti-vated my acquaintance because I was the wielder of Fallowblade, his key to freedom. He charmed me for his own insidious purposes, not because he genuinely held me in high regard. She told herself she was stung by this sudden hurtful insight, although in her heart she knew such a sting was non-existent, even if the conjecture were true. She was making an attempt to tarnish the love she could never realise. Thus deceiving herself, she vowed that she would shun Zaravaz whenever possible; that she would make every effort to excise him from her heart.

There was nothing further she could do but bide in discontent, pacing up and down the promenades overlooking the bridge and the bivouac, with fleets of clouds racing past above and below like sailing ships made of steam. The wind battered her garments and hair. Temperamentally the alpine gale increased in velocity, gusting to such magnitude that it threatened to push her over the side. Thereupon she returned to her suite, to lounge sullenly upon her window seat and brood.

Towards morning the trow-wife Hulda came and told her that Lieutenant Zwist was in the anteroom, waiting to conduct the damsel to a banquet.

'Oh, a banquet,' Asrăthiel said caustically. 'How delightful. Prithee tell him I will not attend.'

Dolefully the trow-wife trailed off. She returned a moment later saying, 'If tha pleases, ma'am, da chiarn, he say tha must. He bide ootside.'

Asrăthiel flounced to the door and flung it open. Zwist loitered there; elegant, erudite in ebony and silver, begemmed with black opals and jet. He bowed and offered his arm.

The damsel ignored the invitation. 'Regrettably your journey is wasted, sir,' she said. 'Convey to your liege, I do not wish to favour any more of his banquets.'

'That is a pity,' said Zwist, 'for I am sure Prince William will look for you.'

'William?' the damsel was astounded. 'Surely you do not mean he is to be present?'

'Indeed, he is to be our guest,' said the knight, smiling slightly, 'along with many of his officers.'

Asrăthiel's blood chilled. What new chicanery was this? What horrors had the goblin king inflicted upon William Wyverstone and his men? She must find out at once. 'Very well, I will come with you,' she said hurriedly, her pulse thundering.

Zwist responded, half laughing, 'I will wait for Lady Sioctíne to attire herself.'

Catching a glimpse of herself in a glass, Asrăthiel saw a wild-maned damsel in a torn dress. 'No, no, my appearance matters not.'

'Unkemptness can be interpreted as incivility,' admonished svelte Zwist, and she perceived she would not be able to cajole him.

With all speed Asrăthiel ran back to her dressing table, calling for her handmaidens.

Soon afterwards Zwist accompanied Asrăthiel along gorgeously carved and ornamented galleries to a dining hall she had not seen before. As they walked, the knight was obligingly regaling his companion with arbitrary facts in which she took no interest whatsoever, being overcome with anxiety and preoccupied with what she might soon discover.

'Although we call ourselves the Silver Goblins,' said Zwist, 'all the clans of the Glashtinsluight have an intrinsic relationship with silver. It runs in our blood. Pure silver is our most favoured metal; nonetheless we appreciate other metals with similar colour and lustre. Titanium, for example, and zirconium.'

'Yes, yes,' said Asrăthiel distractedly. 'How has your lord treated William?'

'With all courtesy due to a guest.'

This conveyed nothing. It was a matter of conjecture, what kind of courtesy, or lack thereof, goblinkind considered to be owing to a human visitor. 'Are we nearly there?' she asked.

'Almost. Platinum,' continued Zwist, blasé, 'when mixed with iridium gives a silver-white metal, but when alloyed with osmium it takes on a bluish tinge, not unpleasant. White ruthenium hardens platinum and palladium jewellery. Rhenium, rhodium and nickel are silvery in colour. We are quite fond of pewter, niobium and osmium. Electrum gleams like frost and would be a great favourite, with us, but unfortunately, as you know, it contains gold. Ah, here we are!' He released Asrăthiel's elbow and bowed once more. 'Conversation passes the time pleasantly, especially when one is apprehensive.'

And she knew then that he had kindly tried to distract her with his eloquence, and wondered afresh how one so wicked could be so considerate.

They entered a rib-vaulted chamber as large as a museum, its marble floor like sheer ice.

This new feast hall was bright with candles, lamps and bright green firelight from flames of burning barium nitrate and copper salts cavorting on cavernous hearths. Naturally formed silver ores with structures of extraordinary beauty could be glimpsed about this space up and down the walls, having perhaps evolved there. Numinous of hue were they, and wonderful of form; surpassingly lovely treasures of the deeps; delicately branching argent ferns with miniature lobes as fine as misty rain; coralline structures exquisitely formed; tiny jewelled fans and crystal lyres; gemmy birds and lizards of bijouterie; the jewelled silvers of the underground. The skeleton of a tiny raptor crouched in an alcove, fossilized by pure opal; a little, rainbow-hued work of art. Crossed swords, axes and other weapons of eldritch make were displayed on the walls, between fantastic tapestries, many yards long.

To Asrăthiel's surprise the Narngalish were indeed present in the hall; perhaps forty men; a handful of equerries and other retainers, eighteen noncommissioned officers, six captains, two majors, King Warwick's lieutenant-general, Sir Gilead Torrington, and William himself.

William! When the damsel caught sight of him moving amongst the long tables, she paused in the doorway. Almost at the same instant he spied her, and stopped in his tracks. But only for a mayfly's wing-beat; then he pushed his way through the crowd of men, goblins, trollhästen, and trows, and they approached each another. As they met, she curtseyed.

Here in this place, under the sharp scrutiny of this assemblage of knights both eldritch and human, the proper decorum must be shown. Though the damsel longed to greet William effusively she held back, behaving as propriety dictated.

The prince let his gaze rest upon Asrăthiel. She saw herself mirrored in his eyes; his expression clearly showed that he was recalling every detail. It had always entranced him, she knew, that even when she was in a solemn mood, the outer corners of her mouth curled upward, so that it almost seemed as if her lips curved in a faint, enigmatic smile. His glance took in her gown, fashioned of a web like sea foam and decorated with crystals of transparent tourmaline. Against the pallor of her raiment and jewels, her hair contrasted startlingly black, and her own eyes - it was as though two lucent panes of lapis lazuli had been set in ivory. Her lips were the crimson petals of a rose, her waist pliant as a whip, and slim as a reed.

For her part Asrăthiel beheld a statuesque nobleman, dark-haired, slender and able-bodied, with a grave mien. She noticed a few freckles across the bridge of his nose, and a trifling asymmetry in the set of his shoulders. It was almost imperceptible, but ever since she had dwelled in the company of eldritch flawlessness the slightest disproportion leapt out conspicuously. He had cultivated a moustache, since last they met, and a close-cropped beard sprouted on his chin. Beneath his woollen doublet and trousers he wore a shirt of linen. No sword hung at his side, only a small dagger.

'Are you hale?' William murmured, gazing searchingly at the damsel.

'I am.' Her throat felt constricted. She wanted to shout with joy at this meeting, but must swallow the exclamations that threatened to spill from her tongue. Nonetheless he read her delight in her face; she could tell. 'And you?'

'I too. I am jubilant to see you.'

It was obvious he ached to embrace her, but not here in this eldritch hall, in full view of the assembly, who watched them covertly, casually.

'How came you here?' Asrăthiel asked uncertainly. 'Are you all prisoners?'

'Unpredictably the goblins promised us safe conduct into Sølvetårn. We have been received cordially, and this feast has been given in our honour, to our amazement and suspicion.'

'They are masters of equivocation!' she warned softly.

'Of that I am aware. Be assured, my captains closely examined the phraseology of their promises before we accepted the invitation. They assured us their victuals would do us no harm and our freedom would not be compromised. Yet, had the goblins vowed to cut us to shreds after our visit, still I would have come to Minith Ariannath. I longed to see you.'

'You carry no sword, though I see they allowed you small side-arms.'

William said, 'I brought a blade of gold from King's Winterbourne. We have manufactured many gold-plated swords during the time since you left us. None like Fallowblade of course. But our hosts made us leave all our bullion outside the doors of Sølvetårn, as a condition of entry.'

The prince looked so unreservedly steadfast and honest, so chaste, standing there before Asräthiel; he who had been coura-geous enough to enter the lairs of iniquity for her sake, though with no adequate defence.

'Words cannot describe what a joy it is to look upon you again!' she said earnestly.

'Nor can they convey,' intervened a musical, derisive voice, 'what joy it gives me to have reunited two such intimate acquaintances.'

Both human beings flinched as a tall figure partially eclipsed the candlelight. Zaravaz was beside them, clad in shadows and dazzle, as provoking as insolence and as tantalising as secrets. As ever, his beauty, stature and bearing exacted attention. He smiled, but not as he had smiled before. It was such a look as might be the last sight a condemned man witnessed before his execution; the expression of a hunter who leans to slit the throat of a fallen deer.

'Prithee, condescend to grace my table,' invited the goblin king, glancing from one guest to the other in the manner of some generous benefactor. 'You shall be seated side by side.'

William frowned, manifestly unsettled, but although the demeanour of the goblin king was fraught with sarcasm and sinister overtones, there was nothing overt in his words to give offence.

When all had taken their places at the tables, the first course was served.

The banquet was the most socially uncomfortable occasion Asräthiel had ever experienced. Tension was so extreme as to be almost visible. It was as if the veneer of civility were a pane of thin-nest glass, so fragile that the merest ill-chosen word might shatter it into a myriad shards of lacerating violence. No one in the hall, not even the most slow-witted trow, could fail to be aware of the barely battened- down hostility between the two warrior corps. To begin with there was no exchange of words between the groups - none could bring themselves to it. The men strained to behave with utmost urbanity, yet ever and anon their trained reflexes were triggered by a suspicion of alarm, or their knife-edge pride took some subtle buffet, and their hands sought the hilts of their daggers beneath the table. The goblin knights, begemmed with black gauds - morion, jet, hematite, obsidian, rutile and black onyx - took pains to conceal their rancour, but it was evident nonetheless. They looked as if, rather than sharing a table, they would prefer to seize their guests and tear out their throats, and were keenly seeking an excuse to do so.

The damsel herself endured the dinner in torment of spirit, unsure as to the intentions of the Argenkindë, expecting every moment that a fight would break out, which would ensure doom for the men.

A low murmur of voices permeated the refectory, but at the table occupied by the goblin king and his foremost officers, William's company and the weathermage, there was only desultory conversation punctuated by awkward pauses, during one of which, Zaravaz turned to one of his knights and was heard to ask, 'Is there such a thing as death by boredom?'

Presently Zauberin made some lewd reference, aside, to his fellow diners, whereupon Asrăthiel heard the goblin king say to his first lieutenant, 'We will have none of your coarse jests tonight, my rag-rannee.' Zauberin, thus reprimanded, fell silent.

Aristocratic trollhästen roamed at will, adroitly, amongst the tables, their glimmering coats washed by the green glow of their manes. As ever, knights and daemon horses mingled amiably. Now and then a trollhäst would extend its expressive head between two diners and delicately remove some viand from a platter. Solemn eagle owls watched over all.

'They are barbaric and uncultured, to dine amongst their horses,' whispered William's knights.

'I never thought to see the inside of Minith Ariannath,' others muttered, as they stared about at the magnificence of the hall, 'I never dreamed of beholding the fabled setting of their wickedness and revelry.'

'I did not believe it existed!' said one of the officers.

'Those are fine weapons,' diplomatic Sir Gilead Torrington said aloud, surveying the armaments displayed on the walls. 'Marauders were seen to be scouring the battlefields for eldritch blades, but they could find none.'

Zauberin, his eyelid drooping indelicately, said, 'No *graihyn* let fall his sword during those games. Even if there had been any blades to find, no mortal *feiosagh* could wield them. In the hands of *sallagh* men, goblin weapons burn and dissolve.'

'In right sooth, they left very little that belonged to them on the battlefield,' William muttered to Asrăthiel. 'No blades, no corpses. We saw the way their fallen were transformed.'

Persisting in his endeavours to engender small talk to fill the difficult lulls Torrington again addressed the goblin knights. 'However, there was armour. I recognised your plate; I had seen pieces of it before. People named them 'gypsy leather', and sold them as valuable articles, supposed to bring luck.'

'What kind of luck?' Zaravaz asked innocently. 'Good or bad?'

'Good, methinks,' was the sharp reply.

'There's a fascinating superstition,' murmured Zauberin, with a contumelious grin which put an end to that topic.

Waving his hand in the direction of an appetizing display of provender Zwist said to the human officers, 'Pray sample all our dishes. We would not stint those who dine at our tables. Here is a great favourite, smothered in a sauce with bite; we call it 'Wolves Eat the Stranger'. Over here is a tasty triumph made with blood plums, known as 'Abruptly the Fool Blushed'.

'You jest, sir,' William said stonily. 'Perchance at our expense.'

Asrăthiel touched William on the arm. 'No not at all,' she hastened to assure the prince. 'Goblin recipes truly have such names. And I am sure those are delicious.'

She took a spoonful of one of her preferred dishes – a fragrant concoction quirkily named 'Envision an Avenue of Incense-Scented Trees Leading to a Translucent Palace' - and placed it on his plate, whereupon the prince thanked her with a smile.

Seated amongst his lieutenants, Zaravaz cast William a glance of bitter irony. 'Here's to your continued good health, your Royal Highness,' he said, raising high a chalice. 'I trust the wine is to your taste.' He took a deep draught from his cup.

It is probably poisoned, thought Asrăthiel, but it was too late now, for William had already sipped. He sustained no ill effects, however, and soon proposed a toast to the health of Zaravaz. King and prince exchanged nods with impeccable etiquette, each salutation representing a stab to the centre of the heart and a twist of the knife in the wound.

William cleared his throat. 'I, at least, was not aware,' he said to the eldritch knights, 'until you spoke to us in parley on the battlefield, why you felt such animosity toward our race. Now that the reason is clear, allow me to point out that in Narngalis certain laws have always been enforced. Earlier generations of Wyverstones banned the lighting of fires under downed cart-horses to make them get up, the chaining of dogs, the use of steel-jawed spring traps, cockfighting, bear-baiting, the tying of chickens by their feet in markets, and the beating of animals. Of all kingdoms, Narngalis is the most humane.'

Lieutenant Zaillian remarked acidly, 'Better to ban cages, chains, wagon shafts and captivity altogether.'

'Better to ban those who deal in such depravities,' said Zande, scowling.

Men and goblins watched each other, seething with resentment.

'One is overjoyed to hear your news,' said Zaravaz, replying to the prince's declaration, 'though I am not certain which one.

For our part, we have also banned similar abuses of human beings. When our draught-men collapse in exhaustion between the shafts our kobolds merely prod them until they rise to their feet and stagger a little further. Fire-goading is so outmoded.'

'I perceive that nothing I can say will satisfy you,' said William, the blood rising to his cheeks. 'You consider human beings to be no better than animals. That is where man and goblin can never agree.'

'If your heart and mind were not closed against logic,' said Zaravaz, 'you would not speak thus. You say your kind is better than other species. Can you navigate like a pigeon, swim like a dolphin or track like a hound? Can you run as fast as deer or see ultraviolet, like bees?'

William glowered.

'Animals, sir,' Torrington declared, 'are not as intelligent or as advanced as human beings. Therefore they are inferior.'

Leaning towards the foremost of his lieutenants, Zaravaz spoke to them in the goblin language. He bestowed a look of utmost contempt upon Torrington before sitting back in his chair, placing one booted foot on the table and proceeding to whittle an apple with a knife, as if absorbed in the pastime.

Taking up the debate on his liege's behalf Lieutenant Zande said to Torrington, 'You are gravely mistaken, guest of Zaravaz. But even should you be correct, does possessing superior intelligence entitle one of you *boanlagh ny theayee* - as is one of our terms for human beings - to abuse another? If for example I gave you a blow to the head that addled your brains, would clever men have the right to trample over you because of your stupidity?'

'Nay, but - ' Before King Warwick's lieutenant-general could frame a reply Zaillian interjected, 'In any case, there are animals who are unquestionably more intelligent, creative, aware and communicative than some *boanlaghyn*.'

'I do not believe it!' Torrington said.

'Perhaps you know what a chimpanzee is?'

'Indeed. They are a species once found in remote areas of Ashqalêth.'

'Before the *boanlagh ny theayee* rendered them extinct,' murmured Zwist, helping himself to a slice of 'Moonlight is Cruelly Deceptive', a spicy cake profusely decorated with edible leaves of thinnest silver foil.

'Compared to a human infant,' said Zaillian, 'or to one of your village idiots, an adult chimpanzee is far more advanced. By your reasoning the monkey should take precedence over the tot, *red ommidjagh.*'

'That is not what I meant,' Torrington replied with some asperity. 'You fail to perceive the point. The druids teach that the Fates gave humankind dominion over all other forms of life, and therefore it is our right to treat animals as we please.'

Apparently paying scant heed to the exchange, the goblin king chopped off a portion of fruit with swift precision.

'Even if that were true, Sir Gilead,' Asrăthiel said, joining the debate for the first time, 'a king has dominion over his subjects but that does not mean he has the right to ill-use them.'

Torrington lapsed into silence, perhaps in deference to the weathermage, perhaps digesting her words, perhaps thinking of Uabhar and his fate, of which Asrăthiel had notified them in her letters.

William said, 'I have learned much on this topic from the Lady Maelstronnar.'

The knife of Zaravaz suddenly slipped right through the apple, as if he had miscalculated an incision. It flew out of his hand and stuck, quivering, in the table. Every head in the hall turned to look.

'Pray pardon the interruption,' the goblin king said pleasantly, retrieving the implement and resuming his new hobby.

Clearing his throat the prince continued, 'The Lady Maelstronnar has expounded on this subject at length, and her argument has largely won me to your cause. She has told me of certain crows that invent tools, for example, and rats that learn to navigate. I have come to realise that animals are not so very different from us after all - '

'Your breed,' Zaravaz interrupted abrasively, looking up from his task, 'takes the position that animals and *boanlaghyn* can only be said to be similar if animals are found to be doing amazing things, rather than when *boanlaghyn* are found to be doing surprisingly mundane things. This implies that respect for other species should be measured in proportion to how humanlike their abilities are. It also suggests that animals are only worthy of esteem inasmuch as they are similar to human *donnanyn mooar*.' Having tossed aside the apple he uttered the last three words in thundering tones, pounding the table with the flat of his hand, as if unwilling to forbear any longer, even for etiquette's sake. The noise of the blows resounded throughout the hall, and the owls took flight, swooping and soaring into the cavernous vaults of the ceiling.

William and several of his men half started out of their seats. A menacing silence enveloped the multitude. Even the daemon horses stood poised like graceful statues. Only a few owls' feathers drifted down in a lazy rain.

Then Asrăthiel leaped to her feet. 'The Glashtinsluight code of honour,' she cried, 'requires that the host protects invited guests while they bide with him. Cool-headedness in debate will ensure this code is maintained.' She looked around, deliberately bestowing her gaze on both parties equally.

'Indeed you have become exceedingly intimate with our ways, Sioctíne,' Zauberin said with a sneer. 'Patently you presume to lecture us on our own precepts.'

But Zaravaz, who now seemed to be intent on paring his fingernails with the knife, said, 'And the Lady Stormbringer is perfectly right, *aachionard*.'

The moment had passed. The Narngalishmen subsided, and the further regions of the hall reverted to their convivial hum. A trow sat at the goblin king's feet eating the remains of the apple. Asrăthiel made herself swallow some food for the sake of appearances, but she could not taste it.

At length Zauberin turned to the prince and said, 'Returning to our previous argument, we grant that your kind possess some benevolent qualities, but all in all, the human race is evil.'

'Quite the contrary!' William cried.

'Oh, but you are,' said Zaravaz. 'Innately. Irredeemably. The eradication of such exorbitant evil must inevitably be an act of moral goodness.'

The men growled their outrage and disapprobation. Fore-seeing the imminent escalation of further antagonism, Asrăthiel intervened again, changing the subject. Loudly she asked William, 'Your Highness, have you seen the man Fionnbar Aonarán? He was here in these mountain halls but they sent him forth.'

With her eyes she beseeched the prince to forsake the intensifying argument. He glowered at his host, but eventually decided that circumspection was the wiser choice. 'Yes, I have seen him,' he said reluctantly, 'for he wandered into northern Narngalis. He is deranged, methinks. When first he was found roaming without purpose, he kept seeking ways to end his life. His attempts became increasingly bizarre. By rope and fire and blade he hunted death. He picked fights with swordsmen, cast himself into bonfires, and hanged himself by the throat. Always he survived, yet not unscathed. His body is blackened, his hair burned from his skull, his flesh scarred and puckered. The pain he must have suffered is unimaginable. His person is warped, and his mind also.'

'After becoming immortal,' said Torrington, 'he came to realise that immortality has not given him happiness. Unable to find happiness, he wishes to 'end it all'.'

The goblins were listening, many smirking, some chuckling.

Zaravaz, however, did not smile. 'For your kind the most wonderful gift of all is life,' he said quietly, 'and it should be enjoyed to the fullest. Having received life, the most wonderful gift is the promise of death at the end.'

The chamber became noiseless, save for the crackling of flames and the patter of kobolds' feet as they removed empty platters from the tables.

'Aonarán Toadstone was not born for immortality,' Zaravaz went on, 'and is unable to come to terms with it. You, however, Lady Stormbringer,' he said, 'were born to it.'

Asrăthiel was seized by sudden concern for her parents. 'What of my father?' she asked, 'and my mother, who might also have become immortal?'

'Your mother is not immortal, for she never drank the Draught. She is merely long-lived. Extremely long-lived. For now, she sleeps, and nothing troubles her pleasant dreams. I daresay your father roams somewhere in the frozen lands of the north. In contrast to Toadstone he has a purpose – to find a way to awaken Jewel to the watch. It might be supposed that his purpose sustains him, even in the face of the nightmare of deathlessness.'

'My wish,' Asrăthiel murmured, 'is to journey to those lands and find him, some day. I long to help him and give him condolence.'

Zaravaz shrugged. 'Then go with us,' he said. 'We have sojourned here long enough. It is time for us to seek adventure elsewhere. Besides, the glories of this place now pall, due to recent intrusions and our memories of the golden caves in which your ancestors so hospitably entertained us.'

Shocked by this announcement Asrăthiel said, 'Do you truly mean to depart from the kingdoms of Tir?'

'We have been contemplating the notion of riding out, of travelling north again. We might ride to Ellan Istillkutl where dwell our kith the Ice Goblins, or to Cheer ny Yindyssyn or beyond, seeking the other clans. It is time we rejoined the *liannyn*. For too long have we been away from them.'

Recalling that the *liannyn* were she-goblins, Asrăthiel felt a pang of jealousy.

'What of your noble mission to save the world from the evil scourge of humanity?' demanded William.

'We have plans,' Zaravaz said coldly. 'You will later learn of them. Do not be in a hurry.'

He called for music then, and as the bagpipes of the fridean began to wail beneath the floor, the susurration of discontented conversation thrummed through the hall.

When at last the feast was over the men, summoning much resolution, formally expressed appreciation to their hosts before they left Sølvetårn. It was no easy task, declaring gratitude to those whom they would much rather be putting to the sword. The lips of the human knights moved, and words were forced forth, but no conviction accompanied the sounds.

'And thus,' said Zaravaz, conducting his guests through the corridors on the way to the front gates. 'As I promised to demonstrate, we dwell quite comfortably here, apparently living on worms and beetles in our dank burrows. As you have witnessed, your weathermage is diligently waited upon by her attendants and lacks no comfort.'

'Let her go with us,' said William.

'You overreach the terms under which we made you welcome,' Zaravaz said scathingly. 'Beware. You agreed to keep silent on that matter. If you rescind your side of the bargain, our temporary treaty shall be annulled, and the lives of you and your cohorts shall be forfeit.'

'Prithee, speak of it again, man,' muttered Zauberin.

After this threat William resentfully remained silent, and they passed through the galleries of Sølvetårn until they exited from the front gates and stood upon the approach to the wonderful bridge that seemed fashioned of glass, and whose stanchions - if stanchions they were, and not weird decorations - resembled icicles dripping from a twig. Alpine gusts whipped their garments and hair, and the sky, cold and remote, seethed with cloud like pourings of steam and smoke and liquid pewter. Beneath the bridge the crevasse dived into dark and secret mouths where the wind whistled like a lost bird. Somewhere in those depths, Asrăthiel thought fleetingly, lies the Sylvan Comb. Or perhaps it is still falling...

There the prince halted, saying to the goblin king, 'Give me a moment alone with Lady Asrăthiel before I depart.'

Zauberin glanced at Zaravaz, who nodded briefly, turned his back and walked away. The goblin king's knights followed him, withdrawing from the presence of their human guests. Out of the gates a freezing wind came funnelling, as if the mountain halls breathed an icy sigh.

'Asrăthiel,' murmured the prince, 'I could not ask this in their hearing, but have those ravishers dared to force their attentions upon you? If they have touched you they will pay dearly, before I rest in my grave.'

She answered, 'I have not been forced. I have been treated with respect.' Aware that this truth was close to equivocation, she felt a stab of self-reproach as if she had been faithless.

'I cannot tell you how glad I am to hear it!' William took the damsel's hand in his own and clasped it to his heart, saying, 'You understand that my heart belongs to you. I shall never rest until you return to us.'

'I know,' she replied, 'but do not be dispirited. I am treated well, here, and incredibly, my opinions and wishes hold some sway. There is still hope that I will escape. Believe me, there is still hope.'

'If they take you away from the four kingdoms, away from these northern marches to the mapless lands, I will follow.'

'Oh William!' Asrăthiel exclaimed with feeling, greatly moved by his constancy and selfless compassion.

He looked at her so sadly, with such devotion and affection brimming from his eyes that she reached up, twined her arms about his shoulders and kissed him upon the mouth. 'Now you must go,' she said, stepping back and quickly glancing, not without trepidation, at the shadowy incarnations looking on. 'I will be thinking of you. Do not fear for me, for I will be secure.'

Before leaving, the prince drew her close and kissed her in reciprocation; savorously, and with prodigious gentleness.

Then officers of the horde came swarming around them, and the Narngalishmen were hustled across the bridge of glass or crystal. The crowd parted and began to disperse. Asrăthiel remained on the spot, looking along the bridge after William, long after he had passed from view into the encampment. Eventually she made up her mind to return to her rooms, but when she turned around she saw someone standing a few paces away and the sight, unlooked-for, struck her to the heart.

The hair of Zaravaz was as black as perjury, limned with flowing gleams, the blue iridescence of a crow's wing. As arousing as battle song, and as dangerous as lightning he was leaning nonchalantly against a wall as if idling the hours away. Suddenly, for Asrăthiel there was nothing else in existence but those matchless lines of symmetry and vigour. Captivated, as ever, she marvelled at his eldritch beauty, the beauty of a supernatural being that no human creature could possibly hope to match, except, perhaps, viewed through love's enchanted glass.

Had he witnessed the kiss? She did not know. They were alone together between the front gates of Sølvetårn and the depthless chasm; between splendour and infinity. Marshalling her scattered thoughts, the damsel spoke to the goblin king. 'What are these plans you have made for the Four Kingdoms of Tir, if the Argenkindë depart?'

'We intend,' he said, 'to leave behind additional mispickels to assist those we have already installed, who dwell throughout the lands, in caverns and warrens, in disused wells and abandoned quarries. These unremitting slaves of ours, both the greater and the lesser, will forever act according to our instructions, never succumbing to corruption. They will regulate and control certain affairs of men, enforcing goblin laws to safeguard and protect nonhumans. The kobold watch, comprising both the red and the blue, will patrol regularly, preventing and detecting crimes. The blues of the Kobold Justiciaries will judge offenders, and pass sentence and condemn them, while the doughty mispickels of the Kobold Avengers and Executioners will operate the penal system.'

'Men shall band together and overrun them! Iron and salt will vanquish them! They will be defeated!'

'Hardly likely. Mispickels are poisonous to your species, and cunning, and strong, and virtually immortal. They will lurk everywhere, frequently changing their place of abode, always delving deeply into lairs dangerous to humankind, tunnelling up to burst forth where least expected. Their armour resists iron and salt. They will wield uncanny weapons, and if the weapons are lost or destroyed they will simply manufacture more.'

'What about giving teachers to my people, instead of punishers?'

'As your lover said at the dinner table, all human beings instinctively know right from wrong. They need no teachers to instruct them to mend their ways. Besides, we tried that avenue long ago, with no success.'

'If you ride north,' said Asrăthiel, 'will you drag me with you?'

'Will you deign to accompany us?'

'I would rather not.'

'You disappoint me, Weatherwitch.' The lavender eyes darkened to storm-purple.

'You can coerce me to go with you, of course,' said Asrăthiel, 'but you won't break my will. My mother had a saying, which she learned from her family in the Great Marsh of Slievmordhu. 'If you love something - '

Zaravaz interrupted, 'Yes, I have heard that old saw several thousand times. If you love something, set it free. If it does not return it was never yours.'

'No! If you love something truly, you would not have caged it in the first instance.'

The goblin king pushed off the wall and drew himself up to his full height. 'Love?' he said scaldingly. 'You flatter yourself. Do you think one wench can please me more than any other? You are all much the same. Do as you please, Witch, it makes little difference. If we leave Sølvetårn you will be free to choose to ride north with us, or to return to the lands of men. Either way I will not yet exterminate the pathogens that infect the face of this fair land, those harm-causing agents which you seem to consider so precious.' Zaravaz raked Asrăthiel from head to toe with one of his measuring looks. 'Think on it,' he said presently. 'Think on whether you would stay, or come with us.'

'I do not have to deliberate,' she said haughtily. 'The choice is hardly difficult.'

He laughed, and with a swish of his cloak that sent biting draughts gusting, he was gone. But Asrăthiel felt torn apart. She had never expected Zaravaz to relinquish her so easily. Now that she was faced with the prospect of freedom the decision was, in fact, much harder than she had expected. Her confusion troubled her; she ought to be joyful, but was not.

Having appeared from some side corridor, Lieutenant Zwist accompanied Asrăthiel back to her suite. She said very little to him along the way, but he kept up a cheerful flow of chatter. At her door, just before he parted from her he bent his head, cupped a hand - beringed with black opals - to her ear and whispered, 'Know that my lord desisted from killing your prince only because he knows you love him. Good morning, Sioctíne!'

After performing an exquisite bow he swung away and strode off.

Zwist's revelation served only to further agitate the damsel's sensibilities. She threw herself upon her couch and lay against the silk-like cushions, staring up at the draped canopy and the long, curved bones of the ceiling, without seeing them.

It was a distressing condition she found herself in. She loved Zaravaz, and longed to be with him, but as she lay musing she recalled his past wickedness and realised, fully, what it entailed. The suffering of innocents was not to be brushed aside - not for the sake of love, not for anything. It came to her that she could never go with him because of the unseelieness in him, because he had slaughtered human beings cruelly, and without mercy, and even with joy.

There was no sleep to be had that day. The weathermage left open the curtains and gazed out through the window at the sky beyond the peaks. Billowy cumulus clouds floated there. The firmament was like some wind-blown meadow clotted with the blowsy heads of lacy umbelliferae: meadowsweet, cow parsley, ground elder, wild angelica, burnet saxifrage, hemlock. The flowing of the clouds against the frozen crags was hypnotic, creating the optical illusion that the sky was motionless and the mountains were crashing down, endlessly collapsing.

Sunset alchemised the snow-dusted landscape to a realm of gold and flame. It was then that Asrăthiel rose from her couch of desolation and went to seek Zaravaz. Throughout the night she searched, but he was not to be discovered.

Toward morning she found him beyond the walls of Sølvetårn, in the company of his knights and many trollhästen. They were congregating beside a noisy, fast-moving alpine stream that poured, glittering, down a rocky channel, deflecting from outcrops on either bank. The water foamed and boiled along its bed of oxide-stained rocks and water-worn pebbles. The goblin knights were dismounting, after a night-long man-hunt. When she saw them, Asrăthiel drew to a halt. She did not approach Zaravaz or call out to him. She was smitten, as always, by the look of him, for it inspired terror to behold such beauty, and her courage began to fail.

But, upon spying the damsel he left his chivalry, and came to her, stripping off his riding gloves. His hair, wind-tossed, was so black it seemed to suck the light out of the surrounding air.

'What is it?' he asked.

'Have you decided,' she said, 'whether you will depart from the Northern Ramparts?'

'I have. We will.'

The damsel felt as if, somewhere, a full-blown flower had shrivelled on the stem. 'In that case, I shall tell you something. You gave me a choice,' she said, forcing out the words. 'I have considered. My decision is this: when you go, I will stay here in the Four Kingdoms of Tir.'

Asrăthiel held her breath. Behind the shoulder of the goblin king she could see the eldritch knights amongst the milling daemon horses. Moonlight rinsed them with a dry white wine. As the mountain stream churned over the rocks in the moonlight it flashed and sparkled with silver streaks. Bright droplets were tossed up into the air like a hurrah.

Zaravaz had merely given her a brief glance, his handsome face betraying no emotion.

He said, 'Well if that is your choice, you might as well go back straight away. There is no profit in your staying a moment longer.'

Shocked by this reaction, Asrăthiel found herself at a loss for words. She had not expected this, but had presumed she would stay in the Halls of the Mountain King for at least a few weeks more – however, from that instant, everything began to happen quickly.

Before she knew it a group of household trows appeared and she was whisked away from the goblin hunting party, along chiselled paths and stairs to the front gates of Sølvetårn. Tormented by anguish of spirit she feared she might never see Zaravaz again, dreaded that he had finished with her entirely, because she refused to acquiesce.

Yet she did see him again, once more, before she was cast forth.

He met her at the gates, accompanied by his ten highest-ranking lieutenants. All of them, all his knights, looked upon their human visitor differently now; even Zwist, who had been a kind of friend. They scowled at the damsel and their mood was grim, for she had displeased their lord, which angered them.

'Go home to your yellow-tongued butter knife over the mantel-piece, Sioctíne,' called out Zaillian. 'Care well for it.'

'That I shall,' she replied defiantly.

'We wish you ill,' Zauberin snarled to Asrăthiel's face, 'for your ingratitude, your ungraciousness.'

'*Bee dty host, jouylleen!*' Zaravaz said sharply, and the first lieutenant subsided, his demeanour sullen.

Before his erstwhile tribute was taken across the bridge the goblin king gifted her with a sword of iridium, forged with gramarye.

'Wield this instead of Fallowblade,' he said, his tone remote, his violet eyes as cold and as fathomless as underground lakes. 'This is *Rehollys*, 'Moonlight', and it will serve you well.'

Before she could stammer acknowledgement Lieutenant Zauberin took a pace forward and declared dismissively, 'At the equinoctial full moon the Argenkindë will ride out into the regions north of these mountains, into the frozen lands.' Stepping back he bowed fleeringly, his manner somehow conveying, We are well rid of the likes of you.

'Farewell,' Zaravaz said to Asrăthiel. '*Bannaght lhiat.*'

The goblin king bowed brusquely and with impeccable courtesy, then strode away without a backward glance. Zauberin and the other lieutenants closed ranks behind him, and Asrăthiel was left with only Hulda and some other trows. 'Come alang! Come alang!' they entreated, pulling at the damsel's skirts, and she allowed them to conduct her across the thin, high bridge. Evidently a message had been dispatched to William in his encampment on the other side of the crevasse, for the prince, with his retinue, was waiting for her.

As Asrăthiel curtseyed before him, for some reason it kept running through her mind that she had not even been given a chance to bid goodbye to Tangwystil.

11
GOLD

Lord Luck, thou comely youth with shining brow,
I beg thee, shower fortune on me now.
Pray heap on me thy bounty in great store,
And I will praise thy name forevermore.

Lord Doom, bold warrior who wields the axe,
Let not thy double blade fall on our backs!
Show mercy; may thy bell toll not for me;
I swear to pay full homage unto thee.

Great Lady Destiny, thou wondrous crone,
In humble state I kneel before thy throne.
Thy wheel spins out the threads of human lives,
Please do not cut them short with cruel knives.

Fair Lady Ill-Luck, siren bright and fell,
Pray do not curse me with thy dreadful spell
If thou shouldst shun me when you pass my way
Then thou wilt have my worship every day.

A DRUIDIC CHANT.

As morning fog slowly dispersed from the peaks, Asrăthiel left the Halls of the Mountain King and started for King's Winterbourne, escorted by William and his troops. On the wooded slopes of the foothills, autumnal maples snagged the first beams of the rising sun, like yellow lamps illuminating the gloomy forests of pine and cedar.

Upon receiving news of Asrăthiel's imminent return, William had despatched the swiftest runners from his encampment to the nearest semaphore station, with messages to key personages. Two days later, while his entourage descended the winding paths of the hills at a walking pace, the wind changed unexpectedly. A sky-balloon appeared from amongst the clouds, whisking along like a bubble on the breeze. As soon as Asrăthiel spied the aircraft in the distance her spirits rose and her footsteps lightened. She could hardly wait to see her friends and family again. When the balloon landed she saw, to her joy, that the pilot was Avalloc himself, and ran to meet him. The Storm Lord, trembling with emotion, greeted Asrăthiel with a single word, 'Welcome,' and a heartfelt embrace. He thanked William and all his men for the part they had played in rescuing his granddaughter, though they refused to take credit for anything except escorting her from the gates of Sølvetårn.

'I am amazed to see you looking so well, after your ordeal, dear child,' Avalloc said to Asrăthiel, tears coursing down his cheeks. 'My knees have been shaking ever since I received word that you had been set free. Such a dreadful burden has been lifted from my shoulders!'

'Oh Grandfather, I am mightily glad you came to take me home,' the damsel exclaimed. 'There were times when I wondered whether I would ever see you again!'

Over meadow and wood, across hill and valley and swift-coursing river, the Storm Lord's aerostat transported Asrăthiel and William to Wyverstone Castle. The return of the weather-mage sparked wild celebrations in King's Winterbourne. From the moment the citizens heard the news that she and the prince were on their way, they began to gather in anxious anticipation outside Wyverstone Castle, braving the chilly Autumn morning. Over the next few hours the crowd swelled to more than a thousand people eager to witness Asrăthiel tasting freedom after two months in the underground prisons of unseelie wights.

Watchmen on the parapets spied the balloon approaching. At the instant they were certain the weathermage was on board they spread the word and bells began ringing all over the city. Even the great bronze bell of Essington Tower pealed out, whose deep voice had not been heard since the end of the Goblin Wars. The city erupted with excitement, and citizens declared the day the most joyful in living memory.

The balloon alighted in the castle grounds, but instead of retreating to the inner chambers Asrăthiel mounted the stairs to a balcony overlooking the gates. As soon as she appeared before the waiting multitude the mood of anticipation yielded to jubilation. She was greeted with cheers, thunderous applause and a throwing of hats into the air. The streets filled with people blowing horns and whistles, shouting and singing, in an outpouring of emotion. Soon after Asrăthiel disappeared indoors the citizens flocked to the taverns and inns to celebrate. The public houses were packed; the celebrations were wilder than previously, when they had received the news that she was still alive. By sunset, cartloads of ale had been consumed. All-day drinkers spilled out of the inns and into the streets, clutching tankards and jugs. Exuberance and elation proliferated. The merrymakers felt bound together by a sense of camaraderie, now that a shared tribulation was at an end.

King Warwick said to Asrăthiel, 'We have all escaped the same prison you were incarcerated in. Our feelings were trapped in the same dungeons. The prayers of the whole kingdom have been answered, in the wake of the shameful bargain we struck to end the war. We all share a great sense of relief.'

It was Warwick's desire that Narngalis' official weathermage should abide at the castle in the care of the Royal Household after her two-month ordeal, rather than returning straight away to her lodgings. Asrăthiel was happy to do so, because her grandfather remained with her. During her stay she received many visitors – family and friends, admirers and well-wishers, representatives from all kingdoms, including a bearer of good wishes from the new Druid Primoris in Cathair Rua. People asked her why the goblins had let her go, and she replied honestly that she could not say for certain, but perhaps the wights had tired of her company. People pressed her on how she had passed her days in Minith Ariannath, and how she had been treated and what she had seen; they wanted to hear every last detail, but Avalloc intervened and bade them leave her in peace. Nor did he ask any questions himself, for he was happy just to have her back, and content to let her tell her story at her own pace if at all, and perhaps also he dreaded what her answers might be. Asrăthiel did not reveal the details of her experiences in Sølvetårn, did not speak of the urisk's true identity, or of what had happened between herself and the goblin king. With her musings and her secrets, she appeared quite withdrawn by comparison with her usual self.

The rejoicing spread throughout the Four Kingdoms of Tir, especially after it became known that the goblins would depart from the northern borders at the equinoctial full moon. The exultation was not much dampened by the additional information that kobold law enforcement corps would be left behind. After all, what were a few dwarfish imps, compared to the might of the goblin knights? Kobolds could eventually be quelled, with some determination, or so many folk liked to believe. King Warwick resolved that after the goblins were gone he would establish a permanently manned watchtower upon the heights of the Northern Ramparts, equipped with the most excellent spyglasses and with beacon fires ready for the sentries to light as a warning, in case the enemy ever returned, or any other unseelie thing came out of the northern lands.

Autumn laid rainbows of soft fire across Tir.

Sunlight slanted into a small courtyard at Wyverstone castle, shining through the leaves of the birch trees as if they were panes of toffee. Avalloc Maelstronnar waited beneath those leaves, hands clasped behind his back, gazing at the low beds of rosemary, marjoram and thyme laid out in symmetrical patterns. He looked but did not see, his mind being occupied with concern for his granddaughter and conjecturing as to Prince William's purpose in requesting a private audience that afternoon. Presently the prince appeared, striding through the colonnaded gallery, his dark blue cloak of quilted linen flaring from his shoulders. As the young man stepped out onto the paving of the formal herb garden, the Storm Lord bowed.

'Perhaps, Lord Maelstronnar, you guess the object of this meeting,' William said after the usual preliminaries. His manner appeared a little awkward, which was not his customary way.

'Perhaps,' said Avalloc.

'I am come to ask for your blessing. I would fain ask Asrăthiel for her hand in marriage.'

With a smile and a gracious nod, the weathermage said, 'You were right, Will. I had guessed your purpose. I know how highly you regard my granddaughter.'

'And how say you, sir?'

'My dear boy, you in your turn must surely guess how well disposed I am to such a connection. Asrăthiel is very fond of you, and I have no doubt you could make her happy. I feel she would be well suited to be Queen of Narngalis when the time comes, for the people love her.'

'And yet I sense some hesitation,' William said, with a touch of unease.

'If I hesitate at all, it is not from disapproval. Only that I have noted that since her return from her dreadful imprisonment the dear child appears quite abstracted. Her temperament is altered; she is not herself, yet. And it is no wonder.'

'I admit, it has not escaped me, either,' said the prince. 'Who knows what horrors she has witnessed, of which she will not tell us for fear of causing distress?'

'I believe it will take some time,' the Storm Lord said, 'before the scars of her ordeal begin to fade. I grant my consent to you and my blessing but, knowing my grandchild so well, I advise you to wait until she has recovered from her trials before making your proposal.'

This, the prince agreed to do.

After seven days Asräthiel flew to High Darioneth to visit her uncle and aunt and cousins, and to pay her respects to her mother.

Jewel continued in her decade-long sleep in the house of Maelstronnar, untouched by time, sheltered by the cupola at the top of the spiral stair. The small room, with its huge windows framed by the stems of climbing roses, trapped warm beams of buttercup-yellow sunlight. The view in every direction was spectacular; sweeping panoramas of mountain, sky and plateau. In this crystalline arbour Jewel's waiting women sat peacefully, their voices, in conversation, as soft and low as running water. One was anointing the sleeper's bare feet with scented creams. As Asräthiel entered they rose and curtsied, smiling gladly. The damsel exchanged civilities with the women before approaching the big, four-posted bed that occupied much of this eyrie.

There, upon crimson sheets and tasselled bolsters she lay, like a magnificent marble statue painted in delicate colours by the most skilled of artists; Jewel, the mother of Asräthiel. Jewel's tresses framed her face like dusky smoke. Fine textured and soft-hued was her skin, brushed with red at the lips and cheeks. Her lids were like the wings of a blue wren. Asräthiel kissed her mother's brow and combed her hair, as was her wont. She spoke to her, telling her where she had been and what she had seen, yet omitting events that might upset Jewel, if indeed she could hear. As usual there was no sign that the sleeper was aware of anything at all, but Asräthiel never ceased to hope.

'One day Father will return,' she murmured. 'He will learn of a way to waken you, Mother dear. Then we will all be together once more.' In her heart she did not believe it.

For a long time she sat in silence by the canopied couch, her thoughts having turned from visions of her father in the north to pictures of the Argenkindë crossing those same remote lands, travelling further and further away from the four kingdoms. Eventually, with a sigh, she bade farewell to the two waiting women and descended to the rooms below.

Fallowblade was back in its cradle above the mantelpiece. After retrieving the golden blade from the battlefield, the Storm Lord had cleansed it of the blood of Gearnach and goblins. His granddaughter stood on the polished floor of the dining hall, looking at the great weapon – the instrument with which she had struck down her eldritch companion, the urisk. She reminisced on all the events that single blow had brought to pass, but did not reach up to touch the heavy scabbard; did not even step towards it. Instead her musings strayed to the silvery blade she had carried from Minith Ariannath; *Rehollys*, sword of moonlight. Avalloc and William disliked the eldritch weapon, so she kept it in a chest of cedar wood, out of sight.

For a week the damsel remained at the Mountain Ring, after which she returned to The Laurels in Lime Grove and resumed her duties, for there was much weatherworking to be done, and too few hands to do it. None of the druids had invented anything to take the place of the weathermasters; their much-vaunted Oracular Workshops had failed to produce anything of greater use than an unreliable method of predicting short-term variations in the weather.

Asrăthiel's world had changed.

It was difficult to accept the changes. War and the advent of the Kobold Watch had altered everything, in ways both subtle and obvious. Most heart-breakingly, her kinsmen were gone. The urisk, too, was gone.

She missed that one. Sometimes she felt as if he had never existed. Other times she felt as if she had never left his side. Either way, she could take no joy in anything. The world seemed a drear and hollow place, hollower than the cavernous silver mines beneath Sølvetårn, soon to be empty and idle and returned to their original darkness.

A dazzling wheel of beaten silver, the equinoctial full moon shimmered in the sky on Lantern Eve, Sun's Day, Otember the thirty-first. Even then Asrăthiel could not quite believe that the goblin knights would really depart. On the following night huge numbers of kobold slaves issued from the northern ranges by night, and crept across the land. The smelly wights with their tapered ears, malignant grins, spreading snouts, barbed tails and long grooves of eyes, began to pop up all over the place, enforcing goblin law with unremitting exactness. In King's Winterbourne it was officially acknowledged that a new wave of kobolds was furtively infesting the alleyways.

Too, the trows of Tir returned to their old haunts. As they had set forth, drawn to the outbreak of moon-bright glory beneath the Northern Ramparts, so now they came gliding back. Between sunset and sunrise they passed like shadows, by ones and twos or half-dozens, along byways and hedgerows, with scarcely a sound but for a faint tinkling of silver bracelets. The human citizens of Tir kept their youngest and fairest under close watch, for fear that the Grey Neighbours would steal them.

It was not until the return of the trows that Asrăthiel finally let go all suspicion of prevarication on the part of the Argenkindë. She gave up all doubt, all hope and dread, and allowed herself to accept the fact that the goblins had departed. Their brief renaissance was indeed over. They had ridden away from the four kingdoms, as they had declared they would, and the Halls of the Mountain King stood abandoned; silent save perhaps for the beat of an owl's wing, the song of draughts through pierced rock, and the soft footfalls of the last trows padding here and there in search of forgotten silver.

Zaravaz was gone.

In rifts torn through Asrăthiel's reality hovered the outline of a tall man with blowing hair; merely a vacuous silhouette of someone who was no longer there. The damsel, chained beneath the burden of forsakenness, wondered how it might have been if she had gone with Zaravaz to the mysterious lands of ice and snow in search of her father. Yet of course, she owed it to her countrymen, to her calling, to her grandfather, to remain and work in Tir. . .

She was immortal, therefore there was plenty of time, she told herself; plenty of time to go roaming in later years.... In private, however, she vowed that when Avalloc's life was over, and when a new generation of weathermasters had arisen to perform the tasks of the old, then, if her father had not returned, she would follow him over the mountains. And if during her quest to seek her father she should chance to meet any of the Glashtinsluight, why then she might enquire after Zaravaz.

Her longing for his presence was so intense, she felt it drain all blitheness and vigour from her life.

Since the Covenant at the Wuthering Moors and the advent of the punitive Kobold Watch, extensive changes had begun to take place across the four kingdoms. Pastures were left to turn into wild meadows, or else ploughed and planted with Winter root-crops. Pheasants, ptarmigan and partridges grew numerous on the moors, no longer in danger from the arrows of hunters. On the upland slopes, cloud vapours raced against the swift shadows of deer, and leaping hares. Forests jubilated with birdsong. Horses, pigs, goats, fowls and cattle had been turned out into the wild places, to roam free. Many, accustomed from birth to domesticity, perished. The strongest survived and banded together in herds or flocks. A new generation was produced; a wild-born, free generation that would prove cleverer and stronger than the preceding one.

Creative human cooks, utilizing beans and nuts, invented new recipes. Butchers, leatherworkers and silkworm farmers went out of business. Nobody was, as yet, daring or foolhardy enough to explore wight-infested caves in search of svartlap, the goblin fabric; fortunately, however, a couple of old herbalists revived the knowledge that the tough and flexible bark of goat willow and paper mulberry made an excellent substitute for leather. Spinners of flax were in great demand. People began trying to harness the power of wind and sun to replace horsepower. Druids invented useless clockwork horses. Cunning artisans made solar powered vehicles that moved slowly and wind powered ones that moved erratically. Lamps were fuelled by vegetable oils. Some enterprising farmers struck bargains with certain Marauders, hiring the strongest amongst them – who were far more powerful than an average man, if not as shrewd – to be labourers. Blacksmiths ceased to make horseshoes and increased their output of man-driven ploughshares.

Discomfiting to Asrăthiel, and to a large part of Tir's human population, was a cult that had grown up amongst adolescents of the four kingdoms. Rebellious schoolgirls were declaring themselves in love with the goblin king, whose reputation for wickedness, prowess and beauty had reached every corner of the land. They claimed they would like nothing better than to meet him, even if they promptly swooned at his feet. Forming little cliques they met in secret to discuss him, draw pictures of him, compose songs, stories and poems about him, act in plays about him, share their dreams of him, and generally ignite the fury of their elders for idolising the enemy.

'I do not know what the world is coming to,' muttered their parents. 'We were never so foolish and feckless in our day.'

Infatuated gentlewomen begged Asrăthiel to tell them every detail about Zaravaz, but she firmly declined. 'I do not wish to relive the memories of my time in Minith Ariannath,' she said, for once glad that human beings possessed the ability to tell untruths.

Despite the fact that women of all ages clandestinely sighed after Zaravaz, and even though it was generally thought that the goblins had left the mountains for good, there remained a strange reluctance on the part of most people to venture to the Northern Ramparts. The memory of lightning-lethal unseelie warriors was fresh in their minds, and the mountains seemed tainted by a lingering terror. Besides, the gwyllion still haunted the high paths, and unknown numbers of trows possibly wandered in the tunnels, and no one could guess how many kobolds continued to infect the underworld. Those who were inquisitive about the Northern Ramparts decided to let the mountains wait awhile.

Except for one man.

Prince William was zealous in his efforts to restore his father's kingdom after the war. He wished to recompense those Narngalish families whose men had fallen in battle; to ensure that the loved ones the soldiers left behind did not suffer from want. Tirelessly he worked towards this goal, and as he did so it came to him that an untapped source of enormous wealth lay within the very borders of his own realm. The goblins had probably taken away with them all their silver and jewels, but they would not have touched any of the gold.

The caves in which the unseelie knights had been incarcerated were lined with a veneer of gold. It could be harvested and sold, and the proceeds used to help the bereaved families. In addition, there was the gold that had been cast into the pit of the Inglefire. Asrăthiel had told William the tale of the goblin lieutenant, Zorn, and how he had perished in those witchy flames, and how, long ago, before the original Goblin Wars had commenced, the horde had commanded their human slaves to cast great quantities of gold into the weird conflagration. The stories had ignited the prince's interest in the elusive and legendary pit of werefire, and he was determined to try to retrieve some of that bullion.

Perhaps, also, he threw himself into his endeavours with some extra zeal, to consume some of his thwarted energy; to divert his attention from the withdrawn, reflective damsel he longed so ardently to love. And perhaps there were elements of anger and hatred behind his plans, for he had witnessed the beauty of Zaravaz, had seen the way the goblin king had gazed upon Asrăthiel, and more than ever he wished to plunder the mountains of their gold and keep some of it for the royal arsenal, that Narngalis might become unconquerable by goblinkind.

Since the forging of Fallowblade the knowledge of the fire's whereabouts had been lost, but many people, including William, had heard the madman Fionnbar Aonarán ranting about a pit of flames he had found while roaming in the dark beneath the mountains. The prince made up his mind to mount a gold-gathering expedition to the Northern Ramparts, taking Aonarán as his guide to the werefire.

When he informed Asrăthiel of his proposal she was dismayed, and begged him to reconsider. 'Go nowhere with that fiendish creature Aonarán, the deathless one,' she cried. 'Whatever he touches he brings to ruin. It is because of him and his schemes that my mother sleeps forever. It is he who freed the horde and caused this war in the first place!'

William, however, insisted that he could deal with Aonarán who, he said, had made of himself merely a harmless gibbering idiot, with all his damaging attempts to die. The damsel would not be persuaded. She was so set against the idea of the prince's adventure that eventually William decided to set off on his quest for the gold without informing her. In fact the quest was kept secret for many reasons; not least that King Warwick thought it best for the denizens of other kingdoms to remain forgetful of the masses of unclaimed treasure beneath the Northern Ramparts. Even though the mountains were within the borders of Narngalis and therefore belonged by right to the Narngalish crown, some pirates might take it into their heads to become salvagers themselves.

Fionnbar Aonarán was fetched from the Asylum for Lunatics, and brought into the presence of Prince William and his father. Upon seeing the immortal madman they could not help but reel with shock. His numerous attempts to slay himself had wrought appalling disfigurements upon his person; he was reduced to a wreck that had once been a man. Black-charred with white scars, his flesh was peeling, suppurating, and ulcerated. His head was bald, his fingertips burned to rounded stumps. A single wobbling tooth remained in his gums. Only his eyes, his pale-blue, swimming eyes like marbles set in cinders, were not ugly and ruined. The wretch moaned and wrung his horrible hands and sighed and whistled. Scant sense could be had out of him, and no one could be certain how much he understood of what was said to him, but he made no clear sign that he refused the scheme.

As soon as his expeditionary party was ready William took his leave of his family and set off northwards. They went on foot; William's most esteemed advisor, Sir Torold Tetbury; a column of knights and men-at-arms including the Knight-Commander of the Companions of the Cup, Sir Huelin Lathallan; a band of miners and engineers, explorers learned in cave lore, and a chirurgeon-apothecary. Aonarán was under close guard, for he could not be relied upon. Several carts accompanied them, drawn by hired teams of monstrous Marauders, strong as oxen, large as bears, chosen for their dimwittedness and lack of cunning. One vehicle carried the expedition's equipment. It was intended that the other carts, which were empty, would be filled with gold on the return journey. William also brought a couple of cages of pigeons, well hidden from Kobold Watchmen, so that he could send a message to King's Winterbourne as soon as the party re-emerged. It was a risky venture, for if the Watch found the avian contraband it would go harshly with the Narngalishmen.

Without horses they plodded slowly; it took more than three weeks to reach their destination. Ninember was waning and the skies were thick with cloud as Aonarán at last guided the party to the high, thin mouth of a cave that opened into a flank of Storth Cynros. Above them towered a sheer rock face with tumbled boulders piled at its foot.

When Aonarán's custodians moved towards the cave's entrance, drawing their charge with them, the pale-eyed man immediately became agitated. He tried to pull away, but they held him firmly in their grasp. When they asked him what was wrong he shrieked that he was afraid of the dark and the creatures that lurked there, afraid of goblins, afraid of the Marauders that accompanied the expedition. 'Here I brought you,' he gabbled, 'but I will not be going in!'

'Look you,' said William's knights, patiently repeating all their earlier assurances, 'we will light your way with the brightest torches. With sword and charm we will protect you from unseelie wights. The goblins have departed, though we have brought gold-plated blades as a precaution, and as for the Marauders, these ones here, who we have employed as bearers, are as docile as lambs and as stupid as cockroaches.' After much ado Aonarán reluctantly capitulated, though he did not let up his whining.

Leaving the carts and carrier pigeons at the cave's threshold, under the care of six men-at-arms, the explorers passed in amongst the shadows of the underworld, entering the labyrinth by way of lower avenues rather than by the bridge into lofty Sølvetårn, because they had no wish to stray anywhere near the Halls of the Mountain King. William deemed it wise to avoid the chance of encountering any eldritch wights lingering around the goblin fastness. More pertinently, Aonarán had assured him that the golden caves and the legendary werefire were situated far from goblin haunts. 'They would not go near it,' he said in a rare moment of lucidity, 'they built their honeycombs far, far away.'

Into the close-walled darkness the party ventured, lanterns held high. A glacial draught was blowing out of the cave's throat, as if to warn that the mountain had a heart of ice. On either side the walls sloped inwards, glistening with a thin film of seepage. The swarmsmen porters were forced to stoop, to avoid cracking their massive skulls on the low ceiling. Underfoot the ground was rutted and fissured, littered with rubble and ankle-wrenching stones. Carefully the men went forward, until the long slit of daylight that marked the entrance was lost from sight behind them.

A moment later Aonarán stopped in his tracks and refused to go on. He threw himself to the ground shuddering and squealing, shouting that the goblins would seize him if he dared to venture any further; that they would torment him without pity and hang him up on the highest pinnacle with two bags of bones for neighbours. It took a great deal of argument to convince him of his security, but in the end he weakened a second time and went on. He seemed, at least, to know where he was going; if he was frightened of the dangers, he was at least confident of the route.

It appeared to the Narngalishmen that their ardour to retrieve the lost gold was matched by an equal and opposing force: the hostility of the deep places. As they followed their marginally sane guide through the echoing tunnels, ever descending, they too were seized by inordinate terror. They sensed, or seemed to sense spectral presences. Half glimpsed movement unnerved them; they felt as if hostile stares from alien eyes were boring into their backs. And they could not help but call to mind the traditional denizens of underground; wights both seelie and unseelie; the dead; worms that ate the rotting flesh of the dead; roots that strangled boulders and sucked nourishment from the casts of worms. Pairs of glowing lights blinked at them from crevices. Footfalls padded alongside them in the gloom, always slightly outside the range of the lanterns' light. It was hard to breathe; the air was alternately muggy and stifling, choking with mould spores, or as cold as the void between the stars; so cold it was like an attack of steel razors shredding the lungs. The men's lamps illuminated milky rock lining the walls; pallid crystal veined with gold. Beyond the reach of the lamplight a watery luminosity strained itself out of some fluorescent rocks. Radioactive ores glowed faintly, and the miniature lights of eldritch miners winked as they scurried away from the intruders. From time to time sounds of agonized squealing, or groaning, or giggling issued from far away in the dimness. Only the Marauders remained unaffected, plodding along, clearly oblivious of the atmosphere of tension.

The miners marked their route with daubs of paint, though none could be certain whether tricksy wights might erase or shift these signposts. They tried, also, to commit their path to memory, for no one trusted their half-mad guide to lead them safely back to the outside world.

Fionnbar Aonarán kept up his complaints of being frightened of the darkness. He baulked and protested, but with bribes and threats his supervisors forced him to proceed, and when he did so he went forth with disturbing sure-footedness, avoiding chasms, easily locating stairs and ramps. The Narngalishmen suspected he could see very well in the dark, like a fell-cat.

In truth, it was more due to the fact that the madman had spent so long in those places, he had become familiar with them. He could read their smells and interpret their air currents. He could recall their layout. So excellently were maps of the underways imprinted on his brain that it only took two days for him to lead the expedition to their first goal.

With their crowbars William's miners levered aside a pile of boulders and there it was – the jagged-edged gap through which the Silver Goblins had escaped from their jail. The engineers examined the structure of the aperture, making certain it would not collapse. Then the prince and several men stepped into the prison caves, brandishing swords and lanterns.

They found themselves inside the first of a series of interconnected chambers, large and low-roofed, all lavishly coated with burnished gold. Diffused images of the intruders reflected from the walls and ceilings. Mellow light gleamed off every surface except the floor, which was covered with flagstones. On closer inspection, having judiciously wielded their picks, the miners discovered that a continuous layer of gold half an inch thick had been inserted between the flags and the ground beneath, thus preventing the goblins from tunnelling their way out.

'Seamless!' one of the engineers cried in approval, squinting at the sombre glory that surrounded him. 'A masterful undertaking, this.'

Austere were the furnishings; they consisted of hundreds of marble couches, with no cushions or coverings. That was all.

'Hard beds,' commented one of the miners.

'Grim indeed is this prison,' said William, holding aloft his lantern as shadows fluttered. 'There is scant comfort here.'

'They gave our forefathers no comfort,' said Lathallan, who stood beside him. 'Therefore it was right that they should receive none. What say you, Captain?'

His second replied, 'Methinks, sir, it was too generous of the weathermasters to provide those vermin with any resting-dais at all. A floor paved with golden knives to warm them through the centuries would have been more fitting.'

'I shall leave here a team of miners and engineers,' declared William, 'along with some men-at-arms, and six swarmsmen to do the heavy labour. While they are busy hacking the bullion off the walls and pulling it out from beneath the floor, the rest of us will go looking for the Inglefire.'

His officers acknowledged the command, and the miners

began to unpack their equipment, but as the prince and Lathallan were about to make their exit from the caves of gold the knight-commander paused and said, 'Sir, an uncomfortable notion has just now struck me.'

'Speak.'

'What if the goblins ever return?'

William stood awhile in dark thought. At length, he nodded. 'I see your point,' he said. 'If they come back to Tir, even if it be many years hence, future generations of mankind will need a ready prison in which, with any luck and cunning, they might incarcerate the wights once more.'

'Yet,' said Sir Torold Tetbury, at the prince's elbow, 'there is much treasure here, and much good would it do the realm.'

'Indeed we face a dilemma,' said William, 'and I would that I had foreseen it ere we set forth on this quest. I was so caught up in my gold-gathering scheme that I did not think through the ramifications. No doubt Asrăthiel pointed it out to me, but I was paying no heed to anyone who gainsaid my proposal.'

On the spur of the moment the prince consulted with Sir Torold, Lathallan and his other close advisors. Ultimately they decided to repair the small amount of damage they had done, then seal the caves, and leave them alone. Instead of salvaging this treasure they would pin all their hopes on the Inglefire and its incalculable hoard. When they returned to King's Winterbourne they would not make public the location of the golden prison. The Northern Ramparts would be declared a forbidden region, and legislation would be enacted to punish any would-be looters who dared to go fossicking there.

After they had reached their verdict they turned to Aonarán and bade him lead them to the pit of flames. The madman flung himself to his bony knees and commenced to wring his hands.

'No!' he cried, writhing in terror, 'Have mercy! I brought you here, is that not enough? Let me be going back to the upper world now! I was trapped here for too long, too long.'

William, however, would not be moved. 'You must lead us,

Aonarán, he insisted. 'After you have done your duty we will take you back to King's Winterbourne, where you may dwell in comfort for the rest of your days.'

'For the rest of my days!' shrieked Aonarán. 'That will be forever! When your proud city has crumbled to ruins, there will I be still! When all of you have turned to dust, there will I be still! How say you now, royal prince? Can you be giving me comfort for the rest of my days?'

For that, William could devise no answer.

It took more expressions of intention to reward or punish to persuade the cringing man to keep going. Eventually he acquiesced once more, having no other choice, and again he began to show them the way. Into the ventricles of the ground they plunged, descending steep ramps and stairs, striding along lengthy tunnels that sloped ever downwards.

For two more days they travelled, pausing briefly for rest stops. Sometimes they suspected that Aonarán might be leading them astray, but his keepers threatened and cajoled, and he vehemently asserted that he was loyal and true. Ill at ease with all this bullying, William privately vowed never again to traffic with the sorry excuse for a man, and decided to make sure he was well treated for his pains upon their return to the city.

Along the way they caught glimpses of wights of many kinds; knockers, resembling pint-sized mineworkers; hag-like spinners at their wheels; a lone family of trows in their trailing rags the colour of smoke. When the adventurers paused and sat down to take a meal they were careful not to leave food unattended on the rocky floor, for if they took their eyes off it, it would vanish. The evasive Fridean haunted these hollows; stealers of victuals, players of eldritch bagpipes. Whenever the men passed underground pools or lakes they had to prepare to resist eldritch temptation, for as often as not, from the dismal water there would arise naked female forms of waif-like loveliness; lovely, despite their unhumanness — the chins perhaps a little too small, the jawbones a fraction too delicate and piscean, yet graceful as grasses, with long, green hair that poured down over their long white backs. Silent in the murk, these wild water-wights would stretch out their arms and beckon. Perhaps for centuries they had hungered for mortal flesh. The men spoke rhymes to ward them off, and clutched at the amulets they wore about their necks, and threw salt at the drowners, but one of the Marauders was tricked, and jumped into a pool. The ravishing girls twined their arms and hair about him, dragging him down despite all efforts to save him. Inky waters closed over the bulky figure and he was never seen again.

Screaming in panic after witnessing this episode Aonarán struggled to escape, but his guards held him, binding him with ropes.

On went the expedition, through the confines of darkness, through the intense cold and unforgiving inimicality that reigned in the underworld, beneath incalculable tons of rock. Three times they chanced upon small groups of roaming kobolds, and drew their swords, ready to fight. Each time, the toxic imps scuttled away and the men put away their weapons.

'Evidently the goblins did not order all their slaves into the four kingdoms,' said Sir Huelin Lathallan. 'Some remain to patrol the underworld.'

'I daresay they did not love the notion of humankind trespassing in the halls of Minith Ariannath,' Sir Torold surmised.

'These are busy dominions, the entrails of the world,' muttered Lathallan. 'Far too busy.'

As they passed down the centre of a long gallery of natural rock, picking their way across a ridged floor on which boulders squatted like toads, there came, from the opening of a tunnel to the left, a glimmer of strange light. The radiance was silver - shafts of pure silver, translucent, like rays of moonlight or starlight purified and concentrated; or long diagonals of virgin ice glimmering ethereally as if lit from within by some numinous force. At the same time the men heard a low rumbling as of distant thunder underground. They halted, drawing their swords and crowding together for protection. The touch of the light upon their skin was tingling, as if a million silver pins sizzled, delightful and excruciating. And the silver pins pushed into their minds, harped on wires across their consciousness, and resonated, and pulled taut their veins.

There was a disturbance in the lightless narrows between spindles of silver.

Shadowy figures were moving there.

Without warning, Aonarán howled and flung himself away from his captors. He tried to run, but the ropes brought him up short and his guards grabbed him. He grappled with them, yowling. Believing the wretch could see in the dark, the men were frightened, for it was evident he had perceived something that scared him from the remnants of his wits; but they held fast and took a firmer grip on their weapons and raised their lanterns high. For an instant of uncertainty they stood poised, like carvings.

Out of the shadows stepped the tall, lithe shapes of men, yet not human.

At first the explorers could not believe what they were seeing; they thought it some illusion, some trick of the senses invoked by glamour. Gradually they comprehended. Those who stood before them were, in truth, knights of the Argenkindë. There were about twenty of them, dressed in sable and silver; handsome beyond dreams, insidious as poison, spirited and sparkling, dangerous as hatred. Their hair cascaded past their shoulders, blacker than midnight in a coal cellar, shot through, here and there, with a crow's plumage sheen of blue iridescence. Silken strands of this marvellous hair rose and fell, buoyed by currents of gramarye, and tiny stars seemed snagged therein. The eyes of the goblin knights were dark, and outlined with slender smudges, as if they had pencilled the rims of the lids with kohl.

When the ogrish Marauders comprehended what it was that stood before them they roared in alarm. They were large and slow, and burdened with heavy packs; for them there would be no escape. Overcome by terror, they cast themselves flat upon the ground and covered their eyes. As one, the men unsheathed their gold-plated swords.

One of the unseelie incarnations was leaning against the side of the tunnel a little way behind the rest, his arms folded across his chest, one knee bent and his foot braced against the wall. His profile could not be described in the gloom. Lazily he turned his head sideways to look at the Narngalishmen, saying, 'Greetings, Your Royal Highness. What brings you to my domains?' and William instantly recognised the voice of Zaravaz.

The goblin king kicked away from the wall and came striding forward, statuesque, smiling pleasantly, his long black hair swinging in rhythm with every step he took.

'What are you doing here?' William cried, incredulous. 'You said you would depart at the full moon.'

'We are not obliged to explain our business to anyone, let alone the likes of you, *boddagh!*' said Zauberin, who had appeared behind the shoulder of his lord.

'In fact,' Zaravaz pointed out to his lieutenant, 'we are not even obliged to explain that we are not obliged to explain.'

'But you said you would go away, and you are unable to lie!' the prince said angrily. 'How can this be?'

Zaravaz spoke a word to Zauberin, who responded, 'It was I who told your weathermage we intended to leave.'

'My *aachionard* was following orders,' said his sovereign. 'I chose to say *tell her we will leave*, rather than *I intend to leave, tell her so.* It is true we do not own your delightful ability to directly utter falsehoods, nevertheless we do not allow that to incapacitate us. We can direct others to speak falsely on our behalf, if they are not aware of the truth. Furthermore, we can change our minds. Perhaps I changed my mind. I will depart when I am ready, not when the moon is in a particular phase.'

'Why does your horde remain here?' Lathallan growled.

'We have told you enough about our own business. What is yours?'

William answered brusquely, 'We have come to salvage our gold from the Inglefire.'

'Indeed,' Zaravaz said politely.

Expecting the eldritch knights to try to block this enterprise the men hefted the weapons in their hands, but Zaravaz said, 'Well you'd better get on with it then,' and merely watched them, his head cocked to one side, a faint smile playing about his fine mouth. Immediately the men suspected a trick of some sort.

'Do you mean to assault us?' demanded Sir Torold.

'We are but casual passers-by. La! We are not even protected by armour. How should we dare assault you?'

'Tell us,' pressed William, determined to penetrate any goblin word play, 'will you try to prevent us from reaching the Inglefire?'

'We will not,' said Zaravaz, '*try* to prevent you.' Once more he leaned idly against the wall, as if bored.

And William silently cursed himself for failing to choose his words more carefully, as one must do with eldritch wights. That statement could be interpreted to mean the unseelie knights would not merely try, they would succeed. Pride, however, prevented him from rephrasing the question and asking a second time. Instead he gave a stilted nod of acknowledgement.

'Oh!' said Lieutenant Zwist, as if noticing the men's weapons for the first time, 'you have dipped your palings in gold! Did you think those yellow sticks would make us run away?'

'Why don't you make your boasts with this sword pressed against your flesh?' invited Lathallan's second, feinting at the goblin knight. Zwist flung a handful of what appeared to be nothing at the captain, whereupon he dropped his blade with a clatter and doubled over, clutching his hand to his chest.

'Desist, Rotherfield!' Lathallan said sharply.

'Those poor imitations of Sioctíne will avail you nought,' Zwist said with contempt.

'Be careful not to stumble and fall on them, or you might cut yourselves!' gibed Zauberin.

He and the other goblin lieutenants were laughing softly as they stood at ease around their king. 'You walk so stooped, men of Tir,' they mocked. 'You jump at every sound and cringe from every shadow. What are you afraid of?'

'We fear nothing,' William's men retorted.

Said the unseelie knights, 'Do not lose your charms, and amulets, for the spinners down here are passing fierce for old biddies! It is fortunate your weapons are so many and so formidable. The worms and beetles of the underworld will surely tremble at the sight of such warriors as you!'

The faces of the men suffused with rage and they were sorely tempted to attack their harassers. Controlling their ire, they held back, for William had too much common sense to throw away everyone's lives, the Companions of the Cup were well disciplined, and the rest were too terrified to make a move.

Wise judgement prevailed.

'We will not be provoked by your taunts,' said William.

At that the beautiful chivalry laughed aloud, but Zaravaz raised a languid hand, whereupon they bowed derisively, turned their backs on the human men and swaggered away. The goblin king had already melted into the dimness. As his lieutenants and other knights disappeared from view they were still jeering and calling out offensive remarks. Zauberin was heard to say, 'Let us go and play with the water-girls.' It appeared the goblins were leaving the intruders to their own devices. The Narngalishmen, however, were leery of being duped again.

The Marauders lumbered to their feet, sweating, panting, and trembling. Still wielding their swords the human men continued on their way. Now doubly vigilant, they lit more lanterns to banish the obscurity that hemmed them in. Aonarán whimpered incessantly, while the Marauders crowded so close to their companions that they jostled them, and Lathallan had to order them to stay clear.

Deeper into the mountain they went. The adventurers had descended a rough stair and were passing through another gallery when their attention was caught by the appearance of a second flicker of light, this time at the far end of the cavern. This new light, however, was utterly unlike the lunar goblin brilliance.

It was a golden glory, like flawless topaz with a piece of the sun at its heart. As they drew nearer the glory intensified, but most wonderfully, this radiance was singing. To William, it produced a soft clear music like the pure voices of children in unison, voicing a wordless melody, and within that pouring syrup of melody there were sudden glints of chimes, as if golden bells were ringing.

The jaws of the Marauders dangled ajar.

'Hark!' exclaimed one of the Narngalishmen, 'that is the sound of goodness! It is the laughter of children.'

'It is the song of the blackbird in the early dusk,' said his comrade.

'No, it is running water,' said a third man.

'It is a mother crooning a lullaby,' said someone else, but others claimed it was the music the stars would make if they fell through the strings of a harp. The song was variously like wind through the leaves of poplars, the beat of a loving heart, the patter of raindrops on a tiled roof, the sigh of the ocean, or the purring of a great cat. The listeners could agree on one point only - that they all heard something different.

Enraptured and intrigued, the Narngalishmen followed Aonarán toward the lustrous source of the music. Around a corner the walls opened out, and there before them in a rocky chamber a bonfire leaped twenty feet high, in full splendour. None had ever before beheld such a phenomenon, yet there was no doubt in their minds that this was indeed that which they sought; the Aingealfyre.

The interior of this light-splashed cavern was sculpted, as if water-worn. A wide and roughly circular well in the floor contained the source of the golden light. Translucent flames flashed in towering spirals from this pit, their glow so bright that the bottom of the well could not be seen, if indeed it had a base and did not pierce right through to the centre of the world, or even to the other side and beyond, to where comets roamed the universe. Spills of jewelled radiance welled up; shimmering crimson and orange were the colours of the flames, now tinged with sea-green copper. Unlike normal combustion this conflagration did not involve oxidation accompanied by the production of heat and light, nor did it give off smoke. It was a self-sustaining blaze of eldritch energies, engendered by gramarye.

The Aingealfyre's chamber was splendid. Its clean, dry walls were veined with glimmering ores. Fractured images of the intruders glanced from countless angles, for the walls and ceiling were not entirely smooth. Indeed, they were pierced with apertures great and small, and fluted, and buttressed, and recessed and niched. Refracted light danced on polished surfaces; brassy and apricot, luteous and rubicund.

Spellbound, the men tentatively approached the barleysugar flames. No fierce heat assaulted them, only a gentle warmth, as of Spring sunshine, yet for some this temperate incandescence was painful, while for others it was like balm. Furthermore, while it did them no harm, they sensed peril in that radiation.

Gazing in fascination, most of the party arranged themselves around the edge of the pit. Aonarán, however, hung back. He ceased his mewling and his tugging on the ropes, and instead became very quiet and still. After a while William recollected himself and said, 'By the Powers, we have found our goal at last. It will not do us much good to stand staring – let us get to work!' He issued orders, whereupon the swarmsmen unloaded the equipment they had carried thence on their brawny shoulders, and the miners unpacked it.

Hesitantly, for the act somehow seemed like desecration, the men, standing as far away as possible from the pit's brink, thrust large iron ladles into the strange blaze, and lowered crucibles on chains. Soon and with astonishing ease, just as they had hoped, they were scooping out lumps of gleaming metal, as soft as wax, sometimes mixed with a few jewels unmarred, sparkling as if rinsed in rainwater. Neither soot, nor ash, nor cinders tainted the precious ore or gems, and to the amazement of the Narngalishmen their booty was relatively cool to the touch, once free of the flames.

Truly, the fire of gramarye was mysterious.

With willing zeal the labourers piled up their gleanings. They accumulated quite a quantity, which they stowed in bags of hempen canvas and stacked against the walls, later to be loaded onto the shoulders of the bearers. Every member of the expedition became engrossed in the task. As the men hauled out their salvage Aonarán stood silently by with a look of awe on his hideous face, never taking his eyes off the fire. He had tilted his head, like a man listening for a far-off sound, and wore a slight frown as though trying to understand a foreign language or to grasp a message.

'All seems to be going well,' Lathallan murmured to William as he and the prince watched over the proceedings.

'The men feel safe here,' said William. 'They know the goblins could never come near this place.'

'Is that true?' asked Lathallan.

'I believe so,' the prince replied. 'The weathermasters say that if a mortal man should enter the Inglefire he would not perish immediately, but fade, gently, without pain, in a dream or trance, as it were. Those who are chaste of spirit survive longer than those whose hearts are corrupt. For unseeliekind it is a different story. They also perish slowly, but as they decline they suffer unimaginable torment, shrivelling slowly until they become a wisp of dust or soot, still alive and sentient. Eventually they float away, doomed to drift on the wind until time's end. Even to view the werefire from afar is painful to them. They will not come here.'

'Nonetheless, we had better watch out for goblins as we depart through the tunnels,' said Sir Torold. 'They are our sworn foes, and no doubt will assail us on our way out.'

William was about to respond with a suggestion, when all of a sudden someone rushed past him and ran straight toward the pit. It was Fionnbar Aonarán.

'Stop!' yelled the prince, dashing after him, but it was too late.

Everything happened swiftly. Aonarán deliberately let himself drop over the brink into the fire. At the instant he toppled, William, who was hot on his heels, grabbed him by the shirt. As Aonarán fell, William was still hanging on. Aonarán's flailing arms knocked the prince's head against the pit's edge and William, fainting, was dragged into the blaze by the weight of the man he was trying to rescue. Both of them vanished into the inferno.

Throughout the Northern Ramparts millions of tons of rock arched and strained, fighting the slow battles of geological evolution; shaped, made and unmade by tectonic, volcanic, gravitational, chemical and climatic forces. In underground chambers, solutions of calcium carbonate dripped leisurely, depositing travertine to form stalactites and stalagmites. Far below the cavern of the Inglefire, molten lava, ash and gases forced their way through crustal vents, a sluggish ooze of volcanic release. On the exposed peaks thousands of feet high, lacy snowflakes fell, blanketing the firn, while crazed winds scraped along the skies at full pelt, sharp-edged and cold as scalpels, as if attempting to chisel the stars from their niches.

The wind veered. It began to blow hard from the north. High in the upper atmosphere miniscule ice crystals were borne along on an air stream, in ribbons so fine as to be almost invisible. The crystals passed southwards across Narngalis; over the foothills of the Northern Ramparts, the Harrowgate Fells, the town of Paper Mill, and the Wuthering Moors, until they reached King's Winterbourne, where they descended, melted to become airborne droplets, and tamely mingled with the other atmospheric humidity.

One speck of moisture drifted through a cranny in a house called The Laurels. It was inhaled by a weathermage, and temporarily became part of her substance. Later it vaporised from her dewy skin and floated away to resume its innocent, ancient, elemental journey.

Asräthiel had not seen William for weeks, yet she was unconcerned about his absence. She knew he was away attending to important matters of state, and for her part, she was busy with her own tasks. Avalloc was staying at The Laurels, helping her train three prentices who were lodging there also. In addition her weathermaster skills were much in demand, for Autumn, the fruitful season, now stirred up storms aplenty.

Days were becoming shorter. Early on misty Ninember mornings the hedgerows of Narngalis would be silver-netted with the dew-spangled webs of orb-spiders. The first frosts froze the last of the butterflies and other winged insects. Wood pigeons pillaged the countryside in large flocks, feasting in fields of clover, gorging on the wild bounty of grass seeds, hedgerow berries and acorns. Along the margins of meadows the last lingering blossoms mingled with the bronze and gold coinage of fallen leaves; speedwell and wild pansy, mayweed and white deadnettle. The brilliant red domes of fly agaric toadstools studded woodland carpets.

On the final morning of Ninember Asrăthiel had strolled with her grandfather through a beech wood just beyond the outskirts of King's Winterbourne. Both wore their robes of weathermaster grey; they walked like two shadows side by side, one with hair like pourings of alabaster, the other with torrents of ebony, flowing from beneath embroidered caps. Early sunlight was shining through the foliage. Amongst the dark stems of the trees floated great drifts and bowers and spangled clouds of colour; points and splashes of rich bronze and cinnabar, poignant green, fabulous gold, shimmering in sun and air, fair as some enchanted realm.

'Of all seasons,' said Asrăthiel, gazing up at the overhanging boughs, 'I love Autumn best.' But saying this she was suddenly overwhelmed by a wave of sadness, for the beauties of the season, being ephemeral, would soon pass away, and reminded her of the transient nature of mortal lives. To be immortal amongst mortals is to be doomed to sorrow, she thought. If I am always to lose those whom I love, fain would I love no more.

A flock of swallows winged slowly overhead like drifts of dark leaves, navigating southwards.

'Tomorrow,' said Avalloc, 'will be the first day of Winter. Already, townsfolk and villagers are making ready for the year's end celebrations.'

'The first of Tenember?' exclaimed Asrăthiel. 'So soon? The weeks have flown!' She pondered. 'It strikes me that William's absence has been much prolonged.'

'Where has he gone?'

'I know not, for he would not say. But after my return from Minith Ariannath he was surpassingly attentive, writing to me almost every day and visiting frequently. The letters have ceased. It is unlike him to be away for so long, and to send no word. It seems odd. I wonder…' She broke off, pondering.

'What are your thoughts, my dear?'

'I wonder whether he has gone looking for the Inglefire. He spoke to me of such a mission but I declared I was against it.'

'Then if he has gone to find it, doubtless he deliberately refrained from telling you so, to avoid distressing you. Will asked me for permission to wed you, you know.'

'I guessed as much,' the damsel admitted.

'If you are anxious about him, petition Warwick for enlightenment. I am certain he will set your mind at ease.'

'I will do that.'

That evening Asrăthiel took her grandfather's advice. Together they paid a visit to Wyverstone Castle, where the sovereign frankly informed her of the whereabouts of his son. 'He has taken an expedition to seek the goblin prison and the Inglefire. His intention is to gather the gold that, according to legend, human slaves threw into the flames.'

'I am dismayed that he would undertake such madness!' Asrăthiel exclaimed on hearing this. 'The goblins may well have left guards. The fire itself is reputed to be dangerous – that is, if they ever find it in that labyrinth, with tricksy wights rolling boulders hither and thither to change the configuration of the tunnels. My liege, have you heard from William of late? Has he sent any message at all?'

'Not since the expedition passed beneath the mountains,' Warwick answered gravely. 'I confess; I am troubled. William's party had homing birds in their care, concealed from the Watch, but so far, we have received no news.'

'I, too, am troubled,' said Asrăthiel. 'Did he take that knave Aonarán as guide?'

'That he did.'

'The fellow is not to be trusted, besides which the Northern Ramparts are riddled with the perils of chasm and slippery slope, not to mention being haunted by unseelie wights. The Companions of the Cup are brave fighters, yet there are some things in that region which cannot be combated by warrior's sword, or charms of iron and rowan. I ask your permission to depart straightway by sky-balloon to seek the expedition, that I may render them my assistance if they are in some straits.'

'Granted,' the king said at once. 'In hindsight I wish I had sent a weathermage with them, but William would insist on keeping it all secret. I hope I do not live to regret that omission.' Earnestly he added, 'Go with good speed, Asrăthiel.'

12
TEARS AND FLAMES

When weatherlords to battle fared, the glinting of the yellow blade
Was spied from far off. Wild and strange the melody, the
  blood-song played
By winds against the leading edge. The wielder of the golden sword
Smote wightish heads, hewed pathways of destruction through
  the goblin horde.
Their smoking blood blacken'd the ground. Unseelie wights were
  vanquished. Then,
'To victory!' sang Fallowblade, 'Sweet victory for mortal men!'
Upon a dark time long ago.'

A VERSE FROM THE SONG 'FALLOWBLADE'

On the morning of the very day that William's expedition discovered the Inglefire, Asrăthiel's sky balloon *Icemoon* arose from King's Winterbourne. With her she took two prentices and the sword *Rehollys* – a wand of argent gaslight - its sheath buckled at her side. The brí-summoned wind was swift and strong. In a single day her aircraft made the journey, passing above the Wuthering Moors, over the remote township of Paper Mill and across the Harrowgate Fells to the foothills of the northern ranges. The landscape rushing past underneath the basket was still brushed by the fading flames of Autumn. Sere and shrivelling, the last leaves clung to black boughs as Winter began to set in. Rivers and lakes gleamed like new-minted pewter.

The aeronauts reached the northern ranges late in the afternoon, as the sun was beginning to sink and lines of birds were flying home to roost, calling to one another like echoes from a distance. Magnolia and fuchsia clouds straggled in elongated rows across the west. The mountains were partially submerged in a flood of mist, only their rugged peaks showing, snow-crowned and floating rootless on the pearly haze. Overhead, the clear skies deepened to indigo.

Asrăthiel murmured words of power, sketching invisible signs with her hands. Her copilot tugged judiciously on a cord, allowing heated air to escape from the envelope. The weathermage and her crew spied the cluster of carts, swathed in evening shadows, whose location indicated the cave mouth through which William's party had entered under ground. As the balloon was commencing its descent towards the carts Asrăthiel strained her eyes to see if she could pick out the shape of the fantastic bridge and the gates of Sølvetårn, further to the right. All at once she spied a band of horsemen clustered on the heights and, unexpectedly, her heart began to hammer. The sight of riders near the bridge reminded her of goblins, but it was impossible that the Argenkindë could still be in the mountains. All the same, she was puzzled as to how men on horseback could have escaped the attentions of the kobold watch, who were ever ferocious to persecute and prosecute mortals who made burdens of themselves upon living creatures. It was particularly unusual that riders should have ventured so far north, to the very doorstep of the kobolds' erstwhile abode, placing themselves in extreme danger. With a whispered word she changed the aerostat's course and headed for Sølvetårn's gates.

As the balloon drifted down she suddenly clutched at the edge of the basket, giddy with hope and dread. The riders were not human at all. They were indeed goblin knights, mounted upon daemon horses. Eagerly she scanned their faces as they came into view. She recognised Zaillian and Zwist, and several other foremost lieutenants of the Argenkindë, but the one she sought was not amongst them. Nevertheless, she could hardly restrain her excitement.

'My lady, those horsemen are of the unseelie horde,' the prentices pointed out nervously. 'Some still linger here! Perhaps all! If goblins are abroad, what mischief might they have worked upon Prince William?'

As the truth of his words sank in Asrăthiel uttered an exclamation of horror.

'We must be careful to choose a landing spot far away from them,' said her crewmember, 'and take all precautions.'

'No,' Asrăthiel said decisively. 'I wish to speak with them. Fear not. As I am with you, they will not harm you.'

Alarm was plainly written upon the faces of the prentices, yet they respected Asrăthiel too well to remonstrate with her, and said nothing more about their misgivings. With all haste the weather-mage set the balloon down upon a rocky shelf. As the floor of the basket knocked against stone the goblin riders swiftly approached, sombre and splendid, arcane and hazardous, their black cloaks fluttering like wings on the wind. The hooves of the svelte trollhästen clapped against bare basalt.

The demeanour of the eldritch knights was grim, in contrast to their usual light-heartedness. On second glance Asrăthiel noted some even more profound change in their manner since last she had seen them, but she was unable to define it. When she vaulted from the basket the goblin chivalry gathered around. Lieutenant Zwist called out urgently, and without preamble, 'Come quickly, Lady Maelstronnar. Ride behind me.'

The prentices huddled close to the sun-crystal cradled in the centre of the basket. Above their heads the still-swollen envelope swayed and rippled, flapping in the evening breeze and reflecting the shifting colours of twilight. Gently the aerostat bobbed up and down, hovering close to the ground. The riders paid it no heed, their attention being bent upon Asrăthiel. Clearly they were impatient.

'What trouble is afoot?' she asked. 'Where is Prince William?'

'No time for gossip. Be quick!'

'I will come with you,' said the damsel, 'but my companions must wait for me here, and first you must swear not to harm them.'

'On behalf of this company,' Fourth Lieutenant Zande said peremptorily, 'I swear it.'

To the prentices Asrăthiel said, 'If I fail to return by morning, depart without me, for I shall be beyond your aid,' and they nodded mute acknowledgement, their faces drawn and their eyes glazed with terror.

Zande picked up the damsel by the waist and swung her onto the back of a daemon horse behind Zwist. Off they galloped with her, she clinging limply like a doll made of rags, drained of vitality, her mind reeling. What have they done to William? Onwards rushed the riders, the long-legged trollhästen leaping with improbable accuracy from crag to crag. The world went past like a smear. It came to Asrăthiel that she and the goblins were travelling within an eldritch time zone; that weird dimension which enabled them to act with supernatural swiftness. Through some secret portal in a cliff they plunged beneath the mountain. In the dark they raced along miles of underground tunnels, flying up and down leagues of subterranean stairs that went by in a blur of incredible speed, so that the damsel could hardly catch her breath, but she glimpsed enough to know that they now moved through Sølvetårn.

Abruptly the horses slowed and halted. The riders leaped to the ground, bringing the damsel with them, and entered a high-vaulted chamber that she recognised at once. It was a room of gothic loveliness, circular in shape, its walls perforated almost all the way around by unglazed archways exposing the interior to the elements, the ceiling an intricate openwork lattice giving almost unrestricted view of the ice-sharp summits that towered against the magnificence of sunset. To one side, a table upheld a casket of embossed silver filled to overflowing with frost-jewels. In the centre of the chamber stood a divan piled with sleek and glossy cushions.

On that divan a figure lay unmoving, as if dead.

Asrǎthiel and the twenty knights had come in with a rush, in a swirl of cloaks, a clatter of boots and a jingling of jewels and weaponry which the damsel could have sworn was deliberate, since the goblins could move silently at will. At the sight of the prone figure they stopped short, like a blast of wind that had suddenly subsided. Utter silence washed over them like a wave. Outside, even the sky-borne breezes cutting themselves to ribbons on the heights died away.

The strangest and most discomposing aspect of this silence was the fact that the room, though large, was filled to capacity with statuesque goblin knights clothed in black draperies. Their mode was no longer flamboyant, as at feast times, nor was it rakish and dashing, as for the hunt. Neither were they garbed in war harness, with antlered helm and engraved cuirass. Instead these dark and mighty warriors were in the solemn costume of ceremony; robes long and flowing, gracefully arranged in loose folds, plain but exquisitely cut. Impressive of stature they stood composed, as straight as spears. There must have been hundreds, and amongst them, the half-pint figures of several trows.

With folded hands and bowed heads the lords of unseelie stood without stirring or speaking, as if keeping some dreadful vigil. Luxurious swathes of their black hair, untied, fell forward like curtains, partly concealing their wondrously comely features. It was a sight to unsettle the most adamant heart.

Outside, the wind began to croon once more. Only its sorrowful song could be heard, and even that seemed subdued as it sighed amid lonely crags and across chasms of emptiness. This seeming lullaby of the airs, in its tranquillity, contrasted sharply with the taut atmosphere that saturated the gothic chamber from wall to wall, and the sense of coiled energies on the point of raging out of control. So intense was the ambience that the floor beneath Asrǎthiel's feet, indeed her very bones seemed to reverberate below the range of hearing, as if charged with a powerful current. The sense of impending cataclysm was immediate.

When the damsel appeared amidst the watching knights several of them turned to observe her. Some moved to block her path. Of these, Zauberin was foremost, scowling, although even hostile grimaces could not mar the eldritch perfection of a goblin warrior.

'Why did you bring her here?' the first lieutenant gratingly demanded of Zwist. 'She is not welcome.'

'Let me see William!' Asrăthiel cried wildly, ignoring his rancour. 'What has happened? Is Zaravaz here?'

Unreasonably - flustered, perhaps by the swiftness of the supernatural ride and the shock of encountering the Argenkindë - she had at first assumed the recumbent form was that of William, then realised it could not possibly be the prince, because goblin knights would hardly be gathering around in solemn quietude as if honouring someone they revered. With this realisation came a cold surge, as if a breath from the grave had blown out her vital spark.

Zauberin and his close companions hissed censoriously at Zwist's party, and spat invective at the damsel. The two sides began to argue vehemently but softly, speaking in their own tongue. Asrăthiel stepped out of their range, all the while casting agonized glances at the motionless figure in the centre of the chamber. She could not reach the couch; too many figures of impressive stature barred her way.

At length the altercation ceased. The opposing groups moved away from each other, the vast crowd parted, and at last the damsel was led through the assembly to the couch.

Upon reaching it she staggered, almost swooning, and dropped to her knees.

A masculine form, long and lean, lay there with eyes closed –

– the goblin king.

The sight of him was a sword thrust of hurt and ecstasy. In its abandonment to oblivion, his face looked even more wrenchingly handsome. The fans of his lashes were ink strokes against his skin's bronze pallor. His arms rested by his sides, and funereal hair drenched his shoulders with liquid night. At that moment, for

Asrăthiel there was nothing else in existence but his exact lines of symmetry and vigour, his dark beauty that outshone every one of his knights. In all respects he was matchless.

Yet he, an immortal being, was lifeless; as cold and immobile as a statue carved from finest limestone, and seeing this the damsel thought the world had dropped away from beneath her feet. For an instant the sense of unreality was so overwhelming that she felt as if she were standing outside herself, looking on. She dared not touch him, dared not trespass on aloof perfection.

'Does he live?' she whispered, at last. The lords of wickedness who surrounded her offered no answer. 'Prithee, tell me what happened!' she begged, her words catching in her throat, as dry as husks.

After a moment Zwist spoke. 'He is fading,' the knight said slowly, as if he found it difficult to choke out the words.

Fading was an eldritch term for the immortal equivalent of dying. It meant the process of transforming from the original state to some lesser form. For Asrăthiel, a tiny but fierce sun at the centre of all purpose and meaning dimmed and threatened to blink out. Virtually paralysed with incredulity she murmured, 'How can this be?'

'I saw it all,' said Zwist, 'from the sidelines. Your boyfriend brought Toadstone to the cavern of the Skagnyaile, the cursed flames. That is what began it all.'

'Tell me!'

And so the second lieutenant proceeded to describe, in low tones, the events that had occurred in the cavern of the werefire. As he did so, the story unfolded vividly in Asrăthiel's mind.

After Aonarán had inadvertently pulled William after him into the Inglefire, uproar exploded amongst the expedition members. Some flung themselves forward in an effort to save the prince, yet stopped short of casting themselves futilely into the pyre.

'He is gone!' cried Lathallan. Kneeling at the well's edge he shoved his hands in amongst the dazzling corkscrew flames, enduring the suffering it caused, casting about, trying desperately to locate the young man. All the while he screamed, and tears streamed down his cheeks. The effect of the verdant radiance must have been harrowing beyond belief. When he withdrew his hands they appeared undamaged, but he spread out his fingers and gaped at them, saying chokingly, 'I thought the flesh had charred off my bones.'

'A' curse upon the fiend Aonarán!' his companions cried. 'The noblest son of Narngalis has fallen.'

Even as they spoke, the air blurred. A blast from nowhere briefly levelled and parted the flames, raising billows of dust and whipping at the garments and hair of the frantic men. At this onset the Marauders bellowed and ran blindly about. In the confusion, a flaming bundle came hurtling out of the heart of the Inglefire. The Narngalishmen jumped up, drawing back in fear and astonishment. At their feet the naked body of a man lay prone on the rocky floor, limned with wavelets of lemony fire. Suddenly Lathallan uttered a glad cry and threw his cloak over the burning figure, dousing the flames. The men could not believe their eyes. It was their prince who lay there, insensible but miraculously unscathed. His garments had vaporised but not so much as a hair of his head had been scorched, and his flesh was whole. They were too stunned to rejoice, but the chirurgeon-apothecary gathered his wits, tore open his bag of remedies and began attending to his lord.

Next instant someone gave a shout and all turned to stare at the pit. The Inglefire had altered. A tremendous change had taken place in its substance and nature, for now, instead of burning with helical green-gold flames too bright for the eye to penetrate, it roared ruby red. The flames had flattened and clarified, transparent as panes of glass, and through them not one, but two figures could be discerned within the pit, a few feet below floor level. Both were on fire.

In all the commotion the Narngalishmen could not ascertain which of their number had toppled in. One of the two blazing men was standing motionless, as if astonished or numb, while the other desperately tried to climb out but fell back, overcome by weakness, writhing in utmost terror or agony. The first, they supposed, was Aonarán, immortal born mortal, who appeared to have fallen into a trance. The second must be one of their own. Pity moved the observers to immediate action, and they lowered their salvage equipment into the flames, calling out to their comrade, 'Take hold! Take hold!'

The suffering man barely had the strength to grip their chains, but managed to hang on for just long enough that they could haul him up as far as the brink. Knight-Commander Lathallan actually leaned forward and thrust his hands right into the blaze once more, though sobbing all the while. Enduring the most searing pain, impossible to describe, he laid hold of the victim and resolutely drew him out over the edge. They laid him on the floor, wrapping him from head to toe in cloaks to extinguish the flames.

The instant he was pulled out the colours of the werefire changed again, transforming to blinding emerald-citrine. Dazzled by the light's intensity, the men lost sight of Aonarán. For a few moments the tongues of scalding light shrank, as if the fire were guttering out, before bursting upward with renewed vigour. During those moments of low smoulder the fire pit was clearly visible. Aside from the flames, now almost pure gold, it was empty. The men had no idea what to make of this, then one of them cried, 'Look there!' and they spied a figure silhouetted against the glare, crawling along the ground on the far side of the cave. It was Aonarán.

'By the Fates, that reprobate has climbed out of his own accord!' Sir Torold cried in disbelief. 'A prodigious feat. And if I can believe my eyes, he is living yet! Secure him!'

Men-at-arms ran to do his bidding, skirting the pit with care. In a daze, Knight-Commander Lathallan had slumped on the floor, head bowed. The chirurgeon-apothecary and his assistant were still tending the unconscious prince, while the others were ensuring that all the flames lapping their rescued companion had been put out. Enveloped in the folds of the cloak, this man had ceased writhing and lay as still as the prince. As still as death.

'Two went in, and three came out!' marvelled the Narngalishmen. 'How did it happen? Which of us fell in? Who is missing?'

'We shall soon see,' Sir Torold said.

And they began to peel back the cloaks to reveal the identity of the one they had rescued...

The Narngalish adventurers could not know that the goblin king and some of his knights, driven by curiosity and animosity, had followed them to the seat of the Aingealfyre. The immortals had watched, concealed in the walls of the cavern, where the radiance of the eldritch blaze could not reach to scald them. After William was dragged into the pit, Zaravaz had leaped out with supernatural speed, so swiftly that human eyes could detect nothing but a blur. He had jumped into the werefire to save the prince's life, but the flames of purity were too much for him, of course. He paid a very high price.

William had been knocked senseless by the blow to his head. In an act demanding astounding potency of body and will Zaravaz had picked up the prince's burning form and hurled him out of the pit, but the effort, while he himself was alight, cost him all his strength. Debilitated and agonised he could not climb out, and so sank into the flames. Had the Narngalishmen not dragged him out, he would have been slowly consumed.

As the men gazed, dumbfounded, at the eldritch being sprawled upon the cavern floor, Zwist, Zaillian and several other goblin knights rushed from their shielded positions. Heedless of their own anguish under the wickedness-scouring radiance of the werefire they seized their stricken king and bore him away.

'My lord spent only a few moments in the flames,' Zwist said to Asrăthiel; 'it was not long enough to destroy him, but long enough to work him great harm. Now he lies here, comatose, and there is naught we can do. He clings to the last vestiges of life in this form, but with every passing instant the final traces of his vitality are ebbing. When you found us we were riding out to fetch you here, for we are desperately in need of aid. If there is any way to bring him back, we know it not. The remedy for such an affliction is beyond our knowledge, beyond the scope of our healing. Maybe the weathermasters know a cure.' More softly, he added, 'If ever you felt any love for him, Sioctíne, you must help him now.'

Asrăthiel whispered, 'Should I be unable to help him, what will happen?'

'The Skagnyaile will have its way. If my lord has ever deliberately slain a helpless creature, he will perish for certain, and there will be no saving him.'

The damsel stared at the comely warriors without seeing them. In other circumstances it would have been moving to see the Argenkindë, who had never bowed to fear, nor been moved by calls to virtue according to human codes of ethics, nor quailed at any deed, nor flinched at the prospect of brutality, now humbled by this stark reminder of the only scythe that could cut them down, whose edge had touched the one they loved best. 'Well then, there is an end to it,' she said, 'for of course he has done so.'

'I think not,' said Zaillian. 'To cut down someone helpless would be beneath his dignity. Our sovereign was too proud to slay a child or an unarmed opponent, or a man whose back was turned. He has only ever killed in combat – partly out of pride, and partly because he enjoyed the thrill of uncertainty. He delighted in the excitement of being matched against an adversary who could fight back. Nevertheless, I cannot be sure what will happen. Only the cursed werefire knows what his doom will be – ash or life. But even if by great fortune he lives, the fire will have changed him utterly. He cannot again be as we have known him.'

'If his doom is to be withered to ashes, how long will it take?'

'We can only surmise. He would surely be gone by the first moon of Averil.'

'Why did he do it?' Asrăthiel cried passionately. 'Why did he risk himself?'

'I daresay,' Zwist replied calmly, 'he took the chance because of your love for Wyverstone. Most of my comrades blame you for the downfall of our lord, but we who dared to enter the light to bring him back feel differently.' He hesitated, then muttered with a tinge of regret, 'I suspect the cursed flames have somewhat altered the degree of our ability to deal in death.'

His words were wasted, for the damsel was hardly listening. As she knelt beside her fading lover, she thought her heart had been torn out by the roots. She possessed limited knowledge of the arts of healing, but no understanding at all of how to restore health to eldritch beings. There was nothing she could do.

It was as if she had played out this drama before.

Her gaze traced the soft dark weeping of Zaravaz's hair. He lay supine, impossibly beautiful, unmarred by scorch or flame, on a carven bier in the fairest of all halls of Sølvetårn, looking as if untouched by harm in any form.

Just like Jewel.

Asrăthiel's mother slept the slumber of wakelessness, surrounded by roses. The goblin king slept the slumber of the dying, surrounded by silver and jewels, and grieving knights black-cloaked, with arms folded and heads bowed, rank on rank.

The current of gramarye that usually played about Zaravaz, tweaking his hair and garments, was absent. He looked as vulnerable as a sleeping child. The damsel had never imagined she would see him this way, so defenceless, adrift on the mere of the deepest possible sleep, on a voyage bound for eternity. He had been imbued with vigour, the essence of liveliness and energy and quick spirits. Beholding him in the grip of lasting torpor made her feel as if all light and gaiety had been stolen from the universe.

'And in millennia of millennia,' she murmured, 'when the sun has exploded and this world is naught but a ball of seared stone, what shall we be then? Shall we be changeless motes suspended forever in frozen darkness?'

Those were Crowthistle's words. They had branded themselves into Asrăthiel's memory. At this instant, so distressed was she that she wished only for the last second of time to flicker out.

The spirit of Zaravaz seemed to have drifted far away on some dim flood, out of reach, but Asrăthiel remained at his side, whispering to him. She caressed his brow and ran her fingertips through his calamitous hair, entreating him to turn back the boat in which his spirit voyaged, but he never moved; not so much as an eyelash.

Once, she fancied she detected a long slow rhythm of breathing, which made her recall something else Zaravaz had told her. He had described how, as the urisk Crowthistle at her mother's graveside, he had sensed the protracted heartbeat that proved Jewel survived. The recollection prompted Asrăthiel to put forth all her brí-senses and for a while she believed she could hear the faint pulse of his life, fading, fading...

For a long time she spoke to the goblin king and called his name. He did not respond. It was scarcely conceivable that he could hear her, but she refused to leave his side, talking and singing softly until, worn out and drained, she fell into a trancelike state, part dozing, part dreaming.

Some while later a hand gripped Asrăthiel's shoulder and shook her to alertness. The sun had set long since, and the butterfly flames of a thousand candles illuminated the circular room. Like a wood of sombre trees the assembled Argenkindë remained standing in their places, watching over their king.

Some of them, however, had grown restless, and intolerant of the human presence.

'You must go,' said Lieutenant Zangezur.

'I will not,' the damsel answered.

'If you cannot heal him you are useless to us,' said one of Zangezur's comrades. 'We do not want you here. You belong with otherkind, may their hands be torn, and their minds go up in smoke!'

'This disaster is your fault, human bitch,' another chimed in.

'And for that fault,' Zauberin said in gravely tones, 'you should be punished. We ought to hang you in chains from the highest peak, alongside the king and the druid, only you would never perish but remain there forever, battered by the winds, until your clothes grew threadbare and dropped in rags from your body; and still you would hang there, while the hair on your head grew down past your feet, and still you would languish Winter and Summer, through snow and rain, staring at sun and stars and moon, and they staring back at you.'

'Let her be,' said Zwist, stepping between Asrăthiel and her harassers. Extending a hand, he helped the damsel to her feet. 'Can you do nothing to save him?' he beseeched, gazing searchingly into her face.

She shook her head dumbly, overcome by sorrow.

The knight sighed. 'In that case,' he said, 'it would be better for you if you were to depart. I cannot guarantee your safety here indefinitely. Besides, your companions await you. Your William lives, after all.'

'William?' Asrăthiel looked up. To her shame, she realised that since she set eyes on Zaravaz she had not spared a thought for the prince.

'Even so. He and his retinue are still close by, though their number is gravely depleted. We set upon them as they emerged from the cave of the flames, and slew many. We would have destroyed them all, but that our lord's rescue of Wyverstone would have been wasted.'

'You are hateful death-dealers!'

'Go to the survivors now, then return to your home. There is naught left for you here, save for peril and ill will.'

'No. I wish to stay with him until the end.'

'Lady Sioctíne, if you stay your enemies will strive to make good their promise to torment you. Those of us who were burned by the light will strive to prevent them, but it will lead to nothing but anger and strife. The blame for that will be upon you.'

'By all the powers of the Uile,' said Asrăthiel despairingly, 'if immortal human beings could weep tears of water, or even blood, sir, I would do so in this bitter hour.' She hesitated, sighed and then said, 'As you say, there is naught left to me. You give me no choice. I will go hence, and leave the cruel Argenkindë to their lamenting - may you all suffer intensely, as you deserve - but the anguish that I carry with me is more than the sorrow of all your brethren combined. From this time forth I will find no happiness in the world, for I love your lord with a passion beyond comprehension.'

'It is you who have slain him,' accused Zauberin. 'You and your folly.'

Disregarding her persecutor Asrăthiel turned her shoulder to him. Addressing Zwist she said, 'It is in my nature to hope. I beg of you, if your lord survives, send me some sign. I will wait until the first moon in Averil.'

'You are foolish to hope,' said Zwist. 'Who could be more wicked than he? The werefire will work its doom on him for sure.'

'But a sign! I must have a sign!'

'Very well. It is easy to make a promise that will require no action. If he lives I will send you a sign.'

'Beware of turning your back on me, mistress,' Zauberin said sharply, and Asrăthiel whirled to face him. 'May your days be fraught with woe,' said the unseelie lieutenant. 'Look upon the King of the Argenkindë for the last time, Bane of Zaravaz. We will forsake Sølvetårn, bearing him with us, and you will never see him again.'

Asrăthiel shot a glance of scorn and sadness at Zauberin. 'You have your wish,' she said.

Just before she departed she leaned over Zaravaz to kiss him goodbye. Strands of her hair slipped from their jewellery clasps and fell forward, pouring around his face, as his black tresses had showered around hers during their hours of love together.

It was then that a marvel occurred. A tremendous sob shook the damsel's frame and impossibly, she wept. Three glistening tears, conceivably bequeathed by her mortal mother, dropped from her blue eyes. The first tear fell on the mouth of Zaravaz, trickling between his lips. The second alighted on his left lid and the third on the right. But before Asrăthiel had a chance to let her lips brush his, Zauberin's cohorts seized her by the shoulders and roughly hustled her away, expelling her from the chamber of vigil.

In a smudge of speed the weathermage was escorted through the paths of Sølvetårn, and cast forth, and abandoned. She found herself in the open air, on a wide apron of stone amongst a jumbled scattering of boulders. A sheer rock face towered above.

Near at hand the narrow mouth of a cave opened into the hillside. Strong gusts of wind buffeted a cluster of carts, a sky-balloon that wrenched at its moorings, some broken and empty baskets that had been used to transport carrier pigeons - and the people who came hurrying to greet her.

Behind the mountains clouds went up like red fumes and a golden-spoked wheel began to dazzle. The sun was rising.

Besides Aonarán and William, only two men of the expedition had survived the ire of the goblin knights. The Crown Prince was dressed in a white linen shirt and a plain tunic and trousers, looking as if no ill had befallen him – as if he had never been touched by fire in any form. He strode up and greeted the damsel with delight, embracing her gently. His words were few but his gaze lingered upon her, and he smiled often. She stared at him in wonderment, keenly aware that he had been fully immersed and burned within the legendary flames, yet, through his innocence, had lived. It was difficult to know what to say to him.

Lathallan, too, looked well, though he seemed to have become almost as taciturn as his lord. His hands and face had taken no scar from being touched by the werefire, though had he plunged right in, like his lord, his fate might have been different. In contrast to William and the Knight-Commander, the immortal Fionnbar Aonarán was greatly transformed. Not even the Aingealfyre could kill him, but his flesh, which had been charred and ulcerated, was now whole. Smooth and unblemished was his skin, and his fingers no longer resembled talons, but healthy human digits. In all ways the erstwhile monster appeared ordinary, save that not a hair sprouted from his head, nor from his lids, nor anywhere on his person, and nobody could persuade him to utter so much as a single word.

Haggard and deeply agitated, Sir Torold Tetbury cried, 'Lady Asrăthiel, I am overjoyed to see you. One of those unseelie scoundrels bade us wait here for you, and Fates be praised, you have arrived. Let us depart forthwith.'

So they left the Northern Ramparts. William, Lathallan and

Sir Torold travelled in the aerostat with Asrăthiel, which could accommodate no more than four passengers, while the prentices accompanied Aonarán down the winding tracks on foot. The weathermage left them with a promise that she would return for them.

As the airship glided through the clouds on the way back to King's Winterbourne there was much discussion between Sir Torold and the weathermage, punctuated by a few quiet comments from Lathallan. Tetbury told how, after the events at the Inglefire, the Argenkindë set upon the adventurers in fury to take revenge for the burning of Zaravaz. The Narngalishmen fought for their lives, but the goblins overwhelmed them. Only, the unseelie knights would not touch William, nor would they approach Aonarán, and it was not until the fight was over that the bloodstained survivors realised this immunity extended to those who had in some part been immersed in the werefire – Lathallan, who had put his hands in, and Sir Torold Tetbury who had also touched the flames. Evidently the unseelie warriors were held at bay by some quality these brave men had acquired.

In spite of this, Zauberin's coterie might have made a second onslaught, but Zwist and his comrades had shielded the survivors from their wrath. 'Most certainly the ill-wishers would have tried to slaughter us all,' said Sir Torold, 'except that others intervened. A number of our benefactors guided us swiftly out of the underworld to the spot where you met us. To them, we owe our lives. Who would have guessed that any of the horde still loitered in the mountains? Ah, but it is fortunate you came seeking us last night, Lady Asrăthiel. We must escort William to King's Winterbourne as soon as possible. Already the king has been apprised of what has happened, for we sent word by pigeon post.'

As they murmured together the prince stood quietly staring out at the passing scenery. He looked unscathed after his ordeal, but seemed almost radiant, and otherworldly. It was as if he had been made privy to the ineffable secrets of the universe; vast wisdom and tranquillity seemed to rest on his brow, and an aura of peace and virtue emanated therefrom.

'William is altered, now, as you see,' whispered Sir Torold. 'I do not know whether the change will wear off or not. He is like some hermit who has spent years pondering on transcendental matters and has finally reached an ecstatic point of essential understanding. It is curious, but his mere presence soothes our agitation.'

'Yes,' said Asrăthiel. 'He is not as he once was. Almost, he has become a stranger. What of Fionnbar Aonarán, who caused it all, and who was also seared in the Inglefire? I saw him but briefly before we rose in flight. He, too, appeared unharmed but changed in his manner.'

'He is as calm as a meditating priest, or an apothecary dazed by his own smoke-dreams.' After a pause Sir Torold added, 'May I tell you something that struck me as odd?'

'Say on.'

'Aonarán's only word, before he jumped into the Inglefire, was an exclamation of surprise and delight, as if he greeted someone and leapt forward to embrace them: '*A máthair*'.'

'*A máthair*,' Asrăthiel repeated abstractedly. 'It means 'Mother'.' Although she conversed, her thoughts were elsewhere.

'Alas that so many good men have died,' Sir Torold mused. 'Fates be thanked that William lives. He was barely rescued in time. No mortal being could have done such a deed. Only a powerful eldritch wight could possess sufficient mastery of time to pull him from the fire before he perished. One of the goblins saved him, did you know? It is a conundrum. Why should they aid us when they hate us so?'

'Why indeed?' the weathermage said sadly. 'The world is a seethe of mysteries.'

After delivering her three passengers to Wyverstone Castle and picking up three officers of the Household Guard, Asrăthiel flew back to collect her prentices from their plodding southward journey. She refused to take Aonarán in her aircraft, bidding the guards bring him back by road.

When her tasks were done, so distraught was she, so wounded

by the loss of Zaravaz, that instead of resuming her residency at The Laurels she returned to Avalloc in High Darioneth, retreating to her childhood home and the comfort of her family. Her world had changed; now she, too, was fundamentally altered. She revealed to no one the reason for her low spirits, for it was a secret that could not be shared. It was too much to hope that any human being might forgive her for falling for the ultimate foe. The burden of lonely grief, however, was too much to bear. She was inconsolable, sick throughout her spirit, and unable to bring herself to perform weathermastery any more. Since she would not wield the brí, she formally gave up her position as Weathermage to Narngalis and secluded herself at Rowan Green. Neither friends nor family could lift her from her despondency; she lost all interest in pleasurable pastimes.

On that final balloon journey from Sølvetårn, as Asrăthiel had pondered on her last moments with Zaravaz, she had come to understand that for her there could be no other. He meant more to her than she had believed. It was as if his spirit, and hers, had without her awareness melded to become one, and now were split asunder. Gone were her doubts about eldritch-human liaisons; the old tales told of many such, and besides, when faced with eternity, differences faded into insignificance. How could anyone bear to live forever, eschewing the most vital essence of one's inner being?

She could not marry William, who, in any case, was no longer the man she had known. The prince had been transformed, and now she felt distant from him. When he visited her at Rowan Green she guessed why he had made the journey and tactfully fore-stalled his offer of marriage, suggesting he should look elsewhere for a wife, because she could never bring him happiness.

'I am immortal,' she said compassionately, 'and you are not. There can be no hope for contentment between us. I shall never marry, but you have a different destiny, methinks. You shall find one who loves you as you deserve.'

The king's son received her advice with the unwavering equanimity he had possessed ever since the werefire had rinsed him. He gazed radiantly upon the weathermage, saying, 'You are wise, Asrăthiel. I perceive that you are right. I must let you go, though you will always hold a special place in my heart.'

'And you in mine.'

Their parting salutations had been chaste and respectful. He took the role of a fond and dependable friend to her, now, yet sometimes he seemed more like some celestial stranger.

Tenember passed, and a new year commenced.

The Winter of the year 3491 was long and severe. Asrăthiel spent most of her time sitting beside her sleeping mother. The briars entwining the glass cupola grew stark and leafless. Blackened by frost, they resembled twisted iron bars. All through that terrible season the damsel sat sad-eyed in the eyrie while storms raged outside the panes and rampaged across the storths. No carlin or apothecary could heal her. The aged scholar Adiuvo Constanto Clementer, who now dwelled at the House of Maelstronnar, gave kindly counsel to Avalloc's granddaughter; 'You mentioned that lately, under severe duress, you cried,' he said. 'There is a chance that weeping might relieve your suffering. Can you weep again?'

She tried, but could not.

'I have no more tears,' she said.

And as in fancy she fled northwards, across hill and vale, forest and lake to the icy towers of the Ramparts, she thought she heard the sound of small hoofs clattering over flagstones, and peered about in the hope of catching a glimpse of a small, goat-legged figure moving like a shadow against firelight - but it was only a pair of song-thrushes knocking snail shells against the roof.

'Crowthistle', she whispered, allowing herself to acknowledge, now, what she had previously attempted to deny; that Zaravaz had not befriended her, in the first place, solely in order to persuade her to free him from the spell. On the contrary – as an urisk he had shown himself unfriendly from the beginning, ill humoured and inclined to make a nuisance of himself - out of resentment for his plight, perhaps, or for want of any better divertissement. His pride forbade him from fawning on human beings in order to obtain their goodwill. Clearly he would rather have stayed forever cursed than stoop to such measures. No, he had not merely played on her feelings to suit his own ends. Any esteem the urisk had felt for her in those early days when they had fraternised with each other, any friendship he had shown her, had been sincere.

In the most unassailable depths of understanding, she had known it all along.

Similarly, when Zaravaz had cast her out of Sølvetårn so swiftly, she had never really wondered why it had seemed suddenly easy for him to give her up. He was aware of how grievously she pined for family and friends; furthermore she had claimed she loved William, and it was almost certain Zaravaz had seen her kiss the prince goodbye at the gates. Even in his wickedness the goblin king had forfeited his desires for her sake, and that was perhaps the most painful knowledge of all.

Since his immersion in the werefire William Wyverstone had developed a faculty that was quite astounding. Indeed, it was a power worthy of an eldritch wight or a powerful sorcerer or – some said – of a man who had directly received the blessing of Lord Ádh himself. The prince had become capable of healing a multitude of ills, merely by touching a patient; but even he could not succour Asrăthiel. The changes in his character proved permanent; he never reverted to his former self. He had been blasted by the torch of gramarye, and was no longer as he had been, tugged this way and that by the tides of human emotion, but continued always detached and serene, a calming influence on those who surrounded him.

As for Aonarán he never spoke another word; neither did he seek death as he once did, and many said his wits had been burned out entirely. His habit was to sit placidly beneath a plum tree in the courtyard of the Asylum for Lunatics, paying no heed to the antics of those who surrounded him.

A quarter of a year passed. The month of Mars eventuated, bringing the natal swellings of buds upon thorny stems.

At High Darioneth people celebrated the annual festival of Whuppity Stourie. The bells in the tower of Ellenhall, which had hung silent from Tenember to Feverier, recommenced their evening carillon at sunset on the first day of Spring. As the opening peals rang out, children from the plateau and from Rowan Green raced three times around the hall, in the direction of the sun. As they ran, they twirled paper balls on the ends of cords, with which they buffeted each other. After the chorus of the bells came to an end the Storm Lord cast handfuls of small coins upon the lawn. Giggling and shoving playfully, the children swarmed to gather them up. Following the upholding of these ancient traditions, there was music, and everyone feasted in the great hall, Long Gables.

Asrăthiel watched the activities without participating. Seated between Avalloc and Dristan she picked at her meal, listening half-heartedly to the general gossip. People were commenting disapprovingly on the host of women who still fancied themselves in love with the goblin king. There had sprung up a brisk trade in portraits of him, many of them executed by artists who had never set eyes on any of the Argenkindë. Somehow a rumour had arisen that the goblin king had become seelie, having been burned in the werefire, and this gave his devotees courage to sing his praises even louder, flagrantly embroidering on the little they knew of their favourite until they had devised a set of biographies, endlessly and rhapsodically debated. The weathermage could not help being fascinated with this talk, while deploring it at the same time. No one ever asked her about him any more, because she steadfastly refused to speak of her imprisonment.

Other dinner guests were discussing the recent courtship between Prince William and the daughter of Thomas, Lord Carisbrooke. It was a match that met with general approval.

'Lady Meliora is a delightful creature,' they said, 'as even-tempered as the Crown Prince. She would make an excellent queen, if chosen.'

'What a king and queen we shall have!' their companions cried, one adding, 'The dear prince cured my aunt's jaundice with one touch of his hand! People have been coming from all over, to try if he can help them and he never turns them away.'

'Yet he cannot restore everyone to soundness,' someone else interjected. 'He could not save my cousin.'

'Is it not intriguing,' one of the diners commented, 'how our Prince William's outlook has changed since his ordeal by fire. He seems quite beyond the mundane trials and woes of ordinary human beings. Nothing ruffles him. The courtiers say he is never irritable or angry, neither has he been seen to be woeful.'

'Nor ever moved to burst into a roar of thigh-slapping laughter, either,' the speaker's neighbour reminded the listeners.

Not to be diverted from his point the diner continued, 'So beatific is he that the superstitious folk of Slievmordhu have been conjecturing that he has been touched by the hand of Lord Ádh, and has been blessed or sanctified.'

'That makes two of them!' Albiona Maelstronnar rejoined.

'You cannot be referring to that queer fellow in the madhouse!'

'Nay, not at all. There is a rumour circulating amongst the peddlers that a most singular stranger has entered Narngalis and now walks – nay, runs southwards along the roads and lanes. He wears ordinary countryman's raiment, but his unexplained haste makes him an object of curiosity. More than that, he has a certain air that makes people suppose he too has been touched by the hands of the Fates.'

'What is unusual about him?'

'They say he appears serene, yet there is a vigorous excitement about him. He looks to be in his early thirties, yet somehow he is also much older. It is clear he is no eldritch wight, yet something about him hints of the supernatural. He has two aspects rolled into one.'

'Oh well, I don't call that odd. Half the folk in my husband's family are two-faced.'

Both women chuckled.

The matter piqued Asrăthiel's curiosity, but only for a short while. Soon she relapsed into her customary apathy.

Her listlessness was somewhat diluted by the prospect of her mother's birthday, on the eleventh of Mars.

To her grandfather she declared, 'I shall fly *Icemoon* down to the lowlands to gather the blossoms of early Spring. I intend to deck my mother's room with the golden-yellows of lesser celandine and forsythia, and wild daffodils, and fragrant gorse.'

'Do so with my benediction dear child,' said Avalloc. 'Anything that might make you smile brings warmth to my heart.'

On Jewel's birthday Asrăthiel – immune to the prickles of gorse - adorned the bedchamber with wildflowers, and combed her mother's hair across the pillow, while singing the songs of Spring. From time to time she glanced out of the briar-framed window panes. There was no way for her to know, but it was a morning strikingly similar to the first morning her mother had ever spent in Rowan Green. Across the garden she gazed, and through the foliage of a rowan tree, and past the parapet bordering the cliff edge. On one hand the fertile plateau of High Darioneth stretched away, shadows resting serenely across misty fields and orchards. On the other, steep slopes climbed into the sky, where clouds drifted around the peak of Wychwood Storth. The melodies of falling water and the twittering of blackbirds embellished the wind's low murmur.

That very afternoon a man in peasant garb arrived at High Darioneth. Alone, or seemingly alone, he entered through the East Gate, and ran, with a steady, enduring gait, all the way to Ellenhall. Quite a stir he caused, because he was the stranger whom rumour had described; the man of two aspects. Watchmen accompanied him, and although he would not tell them his name they did not hinder him, for there was something familiar in his voice, his bearing, his face…

By the time the newcomer reached the road leading up the cliff to Rowan Green a crowd had formed around him, chanting and singing. Children were skipping and shouting. They had recognised him, at last. Tall and lithe was he, with a dark brown beard, and hair that rained across his shoulders and down his back. His eyes were as green as leaves.

News of his approach travelled ahead of him. The bells of Ellen-hall began to chime in celebration. By the time the traveller arrived at the top of the road, Avalloc, Dristan and Asråthiel Maelstronnar were waiting. Their arms were extended wide, and the look of incredulous joy in their eyes was so moving that it was painful to behold. As the four, reunited, enfolded each other in a quadruple embrace, the old man wept.

Arran Maelstronnar had returned.

The newcomer was deeply affected by greeting his father, brother and daughter after the prolonged separation, and although he was clearly anxious to be reunited with Jewel he remained with them at the threshold of Rowan Green for a long while. The four were oblivious of the jostling throng that milled about them, remaining at a respectful distance but unable to keep their voices down.

'It is he!' the well-wishers jubilantly cried, 'Arran has returned from the ends of the world! The Storm Lord's son lives!' More people were running up the road on the heels of the first crowd, and many clustered around Albiona – who was laughing and crying at the same time – and pelting her with questions, as if she were already an authority on every detail of Arran's travels. Cavalon and Corisande, overwhelmed by the enormity of the event and the excitement of the onlookers, hung back with mouths agape.

For those at the centre of the maelstrom, time became mean-ingless. It might have flown, it might have stood still – they had no notion of it. The whole world might have suddenly become silent and blank for all they knew – the scope of their entire thought was filled with the presence of each other; they could not stop them-selves from simply gazing and smiling. Arran's relatives seemed unable to let go of him, as if he might vanish if they should lose their grasp, and he was in the same predicament. One minute Arran's fingers dug into Dristan's shoulder, next he grasped Aval-loc's hand with a grip of iron, but all the while he was enfolding Asråthiel beneath his arm as a pen folds her cygnet under her wing; holding her close against him, and she clinging to him as if she would never give him release; like a climbing rose clinging to the wall that supports it. Presently they found themselves murmuring questions and answers, but they hardly knew what they said or heard; nothing sank in, and it would all have to be repeated later. By degrees, Asrăthiel recovered her senses sufficiently to take a second look at her father. Of course, he had not aged much, if at all, but she fancied she could see subtle changes that perhaps no one else would.

By then Dristan's children were doing their best to squeeze themselves between their father and uncle, without success until at length Dristan noticed and drew aside to let them in. Looking up, Arran noticed Albiona amongst the onlookers, and beckoned her over. She fell upon his shoulders with a flurry of exclamations and he kissed her on both cheeks.

At last Arran said, gently disentangling himself from everyone's warm embraces, 'Is it still in the cupola, her sleeping place?' And like a jot it came home to Asrăthiel that her father would not have returned if he did not bear with him some hope for her mother's awakening.

'She is there,' Avalloc affirmed, whereupon Arran ran across the green and into the house ahead of them, heading straight upstairs to where Jewel lay asleep. Albiona hastened to position herself at the front dor, where she endeavoured to impose some sort of order on the steadily growing deluge of joyous friends and acquaintances, while the rest of the family followed in Arran's wake. When they had assembled around Jewel's couch, amongst the wildflowers, they watched him lean down and kiss his wife, then draw back.

Only then, as he gazed lovingly at her flawless face, Arran hesitated.

'Jewel,' he murmured, 'can I awaken you?'

'Is it possible?' exclaimed Asrăthiel. 'Father, have you found a cure?' It was too much to hope for, too much to comprehend. She felt excited, terrified and amazed. Suddenly light-headed, the damsel leaned on her uncle Dristan for support.

'I do not know for certain, my darling,' said Arran. 'If it is not a cure, then all my labours and travails these past years have been for naught.' He made to take something from a pocket in his tunic, but thought better of it. 'Now that the moment of proof is at hand I find I am reluctant to try my remedies, for they are the last hope. If they fail, all is lost forever.' Sweat beaded Arran's brow, and he was trembling.

'My dear boy, let us bring you refreshment,' said the Storm Lord.

'Gramercy but no, Father. I have vowed that once I entered this house I would neither eat nor drink until I had tried to waken Jewel.'

'Bide awhile and compose yourself,' the sage Clementer advised gently. 'Jewel has waited all these years. She will wait a few moments more.'

'You are right.' Arran sat down at his wife's bedside, never taking his eyes from her face, with his daughter sitting close beside him, holding his hand. Tiny hands parted the strands of Arran's hair that fell across his shoulders, and a pair of eyes the size of cucumber seeds peered out.

'Hello Fridayweed!' Asrăthiel said to the impet, who was sitting next to her father's ear. 'I am glad to see you.'

The little wight bowed politely. Avalloc rested his hand on his son's shoulder and, clasping Asrăthiel's hand more tightly in his, Arran began to speak.

'There is no single straightforward remedy for such a unique and complicated malaise, this endless sleep,' he said, 'caused as it is by poison and flawed sorcery. I searched long and hard to ensure I had explored every possible avenue. My path to the truth was beset by impasses and swindles, false leads and useless clues, but eventually I happened upon three – nay, four treatments that held promise; one for the flesh, one for the breath and one for the blood. One also for the spirit, and that is the simplest and most powerful of all. Together they may have efficacy.'

'They will work!' cried Asrăthiel. 'I know they will!' She directed an agonised glance at her grandfather. Avalloc attempted to smile reassuringly, but could not conceal his doubt.

A second time Arran made to remove something from his pocket and a second time he stopped short. 'Let me dwell in hope a short while longer,' he said. 'I will tell you the story of my wanderings, and at the end of it I will try the remedies. Ah, Jewel, can I waken you?'

Then he told his father and daughter a tale of a deserted coast where gulls swooped in changing skies, where serried lines of foaming waves rolled in to crash upon the rocks, spreading out to become white lace edgings that fizzed as they drew back into the ocean. Curly shells littered the beach, mingled with strands of brown bull-kelp, and tiny uncut gems, blue and green; jewels of the sea. Silvery leafed saltbush clung to crevices in the cliffs. It had taken a year to reach this shore.

In the morning, at low tide, Arran rose from his sleeping place in the dunes and picked his way amongst the rock formations along the low tide mark. He heard the sound of sobbing and, following it, entered an airy cave sea-scooped from a precipice. A mermaid lay there in a clear rock pool, her fish's tail of shining, overlapping discs coiling through gardens of sea anemones and chains of seagrass, her pearly skin gleaming, her yard-long green hair sliding like wet paint around her strange face. She cried and moaned, talking in an outlandish language, but it became obvious to Arran that the reason for her lamentation was that she had been stranded when the tide went out.

Sailors told grim yarns about these cold-blooded wights but, unafraid, Arran lifted her in his arms and carried her down to the water's edge. As soon as he touched her he discovered that he could understand her talk. When he laid her down gently in the foam she crowed with delight, saying, 'Now I can return to my water kingdom and, man, thou mayst come with me! Never fear, for thou wouldst not drown; in sooth, thou canst not die, methinks. Come and be a king under the sea! Rule over a fair realm of exotic delights, pampered by concubines who are immortal, like thee. Never know sorrow or loss!' But Arran would not accept the invitation, though she asked three times. 'Very well,' said the sea-girl, 'Instead I will give thee a gift in return for thy kind deed. What would'st thou like?'

He said, 'A cure. A cure for my wife, who sleeps in a coma.'

With a splash the mermaid darted away. Arran waited, but when she did not return he thought that was the last he had seen of her. Just as he was about to walk away she reappeared, gliding into shore on the next great comber, and tossed him a glass phial containing a green substance.

'This is *cneadhìoc*, wound-heal - a poultice made from a rare seaweed that doth grow on a single seashore,' she told him. 'It will not cure all things, but it will heal any wound and draw out any splinter. Once long ago,' she said, 'I gave another gift to a human being, and it was a shirt of fishes' mail.' Then, with a flick of her iridescent tail, the grateful mermaid was gone.

'What use is a drawer-out of splinters?' Fridayweed grumbled softly from beneath his ear. 'What profit is there in healing the wounds of one who cannot be wakened?'

Ignoring the wight, Arran spoke next of discovering a land of ice and snow so cold he named it 'Midwinter'. For years he had travelled along the coast to find this country, because he had over-heard a band of spriggans talking about certain ancient bubbles of air trapped in ice and guarded by frost elves. These airs, the spriggans said, being from a time when the world was new-birthed and pure, sometimes possessed phenomenal properties.

Warmly wrapped in rags that he had bartered from trows along the way, Arran eventually arrived at a region that jutted into polar seas; a peninsula whose hilly spine resembled, in his hungry opinion, a row of gigantic puddings dripping with white sauce and dusted with sugar. In these latitudes the wind was piercing; the cold penetrated to the deepest recess of mind and body. The wind, with its millions of little knives, scraped away the clouds. From clear skies, stars as brilliant as cut jewels shone down upon the land-scape, creating a shimmering twilight. Like glass rods breaking, the air cracked and snapped.

The weathermage had reached the summit of a ridge above the shore when he encountered the first snow troll he had ever seen in his life; a great, hairy fellow some seven or eight feet high, with skin

like brownstone, all gnarled and whorled with warts, an outland-
ishly long nose, jutting brows like snowy cliffs and sad eyes that
drooped down at the outer corners. He was clad in a robe of white
hides, dripping with icicles, and carried a knopped club. The most
astonishing thing about him was his headgear, for he wore a kind of
coronet that appeared to be made from shifting radiance of many
hues, in threads and banners, as if fashioned from the northern
lights. The wight challenged the weathermaster, accusing him of
trespass, but Arran protested that he was just a peaceful traveller
passing through.

'Toll you pay,' grunted the troll, eyeing the weathermage from
beneath beetling brows.

'What shall I pay you with?'

'Coin.'

'I have no money.'

'Food.'

'I have no provisions. I have nothing I can give you as toll price,
unless you'll accept a song.'

'Blood,' said the troll, and it rushed at Arran.

Arran carried no weapon save weathermastery and his own wits.
He fought the troll, there in the snow, and the wight was as strong
as an avalanche, but Arran was fast. Notwithstanding, the impetus
of an avalanche is formidable, and the weathermaster was making
heavy work of it when the impet Fridayweed popped out of Arran's
pocket and jumped across to his antagonist's shoulder. While the
slow-witted troll was twisting its knotty boulder of a head to see
what was shrieking in its ear, Arran seized the opportunity to trip
the creature up and push it off balance. Down the hill tumbled the
troll, gathering layers of fleecy mantle, becoming a massive snow-
ball. It rolled down to the foot of the slope and into the sea with a
tremendous splash.

'Oh well done, Fridayweed!' Avalloc said approvingly at this
point in the story, and Asrăthiel applauded.

Arran did not wait to see how the wight fared in the ocean with
the chunks of brash ice floating and clashing about its lugs, but

hastened on his way. Before he passed out of earshot he thought he heard a deep voice shout out, 'Stora Snötrollet you pass, but reck-you Ice Goblins!'

'Ice Goblins!' exclaimed Asrăthiel, squeezing her father's hand. 'I have heard some talk of them.' With a pang of desolate longing she pictured the Argenkindë riding across a wintry landscape to rendezvous with their long-lost kindred. 'But pray, go on,' she added quickly, banishing the vision.

That night the entire sky became congested with dark and heavy cloud. As Arran plodded through thick drifts he looked up and saw, atop a hummock and outlined against the lowering sky, a pinnacled, throne-like chair carved from a solid block of white ice. Snow had fallen on it, and clung in glistening masses here and there. Seated on this extraordinary piece of furniture was a slim youth clad in shimmering raiment and adorned with sharp diamonds. At his feet sat an arctic wolf and a snow goose. The weathermage guessed at once that this was one of the frost elves of whom the spriggans had spoken, for the youth wore a spiky coronet of icicles, and all his diamonds were, on closer inspection, ice crystals. He was like no other being Arran had ever beheld, with his angular cheekbones, sharply pointed nose, and thin, pale lips. His eyes were the same eerie shade of blue as the bergs the weathermaster had seen floating in polar seas; pieces shorn off the feet of mountain glaciers, once pressed beneath stupendous weight, from which all trapped air had been expelled, so that they took on the luminous blueness of tropical twilight. The elf's skin was like rime; white with a faint sheen. Clouds of miniature, eye-stabbing lights hovered around him like prisms of moonlight.

'You should know fear. Vy come-you here?' asked the wight, rising from his seat and stepping lightly towards the visitor as the bird and beast looked on. He left no footprints in the snow.

'For the air,' Arran answered. 'The ancient air from the morning of the world, trapped in ice.'

'Ne,' said the elf. 'Our statutes are precise; no man may haf our ice.'

With that he set upon Arran, wielding an ice dagger in each hand. The elf moved as swiftly as the man who, being unarmed, could only dodge and weave, and the weathermage was also hampered by the snow, into which he sank with every step. He was not, however, completely unprepared, for while he had been trudging along he had been putting forth his brí senses to gauge the state of the elements, and marshalling local patterns in such a way that he could call on them in time of need. And call he did. A sudden blizzard swirled around the duellists, so violent that the snowflakes bucketing from the skies were blown sideways.

The blizzard blew the frost elf sideways, too. He was bowled over, but immediately jumped to his feet. Arran, panting from the exertion, used the pause to catch his breath. He expected the wight to resume the onslaught, but the elf put away his daggers, saying, 'Valiant are you, and more dan man, too. Dat vill suffice; you may haf ice.' Without delay, lest the elf should change his mind, Arran struck out on his journey again, but the wight left him with a parting shot: 'You passed Stora Snötrollet, you passed Hrim's chair, but off da Ice Goblins, bevare!'

Asrăthiel who had shivered at every mention of Ice Goblins, interrupted her father's narrative with a question. 'How did you know the way to the place where this ancient ice exists?'

'I did not know at all!' he answered. 'The spriggans appeared to think it was in the far north, so I merely kept heading in that direction. At length I came to a bay shaped like a crescent moon, which was in fact the partly sunken caldera of a live volcano.'

There he had rested, looking out across the water to an island whose long row of snowy peaks seemed to be on fire, white clouds pouring up like smoke from the summits. At his back rose the sweep of the volcano, its slopes streaked with grey rocks, rust-red oxidised iron, alabaster snow and silver slicks of water. Steam was rising along the shore, where cold ocean currents touched the warm black gravel of the volcanic beach. 'This is not the place,' he had said to Fridayweed. 'There is no ancient ice here.'

So on he went, deep into the snowy wastes, and one night, seated beside a little ball of fire he had summoned to keep himself warm, he watched the sun go down. Sunset streaked the snow with subtle colours of pale peach and mauve, and fleecy bars of cloud were cutting off the tops of the mountains. As evening drew in the clouds sank lower, pouring down the slopes until they obscured the feet of the ranges instead of their heads, and the mountains hovered on a raft of mist. He was musing on the notion that mist and cloud seem to come from some unknown world and to dissolve the barriers between this world and the other, when the ground spoke to him.

'Haf you seen,' growled a voice so deep it was like soft thunder, 'a vun-eyed greybeard carrying a shtaff, vis a raven on each shoulder und two volfes at his heels following? Vears-he a broad brimmed hat und a blue traffelling coat.'

The hairs rose on the back of Arran's neck. 'No,' he said, for want of a better response. Looking carefully at his surroundings he spied an outsized, ugly face immersed in a long white beard that dripped with icicles. A giant was looking at him from out of the hillside, as if embedded therein. Some fifteen feet in height, this creature made the snow troll look small by comparison. He could only be one of the *hrimsthursar*, a frost giant, of which the lore books at High Darioneth recorded very little. The giant appeared to be ruminating on Arran's rejoinder, which led the weathermage to wonder whether he had just imparted good or bad news. He knew that frost giants could be benign or malign; also that they might be ignorant or wise, and he grew wary. First and foremost, he must show no sign of fear.

'Man,' said the frost giant, 'vat know-you off ice?'

'I know,' Arran said courageously, 'the ten names of ice bergs, the eighteen names of sea ice, the twenty names of coastal ices, the sixteen mountain ices and the three ices of the ground. I know all the ices of the polar plateaux and all six of the atmospheric ices. I know the shapes and colours of ice, and how they were formed, and how they will dissolve; blue ice, black ice, white ice and jade-green ice from glacial shear zones; frazil ice, pancake ice and the intricate ice flowers of the polar seas, brash, firn, rime; ice pipes, ice falls and ice lenses.'

By good fortune the giant had questioned Arran about a subject he had studied in depth. Few weathermasters had ever frozen an entire lake; Arran was one of those few.

Between snow-shine and star-twinkle the giant rumbled, 'I hight Bergelmir, son off Thrudgelmir, son off Thrym. It is vell, man, dat you know some-ting of ice. Yet dere is much you know not.'

Bergelmir proceeded to tell Arran other names, and secrets of ice previously unknown even to weathermasters. He shared the *hrimsthursars'* knowledge of water and air and fire. By all this Arran knew the giant to be wise and benign, so he revealed his own name. All through the night they conversed, and as day dawned Arran asked the wight what he knew about precious bubbles from a bygone era, trapped in ancient crystals.

The frost giant told him that the air ensnared into that special matrix was scorched by the passage of stars that fell from the sky and created the wells of immortality, thousands of years ago. Winds drew that star-burned air over the frozen plains, and snow fell, which turned to ice and remained thus in the eternal cold. Those antique gases, called *skjultånd* - hidden-breath - had special properties, but their exact science was unclear.

'Prithee Bergelmir, son of Thrudgelmir,' said Arran, 'tell me how to find this *skjultånd*, so that I may take some home to my wife.'

'Shtay here, Arran son off Avalloc,' boomed the frost giant. 'Shtay here und learn da secrets off da universe from da *hrims-thursar*. Become-you da king off scholars.'

Arran said, 'No, I must go on.'

'Then I vill tell you how to find vat you seek,' said Bergelmir, 'but it may not a cure be.' And the giant told Arran how to make his way to a certain nearby shore, where lay an enchanted vessel in which he must voyage if he meant to achieve his goal.

Just before they parted, Bergelmir said, 'Und ven you return to your home in da south you vill pass srough lands dat vunce vere varmer. In dose days dere vere human farmshteads, und at dose shteadings da tömte used to dvell. Da human beings haf gone, since da cold south-crept, but some off da tömte remain. If find-you any, tell dem you vere sent by Bergelmir und dey might you-help. If you spy a vun-eyed gammel greybeard along your vay, 'tvould be best to shtay clear off him. One final vord of varning, Arran son off Avalloc; bevare-you off da Ice Goblins.'

After expressing his gratitude without directly thanking the giant – for he was well aware of eldritch protocol – Arran went to the designated shore. There he found an elegant shell-like boat, just as Bergelmir had said he would. The boat sailed by itself, carrying Arran out onto the sea, where lumps of clear ice floated amidst the brash. Leaning over the side the weathermage scooped up a lump of this clear ice, noting with delight the masses of tiny bubbles crammed therein, like a paralysed fizz of sparkling wine. He chipped off a small piece as the boat took him back to land, stowed it in one of the phials he carried and kept it frozen by means of weathermastery.

That night, with Fridayweed snuggled into his hair, Arran lay down to sleep in the snow, as usual murmuring a heat-summoning to keep them both warm, though he had no victuals to nourish him. But he was excited about finding the *skjultånd* and slept fitfully, half waking from time to time. Once, when he raised his head, he fancied he saw a cavalcade of extraordinary knights and ladies riding by in the distance, lit by moonlight and snowlight or perhaps by a brilliance of their own. He thought he heard them speaking; he could not understand their language but he received the strong impression that they were recalling persons they once had known, persons they yearned to see again. A sprinkling of glitter rained from their hands and garments as they rode by, and lay upon the snow. It might have been a dream, for he felt afraid without knowing why.

The weathermaster woke in the morning to see the colours of sunrise tinting the drifts, and presently he came across a scatter of crystals as pure and bright as diamonds. When the sun's first rays struck these prisms they reflected a series of images. He gazed at them in wonderment; the faces of a crowd of strangers, all comely beyond compare, yet with a cruel look; and one, a masculine countenance, whose beauty outshone the others as a comet to fire-flies. In the sunlight the visions melted away, and with the two outlandish remedies in his possession Arran turned at last for home.

For months he tramped, but he never forgot the frost giant's advice. As soon as he saw the misty peaks of the Northern Ramparts on the horizon, which indicated that he had re-entered the lands that had once been home to human farmers, Arran began to look for a tömte. Tömtes were, he knew from his studies, farmyard helpers; a kind of northern version of brownies. He had spied no such wights on his outbound journey through this windswept country, where clumps of wiry grasses and thistles clung to iron-hard ground between patches of snow; and he saw none on his return. Still hoping, he took to boldly calling out, 'Tömte! Tömte! Come to me!' though the only things that came to him were the croakings of crows, windborne motes, cold breezes and grit that lodged in his worn out boots to make him even more footsore.

He was passing amongst the first foothills of the Ramparts when a white hare started up from the grasses and loped away. It stopped and turned to look at him, and he could have sworn that it was inviting him to follow, so he took off after it. The hare led him a merry chase through the sedges, while in his pocket Fridayweed wailed in protest against the jolting. Before Arran knew what was happening he had tripped and fallen flat on his belly, and a rope net was pinning him down. Bruised and aching he looked up and saw someone observing him with a wry air.

'Why have you done this to me?' the weathermage demanded indignantly. 'Let me up!'

'Ouch,' Fridayweed said in muffled tones, squeezed somewhere in Arran's ragged clothing.

'Man, man, catch me if you can, why call-you the tömte tiptoe tasty treat?' the someone said in a high-pitched voice.

Arran rolled his eyes and sighed. He felt glad that the tömte was fluent in the common tongue, but evidently it had its own whimsical way of expressing itself, like many eldritch wights. He hoped the fellow would keep rhetorical questions to a minimum and be sparing with phrases such as 'If you asked me on a Moon's Day I'd say 'yes' but if you asked me on a War's Day my answer would be 'no'.'

'Bergelmir sent me,' he said.

Up went the net of rope, and Arran was free. Fridayweed poked out his head, glanced about, grimaced and withdrew.

'What said the jotun, slow one ice-pale as a whale, that Bergelmir yesteryear?'

'He said you might help me. My name is Arran, son of Avalloc.' Sitting up, the weathermaster came face to face with a wiry little chap who had a weatherbeaten face, a pale, bushy beard and twinkling eyes. He was wearing a conical red hat that drooped down one side of his head, a long coat of polar bear fur with a high collar, mittens, green trousers, and reindeer-hide shoes with turned-up toes. The tömte was stowing the entire net - obviously a magickal one - in his sleeve. White tufts of pointed ears, like a hare's, jutted from beneath the furry brim of his cap.

'I am seeking a remedy to bring my wife out of her long sleep,' Arran said. 'I have found *cneadhìoc* and *skjultånd*, but there is no knowing if they will be of any use. Her sleep is deep, only one step from death, and if there is anything more that might help her, pray tell me. The weathermaster gingerly rubbed his chin where a leaf of crowthistle had prickled it when he lay on the ground. After a while he said, 'Good tömte, did you hear me?'

'Rognvald is thinking, blinking,' the wight said sharply, opening and shutting his lids. 'Blink-king of spades to dig for answers! Did a lot of drinking when farms thrived, bees hived, honey for the mead, there is a weed.'

'A weed?'

'Beneath the snows something grows. Snow melts in Summer daisy dozy lazy days, and three leaves.'

'What is there, when the snow melts?'

'Little lobes of lichen like lace lick the lovely face of rocks. Misty, moisty moss, fairy floss, green as emeralds for the queen, have you seen? And the prickly one, the stickly one thickly grows purple-petalled in Summer sun of Avalloc. Pricked your chin! Needles in!'

'Lichen, moss, and crowthistle,' Arran translated. 'What of those three herbs, friend Rognvald?'

At the mention of crowthistle, Asráthiel drew breath sharply. The term triggered agonising memories. Her gasp passed unnoticed, for all attention was focussed on her father. The barely intelligible wight had told him about some rare varieties of those plants, which grew nearby. Taking these ingredients in specific proportions and treating them in certain ways, a health-giving remedy, *trebladen* could be made, to be taken by mouth. 'They may not cure, to be sure, the leaves of herbs upon the moor,' said the tömte, 'but they oust bloodsuckers, feather-pluckers, liver flukes and leeches, creechers what bites, toads and nematodes, spongers and scroungers, lollers, lawyers and other parasites.'

'Mistletoe is a parasite. Prithee give me some of this remedy.'

'Cannot give it, haven't any; not a penny. If you would take it you must make it; pick and grind and boil and bake it, pat-a-cake it.' The wight flicked its tufted ears and made to skip away, but Arran jumped up saying, 'Wait! Prithee help me with this task!'

'Why should I? Good bye apple pie, apple of your father's eye'll be going now.'

'I will pay you. No coin or food have I, but I can move the winds. I can call or banish snow.' In his desperation Arran was again ignoring his kindred's prohibitions on meddling at whim with the weather. 'Do you dislike snow, Rognvald, since the cold drove your farming families away? I can make the snow melt, for a while, here where you dwell, so that the earliest flowers of Spring will blossom for you.'

'What care I for snow to flow away, blow away with the fairies at the bottom of the garden?' The tömte skipped a little further off.

'I can entertain you,' Arran said wildly, uttering the first words that came into his head. 'I can tell stories. I can sing and dance.'

'Sing?' said the tömte, pricking up his ears. 'That's a pretty thing.'

So it happened that Arran Maelstronnar sang for the tömte of the foothills, while the enraptured wight sat at his feet, hands clasped around his stringy knees. The weathermage sang a ballad of love; of parting and longing, which he himself had composed during the years of his travels. The theme appeared to suit the tömte, for after Arran sang the final verse he brooded in silence for a few moments, then leaped energetically to his feet saying, 'Come with me to wild-weeds three. *Trebladen* we shall blend, before day's end of the world as we know it.'

Away they went together, the man and the wight. Rognvald showed him where to pick the ingredients - including some early buds of a stunted variety of crowthistle - how to measure them precisely, pound them to pulp in the mortar of a hollowed-out stone with a pestle of granite, and boil them in a little distilling apparatus the tömte retrieved from a hole in the ground, which he usually employed to make a kind of *akvavit* from wild roots and tubers. The purple juices of the crowthistle petals coloured the entire mixture. Arran wondered if *trebladen* might be poisonous, so he placed a drop on his tongue. It tasted bitter, but there were no ill effects; indeed, he felt invigorated. 'No toxins taint *trebladen*,' the tömte assured him, 'but bitter bites the purple petal; feral flower has fierce flavour of the month.'

When all was finished Arran filled one of his phials with the mixture, expressed his gratitude to the wight without thanking him, and took his leave. Just as he was setting off, the tömte said, 'Did you see them? Flee them? Disagree with them, so nice, the lovely lordly lethal goblins in the Land of Ice?'

'No,' said Arran, 'I did not see the Ice Goblins.' But later, when he thought about it, he said to himself, 'Perchance I did.' And he was glad he had not met with them, for there could be no doubt they were dangerous; but he wondered, again, about the beautiful, cruel faces mirrored so briefly in crystal, and it came to him that they might have been the imprints of memories.

Late one evening he was climbing the rising ground beneath a stormy sky. Dark clouds swirled overhead and the wind blew in sharp gusts, tossing the thistle-strewn sedges and stunted heath. As he trudged he was suddenly gripped by fright, and became aware with shock that a tall, humanlike figure was walking alongside him. It looked to be an old man in blue robes, using a wooden stave as a walking stick. His long beard and ragged hair, the colour of sleet, were blowing in the wind, and his garments flapped like wings. Beneath his broad-brimmed hat he wore a patch across one eye, and strangest of all, a great black bird was clinging with hooked claws to his left shoulder.

Show no fear, Arran said to himself, but he could not prevent a swift, involuntarily glance behind him. Dimly outlined against the scrub, two spare, svelte creatures were slinking; wolves. So, this was the patriarch of whom the frost giant had spoken. Arran sensed great power in this personage and remained silent, subdued by awe and dread.

Presently, in a deep, resonant voice, the stranger asked what he carried, and Arran answered truthfully, for he was reluctant to lie to this formidable manifestation, even though he was half fearful that the old man might seize the medicines and take them for himself.

'Show me these remedies,' said the greybeard, and Arran did him this service, upon which the stranger threw back his head and laughed, but without mirth. He uttered no further word but shook his grizzled head, as if to indicate, There is a new fool born every minute. Still chuckling he strode away, his two lean wolves trotting in his wake, leaving Arran angry and baffled and on the point of following him and asking what he meant by it: but Fridayweed squeaked, 'Let us go! Quickly! Let us get out of here while our luck holds, before he turns back. If he sees us here still, I trow there will be no small disturbance and gnashing of teeth!'

Discomfited by the note of urgency in the little wight's tone, Arran heeded his advice and hastened away, but his heart curled up in his chest, as heavy as an embedded fossil.

The weathermaster had put a good distance between himself

and the stranger. Now that the danger was past and he was close to home, with three plausible remedies in his possession, his excitement began to rise. He could hardly wait to see his family again, and to try out the treatments he had gathered. So pressing was his need that as he crossed the Northern Ramparts he broke into a run, and had been running ever since, barely stopping to rest or take refreshment, neglecting niceties such as shaving off his sprouting beard. He sprinted through Narngalis; across the Silverton region and the Harrowgate Fells, past Paper Mill and the Wuthering Moors, through King's Winterbourne and down the Mountain Road to the East Gate of the Mountain Ring.

'And here I am,' said Arran in conclusion to his tale.

'You mentioned there was a fourth remedy, dear boy,' Avalloc reminded him.

'Ah yes. As I returned through my homeland, everywhere I looked I beheld the aftermath of war. I heard about Uabhar and his schemes, the slaughter of my kindred, the invasion of Narngalis, the coming of the goblins, the rise of the kobold watch and all the tragic events that have taken place during my absence. Folk were picking up the broken threads of their lives, and piecing them together, and I was astounded at their resilience. No matter how much they had suffered, no matter how much was lost to them, they persevered. They loved life, and laughter, and each other, too dearly to give in. Thus, without the help of any eldritch wight, I came to the conclusion that love and laughter in themselves can help to heal the spirit. That is the fourth remedy.' Leaning over his wife he murmured again, 'Jewel, can I awaken you?'

And Asrăthiel cried desperately, 'Of course she will waken!' but she perceived the uncertainty in the faces of those who surrounded her, and pictured the old one-eyed wight with the staff throwing back his head and laughing, and she came close to despair.

From a pocket in his tunic her father took a wide-necked glass phial containing a green paste. He placed the container on a small side table, then with utmost tenderness unfastened the lacings of Jewel's bodice and laid aside the fabric, exposing the wound made by Fionnuala Aonarán's mistletoe quarrel, just below her breastbone. The injury had never quite healed. Picking up and unstoppering the phial, Arran said 'Here is *cneadhìoc*, a poultice to draw out any lingering splinters of mistletoe.' Gently he dabbed green ointment on the lesion, while the crowd – now augmented by the entire household - looked on in silence.

'Awaken,' said Arran. 'Jewel, awaken, love, laugh, live.'

Jewel's lids fluttered like the two wings of the Blue Lycaenidae Butterfly. That was all. There was no more; yet it was a sign where no sign had existed before.

The watchers gasped, but before anyone could make a comment Arran bade them hush. He said in a commanding, nervous tone, 'Fridayweed, give me the phial of ice,' and an impish face peered from another pocket of his tunic. A small, wizened paw handed Arran a second flask. This one was filled with a colourless substance, veined with whiteness.

'Here is the ancient ice, *skjultånd*,' said Arran, 'from the heart of the Land of Midwinter, filled with trapped bubbles of air that was burned by falling stars, kept frozen by the use of the brí. Never have I been so glad of my weathermaster's powers.' As he was speaking he allowed the ice to melt in the phial, warmed by his hand. Removing the stopper he placed the container beneath the nostrils of Jewel. 'Inhale the world's first breaths,' he whispered. 'Jewel, awaken! Love, laugh, live!' and he held the phial in place until even the water had evaporated.

The rate of Jewel's breathing increased, and the colour of dawn flushed her cheeks, but she did not wake up.

Nobody stirred.

What could it mean? Was she really coming back to life or had the queer galenicals tipped the balance the other way, from sleeping to death, and the onlookers were witnessing Jewel's final gasps?

Said Arran to the onlookers, his voice unsteady, 'Do not rejoice. I warn you, she is not safe yet. She is not back with us, though the wheels of that machinery seem to be in motion. This is the most dangerous time. I beg you, do not distract me. The power of her forefather's benediction was as strong as his curse. Jaravhor of Strang never properly completed the enchantment of invulnerability that he laid upon his descendants. Through laziness, or incompetence, or carelessness, or arrogance, he omitted the spell that protected them against mistletoe. I have here something to complete that spell. If this does not bring her back, then I have failed.'

Between his fingers he held a purple phial.

'What could protect against mistletoe?' he continued. 'It turns out to be something inconsequential, something common. Trebladen is the essence of flowers of crowthistle, mixed with other things and distilled in the same manner as attar of roses.'

Arran unsealed the purple flask, parted Jewel's lips with one finger, and allowed a few drops of a purple liquid to fall on her tongue.

'It tastes bitter, I know,' he murmured, 'I am sorry. Awaken, dear love. Love, laugh, live!'

Jewel opened her butterfly lids.

The blueness of her eyes was moonlight shining through sapphire. Gazing up at her husband, she smiled faintly. She had woken.

Overcome by emotion Arran lifted his wife into his embrace, buried his face in her luxuriant mane, and rocked her back and forth as if she were a child. Asrǎthiel's were the only dry eyes in that house.

'Let the bells ring out!' cried Avalloc Maelstronnar. 'Spread the news! Let there be holiday and dancing in the streets!'

The household's outpouring of joy was like an explosion. Albiona, the children and all the servants ran outside, proclaiming the tidings to all and sundry. Word travelled swiftly around Rowan Green and down to the plateau below, then flooded across the kingdom by means of semaphore.

In the House of Maelstronnar the carlin Lidoine swooped upon Jewel, who vainly protested that she was in perfect health and needed no physicianly assistance. Multitudes converged on the house, bringing bunches of flowers and foliage. Albiona shooed away the well-wishers with the words, 'You are too kind, but Jewel is not yet fully hale, and we must give Arran time to rest. You may not visit them yet.'

This did nothing to dampen the celebrations. The royal family sent their respects and gifts, and the Maelstronnar miracle was the talk of every town and village in Narngalis.

After so many long years the mother of Asrăthiel had been roused from her suspended animation. It would take some time before she regained her customary wellbeing, but they had time aplenty, now, the Maelstronnar family; time to enjoy their long-desired reunion, time for such rejoicing as had never been known in High Darioneth.

13

REPRISE

How many bitter hours have passed since my last sight
Of thy belovèd face, more beautiful than night?
No balm to soothe the pain, no hope of remedy
To ease my tortured mind. Obsessed am I with thee.
Methinks I hear a sigh resound from days of yore,
Up in the lofty void where these dark arches soar;
The voices of the past lament for what was lost;
Thine unforgiving heart, redeemed at such a cost.

Here I linger alone in this dim forsaken place
I am cursed by my longing to look upon thy face.
I have been thy downfall, thou art bound for some dark shore,
With thee goes my heart's passion and all that came before.

A SONG OF THE FORSAKEN

So it happened that as the returning sun warmed the Four Kingdoms of Tir and Spring embellished the countryside with a froth of gleaming blossom, there began a season of unparalleled joy at the House of Stormbringer.

Avalloc was ecstatic, now that his heir had returned and his daughter-in-law had been restored. He called for the election of a new Storm Lord, and began preparing to resign from his office. 'I have captained the Council of Ellenhall for long enough,' he said. 'Since the betrayal and slaughter of my dear kindred, my heart is no longer in the task. It is time for a new leader to take over.'

Albiona and Dristan could not be more delighted at Arran's homecoming and Jewel's recovery. Their children Cavalon and Corisande were likewise elated, and even the household brownie seemed more cheerful on the rare occasions it was glimpsed. Possibly it enjoyed the congenial and unthreatening company of Fridayweed, Arran's impet.

As for Asrăthiel, she was wildly happy, yet her heart was heavily burdened. Somehow, between two opposite poles of emotion, she existed. Back in the loving arms of her family she dwelled almost in a state of satisfaction, but when the north wind blew she became restless and discontented, as of old. Hardest of all to bear were the haunting memories. Her heart ached for her eldritch lover. Daily life insulated her from the shock and pain of losing him as wrappings of silk stuff and thistledown might muffle a stone. The anguish could be temporarily ignored, but it was always present, cold and hard and remorseless, at the centre of all. And she knew that eventually, when Averil's first moon rose, if there came no sign, no message from Zwist, then Zaravaz would have succumbed to the burning. She would never see him again.

Jewel's health was delicate after her long sleep. She was weak and easily exhausted, lacking appetite and vigour. At length, when she had recovered – much quicker than the carlin had expected – the reunited family assembled in the dining hall one evening, for a celebratory meal.

Tall vases stood about the room against the walnut panelled walls, overflowing with the sumptuous blooms of late spring. A clear, bright blaze danced on the hearth, its flames like a flurry of spun-sugar Autumn leaves. Firelight glinted off diamond window-panes, brass candlesticks and silver tableware, polished oaken settles. Over the mantelpiece Fallowblade rested in its decorative scabbard like any ordinary sword, giving no hint of its strange history, its marvellous qualities. Avalloc sat at the head of the table surveying, with great satisfaction, the shining faces around him; his sons with their wives, his three grandchildren, and his two venerable house guests Clementer and Agnellus. The diners laughed and conversed, exclaiming over each new dish as it was brought to the table, drinking deeply of the cellar's best wines and generally making the rafters ring with the sound of their happiness – except, perhaps, for Asrăthiel, who – the Storm Lord had noted – still seemed more subdued than of yore, as if she were haunted by some sort of indefinable shadow ever since her imprisonment under Silver Mountain.

During Jewel's convalescence the family had taken care not to pester her with questions, plying her instead with delicacies to temp her and joining her for measured strolls in the garden, all the while making light-hearted small-talk and attempting to shield her from the worst impact of the events that had transpired while she slumbered. Patients who were burdened with oppressive sorrow took longer to recover, it was common knowledge. Though the family could not – would not – conceal the massacre of the weathermasters, or the war that had ravaged the four kingdoms, they had painted as palatable a picture as possible. Their efforts had been fruitful. Jewel had grown to become the very picture of robustness. No one had any more qualms about quizzing her as to what – if anything – she recalled about the period when she slept. She remembered, nonetheless, very little – no more than some vague though not unpleasant dreams.

Now it was Jewel's turn to probe for answers. Late that night after the banquet was over and the sounds of rattling crockery issued from the scullery, indicating that the zealous brownie was already at work, the human members of the household were preparing for sleep. Jewel entered Asrăthiel's bedchamber carrying a lighted lamp, which she placed on the dressing table. Asrăthiel was seated in front of the looking-glass, gazing at her image in the mirror, lost in thought. She had been removing the jewelled pins from her hair but had lapsed into this reverie, her coiffure still half completed. Jewel commenced to untangle the last strands and pluck the remaining fastenings from the storm cloud of tresses showering down her daughter's back. Asrăthiel smiled at her mother's reflection in the mirror, recalling the numerous times Jewel had performed this loving service for her throughout her childhood.

'What is ailing you, *a mhuirnín?*' Jewel murmured presently, as her fingers combed searchingly through the soft skeins of hair. 'You seem lost in daydreams these days. Has the North Wind, your new namesake, stolen your peace of mind?' This was closer to the truth than Asrăthiel dared to admit. Your father and I are worried,' Jewel went on, 'because you are not as happy as you used to be. There seems to be a deep melancholy behind your content-ment which, I deem, you have been at pains to mask. Perhaps you are deeply troubled by the suffering you witnessed during the wars. Or are you unable to shake off the memories of your ordeal under the mountain? Or both?'

Asrăthiel did not try to dissemble. Jewel knew her as only a parent could. 'You are right,' the damsel said with reluctance, 'I am assailed by some shadow – sorrow, longing, regret, call it what you will. I do not even have a name for it. But Mother, I beg you and Father to refrain from pressing me for the cause, as I feel that to reveal it would be inappropriate, and besides, I'll warrant that the passage of time will eventually heal the wound and I will be merry again soon enough.'

With tactful understanding Jewel respected her daughter's wishes and did not pursue her inquiries, but Asrăthiel could tell that her mother suspected she was suffering from a broken heart as a consequence of a tragic love affair. Perhaps her parents conjec-tured that she had fallen for some lord in King's Winterbourne or some captain of the Grïmnørsland army, and that a quarrel had severed the union.

Had they learned who was the real focus of her heartbreak, they would, Asrăthiel thought, have been shocked, disbelieving and outraged. She had renamed herself 'North Wind' in memory of a lost loved one. Her parents could not know that now she wore the appellation for the sake of another.

She could not stop thinking about Zaravaz, and whenever she found herself alone she dwelt on him exclusively. Would he live or fade? If he faded, could she bear it? If he lived, could she bear it? Would the highs and lows of passion be scorched from him, as had happened to William? Would he be transformed into a silent dreamer like Aonarán? Or would he be no more than an empty, mindless shell – walking and breathing, but with all character burned out of him?

Unanswerable questions were driving her to distraction. Had the Argenkindë already departed from Sølvetårn, bearing their king with them, or did they tarry still, awaiting the outcome of his silent battle with eternity?

The first moon of Averil came and went, but no sign attended it.

Asrăthiel wanted to be certain there was no misunderstanding, as had occurred last time the goblins had linked their plans with the moon's fickle drift through the heavens; therefore at nights she waited in the kitchen for the household brownie, and when the furtive creature appeared she calmly greeted him, asking him if there was any news from any other eldritch wights concerning the Silver Goblins. The brownie had heard nothing. Every night for weeks, the damsel waited in the dark, and put her enquiry. At last, one night, the brownie told her that he had spoken with some passing trows. The wights stated unequivocally that the Argenkindë had abandoned their fastness and gone forth into the northern wastes. The goblins had gone. There was no mistake.

It was all over.

That night the damsel could not sleep. At dawn some strange birds down on the plateau uttered calls like cries of terrible despair as if bewailing the horrors inflicted by man upon all other living creatures, heart-rending cries of anguish and despair and piercing sorrow.

Now that all hope was gone it seemed to Asrăthiel that the very light of the sun had paled from yellow-gold to dishwater, and the songs of birds were but a faint and scratchy echo of their old melodies. Days seemed long and dreary; so dreary that it seemed difficult to rise from bed in the mornings. Even the colours of the world had faded; the vibrant greens of Summer foliage had greyed to celadon, the intense white of snow on the highest summits dimmed and lost their lustre; the blue periwinkles in rocky crevices beside the streams were nothing but blotches of corroded ink. It was as if a kind of dirty miasma veiled everything. She told herself, desperately, I must not succumb to this mad misery! I have everything I have ever longed for, now that my parents are both at my side. If I succumb to this despondency I will be failing my family!

The damsel tried to find peace in the beauty of her mountain home, and in the pleasant childhood memories triggered by every tree and pool, every house and face. Sometimes, at the end of a joyful day spent in the company of her family, she would make her way to some high place, where she could watch the sun go down over the western ranges, casting its peach-coloured luminescence across orchards and fields. Far below her feet, the immense wooded plateau stretched for miles, encircled by saw-toothed mountain peaks. The fading light would catch the glimmer of a lake, or a shred of smoke rising from the chimney of a distant cottage.

Other times she might descend the steep cliff path from Rowan Green and walk along the cart tracks of the plateau, through groves of budding walnut and chestnut trees, along leafy lanes and byways that crossed brawling streams.

Her mountain home was beautiful, there was no doubting it, but for all its beauty it could not content her any longer. Her spirit soared beyond the storths, beyond the snowy roofs of Sølvetårn's silver halls, into infinity, especially when the north wind came wailing its song of ice.

The amazing news of Jewel's reawakening spread throughout the four kingdoms. It reached the ears of certain men in the employ of the Duke of Bucks Horn Oak; Tsafrir, Yaadosh, Michaiah, and Nasim, now more than sixty winters old. Under the command of their lord they had been helping in the fight to defend Narngalis. Now, with his blessing, they travelled to High Darioneth to pay their respects to the Storm Lord's daughter-in-law, the child of their old friend Jarred. The household of Maelstronnar made these grizzled, honest men most welcome. Mingling with them and listening to their stories of her father set Jewel to pondering about her old home in the Great Marsh of Slievmordhu. She and Arran decided to revisit places in Tir they had known; to reacquaint themselves with people they had loved long ago.

A message arrived from Kings Winterbourne, inviting the weathermasters to a three-day celebration honouring a momentous royal event; Prince William's betrothal to Lady Meliora Morley, eldest daughter of Lord Carisbrooke. Jewel and Arran arranged to visit the Marsh before proceeding to the royal city.

As soon as the merry men of Bucks Horn Oak had departed from Rowan Green, Asrăthiel and her parents set off in a sky balloon, following the Mountain Road, across the Canterbury Water and the Border Hills, passing far to the west of Cathair Rua, until they arrived at Jewel's birthplace. As they travelled Jewel enthusiastically entertained her husband and daughter with tales of the Marsh they had heard before, but of which they never tired. Particularly, they were fascinated by stories about the secretive eldritch inhabitants of the Marsh; dangerous waterhorses that dwelled in the depths, the miniature damsels called the asrai, clad only in their flowing green hair, the gruagachs of the islets, the will o' the wisps that floated upon the Marsh at night.

The Great Marsh of Slievmordhu had altered little since Jewel's childhood days. Its rich and widespread complexity of marshes, streams, ravelled woods and reed-edged lagoons lay peacefully in that low-lying, lush region, fed by pure rivulets from the surrounding mountains. The Marsh's waters were as sweet as ever, being constantly refreshed by gentle currents that barely disturbed the surfaces of the mirrored meres, the black tarns, the secret, overhung channels, and the tranquil shores of more than three thousand islets.

Marsh Town too looked much the same, its reed-thatched houses perched on stilts driven deep beneath the mud, some built on the tiny eyots, others suspended above their own glimmering reflections in the water or floating on rafts. The wooden bridges, boardwalks and network of hidden causeways that connected all buildings were kept in excellent repair, as were the footpaths, duckboard trails, stepping stones and catwalks webbing the entire Marsh system. In open astonishment the Marsh dwellers stared at the newcomers dressed in their flowing raiment of blue-grey linen, until some folk recognised Jewel, whereupon they waved and shouted greetings across the water.

As the visitors voyaged in the boats of the Marsh watchmen, Jewel caught sight of three small children walking across a pond on the buoyant discs of giant lily pads. 'Just as I used to do!' she exclaimed. The boat glided beneath overhanging alders and willows, sunlight glimmering through their foliage. Delightedly the Marsh daughter gazed at the familiar proliferation of bulrushes and reeds spearing up from banks of sphagnum moss and sedge. Sticklebacks glided amongst the waterweeds, frogs uttered notes like bells and drums, and dragonflies twinkled as if they were iridescent lights. Birds darted and splashed everywhere; bright kingfishers, grey herons stalking on their long stilts of legs, ducks paddling and diving in the reed beds.

Regaled with stories and entranced by the water world, the travellers reached, at last, the cottage of the White Carlin, Cuiva, and her husband Odhrán. Earnán Kingfisher Mosswell was eighty years of age, shrivelled by the weight of years, and ailing. He now lived with Cuiva and Odhrán, who loved him as if her were of their flesh and blood. The old eel-fisher shed tears of joy when he beheld Jewel, his step-granddaughter. Sweet indeed was the reunion, and the weathermasters plied the Marsh folk with gifts. Jewel spent many hours reminiscing with Earnán, sitting on the sunlit staithe in front of the cottage, while water lapped beneath the boards and marvellous dragonflies darted, armoured in polished bronze and gold, their fretted wings a mere shimmer on the air. Fondly the two of them recalled Jewel's parents, and Earnán's beloved mother Eolacha, once the carlin of the Marsh.

'Some would say,' mused the old man, 'that life has been unkind to me. After all, I have lost two wives and two children. Unaccountably, I do not feel bitter, but serene now that the worst pangs of grief are past. It is pleasing me more than I can say, to see you and your dear ones so hale and content. Cuiva's family has become like my own, and in my later years a wonderful peace has enfolded me. It is true that life has been unkind to me, but in many ways it has also been generous.

'Let me tell you another thing, a mhuirnín,' the old man said. 'Long ago a stranger came to the Marsh and although he looked to be about the same age as me he resembled your father in many ways. The likeness was quite striking. He said that his name was Jovan and he was the son of a sorcerer, though he was not looking proud of his heritage. He asked after Jarred, claiming to be his father. He had travelled much and seen amazing sights. He told me many valuable secrets, which later I passed on to the venerable Clementer. This Jovan had only a single regret; that he had not visited his wife and son since he left them long ago.

'So Cuiva and I revealed that Jarred had a child and a grand-child, and we told him also where to find Jarred's grave. At this, the stranger wept and said he might once have met Jarred, or so he believed, beneath a dilapidated porch in Cathair Rua - had seen and spoken to him, but had not the courage to reveal his identity because he believed his son would despise him for - as it were - 'running away' from the family home. He, the stranger, was mightily proud of Jarred and wished he had made himself known to him then, because now it was too late.

'In deep sorrow Jovan went alone to the graveside but when he returned he was smiling and happy and tranquil. By this, Cuiva and I knew he had seen what few people have seen at that burial place, and had found peace within himself. Of us Jovan petitioned that if we should again meet Jarred's child or grandchild, we would convey to them his message of love and ask, on his behalf, for their forgiveness. He went away and we never saw him again but later we heard he had gone to a village in the deserts of Ashqalêth, where I suppose he will live out his years and die of old age, just like the sorcerer his father.'

Jewel shed tears when she heard this story, nonetheless she was comforted by the knowledge that her father and grandfather had found each other, after all, even though for such a brief moment.

Muireadach, Cuiva's brother, and Keelin, her sister, dropped by to pay their respects to Jewel and her family. Cuiva's sons Oisín and Ochlán and her daughter Ciara also called upon the weathermasters, as did Suibhne Tolpuddle, his sister Doireann, several members of the Alderfen family, and many other folk who had known Jewel in her childhood.

Most poignant of all – and last, before they departed on the return journey to High Darioneth - Jewel, Arran and Asrăthiel paid their own visit to the graves of Lilith and Jarred, which occupied a lonely islet in a lily-strewn lake.

Evening was closing in. Mist was beginning to rise from the surface of the water. The skies were darkening, and herons called to one another as they flew home to roost. The three visitors stepped from their boat. Wavelets lapped at their feet, and frog notes belled from amongst the mosses.

'Behold,' Jewel said softly, indicating the pair of blossoming trees that grew atop two long mounds, headed by engraved tombstones, 'it is exactly as Adiuvo Clementer recorded in his book, 'The Iron Tree', the story of the lives of my parents.'

'How did he describe this place?' Asrăthiel asked, gazing in awe at the trees.

'I memorised the passage,' said Jewel, her voice quivering with emotion, 'for I love it well. He wrote,

'This is the history of Lilith and Jarred, who found one another and fought against terrible odds. At the last they passed out of life, but not before they gave life to another, for whose sake they sacrificed themselves. Their lives were not yielded up in vain – their cause was successful, and in that their triumph lies. They are gone, now, Lilith and Jarred. Side by side they lie in the ground, and from their mounded graves have sprung two rare trees, the like of which have never been seen in the Four Kingdoms of Tir. The slender boles lean towards one another, intertwining their boughs, and in springtime the blossom of one tree is the colour of sapphires, and tranquility, and all things blue, while the flowers of the other are as red as passion. And when in Winter the winds thread through the leafless boughs, a wondrous music is made, like the dim singing of flutes and bells, and the deep sigh of the ocean; and when autumn unfolds, the trees bear sweet fruit, and it is said that to eat of that fruit is to know joy, and to dwell in happiness forever."

Mother, father and daughter stood regarding the extraordinary trees for a long moment, while the boughs dipped and nodded, stirred by the faintest of breezes.

'And it is so!' said Arran presently. 'I have never seen such flowers.'

A gust shook the trees, whereupon blue and red petals drifted down to become part of the floral counterpane covering the graves.

'Who's that?' Asrăthiel said suddenly. Her parents stared in the direction of her outflung arm.

The half-light of gloaming might have played tricks upon the eyes, but it seemed to Asrăthiel that a young couple was strolling amongst the willows on the opposite bank of the lily-mere, hand in hand.

Their shapes shimmered through the mist, but they looked to be lovers walking by the water's edge, for they never took their eyes from one another. One had the appearance of a woman, whose eyes in the twilight glimmered blue, like two wings of the Blue Lycaenidae Butterfly; the other was evidently a man, tall and lithe, with hair the colour of cardamom spice. As Asrăthiel watched, holding her breath, unwilling to so much as blink lest the vision be snatched away, she thought the lovers paused. They seemed to turn to look straight towards her and her mother.

Then a light of recognition dawned in their eyes and they smiled, tenderly and joyfully, as if they had come at last to their heart's desire.

The lake mist swirled up and obliterated the vision, and when it thinned, no sign of the phantasms could be detected.

Jewel stood laughing and weeping simultaneously, while Arran comforted her with embraces, saying, 'What is it? What have you seen?'

'I am not sure,' said Jewel, wiping her eyes, 'but I am filled with happiness.'

'I saw them too!' exclaimed Asrăthiel.

'You saw them, *a mhuirnín*? Then it must all be true,' said Jewel. 'It must all be true, that our loved ones never leave us.'

'Of course it is true,' said Arran, gently, and placing one arm about the shoulders of his wife and the other about the shoulders of his daughter, he led them away.

After reluctantly bidding farewell to their friends Asrăthiel and her parents left the Marsh and journeyed straight to King's Winterbourne for Prince William's betrothal festivities. The Crown Prince had chosen a bride, and the populace rejoiced. From Southborough to Northgate, from the grand municipal buildings of the west to the fortified towers and Wyverstone Castle in the east, throughout the Port of King's Winterbourne and all along Winterbourne Bridge, the streets of Narngalis's royal city were bedecked with bunting in honour of the celebrated couple. The grey basalt of the city provided a sombre backdrop for the colourful flags. After the sorrow and hardship of war the people were doubly glad of a reason to rejoice, and each night there was music and dancing in taverns, assembly rooms and private houses.

In Wyverstone Castle the royal family, courtiers and guests from other realms were as glad as the commoners, though perhaps less boisterous. Every evening lavish banquets were conducted at the castle, and every day was filled with sports and divertissements of many kinds for the pleasure of the guests. Although the goblins had outlawed the wearing of animal products, the resourceful weavers and tailors of every land were constantly inventing new fabrics from vegetable sources. The magnificent chambers of the royal residence were alive with mirthful crowds in gorgeous raiment; dusky hues and intense sable contrasting with vivid flashes of jewels, brocade, or embroidery, or rich, bright colours crawling with the intricate scrolls of blackwork. The older noblewomen wore lace veils of held in place by ornate chaplets of silver wire. Younger ladies adorned their heads with jewelled cauls, their hair hanging down their backs. Fond of tradition, the men hatted their long locks with capuchons of various styles.

King Warwick's elite knights, the Companions of the Cup, were present throughout the festivities, clad in tabards of velvet and brocade, lined with linen, and appliquéd with heraldic designs. During this peacetime revelry the knights saw fit to lay aside the arts of war and turn to other, equally honourable pursuits such as poetry, music, rhetoric and the study of history.

At the feast on the third and final evening Asrǎthiel, who was seated at a long dining table with her parents, her grandfather, aunt, uncle and cousins, surveyed that fair assembly in the Great Hall of Wyverstone Castle. Shahzadeh of Ashqalêth and her consort were amongst the guests, and Queen Saibh with her companion Fedlamid, and King Thorgild Torkilsalven, and Queen Halfrida. Asrǎthiel witnessed happy faces and merriment everywhere.

Prince William in cambric shirt and quilted doublet, his light-brown-gold hair flowing from beneath a velvet cap, gazed blithely upon his pretty new bride-to-be. Lady Meliora, in faux silk and taffeta returned his gaze with a fetching smile. On beholding William's obvious contentment, Asrǎthiel felt a surge of happiness for him. Her thoughts turned inward, and she visualised herself in her sky-balloon, *Icemoon*, suspended above the battlements and turrets of the castle. Looking around with her mind's eye she saw a kingdom recovering slowly but surely from the ravages of war, as time began to ease the suffering of folk who mourned the fallen. To the west, in the Mountain Ring, a new generation of eager prentices was mastering the brí. Joy and healing abounded everywhere, except in her own spirit where a raw wound bled incessantly.

There is no happiness to be obtained for immortal beings alone in the world of mortalkind, she thought, except for my parents, who have each other. Yet, neither shall the road of deathlessness be entirely easy for those two.

Jewel and Arran found delight and solace and understanding in each other, but she, Asrăthiel, human born immortal, had no kindred spirit and no hope of any, since all the wells of immortality were now dry. In all events, she had no desire for any partner but one, and he had perished to dust or ash by the rising of the Averil moon; alive in a way, but mindless and powerless.

Asrăthiel's young cousin Corisande interrupted her melancholy musings, tugging at the damsel's sleeve. The girl was giggling, her eyes sparkling with glee. Albiona, holding her daughter by the hand, explained the reason. 'One of the servants told us there is an old beggar living in a corner of the castle kitchens,' she said. 'He's the one who did some sort of good turn for Narngalis that earned him repute. King Warwick has given him shelter and food for the rest of his days. The servants say he snores day and night in the warmth of the kitchen hearth, only waking to eat, or tell tall stories. His name used to be Cat Soup but, mindful of the ferocious kobold watchmen, he has prudently changed it to Fruit Salad.'

Asrăthiel forced herself to share Albiona's and Corisande's laughter.

'I've heard his real name is Kevin,' murmured Sir Torold Tetbury.

The revellers lacked for naught, and the junketing lasted throughout the night. As was the custom, performers entertained the diners between each course, and dancing in the ballroom followed dinner. King Warwick presided over the ball, viewing the high-spirited display from a stage where he sat in comfort, clad in his heavy gold collar and long gown of quilted cotton damask, dark purple and trimmed with faux ermine. He was flanked by Avalloc Maelstronnar and the father of the bride-to-be, Lord Carisbrooke.

Toward midnight, supper was served in the Crimson Drawing Room and the Blue, but Asrăthiel, her heart unaccountably heavy on this night of celebration, had no desire for food. Neither, apparently, did William's excited sisters, who clustered around the weathermage, arrayed in embroidered gowns of lace, muslin and cloth-of-silver; demure Lecelina, the eldest, Winona somewhat bossy, the second-born, and Saranna the youngest, vague and fey.

'There are bonfires all over the city,' Saranna said, companionably hooking her arms through Asrăthiel's.

'The biggest is in Coppenhall Square,' said Lecelina.

'Come with us,' said Winona, 'and we'll show you the best vantage point from which to watch the spectacle!' And they guided their friend, along with Corisande and Cavalon, up a steep and winding stair to a high turret.

There was indeed a fine view of the city's festivities to be obtained from this eyrie atop the castle. A large arched window, unglazed, looked out from the turret room. Its sill was low; only two feet above the floor, and as deep as the turret walls, which were two and a half feet thick. Filigrees of living stems, covered in flowers and foliage, clung to the mortar between the stones surrounding the window, framing the starry sky and the midnight cityscape.

'Do not go too near the window!' Lecelina warned the two children, who had already begun exploring the room. 'Next thing you'll be falling out!'

Gasping from the exertion of the long ascent, Asrăthiel and the princesses seated themselves on three-legged stools. They looked out over the many roofs and battlements of the castle to the metropolis extending in all directions far below, lit by lanterns, flambeau processions, celebratory bonfires and fireworks. The night was still, and the river gleamed with sudden bright reflections.

Presently, Winona's attention began to wander. 'This is a strange room,' she declared, gazing about. 'Long ago it was frequented by a carlin called Lenore Frithelstock. See, there is a second door, higher in the wall on the other side. It leads up to a small cloistered roof garden, long abandoned – weeds grow there in the shelter of the walls, for it is a suntrap, but amongst the thistles grow many fragrant herbs and flowers.'

'Some believe this room is haunted,' said Saranna, 'but I believe that if anything haunts at all, it must only be the Cailleach Bheur.'

'Why do people think it's haunted?' young Cavalon wanted to know.

'There is a strangeness about it,' said Saranna. 'Even in the depths of Winter, when most vegetation slumbers, climbing plants somehow grow in the roof garden, and send their tendrils twining about the walls. They always manage to creep through this window. Once inside, the bare stems bloom. Jasmine, clematis, bindweed and all sorts of creepers and climbers burst into flower in this chamber. It is like an indoor-outdoor room, for it is never short of blossoms and leaves, no matter what the season. Our father had a pair of shutters hung on the window, but the shutters could never be completely closed even when workmen nailed them together. Eventually they were removed.'

'It always seems warm in here,' added Lecelina.

'And pleasant,' said Corisande.

'Why is it not used as a greenhouse or a sitting room?' Cavalon asked.

'It is too small and inconvenient. The stair is narrow, slippery and very high, as you have just discovered.'

They ceased to speak and resumed gazing out across the slates and crenelations of the castle, observing the bonfires of celebration. Dim sounds of cheering and singing wafted up from below, and the blaring of horns, the chiming of bells, and the intermittent crack-crack of exploding fireworks. Strains of music swelled from the castle rooms below stairs, interwoven with the hum of conversation. A mood of reflective contentment had settled on them all.

'Is it not wonderful,' Asrăthiel said wistfully, 'to dwell in a land of peace and plenty.'

'Indeed,' her friends agreed.

'No more wars,' said Cavalon happily.

Corisande piped up. 'Asrăthiel,' she said, 'when I am old enough, will you teach me to wield Fallowblade?'

'Come now!' said Lecelina. 'Why should you want to use a great big clunking dangerous weapon like that?'

'In case the goblins come back,' Corisande said energetically, 'the wicked, wicked goblins! I will smite them for their wickedness!'

Seated on her stool the weathermage turned her gaze upon her little cousin, who was standing beside her. Their faces were almost at the same level. Asrăthiel smiled, although the smile did not reach her eyes. 'If you like I will teach you,' she said affectionately.

'I too should like to learn it,' said Cavalon, pushing forward.

'Very well then,' said Asrăthiel, 'We shall do that, starting at this – oh.'

She rose to her feet. Her audience turned around to see why.

'Do not bother,' said Zaravaz from the doorway.

14
WHEN THE NORTH WIND BLOWS

Oh, let me go a-roving, a footloose vagabond,
To seek outlandish fortune, to find what lies beyond!
Beyond the airy mountains, beyond the sounding sea,
Far over known horizons; the traveller's life for me.

Pray, let me find adventure on some exotic strand,
Exciting expeditions, encounters bold and grand.
Let me discover marvels upon some distant shore,
And map the lonely islands uncharted heretofore.

The world beyond these borders holds much I have not seen.
Let not my life be bound these cramping walls between,
For there are countless wonders that wait to catch my eye.
As once I was a fledgling, now I would learn to fly!

SUNG BY A TRAVELLING MINSTREL.

I t was the high doorway leading to the roof garden. He was leaning back against the architrave with his arms folded; a handsome knight with storm-purple eyes and dark lashes.
Intensely black was his hair, yet liquid glimmers ran up and down through it, as if a sheen of blue fire glided there. Unearthly

currents combed and lifted the long, smooth strands. Burning silver blazed from his coal-coloured garments, and his cloak was a furl of occultation. It was exciting to look upon him.

Out of the night, three horned eagle owls abruptly fluttered down to perch on the windowsill. The very stars in the sky appeared to grow larger and more luminous as if, like the birds, they were attracted to the goblin king. Seductive was he, and, sardonic, and eldritch, and he looked at Asrăthiel with a curious intensity of concentrated passion which went straight to the core of her being.

The damsel's spirits soared. Her heart turned over.

'Do not bother,' he announced again, before leaping down and sauntering into the room. 'If your kindred learn to live virtuous lives, no goblins shall ever illuminate your dreary days again.'

'Ah,' said Corisande, agog and cheeky, first to find her voice, 'but *you* are a goblin, sir.'

With a gasp of horror Lecelina seized the child and clasped her in a protective embrace, but the little girl wriggled free.

Zaravaz gave Corisande an avuncular pat on the head as he went past. 'Such a merry mischief you are, young lady,' he said indulgently, and Corisande smiled adoringly up at him.

'So,' said Asrăthiel, her pulse beating so fast it was nothing but a whirr. 'You are here.'

'I am indeed,' said Zaravaz, coming to a standstill in front of her. The sisters, who had stood stunned, picked up the children and made to rush away, but without turning his head to observe them Zaravaz said, 'The door is locked. So is the smaller portal. But pray do not distress yourselves. I mean you no harm.' He flicked a finger at the eagle owls, which unfurled their wings and flapped silently away. 'And I come alone,' he subjoined.

The weathermage could not take her eyes from him. Hardly able to credit that he was here with her, she willed him to exist, willed it not to be a dream, a glamour or a fraud. It was he, her eldritch lover, and if the werefire had altered his looks he had only become – if it were possible – more beautiful than ever. But how had the Burning changed him in other ways, ways that could not be seen? When it scoured the unseelieness from him, how had it influenced his character? Patently he was no witless vegetable, nor was he silent like Aonarán or remote like William, but the differences might be subtle. Would she know him at all?

She was standing with her back to the window. Zaravaz placed one hand on the stones of the frame and leaned upon it, his arm forming a barricade between the damsel and the rest of the room.

'My strength,' he said softly to her, 'has returned in full.'

All those who were present in the room could see at once how matters stood between those two, by the way they looked upon one another. And they were struck with astonishment.

Then Zaravaz said to the audience at large, 'I will harm no mortal creature this night. Leave now, for the door is suddenly unlocked. I wish to speak privately with Lady Asrăthiel.'

It came to Asrăthiel that she had never before heard him speak her name, and the sound of it made her feel as if she had turned to water, so that she must quickly sit down on the wide sill amongst the petals of jasmine. The sky behind her back was like a starry cloth hung upon a wall.

'Go,' she said to her anxious companions. 'I will be safe, I assure you.'

Zaravaz whispered, so that only she could hear, 'So you suppose.' Aloud, he said, 'Wait for us in the chamber you call the Blue Drawing Room.'

Unwillingly, now, the princesses departed, for they were fascinated and captivated by the beauty of the goblin king, and fain would have lingered near him. When they had gone Zaravaz drew Asrăthiel into his arms and kissed her. How long that kiss lasted she neither knew nor cared, though time without end would not have been long enough.

When they drew a little apart she began to speak, but he placed a finger on her lips to seal them, saying, 'I was Crowthistle, your confidant. I know the darkest secrets of your heart. If you want my love, you have it.'

This was the Zaravaz she knew. Seelie he might or might not be, but nothing else had changed.

''Tis all I want,' she said, still struggling to comprehend the enormity of his reappearance.

While she composed herself he sat on the window ledge close beside her and related the story of his recovery, as Lieutenant Zwist had told it to him.

Soon after Zauberin's cohorts expelled the weathermage from the gothic chamber in Sølvetårn where Zaravaz lay insensible, the goblin king had opened his eyes for the first time since being hauled out of the werefire. His breathing deepened. His eyes remained half-open. Sometimes the lids fluttered, or closed for a while but he said not a word nor did he move.

He lay, in a half-swoon for long days and nights, for weeks and months. During that time he was healing in body, mind and spirit. It was the immortal tears of Asrăthiel, three drops so rare that their like had never existed in the world, that had brought him back from the brink and restored him.

When Zaravaz fully awoke it was immediately clear that all wickedness had been scoured from him in the Aingealfyre; burned out, and evaporated. Flames of gramarye had purified him of unseel-ieness, as a blade of steel is tempered in a blast furnace. The influence of the Aingealfyre had actually reached back through time, draining every mote of pain and sorrow he had ever generated, then funnelling it into him, so that while he was writhing in the flames he suffered every last stab of torment he had ever meted out, and every last shred of sorrow he had caused, in place of the victims who had endured that agony and sorrow. He had endured exactly what they had endured, and now it was as if they had never borne it.

The effect of the Aingealfyre was retrospective. It changed history.

Which meant that even though Zaravaz had slain thousands of people he had never inflicted any pain or grief on his victims. To put the seal on his transformation, the cleansing flames had rendered him incapable of violence and cruelty.

He had become seelie.

His powers were not diminished in any way, but now he was forced to wield them only in the cause of justice, generosity, freedom, and every other species of righteousness.

'If I was terrible before,' he said to Asrăthiel, half-jesting, half-serious, 'I am more terrible now.'

She looked up at him, imagining that for love of his beauty the stars must have deliberately twined themselves like tinsel into his hair.

'What of your kindred?' she questioned. 'How did they respond, when you woke to seelieness?'

'My knights' loyalty did not falter in the face of this catastrophe, but they are determined to scour the world in search of a cure, as your father did, having vowed to save your mother – and, I have heard, he was successful. The *graihyn* set a guard of vicious fuathan and other wicked wights around the Aingealfyre, and powerful weavings of gramarye, that no human being might ever again approach the flames to fashion swords of gold, or to fecklessly tumble in and require rescuing. Now the Argenkindë all shout your praises, Weatherwitch, and would welcome you as one of their own, because your miraculous tears saved me. Zauberin is loudest with his eulogies, and calls curses upon himself for having exiled you.'

Asrăthiel smiled, and inclined the weight of her body against her lover's, heedless of the sheer drop from the window at their backs. 'Zwist promised to send me a sign if you lived…'

'I am that sign.'

She laughed, realising that Zwist had not specified when he would send the sign. 'My father has returned, and my mother has reawoken,' she said. 'All my dreams have come true.'

'I know. But are you happy here?' he asked.

'Not without you.'

Taking her hand in both of his, Zaravaz raised her fingers to his mouth and kissed them. 'On my oath, it went hard with me to lose you. Come away with me,' he said, bending closer so that the sweet warmth of his breath fanned her cheek like a feather. 'Come away to the lands and seas that exist beyond these borders. I will show you marvels, and excitement enough that you shall never tire of immortal life.'

'Of that,' she said, 'I have no doubt.'

'As you know,' he said, 'the Glashtinsluight possess antigravity capabilities.'

Lifting her head, Asrăthiel stared at him in bemusement. 'Yes,' she said. 'It means you have the ability to move quickly through time. Also, I have noted, you tend to laugh more readily than humankind.'

He added, 'Also we can fly.'

And he let loose his goblin wings.

Four dark vanes of energy flared from his shoulders; shadowy, diverging rays forming the sharp shape of an X with the fulcrum centred between his shoulderblades. They faded at their tips to a heat shimmer.

The goblin king gathered the damsel in his arms and flew down from the turret.

In the Blue Drawing Room of Wyverstone Castle, where the weathermasters and the royal family congregated with the foremost knights of Narngalis and other noble guests, a take-as-you-please supper had been laid out. Silver glittered everywhere; encrusted on the walls and the heavy frames of the paintings that adorned them, on the embroidered chairs, the ornate ceiling, the firescreens. Tiered chandeliers depended from the ceiling on long brass chains, sparkling like spiral galaxies. The floor was thick with priceless creamy carpets. About the walls, cabinets inlaid with semiprecious stones housed objets d'art. Tall doors at the far end of the chamber gave on to a torch-lit balcony overlooking the gardens. Before these portals posed graceful marble statues, and tall vases of lapis lazuli overflowing with ferns and delphiniums.

Though the architecture and furnishings remained as serene as ever, the feelings of the aristocratic crowd who milled about in the room had soared to an exorbitant pitch of awe and terror, amazement and expectation. The princesses, flushed with agitation, had come running to spread the word; the goblin king was amongst them, and he was about to enter that very room.

The news caused a sensation. Pulses quickened, nerves tingled, tongues wagged and people began looking nervously over their shoulders. He was here - they repeated - in the castle itself; the famous Zaravaz, whose reputation as a despoiler and heart breaker, augmented by gossip and imagination, had reached the status of legend. People were incredulous that after seeing and hearing so much about this wicked creature they were about to find themselves occupying the same room. The princesses vowed he had promised to do them no harm - and they must believe him - but men, though not armed for battle, found their hands straying to the hilts of their ornamental daggers and dress swords. Speculatively they eyed the candlesticks, looking for traces of gold inlay, and some said, ''Tis pity the barbarian is not to enter the Crimson Drawing Room, for it is choked with gold.' Others muttered, 'If one of the horde could steal in so easily, without being spied by the watchmen, how many more might be waiting to storm the gates?' Many women glanced critically not at weapons but at mirrors, all the while smoothing stray wisps of hair, rearranging their garments and covertly practising their most fetching poses.

In great alarm Arran, Jewel and Avalloc descended on the princesses, asking, 'But where is Asrăthiel? Was she not in your company? Surely you would not have left her alone with him!'

'Oh!' exclaimed Winona, suddenly uncomfortable, 'but she wanted – that is to say, they were –'

Lecelina cut short her sister's stammering. 'She is with him,' she said, 'as is her wish.' Lowering her voice she added, 'Methinks some understanding exists between them.'

'Understanding!' Avalloc shouted incredulously, heedless of the surprised looks from those who surrounded him. 'How could that possibly be?'

Jewel abruptly sat down on a chair, fanning her face with an embroidered serviette.

'Enchantment, more likely!' Arran roared, his brow dark with anger. 'He will not get away with this!'

King Warwick gave orders to seal off the Blue Drawing Room, scour the premises for other intruders and double the guard at the castle gates. The sentries posted at the drawing room doors were instructed to allow only the Lady Asrăthiel and her companion to enter. To avoid uproar and sudden headlong stampedes, the news of the mysterious new arrival was not permitted to spread to the multitude of revellers thronging the castle's lower levels; their care-free festivities remained undisturbed.

'Precautions are unnecessary,' Lecelina insisted. 'The Unseelie Lord vowed he meant no harm.'

'And he cannot lie,' appended Winona.

Saranna cupped her hand to her sister's ear. 'But I should certainly like him to lie with me,' she whispered brazenly, where-upon Winona could not help giggling.

'Such eyes,' she whispered back. 'So unusual. The colour of royalty; the colour of wine.'

'Such stature,' said Saranna in an undertone, 'such noble demeanour!'

'Oh, where is Asrăthiel? What has happened to her?' said Jewel anxiously.

'This will be some trick, some vicious snare,' said Sir Huelin Lathallan, adjusting the sword-belt concealed beneath his tabard.

The three princesses assured him that it was not so. 'He has not come here to work us ill,' they said, unable to bring themselves to speak the name of Zaravaz, it being so laden with significance. 'He has not come here to make war.'

'Why, then, has he come?'

But Warwick's daughters refused to conjecture.

The Companions of the Cup drew themselves up in two rows on either side of the closed doors, like a guard of honour, as if showing esteem to the expected visitor but ready to spring to the defence of the household if he should attack. In quiet suspense the gathering waited, all attention fixed on this entryway. So intent were they that they barely noticed when the torches on the wide balcony behind them flickered, as if blown by a sudden draught, but when they sensed a sudden shadow falling across the stars they all turned to look.

Two figures alighted on the stone balustrade and leaped soundlessly down, he with his arm about her waist. Together the Storm Lord's granddaughter and the goblin king walked through the open portals into the room.

The waiting concourse had reckoned on beholding the Lord of Wickedness, having been forewarned, but the actual sight of him, so close at hand, was both terrifying and exhilarating. Half the assembly could not get close enough; the other half could not get far enough away. All attention was riveted on him. People glanced in a casual manner, peering from the corners of their eyes, feigning indifference, pretending not to be utterly fascinated. Some had never set eyes on him before, but had heard much of him in legend. Many had only ever seen him on the battlefield, their avowed foe whirling in a dance of death, slaughtering men with vigorous enjoyment. Now he stood within their very halls, a supernatural knight whose torn-shadow hair framed a face so handsome that those who gazed upon him narrowed their eyes as if dazzled by a brilliant light, yet they could not look away.

As for the fact that the ancient enemy stood side by side with the Storm Lord's granddaughter and it was patently obvious that close affection bound them together – this was too much to countenance. A wrathful murmuring filled the chamber, punctuated with exclamations of shock and horror. Some believed Asrăthiel must have been bewitched and others were enraged at the notion that she had traitorously allied herself with the foe, but most knew not what to think or feel.

The Companions of the Cup stepped forward at once, drawing their blades a couple of inches, but King Warwick waved his hand saying, 'The guest code applies. Do not touch him.' His gesture brought the knights to a halt, and they returned the blades to the scabbards with some violence.

Though there was nothing normal about him, the King of the Argenkindë behaved as if he were a normal visitor. He bowed. 'I am Zaravaz,' he said.

'And you have bewitched my daughter, I see,' Arran said with hostility. 'Asrăthiel, come away. Lidoine will know how to lift this spell.'

Avalloc glowered. Jewel had turned pale.

'Father,' said the damsel, 'you underestimate me. I am no dupe. Before I am generally censured for having formed this attachment, pray hear me out.'

Then Asrăthiel, with rapidly beating heart, pronounced the names of all the people in that chamber so that Zaravaz would know them, although evidently he knew them already, and at the same time she tried to allay the fears of her kindred. She explained how Zaravaz had been burned in the Aingealfyre while saving the life of Prince William, and how all his wickedness had been destroyed, and he had paid in the fullest and most rigorous way for his offences. Finally, she told them that he was her chosen companion.

'Your chosen companion?' Arran repeated in amazement, shaking his head. 'I do not hear aright.'

With more tolerance than Arran, Jewel looked upon Zaravaz, marvelling, and murmured, 'So this is a goblin. So much for the old tales!'

Avalloc merely gazed at Asrăthiel. She averted her head, unable to endure the bewilderment and distress in his expression.

When she had made everything clear, King Warwick stepped forward, his heavy robes rustling as he moved.

'You rescued my son,' he said stiffly to Zaravaz, quite unable to bring himself to address this traditional enemy by any title, honourable or otherwise, 'therefore I thank you, unless your eldritch mores define thanks as an offence. If it is true that you are completely free of wickedness and have atoned for your crimes the way Lady Asrăthiel describes, then I cannot do otherwise than receive you beneath my roof.' The king's stern expression indicated an unspoken adjunct: in consideration of our history, it is not easy for us to accept your kind as hearth guests.

'Warwick Wyverstone, I will not much longer presume upon your hospitality,' said Zaravaz, 'for regrettably the decorative scheme of your home is not to my taste.' He glanced disparagingly at a lightly gilded fruit dish that adorned the supper table. The king nodded tightly.

William bowed courteously to the eldritch lord. 'I am grateful,' said the prince, 'that you risked your life for mine.' As the mortal and the immortal stood facing one another, some who viewed them fancied they glimpsed some ineffable bond of kinship between them. William might have shared that opinion, for he added, gravely, 'It appears we may have become Brothers of the Flame.'

Zaravaz winced, and effected a strained smile. He made no reply, whereby Asrăthiel suspected he did not trust himself to speak as courteously as the occasion required. She could see it cost him much effort to restrain himself amongst his erstwhile enemies; he was like some wild animal on a tether.

One by one the members of the royal families and the weathermasters formally greeted their unexpected visitor, though they stopped short at welcoming him. King Warwick adhered to tradition, impeccably playing the part of host and suppressing his feelings of outrage and condemnation. Avalloc only bobbed his head curtly; disapprobation clouded his brow. There was now no open censure or hostility, though the air of the chamber virtually crackled with tension.

The only royal personage manifestly pleased to salute Zaravaz was Queen Saibh. 'Bold sir,' she said timidly, 'I believe I am in your debt. You made the Druid Primoris say he lifted the curse from the House of Ó Maoldúin, and my sons' days are the better for it.'

'There are no debts, gentle queen,' said Zaravaz, favouring her with an intense and hypnotising look that provoked a ferment of jealousy amongst some of the ladies looking on. 'It is enough that abject superstition is quelled.'

'In that case I myself owe you no obligation, sir,' said Saibh's consort, Fedlamid macDall, 'though you freed me from thralldom to the Grey Neighbours. Yet it is beyond my power to express the depths of my gratitude, for without your intervention I would have been forever enslaved.'

'Had Lady Asrăthiel not petitioned on your behalf, Fedlamid,' Zaravaz said mildly, 'you would still be bound in servitude to the trows.'

MacDall made a low reverence to Asrăthiel.

'Is the Sanctorum's curse entirely lifted, brave sir?' Saibh asked. 'Ronin sometimes wonders.'

'Queen Saibh, there never was a curse,' said Zaravaz, 'but if it means aught to you, send a messenger to the Dubh Linn, the Black Lake on the moors of Slievmordhu. Let your envoy notify the fuathan infesting those waters that Zaravaz sent you. Command them, in my name, to cast out the four wooden toys that the flapping druid threw in, for dry Virosus stipulated that as the charms rotted away, so would the house of Ó Maoldúin. Keep the four sticks preserved in some strongbox, if it puts your mind at rest. I tell you this, Saibh, because you are temperate of spirit, and when you were a child you used to defend the songbirds' nests in your father's woods from your thieving cousins.'

Between surprise that he could have known so much about her, and delight to think that her son's worries might be entirely swept away once and for all, Saibh stammered a suitable response before she and her consort retired meekly from the presence of the renowned and infamous visitor.

It was with much apprehension that Asrăthiel formally presented her lover to her parents. Her father, who had not fought in the recent wars and who had never seen one of the Glashtinsluight – unless it had been a cavalcade of Ice Goblins he had glimpsed in the land of Midwinter, and not a dream – regarded Zaravaz with suspicion, barely overlaid by a veneer of politeness. He took the measure of Zaravaz and, to the damsel's astonishment, right in front of her eyes he appeared to soften his attitude. Indeed, she judged that at length he almost approved. To her surprise he said, 'Methinks, sir, I have seen your face before, reflected in an ice crystal, or else I was bedazzled.'

'In Ellan Istillkutl, Lord Weathermage, the boundary between illusion and reality can be ill marked,' said Zaravaz, who appeared to know about Arran's travels, though Asrăthiel had not told him.

As for Jewel, when Zaravaz kissed her hand as suavely as a gentleman of the highest degree she was clearly entranced and intrigued, though at first she hung back, gazing searchingly at his countenance as if trying to place him. 'I am astonished,' she said frankly, and with some complaint, 'to see that my daughter has found companionship with the lord of an unseelie race. 'Knowing what I do about goblins, I cannot help but be concerned for her welfare.'

A stir and a flurry went through the multitude when they heard Jewel pronounce this implied criticism. From past exchanges on the battlefield they knew well that the Glashtinsluight did not take kindly to adverse comments. Many held their breath in fright as they awaited Zaravaz's response, and made ready to flee.

'My lady,' said the goblin king, regarding Jewel with a gentle respect they had not conceived was possible in him, 'There is no need to fear me. I am no longer unseelie, and besides, your daughter has conquered me entirely. She has bested me, wherefore rightly you ought to be concerned for my welfare, for she has the power to overwhelm me with a word, or merely by crooking her little finger.'

Laughing, Jewel replied, 'and that is as it should be. But I, too, have seen you before!' she exclaimed suddenly, as forthright as ever. 'I saw you in a dream, and in water. It was you!'

With an elegant bow, Zaravaz acknowledged that she was right.

Ever inquisitive, Jewel wanted to know how it had come to pass that she had experienced a precognition, as it were, of the goblin king; wherefore Asrăthiel told the story of the urisk Crowthistle, while the entire assembly listened in. All the time they continued to watch Zaravaz in concentrated awe; every smile, every turn of his head every flicker of an eyebrow was noted, and many longed secretly to exchange a few words with him so that they could later say I spoke with the goblin king.

'Why, you were the little urisk!' said Jewel, upon the closing of the tale. 'I am glad to meet you, sir, for although you were a laggard when it came to housework, you did my family a good turn in the Marsh.'

Two or three courtiers almost swooned with horror at this presumptuous address, expecting the goblin king to bring the castle down around their ears in retribution, but Zaravaz laughed. It was such a striking and musical laugh that one of them fainted anyway and had to be revived with hartshorn.

'Not only in the Marsh, Mother,' said Asrăthiel, 'for it was the urisk who recognised that you still lived after the mistletoe arrow struck you down – he who caused you to be raised up.'

'Then, sir, you have my gratitude in full quantity,' cried Arran, his wonder plain to see.

Albiona, however, was scandalized. 'The urisk!' she cried. 'What, the self same urisk that plagued our house?'

'The very one, madam,' Zaravaz said with aplomb, turning to address Dristan's wife. 'I availed myself fully of your hospitality. Your cook is to be commended for her succulent fruit preserves and seed cakes. In the hiring of staff, madam, your taste is impeccable.'

Much mollified and taken aback, Albiona blushed.

'Pray convey my greetings to your estimable brownie,' said Zaravaz.

Murmuring platitudes, Albiona let the matter drop, being too flustered to take it further.

'Your family,' Zaravaz said to Jewel, 'has a habit of offering me gifts. Generous of you, certainly, but I myself have a habit of returning property to its rightful owner. To whom does this belong?' He held out his hand, and in his palm lay glittering the silver-white treasure from the Iron Tree.

At once Asrăthiel said, 'It belongs to my mother.'

Beaming with delight, Jewel accepted the stone. 'My father's jewel!' she exclaimed, caressing it admiringly. 'There was a time I disliked it for what it represented, but it seems to me that its meaning has changed. This thing has become a symbol of hope and joy, and I am glad to have it back.' At her request, her husband fastened the chain around her neck.

While Jewel continued to question Zaravaz about the urisk's life in the Great Marsh of Slievmordhu, and to reflect on the brief conversations they had held together, Arran asked Asrăthiel whether she would draw aside to speak privately with him. She agreed, not without casting an anxious glance at Zaravaz who stood coolly alone in the midst of his foes, with the king's household guard and the Knights of the Cup glowering at him on all sides, and she his only ally.

Her lover smiled, as if reading her thoughts, and said softly. 'Do not vex yourself, ladylove.' More loudly, and to the indignation of the warriors, he added, 'I could take this football team as if brushing off a speck of dust.' Then in polite tones, as if to rub salt in the wound, 'though tricked out so prettily and no doubt proud of their mothers' best cutlery from the kitchen drawer.'

'Are you still immune to iron and steel?' Asrăthiel asked.

'That I am,' he conceded somewhat more reluctantly, and she had to be satisfied.

When they had secluded themselves out of earshot on the far side of the chamber Arran whispered to his daughter, 'Are you happy?' and when she assured him she was, he appeared somewhat more content, though still unconvinced.

'I can only surmise that this extraordinary attachment began during your incarceration at Minnith Ariannatyh.'

'You are right.'

'And you never told us.'

'How could I?'

'Fridayweed?' said Arran, and the impet, which had been curled up inside his collar, thrust its long nose through the curtains of his hair.

'Wot,' it said.

'Can you tell me whether my daughter is under a spell?'

'Not if that one there would take umbrage against my doing so,' said the little wight, peering, awe-struck, across the room at Zaravaz. 'That there swanking bogle'd claw up both my mittens and use my kneecaps as a pair o' cutty spoons if I fashed him.'

'He would not mind,' said Asrăthiel. 'In any case, there is no spell.'

'Aye, then, I'll do it,' said the wight, and it proceeded to recite a short rhyme in a language unknown to either Asrăthiel or her father. 'Now man,' Fridayweed said to Arran, 'Look through the crook of my elbow and see whether the colour of her eyes has changed.'

So Arran held the tiny creature on his palm, and Fridayweed placed its paw on its hip with its elbow akimbo, and Arran squinted as if looking through a keyhole. Presently the weathermage breathed a sigh. 'The same,' he said, lowering his hand.

'Set me on the table,' said the impet. When Arran had placed his fist on the snowy cloth Fridayweed scampered down his arm and hid behind a tray of comfits, where it plunked itself down, cross-legged, and began to munch with relish on the dainties.

'Do not be tellin' him I am here,' it said, between mouthfuls.

'Why not?'

'I'm mortal frittened o' t' Mountain King. I'll drink a brimmer to his health at a good distance.'

'You were not afraid of a snow troll,' Arran pointed out.

'Man, that's a long way different.'

Asrăthiel returned to the other side of the room with her father, whereupon Arran, who had been casting many a protective look in his daughter's direction said to the singular guest, 'What is your intention by coming here tonight?'

Zaravaz replied, 'The Argenkindë deserted your realms many weeks since, but I returned alone, because there was something I had left behind, which I wished to take with me.'

Jewel, Arran and Avalloc all turned to Asrăthiel, who smiled at her beloved family. The joy that shone upon her countenance was apparent to all.

'And have you found what you sought?' Avalloc Storm Lord enquired somewhat abrasively.

'That I have, noble sir,' said Zaravaz. 'As for whether she will come with me, that is for her to decide.'

'Aye,' burst out Sir Huelin Lathallan, who could no longer contain his wrath, 'you would seize the flower of us all, having already taken the lives of the best men in Narngalis! You reaving firebrand! It pains me to stand by and hear you garner gratitude, shielded as you are by guest code, when what you deserve is to be hanged, drawn and quartered.'

'Hold your tongue, sirrah!' King Warwick barked.

The shocked onlookers retreated from Zaravaz and many rushed from that chamber as swiftly as protocol would allow, in terror for their lives. Those who remained cast their fate in the lap of Providence and fearfully fixed their collective gaze on the goblin king.

He smiled.

There was something about that smile which did nothing to ease their apprehension.

'Sir Huelin,' said Zaravaz pleasantly, 'The work of soldiers is to kill or be killed. For the sake of the Lady Asrăthiel and her honourable kindred I will not bandy words with you. Nor will I bandy blows in this place, for I keep my word.'

'You would not dare fight man to man,' retorted Lathallan, 'not without all your conjurings and cantrips and your unfair advantage.'

Tucking up his sleeves to his elbow, Zaravaz looked away as if wearied by tedium. 'If you challenge me I shall be overjoyed to meet you on equal footing, at a time and place of your choosing.' He smoothed back his hair, like a wrestler about to enter a bout, and glanced enquiringly at the knight as if waiting for an invitation.

'There will be no challenges, Sir Huelin,' said King Warwick. 'Not beneath my roof.'

The knight had no choice but to acquiesce, and did homage to his sovereign to acknowledge it. The crowd's tension abated, though Lathallan scowled, as if bandying blows were the very thing he most desired. 'Had we met elsewhere,' he said to Zaravaz, 'it might have been different.'

Ignoring him, Zaravaz turned to Asrăthiel and said, 'It is time for me to depart.'

'Are you going with him, a mhuirnín?' Jewel asked anxiously.

'No. Not now.' The damsel gave her parents a look full of

significance. Arran and Jewel read her unspoken message, I will discuss this further with you later, in private.

Corisande tugged at the hem of Zaravaz's cloak. 'Are you going away?' she asked, gazing up at him. 'But I want to know why your eyes are purple.'

Albiona made to grab her daughter by the hand and impel her away, however Zaravaz crouched on his heels to bring his face level with the child's. Corisande did not tremble, but instead looked at the goblin king with shining eyes.

'Did you know that purple is the final colour of the visible spectrum?' he said. 'Purple's mystery is that it lies between the known and the unknown.'

The child seemed content with that, although Albiona muttered in her husband's ear, 'He still has not told her why his eyes are that colour.'

'A master of rhetoric,' Dristan acknowledged.

'Will you do something for me?' Zaravaz asked the child. She nodded shyly. 'Will you tell that cowardly Fridayweed over there on the table that too many comfits will give him a bellyache?' Corisande nodded again and giggled, after which Zaravaz rose to his feet with a swift and graceful movement, and only Asrăthiel noted the slight flinch.

Awkwardly, though with rigorous observation of decorum, Asrăthiel's friends and kindred made their salutations as the goblin king took his leave of them. The atmosphere in the Blue Drawing Room remained fraught with strain and incredulity. Most of the mortals were poised between disappointment and relief at the brevity of his visit.

Having said his farewells, Zaravaz conducted Asrăthiel out to the balcony. People stepped back to clear a path before them and nobody tried to follow, for it was clear they wanted to spend a moment alone; nevertheless the entire crowd watched them through the open doors as they conversed briefly together.

'It is well that Lathallan did not challenge me,' the goblin king said, 'whether to a wrestling match or mortal combat. Since the burning made me seelie I am incapable of slaying any thing, and it goes hard with me to do any harm.'

'Is that the only change in you?'

She saw in his eyes that it was not, and guessed that the agony of such a burning as he had endured would always be with him, though he would never admit to it.

'The only important one,' said Zaravaz, 'To the consternation of Zauberin and others, who seek a cure.'

Asrăthiel smiled.

'It is my design to join my knights in the far north, beyond the ranges,' Zaravaz said, clasping both of Asrăthiel's hands within his and drawing her close to him. 'I deem we may safely leave these kingdoms in the hands of the kobold watch. Perhaps some day your people will learn to deplore the eternal catch-cry of the bigot; man to woman, fair to dark, dark to fair, human to nonhuman, 'It is not like us, therefore it is inferior; whereby we have the right to treat it ill."

'Perhaps they will learn. I hope so.'

'If you wish to come with me, set your affairs in order and meet me at Sølvetårn. I will be waiting there for you.'

'I want to go with you,' she said, 'but I cannot do so if my leaving will bring sorrow upon my family. And, should they give me their blessing, I cannot know how long it will take to make the necessary arrangements. How long will you wait?'

'I have all the time that ever will be,' said he, looking down at her with eyes the colour of storms, 'and so do you. I will wait until you come to me.'

With those words, and with a parting kiss that rendered her speechless, he sprang onto the balcony parapet, let flare his aerofoils of dark energy and flew away.

No sooner had he done so than hoarse and shrill screams arose from the Blue Drawing Room. The damsel ran back inside, where she encountered a low level of chaos. Ornamental daggers, knives and dress swords lay strewn across the floor. Their owners were regarding them with suspicion, or sheepishly picking them up and examining them.

Albiona was standing with her hands on her hips, surveying the scene. 'He could not help himself,' she declared severely. 'He had to leave a parting gift, that bothersome urisk!' She was laughing, despite her cross words.

'What happened?' Asrăthiel asked her aunt.

'Oh, as soon as he had gone the blades all turned into serpents,' she replied. 'You should have seen the men's faces! And the way they all leaped into the air, casting the vipers from them and yelping as if they'd been bitten! It's a wonder no one was hurt, with people and objects flying in every direction.'

'A glamour, just a glamour,' said Asrăthiel, trying not to smile. 'Of course the snakes would not be real. He would not wish to harm the creatures.'

The three princesses then proceeded to cross-question her, wanting to know all that Zaravaz had said to her and all she had said in reply, but she refused to satisfy their enquiries.

Later that same night, when the rest of the household was abed, Asrăthiel consulted with her parents and grandfather. Their discourse was intense and candid; all facts were laid bare, all feelings expressed.

'You have found happiness, a mhuirnín,' Jewel said, her joy bittersweet. 'We love you too much to keep you from it.'

'Zaravaz could never live amongst us,' Asrăthiel began hesitatingly.

'Of course not,' said Jewel. 'We cannot expect you to stay with us now, though it costs me dear to even contemplate your departure.'

'Mother!' the damsel wrapped Jewel in a loving embrace.

Said Arran, 'Though it hurts me to say so, it is clear how matters stand between you and he, Asrăthiel. Every bird must fly some day.'

'No!' Avalloc said vehemently. 'Not if they fly towards the hunter's arrow! My dear child, I cannot condone your going off with this – this wight. For a start, there is an age difference of thousands of years!'

'You speak of Zaravaz,' said Asräthiel, 'as if he were human. With eldritch races vast time spans are meaningless. For example, they are always in their prime – '

But her grandfather interrupted. 'Nothing you can say will persuade me, Asräthiel. Zaravaz is of unseeliekind. I do not know what fires have burned him, but he is King of the Silver Goblins, who have wrought us great ruin, and of all men, human or unhuman in Tir, I deem him the least worthy of you.'

A surge of pent sorrow and other emotions threatened to over-whelm the damsel, but out of love and respect for the Storm Lord she bowed her head. 'If that is your opinion, Grandfather, I will not oppose you. I will not go with him.' In her mind she said, I will stay here as long as you live, but after that I will consider myself free.

'That is well!' Avalloc said grimly, ignoring Jewel's reproachful look and Arran's questioning expression.

As soon as their meeting ended Asräthiel went out into the night. She took herself down the road from Rowan Green to the plateau, far from human habitation where, alone, she walked for hours through starlit orchards and wild places, and the thoughts on which she dwelled were profoundly stirring to the spirit.

In her mind's eye she pictured Zaravaz and thousands of Silver Goblins racing across the white wastes of Midwinter, the hooves of the trollhästen kicking up glittering clouds of snow crystals. And riding in cavalcade to meet them, she envisioned, came the Ice Goblins, lords and ladies both; *graihyn* and *liannyn*. Then the two groups merged, and with great rejoicing they wheeled and sped off into the unknown, and nothing was left to show that they had ever existed, for the snow sifted across their tracks, and all became pathless.

When, after dusk, Asräthiel returned home her grandfather met her at the door with a lantern in his hand, his eyes of clear jade glimmering with tears.

'Forgive me,' he said. 'What right has anyone in the land to deny you happiness?'

'What are you saying?' The damsel was afflicted to see him so distraught.

'I am saying, my dear, I have thought it over and I see now what a selfish old dotard I have been. Go ahead and seize your dreams. If you want to venture into the wider world with someone who has captured your heart, then do not hesitate.'

But Asrăthiel said, 'I will hesitate, grandfather. My mother and father will live on, but if I go now, I may never see you again.'

'Do not allow that to hold you back,' said Avalloc.

'But I must,' she insisted, clinging to the old man as if she were a child again, and he as strong and hale as he once had been. 'I have all the time in the world. My destiny lies north of the mountains, but I will not leave High Darioneth before you do.'

'I am but seventy-two Winters old,' said the Storm Lord. 'Let me tell you, my dear, that it was given to me to know the exact span of my life. I will live for another forty years. You may go away now, and return to visit us every once in a while. I'll still be here.'

When she heard his words, the damsel's happiness had no boundaries.

She returned to the mountain ring with her family after the betrothal celebrations came to an end, and took a week to put her affairs in order and make her preparations. When it came time to pack her belongings, the only thing she took with her was the gift of Zaravaz, the iridium sword *Rehollys*. After saying all her good-byes she made one final tour around the house of Maelstronnar. She gazed long at the portraits of the beloved weathermasters who had lost their lives on the ferny hill, visited the places where she used to play as a child and the library where she had conversed with Crowthistle, ran upstairs to the deserted glass cupola where her mother had slept for so long, viewed the antique fishmail shirt displayed on the wall, the jewel of Strang in her mother's trinket box, and Fridayweed lying asleep, curled up in a sunny nook with his tasselled tail twitching as he dreamed eldritch dreams.

With each familiar object she saw and touched, the damsel felt a pang of wistfulness and a frisson of fear, to think of leaving behind all that was so dear and so familiar. Simultaneously she looked forward to the future with a thrill of excitement, and if at times she became so overwhelmed by nostalgia that she thought she could never depart, she would think of her lover waiting on the heights, and imagine the lands beyond the borders, that had yet to be explored, and she would whisper to herself, *It is time to put aside old things. I cherish the past, yet it lies at my back. A new life beckons.*

It was in the dining hall, the wide, low-ceilinged chamber panelled with walnut and arrayed with comfortable furniture, that Asrăthiel's eyes were drawn to the great sword in its scabbard hanging on the wall above the mantelpiece. There it was; Fallowblade, the golden sword, slayer of goblins, and heirloom of the House of Stormbringer. From beyond the casements came the musical notes of small songbirds twittering, and the soft cries of children playing on the greensward. The mountain wind, ever unquiet, sighed and murmured as it prowled the eaves and ruffled the rowan leaves with cool fingers. For a long moment Asrăthiel stood motionless, looking at the mighty weapon. One last time she climbed up, lifted it off the wall with both hands, and drew the blade from its sheath.

The fluted tongue of Fallowblade was a pillar of golden flame. Gripping the hilt firmly, Asrăthiel held it vertically in front of her body, as she often had done before. White-gold spangles ran up and down its glimmering length. The atmosphere seemed to sing with arcane voices where the sharp edges of Fallowblade severed the very air, particle from particle. Gently Asrăthiel hefted the sword in her hands, swishing it slightly, almost imperceptibly, from side to side, her gaze never shifting from the blaze of aureate loveliness around this beautiful, shimmering, lethal thing.

'Thank you for what you have done,' she said.

Then she slid the sword back into the scabbard and replaced it on its mountings.

The mountain tops around the rim of High Darioneth had disappeared into a layer of vapour. Giant cloud formations billowed and surged overhead, mist-edged for the most part, their borders hard-stencilled with silver-gilt when they churned across the face of the rising sun. The niveous dome of *Icemoon*'s inflating envelope could be seen rising tremulously behind the tiled roofs of the houses on Rowan Green, glimmering palely against the darkness like an imitation of the moon.

At the launching-place, on the apron carpeted with small-leaved creeping mint, a large assembly thronged about the wicker gondola suspended beneath the balloon. They had gathered to bid Asrăthiel farewell. She kissed and embraced her parents, torn between sadness and exhilaration, but never for an instant doubting that she was setting out along the road to her rightful destiny.

Almost fully buoyant, the aerostat was anchored to the ground by four thick cables. The enormous satiny envelope shivered and swayed high above, its multiple gores rippling as the interior temperature increased. The triangular facets of the sun-crystal beneath the balloon's mouth gleamed and winked like water in moonlight, but in its heart dazzling white-gold rays bristled like a miniature star, or like a pincushion stuck with white-hot needles, and none could look directly into those depths without being blinded, for some quality of the sun was trapped therein.

Asrăthiel's copilot caused the crystal's heat to be gradually released, flowing out from the crystal's peak. Meanwhile, balloon stewards held open the sprung steel band at the lower edge of the fire-proof skirt clipped to the mouth of the balloon, so that all heat was directed inside the silken envelope.

As the air warmed, *Icemoon* began to inflate. Greater it grew, like a swelling bud, until at last it lifted from the ground, still anchored. Then, the gondola was set upright and the copilot climbed inside. The crystal rayed forth more energy and the envelope dilated like a bubble. Slung beneath, the basket strained at its moorings. Watching this scene Jewel was reminded of her first balloon launch, years ago, when young Arran Maelstronnar had been the flight-commander. She smiled at the recollection, and linked arms with her husband, who stood at her side, though privately she was filled with anguish at the prospect of losing her daughter so soon after regaining her.

The sky glimmered like a reflection of fire on water, and clouds blew away from the back of Wychwood Storth. Just as Asrăthiel was about to board the aerostat, Corisande called out to her, 'What about Fallowblade? Who will teach me to wield him?'

Asrăthiel kissed her cousin lightly on the brow and replied, 'Let him alone. May he rest in his scabbard for a thousand years and more.' With that, she leaped into the gondola and gave a signal for the moorings to be cast off. The gondola skated a few feet sideways, before *Icemoon* rose straight up.

Clad in weathermaster garments, the damsel stood with feet braced apart, her black hair streaming down her back, murmuring soft words that unleashed potency with every syllable. Her hands moved in a swift, intricate design while she commanded a rising wind to blow nor'-nor'-east. As she watched the land drop away the line of her body was taut, as if her spine were a metal rod, receptive to every nuance of atmosphere; the changing masses of air, electrified particles, fluctuations in temperature and humidity, and subtleties beyond imagining. The waving crowd below dwindled to a scatter of tiny upturned faces, like daisies in a field. When she had ensured the wind vectors were under her control Asrăthiel waved back, until her family and friends dwindled to specks and vanished from sight.

To the Northern Ramparts they flew, the weathermage and her copilot; to Sølvetårn, high amongst the gables of icy Storth Cynros. In the evening they looked upon the citadel of the Silver Goblins, all spires and starlight, eyries and soaring halls, glittering with jewels delved from beneath ancient fog-cowled mountains, its gorgeous walls hewn from sparkling basalt. The turrets were wrapped in mists, the roofs spangled with snow. Legend had named it Minith Ariannath, the Silver Mountain. Once its halls had teemed with immortal beings, but now they echoed only to the sounds of falling water and cracking ice.

He was waiting there impatiently, Zaravaz, accompanied by two daemon horses with manes and tails of emerald fume, with the wind revelling in his hair. What passed between the damsel and her lover when they met again is only for them to know, for it shall not be disclosed here. Seated on the back of a Tangwystil, Asrăthiel watched her sky-balloon ascend, beginning its return voyage to the south, and kept her eyes on it until it had faded into the clouds. Then she rode away into the mountains with the goblin king and the full moon was rising before them in glimmering splendour, soaking everything with liquid silver; so vast it took up half the sky, like some beautiful alien world suspended in space and time.

AFTERWORD

One year later, Ronin of Slievmordhu wed Solveig of Grïmnørsland. She became his queen and deliverer; the only one who, over time, was able to convince him that he was not to blame for his father's demise, that there was no curse on the house of Ó Maoldúin, and that more than enough happiness to cure old sorrows could be found in everyday events.

Three had entered the Aingealfyre, and three emerged from it. One was mortal, one immortal, and the third was something other. What of that man born mortal, become immortal, Fionnbar Aonarán - he who could conceivably be called the third Brother of the Flame?

'For your kind the most wonderful gift of all is life,' Zaravaz had once said, in reference to this poor creature, 'and it should be enjoyed to the fullest. Having received life, the most wonderful gift is the promise of death at the end.'

Fionnbar, after drinking the draught of deathlessness from the Well of Rain, had come to understand that immortality on its own could not give happiness. Unable to find contentment, he had tried many times to destroy himself. After each attempt he came forth alive but with his mind in worse torment. His life had become an endless search for death – an ironic and perhaps fitting punishment for whatever transgressions he might have committed in his folly.

The coward Fionnbar had brought much grief to the Four Kingdoms of Tir, and especially to the family of Jewel Heronswood Maelstronnnar - yet in the end his misdemeanours had sprung from desire for immortality, cowardice, deception, and a craving for freedom from confinement.

Ultimately, the flames of the werefire had consumed his inner hungers. They had devoured most of his needs and wants, even depriving him of the requirement for sleep. He existed in a kind of vacuous tranquillity, sitting alone in contemplation for hours on end, seldom roused to activity.

For years he remained in the Asylum for Lunatics, every Lantern Eve patiently requesting that he might be released and given some useful employment. When at last Warwick of Narngalis reached the end of his own long span of years, the old king decided to grant him this wish.

After the Argenkindë had departed, Warwick had caused a series of fortified watchtowers and beacons to be constructed along the peaks of the northern ranges. Their purpose was to provide stations from which sentries could ceaselessly look towards the north, in case the goblin horde ever returned.

Manning the towers was a dangerous undertaking; only the brave volunteered, only the hardy survived. Unseelie gwillion and fuathan haunted the mountains, seeking human beings to slaughter. The winds raged at high speed, the cold chewed into the bones of mortal things, and a terrible sense of loneliness stalked the peaks and chasms like some unseen hunter.

The Companions of the Cup took turns at the task of keeping watch, but even they, the pick of mortal knights, could endure the solitude, the icy weather, and the constant peril for no more than three months at a stretch.

The most remote and desolate watchtower of all sprouted like a jagged stump from the bitter heights of Storth Cynros. King Warwick decreed that Fionnbar Aonarán should be stationed there, alone, where no mortal man could last. He named Aonarán 'The Watchman on the Northern Ramparts', whose task was to keep a sleepless vigil, scanning the horizon for all dangers. If the sentry spied approaching peril, he must light the Beacon Fire. Grateful for being given a useful role Aonarán swore fealty and obedience, and after his immersion in the werefire, no one could doubt his honesty. He feared neither gwillion not fuathan; nor did he fear the eternal cold. Compliantly he took up his post in the loneliest watchtower of all. There he remained while the years rolled by, and the weather eroded the mountains, and the world grew older. Forever he kept vigil, staring out across the bleak, uncharted lands.

ACKNOWLEDGEMENTS

T hanks to the following people:
For valuable information about swordsmanship, Elizabeth Bear, Mike Dumas, Elizabeth Glover, Steve K. S. Perry and Nancy Proctor.

For help with research into snow trolls and tömtes, my Swedish friend Therese Kennedy.

Thanks also to the inimitable Kevin Morgan for sharing with me his limitless knowledge of geology, much of which was unable to be incorporated, but which provided me with fascinating insights. If there are any inaccuracies in my reportage of mines and mining, it is I who has included them during the weaving of this tale.

REFERENCES

Gold as a ward against evil:

In the folklore of the Philippines it was commonly believed that demons were afraid of metal objects (a belief echoing the tenet of British folklore that faeries could not abide the touch of cold iron). Particularly, metals with the colours of fire and light, such as gold, copper and brass, were believed to be most efficacious against demons. Tanith Lee explores this association between gold and demons in her wonderful 'Flat Earth' series.

In western mythology silver is used as a charm against vampires, who can be slain with a silver bullet. Gold, however, seems a more logical choice as the anathema of evil, since silver tarnishes but gold does not; also silver is the colour of the moon and stars; lights that can only be seen during the hours of darkness, which traditionally belong to wicked creatures. The peoples of ancient Peru associated gold with the sun and silver with the moon.

In British and Celtic folklore lesser faeries are not driven off by gold: many, in fact, are known to handle it, for example faerie spinning-hags who spin straw into gold, and leprechauns who own pots of the stuff. Much supernatural gold, however, is only an illusion. When the glamour wears off, 'gold coins' regain their true shape: withered leaves.

Terminology:

I have avoided the anachronistic use of the verb 'to fire' when describing the action of bows-and-arrows, catapults and other pre-gunpowder ballistic weapons. The term in this context only came into usage with the first 'firearms', whose explosions were actually set off by a flame. Even in association with flaming arrows, I am not aware of the command 'Fire!' being employed by genuine battlefield archers before gunpowder was employed in weaponry.

Goblin music:

It was well after I had written the passages referring to goblin music that I became aware of the band 'Apocalyptica', who play heavy metal music on cellos. After viewing some of their energetic performances I was struck by how close they came to my vision of unseelie warriors playing wild, raw, stirring melodies on stringed instruments. Apocalyptica's rendition of Metallica's 'Unforgiven' might almost have been written as the 'dance track' for Chapter 6.

Other music that seems to augment the story:

For me, the perfect theme for Asrăthiel and her lover is Metallica's 'Nothing Else Matters. The poignant 'Pearlin' Peggie's Bonnie' as played by Chris Duncan on the album 'The Red House': The heritage of the Scottish Fiddle' represents, for me, the feelings experienced by Asrăthiel when she believes Zaravaz has perished. When listening to it, it is easy to imagine her grieving, but remembering, as she wanders among the forests, lakes and hills of a beautiful, wild landscape under a stormy sky, the wonderful times with him, and their moments of terrible, tender intimacy.

Medieval-style dentistry:

From: 'Medieval teeth better than Baldric's, an online article by Jane Elliott of the BBC News Online health staff. 'A paper published in the British Dental Journal shows that medieval

(12th – 14th century) literature even makes reference to creating false teeth... dentures made of human teeth or cow bone. They also knew how to fill cavities...'

Reference to gold used in dentistry goes back as far back as the Etruscans in 450 BC., and in Pope Julius's Museum, in Rome there is a gold dental appliance (a gold cap) surviving from ancient times.

To readers of the Bitterbynde Trilogy:

Some themes in Fallowblade and The Battle of Evernight run parallel. This is typical of fairytales and folklore, which often repeat certain motifs. In hindsight I have also perceived the influence of 'Beauty and the Beast' upon this tale, among other classic *märchen*.

GOBLIN LANGUAGE

Manx Gaelic in its written form to me looks perfect as a goblin language, although to my regret I have never heard it spoken. My usage of Manx Gaelic is not grammatically correct. Here is a guide to the way I have dealt with the language:

'*Glashtinsluight ny beealeraght lesh sheelnaue.*' This translates roughly as 'Goblinkind do not love to chatter with human beings.'

Aachionard: lieutenant commander,

Ard-veoir armyn: King of Arms,

Armyn: weaponry,

Bannaght lhiat: farewell, goodbye

Bee dty host, jouylleen!: Hold your peace, imp/villain!

Beishtyn: vermin

Ben drultagh: enchantress

Boanlagh ny theayee: scum of the earth

Boanlagh: rubbish

Boddagh: boor

Brouteraght: dirt

Chiarn: lord

Cloie yn ommidan: fool

Cooilleeneyder: revenger,

Crooagen: lice, weevils
Crout ghraney: shabby trick
Donnanyn mooar: great wretches
Drammane: a fine mist
Feiosagh: weakling
Flaieen: imps
Graihyn: male goblins
Liannyn: female goblins
Meeylen: bugs, insects
Ny hashoonyn mooarey: the great powers
Ooyl villish: dessert apple
Peearen ayns lavender: pears in/with lavender
Rag-rannee: good-for-nothing
Red ommidjagh: piece of folly
Sallagh: dirty
Slane vie: very well
Sneeuane ushtey: water spiders
T'eh lhien!: Thumbs up!
Y Hiarn: my lord

The kobolds' song:
'*T' fuill-yiarg er yiarn, t' glassoil er copuir, t' gormaghey er kob-olt, t' geayney er nickyl.*'
'Iron is blood-red, copper is greenish, cobalt is blue, nickel is green.'

INSPIRATIONS AND RESOURCES

King Uabhar views the deployment of his troops:

This paragraph was adapted from - The White Company, by Sir Arthur Conan Doyle, in Cornhill Magazine, 1891.

'Close at the heels of the horses came two score archers, bearded and burley, their round targets on their backs and their yellow bows, the most deadly weapon that the whit of man had yet devised, thrusting forth from behind their shoulders. From each man's girdle hung sword or axe, according to his humour, and over the right hip there jutted out the leathern quiver, with its bristle of goose, pigeon, and peacock feathers. Behind the bowmen strode two drummers beating their nakirs, and two trumpeters in particoloured clothes. After them came twenty-seven sumpter-horses carrying tent-poles, cloth, spare arms, spurs, wedges, cooking kettles, horse-shoes, bags of nails, and the hundred other things which experience had shown to be needful in a harried and hostile country.'

Animal rights:

'Compassionate people have to show opposition to cruelty, and at times we have to run the risk of having unflattering labels placed on us, because there are some things for which we should display no tolerance.' This quote is not my own, but I have been unable to find the source.

The pixie at the Sillerway Bridge:

This passage ended up in 'Weatherwitch', but it was inspired by the story, 'The Pixie at the Ockerry', from William Crossing's 'Tales of the Dartmoor Pixies: Glimpses of Elfin Haunts and Antics', W. H. Hood, London, 1890.

At the Gate of Ironstone Keep:

The tale of Halvdan, Kieran and Conall Gearnach is inspired by part of the story 'Deirdre', an ancient Celtic legend. This tale, also known as 'The Exile of the Children of Uisnach', is often related as a prologue to the oldest prose epic known to Western literature: 'The Cattle Raid of Cooley' (Tain Bo Cuailgne). It has existed by word of mouth since the 1st century AD and was written down by Irish scholars during the 7th century AD. The story has been rewritten many times in the form of books and plays, and remains popular to the present day.

The names of Uabhar's weapons:

King Uabhar's weapons are named after the weapons of King Conchobar in the Celtic legend 'Deirdre'. 'My shield, Ocean; my knife, Victorious; my spear Slaughter, and my sword Gorm Glas, the blue-green.'

'How many bitter hours…'

I wrote this poem after listening to Metallica's song 'Unforgiven', while the rhythms and the haunting, gothic melody were still in my head. It is partly inspired by a verse from Joanna Baillie's 'Orra: A Tragedy' and also influenced by a chapter in Sir Walter Scott's 'Ivanhoe'.

'There stands a fastness high against the stars…'

This poem was greatly influenced by lines 593 to 602 of Keats's 'Endymion' Book II, and borrows some phrases here and there.

The verse 'If it's going to rain':
'If it's going to rain, it'll rain,
And if it's going to shine, it's going to shine,
And if you're going insane, you'll go insane.
Now you've lost your mind.'
Lyrics from a song by Courtney Egan.

Inspirations from the classics:
(i)'The horde drew together... and recoiled from their forward line.'
(ii)'Have mercy on me, proud sir ...All the more shame to those who let you live so long.'
Inspired by passages in Sir Walter Scott's 'Ivanhoe'.

The Goblin King:
The concept of the goblin king was probably inspired by Jim Henson's marvellous movie, 'The Labyrinth', which will always be one of my favourites.

Again, Tanith Lee's 'Flat Earth' series also influenced the creation of Zaravaz.

Names of Goblin Dishes:
'As if to Celebrate, I Discovered a Mountain Blooming with Red Flowers' is the title of a 1981 sculpture by Anish Kapoor.

'Here is a Lush Situation' was inspired by the title of a 1958 painting by Richard Hamilton, 'Hers is a Lush Situation'.

'The Passion for Pepper Burns Like a Flame of Love" is adapted from a comment by Joseph Conrad.

Goblin Philosophy:
a) Sections of Zaravaz's declaration are inspired by an article by Ingrid E. Newkirk, founder of PETA. 'Animal Times', Summer 2003, Page 2.

b) 'More troubling is the implication that our respect for other species should be measured in proportion to how amazingly human-like their abilities are.' This statement, made by Drew Rendall and John Vokey of University of Lethbridge, Alberta, Canada, inspired some of the goblin philosophy. New Scientist magazine 2457, 24 July 2004, pages 28-29.

Avalloc's letter to Asrăthiel in Chapter 7:

This was partly inspired by journalists' reports of the euphoria that broke out in Tasmania in 2006, at the news that two gold miners trapped by a rock fall were still alive.

Mining:

Some of the knocker guilds are named after silver miners' guilds at Cesky Krumlov.

Verse:

'…My arms reached upward. I was not to blame.
For all my heart seemed hungering to feel
The strange delight that made my senses reel.
It seemed so strange that pleasure should be pain,
And yet I fain would suffer once again.'

This is an extract from 'The Merry Little Maid and Wicked Little Monk'. It is very old and catalogued as 'An anonymous poem'.

Ronin's advice:

'To see what is right, and not to do it, is want of courage.' Confucius, 551 BC – 479 BC

'A good leader inspires others with confidence in him, a great leader inspired them with confidence in themselves.' Unknown.

Animal Experiments:

Many scientists now acknowledge that testing on animals is futile, because their physiology differs radically from ours. It is also profoundly cruel and inhumane. You can read more about it on the Internet by Googling the Humane Society or the MAWA Trust – Medical Advances Without Animals.

The latter is a registered charity comprising a body of scientists working on solutions to appalling laboratory practices. With your support they can do much more.

The MAWA Trust
PO Box 4203
Weston Creek
ACT 2611 Australia
Telephone +61 2 6287 1980
Email info@mawa-trust.org.au

Boycott companies that test on animals. Do not buy their products. Lists of these companies (and lists of the kind ones!) can be found at Caring Consumer: a Guide to Kind Living, www.caringconsumer.com./resources_companies.asp

More (and more uplifting) information on animal rights can be viewed at PETA, People for the Ethical Treatment of Animals – www.peta.org Animals Australia www.animalsaustralia.org/

The MAWA Trust
www.mawa-trust.org.au/

The Humane Society
www.hsi.org.au/

People for the Ethical
Treatment of Animals
www.peta.org/

Animals Australia
www.animalsaustralia.org/

OTHER BOOKS IN THE CROWTHISTLE SERIES

Cecilia Dart-Thornton
The Iron Tree

BOOK I OF THE CROWTHISTLE CHRONICLES

Jarred, recently come of age, is leaving the sun-scorched desert village that has always been his home - and to seek out the truth about his father, disappeared when Jarred was ten, never to return.

After he and his companions are set upon in a ravine, they seek shelter in the Marsh, a place of cool, green water and dazzling beauty. Here Jarred meets Lilith, and in a single moment he realises that his life can never be the same again. But neither realises how closely linked their fates - and their past - really are. During a visit to Cathair Rua, the Red City, Jarred stumbles across the secret of the Iron Tree, and with it an unbearable truth about his father's identity...

'Strong appeal for readers who love language and appreciate it thickly applied, and who revel in the detail of a fantasy world.'
COURIER MAIL

Hidden identity, doomed love and kismet... Dart-Thornton conjures up her world of Tir in the luminous yet hard-edged manner of Jack Vance and Mary Gentle.
WASHINGTON POST

Cecilia Dart-Thornton
The Well of Tears

BOOK II OF THE CROWTHISTLE CHRONICLES

After Jewel and Eoin have fled from their native Slievmordhu to the kingdom of Narngalis, they tread a perilous path which ultimately leaves Eoin in the hands of the deadly unseelie wights. With nowhere else to go Jewel finds refuge amongst the plateau-dwellers at High Darioneth. Teeming with siofra, trows and other eldritch wights, their land is under the tight rule of the weather-masters and Storm Lord Avalloc, who have the power to tame and summon the winds...

When Jewel learns that the legendary Dome of Strang is no longer guarded, she decides to continue her journey to Orielthir to unravel the mystery of the hidden stronghold and with it the truth about her father's legacy. Jewel's discoveries lead her on an unexpected quest, accompanied by a handsome young weathermaster who has secretly fallen in love with her. Together they encounter marvels and misfortunes and discover that the key to all their riddles ultimately lies with the extraordinary Well of Tears...

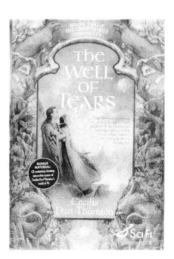

Cecilia Dart-Thornton
Weatherwitch

BOOK III OF THE CROWTHISTLE CHRONICLES

Asräthiel, granddaughter of the Storm Lord of Ellenhall has come of age and received her title of weathermage. As she sets out into the world, her happiness is marred only by her inability to wake her mother from the enchanted sleep that holds her captive, and by curious visits from a perverse yet intriguing faerie-creature.

But rumblings of discontent have begun to circulate in the Four Kingdoms of Tir: the bandits known as the Marauders are attacking the populace with greater frequency, and taxes are being raised to fund the defence against them. Then the people begin, seemingly unprovoked, to turn against the weathermasters, whom they have always held in such high esteem...

The [Crowthistle Chronicles] has spanned three generations of a family whose destiny is wreathed in enchantments and curses... Dart-Thornton writes lavishly descriptive fiction you can immerse yourself in... there are exciting developments in store.'
THE AGE

Cecilia Dart-Thornton
The Ill-Made Mute

BOOK I OF THE BITTERBYNDE TRILOGY

The Stormriders land their splendid winged stallions on the airy battlements of Isse Tower. Far below, the superstitious servants who dwell in the fortress' lower depths tell ghastly tales of evil creatures inhabiting the world outside, a world they have only glimpsed. Yet it is the least of the lowly, a mute, scarred, and utterly despised foundling, who dares to scale the Tower, sneak aboard a Windship, and then dive from the sky.

The fugitive is rescued by a kind-hearted adventurer, who gives it a name, the gift of communicating by handspeak, and an amazing truth it had never guessed. Now Imrhien begins a journey to distant Caermelor, to seek a wise woman whose skills may change the foundling's life.

Along the way, Imrhien must survive in a wilderness of endless danger. And as the challenges grow more deadly Imrhien discovers something more terrifying than all the evil eldritch wights combined.: the shunned outsider with an angel's soul and a gargoyle's face is falling in love...

In a thrilling debut combining storytelling mastery with a treasure trove of folklore, Cecilia Dart-Thornton creates an exceptional epic adventure.

'Not since Tolkien's *The Fellowship of the Ring*... have I been so impressed by a beautifully spun fantasy.'
ANDRE NORTON, GRAND MASTER OF SCIENCE FICTION.

Cecilia Dart-Thornton
The Lady of the Sorrows

BOOK II OF THE BITTERBYNDE TRILOGY

Though Imrhien's memory is clouded by sorcery, she must take vital news to the King-Emperor of Caermelor, where she hopes she may also find Thorn, the fearless ranger who has won her heart. Since no commoner may approach the royal court, Imrhien assumes a new identity as Rohain, a noble visitor from the distant Sorrow Isles.

She soon discovers that the King and his rangers have departed to battle the unseelie wights which have suddenly declared war against mortals. Atacks by nightmare monsters of the Wild Hunt, led by the unseelie Lord Huon, grow ever more frequent and brutal. And when evil forces lay siege to the royal sanctuary on a hidden, mystic island, Rohain is confronted with a horrifying discovery.

To protect those she loves, the Lady of the Sorrows must undertake a desperate quest to discover who she is and why an unhuman evil would wreak such destruction. But the truth of Ronain's past will prove more incredible - and far more tragic - than she could possibly have imagined.

'A narrative tapestry that is richly imagined and teeming with enchanted beings; a *Goblin Market* meets *Lord of the Rings*.'
SUNDAY AGE

Cecilia Dart-Thornton
The Battle of Evernight

BOOK III OF THE BITTERBYNDE TRILOGY

With vital fragments of her memory restored, Tahquil-Ashalind also regains the Langothe, a terrible longing for the world of the Faêran, for which there is no cure but to return there. She undertakes a journey to seek the Bitterbynde Gate, the only remaining way into the world. But when Tahquil's companions are ruthlessly abducted, she abandons this purpose in spite of the dreadful yearning, and sets out to try to rescue them, venturing into the land of Darke, and the blackness of Evernight...

'Dart-Thornton's Bitterbynde Trilogy - each book, and all three together - deserve to win every fantasy award there is.'
TANITH LEE

'*The Ill-Made Mute*, *The Lady of the Sorrows* and T*he Battle of Evernight* are marvels of descriptive prose... a diamond sparkling in the coalmines of descriptively impoverished fiction.'
THE COURIER MAIL

 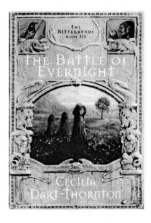

Cecilia Dart-Thornton
The Midnight Game
A fantasy for young adults.

When red-haired Alizarin Hall leaves the city to join her brother far away in the countryside, she has no idea what extraordinary adventures she will encounter. The isolated seaside town of Port Angel, seemingly locked in a nineteenth century time-stasis, harbours secrets beyond imagining.

Dark are the clothes of the populace, as if they dwell perpetually in mourning. Dark are their superstitions and mysteries - in particular the mysteries surrounding the wealthy Devlin clan, whose chieftain is a young man so handsome that beholding him is like falling under a spell.

But why do the villagers dread the coming of the winter solstice? And why do they bedeck their houses with charms to ward off evil?

As the first tendrils of evening mist glide across the lake, and the sea birds utter their piping calls from the dunes, Alizarin discovers a terrible secret.

And the bells begin to toll for the Midnight Game...

CPSIA information can be obtained at www.ICGtesting.com
Printed in the USA
LVOW12s2327251214

420349LV00001B/67/P